Y ou *monster*." His voice was louder "Why didn't you just kill me, too? You sick, evil, inhuman *thing*. You know my little sister was only six years old? And you just go and wipe her out like she was nothing . . ."

Luce bit her lower lip, hard, to stifle the shriek that nearly tore from her. The words raked through her chest; she felt as if the boy had reached inside her, jerking the halves of her rib cage apart.

"You know they made us read a poem in class today?" The question was oddly bland, everyday-ish, but that only made the poisonous grief in his voice seem worse. "It was a poem about you, or anyway about mermaids, and I completely lost it. They make it sound like hearing the mermaids sing is this beautiful, incredible experience, when really, even if you live . . . You know your song is *stuck* in me? I'd be better off dead than hearing something like that all the time, and there is *nothing* that will ever make it go away. And your face . . . Maybe the most evil thing about you isn't even that you kill people. It's what you do to the ones who survive."

But it's the same for me! Luce wanted to tell him. *You're stuck in me, too, and you're not even magic. You're just totally, boringly human.* And wasn't that even worse, in a way?

Luce really understood, for the first time, why the timahk had that rule, that insistence that no human who heard the mermaids sing could ever be allowed to live.

It was so much easier to forget them if they died.

Waking Storms

SARAH PORTER

GRAPHIA

HOUGHTON MIFFLIN HARCOURT
BOSTON   NEW YORK

www.hmhbooks.com

The Library of Congress has cataloged the hardcover edition as
follows:
Porter, Sarah 1969–.
Waking storms / by Sarah Porter.
p. cm.
Sequel to: Lost voices
Summary: As a mermaid versus human war looms on the horizon,
Luce falls in love with her sworn enemy Dorian and
assumes her rightful role as queen of the mermaids.
[1. Mermaids—Fiction. 2. Supernatural—Fiction. 3. Love—
Fiction.] I. Title.
PZ7.P8303Wak 2012
[Fic]—dc23
2011027322

ISBN: 978-0-547-48251-4 hardcover
ISBN: 978-0-547-48254-5 paperback

Manufactured in U.S.A.
DOC 10 9 8 7 6 5 4 3 2 1

4500410722

For Jennifer Lemper,
land mermaid

Oh pride is not a sin,

And that's why I have gone

On down to Walmart with

My checkbook, just to get you some.

Like waves in which you drown me, shouting . . .

Soul Coughing, "Pensacola"

1

Each to Each

The last words he had absorbed were the ones about Lazarus, come back from the dead to tell everyone . . . everything. That was all wrong, bogus. If you've seen death from the inside, Dorian thought, you keep your mouth shut. You don't say a word to anybody. They wouldn't understand you anyway.

"Dorian? Can you continue?"

He looked up, blank. Images of plummeting bodies still streaked through his head.

"'Shall I part . . .'" Mrs. Muggeridge prompted. Dorian pulled himself up from terrible daydreams and forced his eyes to focus on the page in front of him. Acting normal was a way to buy himself the privacy to think not so normally. He found the line and cleared his throat.

"'Shall I part my hair behind? Do I dare to eat a peach?'"

His voice sounded too flat. He tried to squeeze more emotion into it, though the words seemed uninteresting. "'I shall wear white flannel trousers, and walk upon the beach.'" Now Dorian saw what was coming in the next line and started to panic. He struggled to suppress the memory of those dark eyes looking at him from the center of a wave, the gagging taste of salt, that unspeakable music. Did Mrs. Muggeridge have any idea what she was doing to him? "'I have heard the mer . . .'" He choked a little. "'The *mermaids* singing, each to each.'" Now there was an audible tremor in his voice, and something rising in his throat that felt like a throttled scream.

"Please read to the end."

"'I do not think that they will sing to me!'" Dorian spat it out aggressively and dropped the book with a crash. The rest of the students in the tiny class were staring, too shocked to laugh. But what did they know, anyway? "This poem is garbage! It's all lies!"

"Dorian . . ."

"If he'd heard the mermaids singing, he wouldn't be blathering on like this! He would be *dead!* Is this poem just trying to pretend that people *don't have to die?*"

Mrs. Muggeridge didn't even look angry. Somewhere between alarmed and amused.

"If you could read on to the end, Dorian, I think you'll see that T. S. Eliot isn't trying to evade intimations of mortality." Students started snickering at that. She always used such weird words. It was a mystery to him how Mrs. Muggeridge had wound up in this town. She was even more out of place than he was, with her dragging black clothes and odd ideas.

"No!" Dorian didn't remember getting out of his chair, but he was standing now. His legs were shaking violently, and the room seemed unsteady. Mrs. Muggeridge looked at him carefully.

"Maybe you should step out of the room for a few minutes?" He couldn't understand why she had to react so *calmly*. It wasn't fair, not when she'd made him read those horrible lines. He stalked out of class, leaving his English anthology with its pages splayed and crushed against the floor. In the hallway he pressed his forehead against the cold tile wall. His breathing was fast and hungry, as if he'd just come up from under the deep gray slick of the ocean.

He could hear Mrs. Muggeridge serenely reading on. "'We have lingered in the chambers of the sea, by sea-girls wreathed with seaweed red and brown. Till human voices wake us, and we drown.'"

He felt like he was going to faint. But at least the poem got something right. Maybe he'd survived the sinking of the *Dear Melissa*, but he still felt like he was drowning all the time. Every time his alarm clock went off, he lunged bolt upright in bed, gasping for air.

When the class finally poured out into the hall, he straightened himself and trailed after them to chemistry. It was such a suffocating, sleepy, ragtag school, with only sixty students and three teachers. His high school in the Chicago suburbs had been twenty times the size of this place. Everything felt crushingly small.

Other students turned to stare at the two men in dark suits standing near a drinking fountain, but Dorian didn't notice them. He was concentrating on fighting the wobbly sensation of the floor.

The men noticed him, though. Their eyes tracked him intently as he walked away, sometimes leaning on the row of lockers. A few minutes later Mrs. Muggeridge emerged, gray corkscrew curls bobbing absurdly above her head as she chattered to another teacher, the scarlet frames of her glasses flashing like hazard lights. "I suppose I'm behind the times. Apparently now it's politically incorrect to make your students read poems with mermaids that don't kill people. What a thing to get so upset about!"

The suited men glanced at each other and followed her.

* * *

Dorian kept trying to draw the girl he'd seen. If he could set the memory down in black ink, slap it to the paper once and for all, then maybe he could finally get her out of his head. He drew exceptionally well, but every time he finished a new picture he couldn't escape the feeling that something was missing. The drawing he was working on now showed a towering wave with a single enormous eye gazing out from under the crest. The eyelashes merged with curls of seafoam.

He couldn't understand why he hadn't been afraid at the time. The fear had come much later, after he was obviously safe, and the fits of nauseous terror that seized him were infuriatingly senseless. But when the ship was actually crashing, wrenching up under his feet, and people were dying all around him, he'd felt perfectly composed and confident.

He also didn't know where the instincts that had saved

him had come from. If he'd done even one thing differently, he knew, he wouldn't be the sole surviving passenger of the *Dear Melissa*. He'd be as dead as the rest of them, as dead as his whole family. If he hadn't faced down that girl in the waves—or that thing that wasn't a girl, not really, but a monster with a beautiful girl's head and torso—if he hadn't sung her own devastating song right back at her, then it would have been all over. She would have murdered him without a second thought. But sitting under the cold fluorescent lights of the chemistry lab, he knew that singing in the middle of a shipwreck had been a bizarre impulse. Inexplicable. How had he known?

Who would have ever guessed that the way to stop a mermaid from killing you was to *sing* at her?

She'd dragged him out from the wreckage, swimming away with him clasped in one arm. They'd raced at such speed that the blood had shrieked in his head. The foam-striped water had rushed across his staring eyes. He'd struggled not to inhale it, and he'd failed again and again. Salt burned his lungs, and the cold water in his chest swelled into a bursting ache. But every time he'd thought that he was really going to drown, she'd pulled him up above the surface and let the water hack out of him, fountaining down his chin. She'd let him *live*. Only him, out of all the hundreds who'd set sail together.

She'd even spoken, once. Now that he had time to think it over, he realized one of the weirdest things about it all was the fact that she'd used English instead of talking in some kind of mermaid gibberish. *Take a really deep breath, okay? We have to dive under again.* Her voice was gentle and much too innocent-sounding for something so utterly evil.

He hadn't answered. He'd been too pissed off to speak to her, though now looking back, he realized that he hadn't felt nearly furious enough. He'd felt the kind of anger that would have made sense if he'd been having a fight with a friend, say. As if that monster with the silvery green tail was just a girl he knew from school or something. Worse, as if she was someone he *liked*.

She'd belonged to the pack that murdered his mother and father; his sweet six-year-old sister, Emily; his aunt and her husband; and all three of his cousins. He should hate that mermaid girl more than anything in the world. He should dream about dismembering her with his bare hands.

Instead he dreamed about her dark eyes watching him as he sprawled on the shore gagging up a flood of sour, brackish liquid. She hadn't swum off right away after she'd shoved him up onto the beach, and he'd had time to memorize her pale face and dark jagged hair set like a star in a gray-green curl of sea.

He dreamed about her song.

* * *

"Charlotte Muggeridge? We were wondering if we could speak to you for a few minutes." The taller of the two men folded back his suit lapel to show her his badge. Mrs. Muggeridge goggled at him in absolute confusion.

"Anyone can speak to me!" She was alone with the men in the teachers' lounge. The grubby vomit orange sofas sagged in patches like rotting fruit. Inspirational posters urging them to strive for their dreams had faded to anemic tints of jade green and beige. No one sat down. Instead she swayed a little, staring from one glossy, polite face to the other. Both the suited men met her gaze with bland determination. Both had empty blue eyes and freshly shaved cheeks. "You can't actually be FBI! That is, of course you can speak to me, but . . . I couldn't possibly have anything to say that you might find interesting . . ." She trailed off, then glanced up at them with new sharpness. "I hope none of our students is in trouble."

"No one is in any trouble, ma'am." Mrs. Muggeridge's eyes were darkening with a feeling of aversion for the tall man, though she couldn't justify her dislike. He was perfectly well-mannered. "There was an incident in your third-period English class?"

That bewildered her, again. "Certainly nothing I couldn't handle without help from the FBI!" She gaped at them. "Don't you have more important things to worry about than an out-burst from a fifteen-year-old boy?"

"In this case, ma'am, we think it might be important."

"A tenth grader didn't *care* for T. S. Eliot. Send in the feds!" Her voice was heavy with sarcasm. The agents were glowering at her.

"Just describe the incident. Ma'am." The politeness was slipping now.

"Well . . . It was only that we were reading 'Prufrock' in class. We reached the closing stanzas, about the mermaids. And Dorian Hurst became very upset, for some reason. He jumped out of his seat and started yelling. But he's generally been a very good student since he enrolled here."

The two men were obviously trying to keep their faces smooth and vacant, but something excited and a little disturb-

ing started to show in the quick pointed looks passing between them.

"And what did Dorian say?" It was the smaller man speaking now. He had hanging jowls and a high, almost girlish voice.
Mrs. Muggeridge thought it contrasted unpleasantly with his
blocky gray face.

"He said that if Prufrock had *really* heard the mermaids singing, he wouldn't have lived to talk about it." An eager twitch
passed through the shoulders of the taller agent. He leaned in on
her, and his blue eyes were as brittle as hunks of ice. But why
on earth did he care? "It was a peculiar detail to quarrel with,
but Dorian seemed very passionate about it. He accused Eliot of
pretending we don't have to die."

"I thought you said the name was Prufrock?" It was the
shorter agent squeaking again. Mrs. Muggeridge looked at him
with fresh outrage.

"T. S. Eliot is the poet who *wrote* 'The Love Song of J. Al-
fred Prufrock'! How can you be so ig—" Mrs. Muggeridge stifled a number of extremely rude endings to the sentence.

"Did he say anything else?" The tall man sounded bored.

"That was all I *let* him say. He was being disruptive, so I
asked him to step out of class." The shorter man's upper lip suddenly jerked up in sneer, as if Mrs. Muggeridge had just confessed to doing something extremely stupid. It was all too much
for her. "Now, would you *please* explain why all of this is
important?"

"We don't discuss ongoing investigations, ma'am." The tall
agent turned abruptly toward the door, rapping a pen against
his mouth.

"Do you know anything about Dorian's family?" The short agent twittered the question in a shrill, malicious tone. His eyebrows arched suggestively. The tall one swung back around, shooting what was obviously meant to be a quelling glance at his partner, but the little man only grinned.

"His family? No, I don't. I think someone mentioned that he doesn't live with his biological parents, but that isn't so uncommon."

"They're dead, is why. Sister, too. They all died in June." He seemed to enjoy the look of shock on Mrs. Muggeridge's face. "Drowned."

Mrs. Muggeridge felt her mouth fall into an O of dismay as the tall agent jerked his partner's arm and towed him from the room. She stumbled a few steps to the sofa and flopped down, leaning her head on her hands. "Oh, that poor boy!" She gasped the words out loud. "Oh, no *wonder* he was so upset!"

It still didn't explain why they were so interested, though. Not unless they thought Dorian was hiding something.

* * *

His father's second cousin once removed Lindy and her husband, Elias, had made it clear that they didn't want to keep Dorian permanently. They were too old and tired to cope with a teenager. It was just their bad luck that they happened to live right in the town where he'd literally washed up and that his parents had included their phone number on some form they'd filled out. The result was that Dorian had been left with them more or less by default. They reminded him occasionally that this was just a temporary arrangement until something *better* could be worked out, but since nobody else was exactly clamoring to take over as his guardian, he had the impression that he'd probably be stuck with them for a while. They acted skittish around him, mincing and whispering in a way that made him queasy and impatient. The only good thing he could say for them was that they'd at least followed the psychologist's advice to keep quiet about his connection to the sinking of the *Dear Melissa*. No one in his school knew he'd been on the ship, not even the principal, and he liked it that way. If everyone had kept asking him questions about it, he was pretty sure he would have gone insane.

He'd been asked way too many questions already, by a parade of out-of-towners flown in to investigate the ship's crash. Therapists and cops, insurance agents, and even someone who claimed to be from the FBI. What had happened? Had he noticed anything unusual? And, of course, how on earth had he swum twelve miles alone in less than an hour? Some of them seemed to doubt that he'd been on the ship at all, though his name was right there on the passenger manifest.

He gave the same answers to all of them: he didn't remember anything. He'd been standing on the deck, and everything had gone black. He'd come to on the shore.

It had turned into a kind of game. They asked the same questions; he gave the same answers. Like some kind of nightmare merry-go-round: *I don't remember, I don't remember, I don't remember.*

He wasn't about to tell them that he'd been rescued by a killer mermaid.

His reserve wasn't only because they wouldn't believe him or that they might even throw him into an asylum for hopeless lunatics, though those were definitely factors.

It was all just too *private*: the mermaid girl's painfully beautiful face, the searing amazement of those voices, the squeezing closeness of death. He wouldn't have described it even to his best friend, much less to a bunch of pushy, self-important strangers.

For all he knew, he might be the only person on earth who had heard the mermaids singing and lived. The memory was *his*. It was all he had to make up for the loss of his family. The dark-haired mermaid's song burned his sleep, twined through all his waking thoughts.

* * *

Over dinner Lindy asked him at least five times if he was enjoying his macaroni and cheese mixed with hamburger meat; every time she asked in precisely the same simpering, anxious voice. Pink scalp winked through the wisps of her fuzzy, apricot blond hair, and her pale eyes looked permanently frightened inside their red rims. She made Dorian think of a sick, senile rabbit.

"It's delicious," Dorian replied automatically. He kept looking over at the window, where early twilight glowed between red checkered curtains. The kitchen was prim, secure, and always extremely clean. A painted wooden bear in a chef's hat and apron stood on the counter, forever frying a wooden egg. A game show host jabbered on the TV about how fabulous that evening's prizes were. How long would it be before he could get away? "I'm going to go study at a friend's house. Okay?"

Lindy and Elias both nodded so cautiously that it was like he'd just confessed to suicidal impulses and they were terrified of saying something that would push him over the edge. Not that suicide seemed like the worst idea ever sometimes.

Dorian scraped and washed his plate. It was important to keep going through the motions. Convince them that he hadn't been driven totally crazy by the trauma. It was bad enough that he screamed in his sleep sometimes. They were probably already afraid that he was going to come after them with an ax.

He had to find the mermaid who'd saved him. Not to prove to himself that she hadn't been some kind of hallucination—he knew what he'd seen. But she owed him an explanation at least. After all, what kind of reason could she have had for murdering so many people? Absolute evil? If that was it, though, why make an exception for him, singing or no? He didn't deserve to be alive when his parents and Emily were dead.

He needed to talk to her, needed it urgently, and he told himself that it didn't matter why. He just had to hear what she would say. But how was he supposed to find a mermaid? Steal a rowboat and go paddle around in the open sea like an idiot? He'd been brooding over the problem for weeks, and tonight he thought he might have found an answer. It was worth a try at least.

It was only the middle of September, but it was already cold enough that he pulled on a parka and hat before stepping out into the wild dusk, where the wind reeked with the weedy, fishy breath of the harbor. The smell always brought back the sickening taste of mingled bile and salt water horribly flecked with the sweetness of the previous night's chocolate cake that he'd disgorged that day on the shore. His stomach lurched a little from the memory, but he did his best to ignore it.

The small tan house stood on a narrow street that ran straight down to the tiny harbor. The hill was steep enough that the sidewalk was a staircase with broad cement steps. He could see the black masts of a few sailboats crisscrossing like chopsticks in front of the electric blue sky while farther up clouds sagged in a violet jumble. He walked between glowing windows, heading for the sea. It was obvious he'd have to walk for a mile or two, past the beach north of town where she'd left him, then up onto the low, ragged cliffs where a path wound through stands of half-dead spruce. The farther the better, really. She wouldn't want to come too close to a town.

He didn't want to care how she felt about anything, but sometimes he couldn't help wondering if she still thought about him. Maybe she'd completely forgotten him in the three months since she'd swum with him in her arms.

Then he'd remind her. He wasn't about to let her forget what she'd done. He'd show her what a big mistake she'd made by letting one of her victims survive. Especially since that survivor was him.

2

The Voice on the Cliff

"Luce? Oh, Luce, it is you! We've been trying to find you for weeks!"

The dreamlike thrum of Luce's song dropped into silence, and she glanced up in surprise at Dana's warm smile, already very close to her own face. Dana leaned back with her elbows on the pebble beach and glanced around the small cave with its smooth, rounded ceiling. Her long tail stirred under the water, flicking up glimmers of ruby and coppery shine. Luce's cave didn't have any cracks that could let the sun in. The only light came through the underwater entrance set in a deep crevice between cliffs, so that a nebulous, dusky glow refracted up through the water. The dimness didn't keep Luce and Dana from seeing each other clearly, though; they could see without difficulty in any degree of darkness. Dana was stunning even by mermaid standards, with a mouth like a heavy rose and faintly luminous brown skin. As with all mermaids, a dark, subtle shimmering hung in the air around her. Her thick black hair was parted neatly in the middle and fanned out around her shoulders in a dozen puffy twists. Unlike Luce, who was completely naked, she wore a red bikini top. But at least, Luce thought, Dana wasn't wearing a lot of stolen human jewelry the way she'd done before.

"It's a nice cave. I was worried you'd just, like, taken off somewhere, but then Rachel said she'd heard your song in the water, really faint. I didn't know if I should even believe her, but some of us started looking. And here you are!" Dana's voice was too enthusiastic, trying to cover up the awkwardness that kept growing as Luce stayed quiet. Still, she felt better about Dana than she did about the rest of them. Dana and Violet were the only ones who hadn't participated in the assault on Catarina.

"Hi, Dana," Luce finally yielded. She couldn't imagine why any of them would bother looking for her, though, unless Anais had something nasty in mind. Luce kept out of their way; they should keep out of hers. "Were you trying to find me so Anais can finally kill me?" Dana jerked backwards so sharply that Luce felt the shock transmitted through the water. Hurt widened Dana's huge brown eyes.

"Luce, that is *so* unfair! I mean, I know you must hate Jenna now, and maybe you think she'd help Anais . . . do something to you . . . But why would you say something that paranoid to *me*? I mean . . . I didn't even touch Catarina! You know I didn't! And I *always* stood up for you!"

Luce didn't exactly remember it that way, and she didn't much want to be reminded of all the times when Dana had been nice to her.

"You didn't start clawing at Catarina, but you didn't do anything to help her either. You would have just let the tribe rip her apart right in front of you!" Luce was surprised by the savagery in her tone, the sudden racing of her heart. She hadn't realized how angry she still felt until she'd seen Dana's beautiful face again. Dana was shifting from hurt to aggrieved now, her lips tightening and a golden heat in her eyes. Dim bluish light wavered on her cheeks.

"Like we had a choice! Me and Violet! Like, you think if we'd gotten in their way they wouldn't have beat the crap out of us, too, or just killed us? Luce, everyone was *wasted*. We'd all drunk like a ton of scotch that day. And Anais got them totally crazy. Jenna and everyone, they didn't know *what* they were doing."

"You're trying to tell me your own sister would have helped Anais kill you?" Luce's tone was cutting, but in her heart she had to admit that Dana had a point. The mermaids *had* been out of their minds when they'd thrown themselves on Catarina; they'd been in an alcohol-fueled frenzy, wild with hysterical cruelty. Of course, Luce's uncle had been drunk when he'd tried to rape her, too, back when she was still human. And no mermaid would have thought that was an excuse for *him*.

Dana didn't answer at first. She suddenly looked horribly sad, gazing down at the flash of her own scales under the water. "I think Jenna might have killed me then, actually. Yeah. I do." Dana whispered the words. It took Luce a moment to under-

stand her, and another moment to absorb the mournful helpless-
ness of her tone.

"Dana, I . . ."

"Luce, that's the *problem!*" Dana looked up, the golden light
in her brown eyes broken by urgency and awful regret. "I mean
with having Anais be queen. Having her *get* to people. Like,
Jenna and some of the others, they're just completely different
now than they used to be, and I have to look at them every day,
my twin sister and my best friends, and think how they'd probably strangle me in my sleep if Anais told them to!"

"Dana, I'm *sorry!* I mean, I'm sorry I blamed you . . ."

"I want you to be more than sorry!" The words lashed out.
"I want you to care! I mean, you're sitting here alone in this cave
for months, when you're the only one who could help us. And
all you can think about is Catarina and how pissed off and, like,
superior you are, but you don't care about the rest of us at all.
Everyone keeps acting crazier all the time, Luce. Like, as long as
there were ships we could sink, it kind of took the pressure off,
but now that the ships have completely stopped coming this
way . . . I keep thinking we might wind up fighting each other,
or maybe some of the girls will go like Miriam!"

Luce winced at the mention of that name. Miriam's suicide
had left a crater of pain in her heart; it wasn't right for Dana to
use that pain to make Luce do what she wanted. Not that Luce
was clear on exactly what Dana was after.

"What do you want from me, Dana?" Luce snapped. Dana
looked surprised, then assessing.

"You've changed a lot, too. God. You used to be such a marsh-
mallow." Luce tensed with annoyance, but she didn't say any-

thing. "But maybe that's a good thing. I mean, you'll have to be pretty tough to go up against her!"

So that was it. "You think I'm going to get rid of Anais for you?" Luce asked.

A quick, contorted smile bent Dana's mouth. "You're right that she wants to kill you, you know. I'm not going to tell anyone where you are—at least, not anyone but Violet, she's dying to see you—but if somebody on Anais's side finds out they'll come after you for *sure*."

Luce halfway smiled. Did Dana think, if she couldn't manipulate Luce with heartache, then she could control her with fear instead?

"Tell Anais not to bother. It's a waste of her time."

"Luce, you don't get it! Anais knows you're the rightful queen. And she knows we all know it, too! No one really talks about it, not straight out, but we all saw what you *did* . . . using your voice to move the sea . . ."

"I knew what you meant, Dana. You can tell Anais not to worry. Tell her I don't even want to *look* at anyone in our tribe who hurt Catarina, and I definitely don't want to be their queen. Tell Anais I think she's the queen they all deserve!"

Dana reeled back so hard her shoulder banged the stone wall. Her tail slashed back and forth, kicking up small recoiling waves. "Just because they all broke the timahk, and you *didn't* . . ." Luce flinched at that, but luckily Dana was glaring past her and didn't notice. "What, you think that means you're so much *better* than they are? You're too good to even give them *orders*?"

Luce sighed. She still felt angry, but she understood that Dana was in an awful position, stuck with a psychotic queen.

And it sounded like Luce's old tribe might be on the verge of some kind of internal war. Dana was trying to do the right thing.

"It's not *about* the timahk, Dana." Luce's voice was much gentler now. "I don't know if I even believe in the timahk anymore, or not in all of it . . . But I really loved Catarina, and she's gone now, and there's no way I can even find out if she's alive or not. I can't be around a bunch of mermaids who tried to kill Cat and just somehow pretend to feel *okay* about them!"

Dana stared hard at Luce, as if she couldn't make up her mind whether or not to be mollified.

"Why didn't you go with her, then? If you *loved* her so much?" Dana's tone was still sharp, but Luce could tell that her heart wasn't in it anymore. She was forcing herself to act angrier than she really felt. Still, the question made tears start up in Luce's eyes, and she turned her face away. "Luce? Actually, that was what we all thought at first. That you and Cat had just gone off together. Even if it seemed weird after how bad you two had been fighting . . ."

"I wanted to go with her. She wouldn't let me." She looked back at Dana, whose face had gone blank with disbelief.

"She wouldn't *what*? No way, Luce! There's no way any of us would just swim off alone like that. Not if there was any choice! I mean, with how dangerous it is . . . and not having *anyone* to help you . . ."

"Catarina did, though." Luce could hear how bitter her voice sounded. Dana was right; she *had* changed a lot in the months since Miriam's suicide and Catarina's near-murder. "She even tricked me. She waited until I went out to look for food and then sneaked off. To stop me from following her. Because she knew I would."

"Crazy! You didn't think of chasing after her?" Dana wasn't asking it to be cruel, Luce knew, but the question still grabbed her stomach in a knot of shame. The fact was she couldn't completely explain to herself why she hadn't done exactly what Dana suggested. Catarina had been battered and terribly weak when she'd disappeared. If Luce had rushed south after her, searching all the caves she'd passed, there was a good chance she could have caught up with the wounded ex-queen.

Something heavy and sad and secret had urged her to let Cat slip away, to linger where she was. In her darker moments Luce accused herself of disgusting cowardice. But, if she was completely honest with herself, the truth was something even worse than that. Luce suddenly realized that her own silvery green tail had started swishing nervously without her being aware of it.

"Luce? I guess I should admit I was kind of lying before. Saying that Anais would come after you. I was mostly trying to scare you." Luce looked up, smiling in sheer relief that Dana wasn't pursuing the question of why Catarina had left alone. "I mean, Anais would practically cut off her own fins to see you dead, like killing you would be the most amazing thing that ever happened to her, but the thing is . . . there are probably only a handful of girls who'd go along with it now. And she knows that." Luce noticed that Dana refrained from mentioning that one of those girls was almost certainly Jenna. "The tribe is barely holding together, and if Anais pushed everyone to kill you for no reason . . . I don't know, a lot of us might just leave her, or fight on your side. She's not going to risk it unless she can come up with some really good excuse."

Luce watched Dana's wide brown eyes staring off into a corner of the cave. Delicate curls of blue light flickered across Dana's irises, and Luce had a sudden flash of insight: more than anything else, Dana was afraid that she'd wind up fighting her own twin sister, maybe even killing her. Dana must know that if Luce challenged Anais there would almost certainly be a battle, mermaid blood unraveling through the water. And Dana was prepared for that, ready to face her own worst fears for the sake of the tribe. It was stunningly brave of her to come here and to say these things. Luce almost felt ashamed of herself, but she still wasn't ready to give in.

"It's wonderful to see you, Dana. I really missed you." Luce was startled to hear herself say it, and just as surprised to see Dana suddenly grinning back at her with the same open-hearted warmth she'd had before everything in their tribe had gone so hideously wrong.

"You know I'm not going to stop bugging you, Luce. About the whole queen thing. Now, you just *know* you want to take that screwy blond bitch down! Admit it!"

Luce burst out laughing. Then she realized with a hard jolt of sorrow that it was the first time she'd laughed in three months.

* * *

It was already twilight by the time Dana left, and Luce drifted over to the nearby beach where she usually foraged for dinner. Tall rock formations protruded from the water there, sheltering her from view in case any boats came by. They were at that juncture in the early Alaskan autumn when the night began to swing as if it were on hinges, closing steadily in on the daylight. By December the days would be no more than a dim grayish haze seeping through as the door of night was briefly knocked ajar. It was the first time Luce had really wondered what it would be like to spend a deep northern winter out in the sea. She'd only been a mermaid since April, after all, but she had a vague recollection of Kayley saying that in years when the ice got bad the tribe would be forced to migrate south for a while, out past the Alaskan Peninsula, slipping through the Aleutian Islands. She could just make out the Aleutians from here, a dark uneven band wrapping the southern horizon. Maybe she should just leave now and look for Catarina.

She knew she wouldn't, though. As she leaned between two boulders and cracked oysters for dinner, Luce admitted to herself that there was still something holding her here. Not that she had any reason to believe that the boy with the bronze-blond hair would have stayed in the area. It was highly unlikely, in fact. Assuming his parents had been with him on the cruise ship Luce's tribe had sunk in their furious grief over Miriam, then the boy would now be one of the lost kids, just as Luce herself had been, dumped on whatever grudging relatives could be persuaded to take him in or else passed around from one foster home to the next. He could be anywhere in the country. What were the odds, after all, that he'd have family on this desolate stretch of the Alaskan coast? She should picture him living in Montana or New York or Georgia: anywhere but here. That was simply logical.

But she couldn't shake the sense that he was still some-where nearby. Wishful thinking, Luce knew. The kind of lonely delusion that would send her out of her mind if she let it. She wasn't sure which was stupider: imagining that someday she'd see the boy she'd saved again, or *wanting* to see him. He must hate her utterly, and it would be a violation of the timahk, the mer-maids' code of honor, for Luce to speak to a human at all.

It had also been against the timahk for her to save his life, of course, no matter how she tried to rationalize what she'd done. Luce knew there were good reasons for the law she'd bro-ken—the one which demanded that any human who heard the mermaids singing had to die—but she couldn't think about those reasons now without feeling a surge of rebellious stub-bornness. Her resentment of the timahk's insistence on murder had been in the back of her mind when she'd spoken those reck-less words to Dana: *I don't know if I even believe in the timahk anymore.* In retrospect, Luce knew it was a terrible idea to say that out loud. She'd been living in dreamy isolation for so long that she'd forgotten the importance of keeping her most dangerous thoughts to herself.

There was a nudge at her hand. Luce looked down, glad to be distracted. It was one of the two larval mermaids who lived beside this beach: little girls, maybe eighteen months old, who'd changed into mermaids before they'd even learned how to talk right. Now they were stuck being that age for as long as they lived—and for most larvae that wasn't very long. Larvae were slow, awkward swimmers, easy prey for orcas; Luce was glad that these two were too babyish to understand that. They squealed and tumbled together in the water, nuzzling Luce so that she wouldn't forget to crack extra oysters for them. Sometimes she'd sing them to sleep, even tell them half-remembered fairy tales. Not that they understood anything, but they loved the attention.

"Here you go. Wait. Want a few more?" The larvae crooned wordlessly, snuffling at her and gobbling up the shellfish. One of them was pale, but the other was probably Inuit, and gazed at Luce with eyes like black pools. Sometimes Luce thought of giving them names but then thought better of it. That would only make her feel worse when they died.

Late twilight brushed the cresting waves with strokes of indigo, moody purple, slate gray. A few scattered islands cut black patches from the blue-glowing distance. The spruce-fringed slopes of the coast began to call to Luce, and she felt the tidal pull of desire to give herself to the sea. To spiral out through the night blue water, caress each wave with soft curls of her own song, and then maybe—just for a little while—float farther north, out past the fishing village where she'd thrown the bronze-haired boy onto a pebble beach. Not that she expected anything to come of this expedition besides some painful memories . . .

She was careful to keep her singing quiet as she swam out, even though hardly any boats seemed to come through this way anymore. Probably the crews had finally gotten spooked by all the shipwrecks and decided that this part of the coast was simply unlucky. Every time Luce noticed a big commercial fishing boat or a cruise ship, it would be swinging out toward the horizon as if it wanted to avoid the area on purpose. That was fine with her. She knew, though, that Anais and the others had to be seething with frustration, watching their prey repeatedly glide out of range. Still, there was the occasional small fishing boat or kayaker, and Luce couldn't take the risk of anyone hearing her sing. She played with the water as she swam, sculpting it with rivulets of music. Several months before, she'd discovered the secret of controlling the waves with her voice, and she'd been practicing obsessively ever since Catarina had left. Now as she skimmed along the surface she let out a series of high, bright, concentrated notes, calling up a row of perfect jets of water that splashed down again as she swirled away. Then she dipped below, still singing, opening ribbons of air inside the sea.

She could even make small blobs of water levitate now. She'd been working on sculpting water in midair with tiny variations in her song, shaping transparent fish and seabirds, stars with dangling tentacles, human faces . . .

A spangle of shining windows to her right marked the fishing village set back in its small crook of harbor. Luce reflexively edged a bit farther out to sea. Even if no one saw her, human settlements always had an air of discomfort around them, a subdued menace. Farther on was the beach where she'd left the boy, followed by a wall of low, uneven cliffs thick with half-dead spruce. Luce swam in closer again, gazing up. Trees stripped naked on the windward side tilted forlornly out of jags in the rust-colored rock, their bare tan branches like decaying lace. She caught the flash of something white and plummeting, probably a hunting owl, and heard an animal's cry from the edge of the woods. It was loud and determined, and Luce stopped singing to hear it better. Maybe a rabbit was screaming as the owl carried it gripped in piercing talons.

No. The cry went on too long for that and, it occurred to Luce, it was oddly musical, though to a mermaid's ears it was much too coarse and graceless to count as actual music. Not really like an animal's voice at all. Almost human, in fact, and now that she thought about it there seemed to be something peculiar about the sequence of notes. There was one note that soared up, high and feverish, followed by a tumbling fall . . .

Luce heard her own small cry of astonishment. She stopped where she was, her tail flopping straight down in the water. She wanted to clutch at something, but there was nothing to hold on to, only the lift and fall of waves.

It *couldn't* be, Luce thought. It just couldn't! The voice from the cliffs faded away, leaving only the sigh of wind behind. Maybe it had been her imagination after all. Much as Luce had wanted something like this to happen, she found her heart pounding with relief at the rushing silence. She waited another minute for the voice to come back—the voice that had seemed, for a moment, to be singing Luce's own very distinctive song of enchantment—and the cold wind throbbed alone in her ears. It *must* have been an animal; didn't certain animals sound almost human sometimes? It was better this way, Luce told herself. She circled away, ready to head back to her cave.

In the evening dimness at her back a single high note emerged. It hovered over the sea. Then the voice released it, letting it roll through descending tones then drift and spread. The melody wasn't made to be carried by a human voice, but even denuded of all magic, its notes knocked askew, its velvety harmonics missing, it was unmistakably Luce's own song.

Her fellow mermaids knew Luce's song, of course, but there was only one human who had ever heard it and survived. She'd heard the exact same voice singing once before, in fact, as she'd watched the boy lean against a white railing, ignoring the flailing shapes of the people who hurled themselves overboard right beside him. Luce swirled in confusion. The boy with tousled bronze hair must be standing between the trunks of dying trees, dusk light reflecting in his wide-set golden eyes. There was no other explanation for what she was hearing. He'd gone to a lonely spot on the cliffs to pour out this song, gone to the kind of place that humans generally preferred to stay away from, especially after dark. He'd deliberately sought out a refuge where no one would hear him.

No one, that is, unless someone just happened to be drifting along the sea swells nearby. Was he actually *calling* to her?

Luce slipped cautiously nearer to the shore, until she was just below the spot where she heard the voice. It seemed to echo out from the top of a sloping cliff where the rock cracked in a pattern of elongated diamonds. He was only twenty-five feet above her now, maybe less; Luce could just make out a hint of something golden shifting between the trees, a pale hand holding a dead trunk. She kept her body straight down in the water so that the shimmer of her tail wouldn't give her away. Even if he looked right at her, her dark hair would blend into the dimness of the night-streaked waves, and the subtle glow of her skin was no brighter than the natural phosphorescence of the water here. The song lapsed into quiet, but Luce was so close now that she thought she could hear his breathing mingling with the steady whirr of the wind.

Now that she was so close, Luce realized the impossibility, even the horror, of trying to speak to him. She'd helped kill his family. Anything she could say would be outrageously cruel. It would even be wrong to ask for his forgiveness. She had no right.

"Fuck," the boy said. His voice was weary but distinct,

and he pulled his hand back and slapped the bare trunk, hard. "Fuck, fuck, fuck." He grabbed the trunk and shook it till it creaked. It sounded like he might be crying.

Luce's body lifted and fell, tugged toward the rocks and then shoved back again. The waves shattered on the cliffs, flinging blots of foam against her face.

"I'm sorry," Luce whispered. She knew that the moan of the sea would drown out her voice; she'd probably have to shout to make herself heard. "I'm sorry. I do understand how much I hurt you. I do. I'm an orphan, too."

"You *monster*." His voice was louder now. A long rasp of pain. He couldn't know she was there, could he? She couldn't see his face, only his forearm and hand emerging from the trees. "Why didn't you just kill me, too? You sick, evil, inhuman *thing*. You know my little sister was only six years old? And you just go and wipe her out like she was nothing . . ."

Luce bit her lower lip, hard, to stifle the shriek that nearly tore from her. The words raked through her chest; she felt as if the boy had reached inside her, jerking the halves of her rib cage apart.

"You know they made us read a poem in class today?" The question was oddly bland, everyday-ish, but that only made the poisonous grief in his voice seem worse. Did he really not know that she was just below, listening to him with a sharp ache tearing through her heart? "It was a poem about you, or anyway about mermaids, and I completely lost it. They make it sound like hearing the mermaids sing is this beautiful, incredible experience, when really, even if you live . . . You know your song is *stuck* in me? I'd be better off dead than hearing something like that all the time, and there is *nothing* that will ever make it go away. And your face . . . Maybe the most evil thing about you isn't even that you kill people. It's what you do to the ones who survive."

But it's the same for me! Luce wanted to tell him. *You're stuck in me, too, and you're not even magic. You're just totally, boringly human.* And wasn't that even worse, in a way?

Luce really understood, for the first time, why the timahk had that rule, that insistence that no human who heard the mermaids sing could ever be allowed to live.

It was so much easier to forget them if they died.

The moon floated up over the horizon. It hung just above a distant island, immense and sullenly, gloriously golden. Its light reflected off the water so brilliantly that Luce seemed to be surrounded by an armada of burning paper boats.

She leaned away from the rocks, pushing back with slow swirls of her tail. She didn't know when she'd started crying. She closed her eyes and slid up the curl of a wave on her back. Darkness swayed in her head, and everything was cold apart from the hot stripes of her tears.

"Oh my God! Wait!" It was the bronze-haired boy yelling down at her. He was leaning recklessly far out now, his slim body curved like the sail of a ship. Only the hand still clutching the spruce trunk kept him from tumbling down the slanted cliff. Luce gazed straight up at him in shock, wanting to scream at him to be more careful, but her voice knotted in her throat. How could she say anything to someone who felt such perfect loathing for her?

It had been so thoughtless of her to show herself, stretching out on the water like that. She should dive deep under the waves, vanish and never come back. But his eyes fixed on hers pinned her where she was. She hadn't really expected she'd ever see that face again, those ochre-gold eyes set far apart, that bronze hair, longer than it was last time, flicking wildly in the wind.

"Look. I need to talk to you, okay? You *owe* me!"

I've already heard what you have to say to me, Luce thought. *Evil, sick, inhuman . . .* She felt a sarcastic impulse to point out to him that in some circles "inhuman" would be considered a compliment. Now he was peering over the edge as if he was evaluating his chances of making it down that precipitous slope of loose, blade-sharp scree without breaking his neck.

His chances weren't good. But what if he tried it anyway?

He turned his gaze back on her, hard and taunting. Luce was reminded of the way he'd looked at her right before he'd dived off the rail of the buckling cruise ship. She had to vanish. Get away from this place, before the sight of her goaded him to do something idiotic.

"If you don't get over here and talk to me," he announced harshly, "then I'm coming after you!"

Luce dove. It *had* to be an empty threat, she told herself. It had to be. He'd seen at first hand how incredibly fast she could swim, after all. No matter what he said, he'd have to realize the absurdity of trying to catch her in the water. She swooped down through dim regions at the base of the cliff, weaving among loose boulders palely crusted in barnacles. She wasn't about to go far, though. She had to find a spot where she could slip up and watch him unseen, just in case . . .

Just in case he needed her help. But she shouldn't even want to help him, Luce told herself. Why should she feel that saving him once bound her to him, obligated her to rescue him again even if he did something that was purely self-destructive? He'd said himself that he'd prefer to be dead.

A square of pitching moonlight above showed the way to a narrow opening between two straight planes of stone. Luce skimmed her way into it, the rocks pressing in on her shoulders, and slipped her face halfway into the air so that the water still played around her mouth. She looked carefully up and saw him from behind now. He was still leaning out but not quite as far. His head was pivoting back and forth as he scanned the waves, searching for her. But she'd been right. He hadn't tried to make it down to the water. Luce strained to repress a gasp of relief.

"Fine. You're still hanging around listening, aren't you?" Luce was irritated with him for guessing right and also with herself for being so predictable. "I'll be back. Same time tomorrow. You wouldn't have come this close if you weren't at least curious about me." He kicked at the cliff's rim, sending a small avalanche clattering down into the water. Dark rocks split the golden film of moonlight. "Or did you just want to make sure I'm still suffering?"

Luce almost felt provoked enough to say something, but before she could figure out the right retort he'd gone, scuffing off down the path where the trees blocked him from view. After a moment's fury she was glad. Answering him would have been momentarily gratifying, but it would have also been a huge mistake.

Almost as big a mistake, she thought, as saving him in the first place.

3

The Paper Boat

He'd gone to the cliffs four nights in a row now, crying out his best imitation of that monstrously beautiful song. But the dark-haired mermaid hadn't come back, or at least she'd been careful not to let him see her. For all he knew she might be somewhere out there every night, hidden behind rocks or sliding along below the water's surface. Either way, she was still stubbornly refusing to let him confront her. Let her be like that, then. He'd find another way to make her deal with him.

He kept thinking back to the morning of the shipwreck. He'd been so consumed by remembering her song, he realized, by remembering the overwhelming presence of death, that he hadn't paid enough attention to certain details. After the crash he'd pulled himself up onto the ship's railing and dived overboard with the hazy determination of swimming for the rocks nearby. She'd caught him around his rib cage, pulling him away from the wreck, and surfaced with him maybe a hundred yards away. He'd replayed all that in his head at least a thousand times.

What he hadn't given much thought to was the way she'd acted when they emerged into the air. She'd looked around nervously, staring toward the fractured ship, then toward the water where mermaids trilled in unearthly voices to the drowning crowds. Now that he was bothering to focus on that particular moment, he realized the way she'd glanced back was furtive, embarrassed. It was exactly the way a girl in high school would act if she was talking to someone seriously unpopular, worried that another girl in her clique might catch her at it.

And a second after that she'd told him that they had to dive. She'd wanted to get out of sight. It all made sense now. She didn't want any of the other mermaids to know what she'd done. She was afraid of getting in trouble with them. Dorian couldn't help laughing nastily when he realized it. He *had* something on her. He could use it. Now that the plan was forming in his mind, he couldn't sit still. His eyes roamed around the bedroom they'd given him, one wall completely covered in an incongruous photographic mural of koalas and bamboo. Everything else in the room was lacy or floral; his few scattered belongings were clearly intrusive, disturbers of the peace. Lindy's sewing machine and knitting supplies took up a large corner. Dorian kept jumping off the bed, pacing twitchily back and forth, even though it was after two in the morning and he definitely didn't want Lindy waking up.

He was going to *blackmail* a mermaid. Excitement jumped

in his muscles at the prospect, speeded his breath. He wrenched open the bottom drawer of the hideously ornate, baby blue dresser with its painted wreaths of bloated purple roses. He'd finished well over a hundred drawings in the months since he'd first seen her, and now he pulled thick messy stacks of them out from under the tangle of jeans and hoodies. Not all of them would work—there were dozens that showed cresting waves crowded with staring eyes, or sometimes with one huge eye all alone. Cyclops waves. But there were others where he'd made a painstaking effort to capture her face, drawn her framed in peaked slopes of water. A number of those portraits showed a decent likeness, though somehow getting her features right didn't begin to convey how phenomenally beautiful she was. When Dorian drew her, she was never more than very pretty. But one thing was obvious about her: she didn't look anything like mermaids were supposed to, with her short, spiky, almost punk, dark hair and long, shadowy eyes. He felt confident that if any other mermaid found one of the drawings, they'd recognize that face right away.

They'd realize the truth, too. Probably she wasn't supposed to let anybody see her. If the mermaids weren't all seriously careful to keep out of sight, he wouldn't be the only person in the world who knew they were more than an old myth.

It was lucky that he'd used black permanent marker on glossy paper. The images wouldn't bleed in the sea. Dorian began sorting through the stack with his hands trembling, pulling out the best ones and setting them to the side on the matted carpet. He'd just do one or two to start with. If she still wouldn't cooperate, well, he could draw as many more as he needed.

He took out his pen, thinking of a message. It seemed bizarre to imagine that she could read, but then it was also inexplicable that she'd known English. In a movie she would have learned by secretly watching TV somehow, but Dorian knew that wasn't it. Say she could read, then, freakish as that sounded. It wasn't any more freakish than the fact that she existed. He thought for a minute before writing in clear block letters in the empty space above her head: *If I keep putting these drawings in the water, your friends will find out what you did. So you'd better come talk to me. I'm not playing.* He hesitated briefly and then decided not to sign his name. There was the risk his message would be discovered by a person instead of a mermaid. Dorian took the inscribed drawing and folded it into a crude boat. He stuffed it in his pocket and clambered out his ground floor window, dropping into a narrow channel of bracken that ran between the houses.

By the time he'd made it to the beach where she'd left him he'd started to feel just a little bit sorry for her. For all he knew, he was about to mess up her life completely. And she'd saved his, no matter what else she'd done. No matter whom she'd killed . . . He sat on the shore, the cold lumps of the stones digging into his legs, and looked up at the sky. The stars here were bigger than he'd ever seen, outrageous in their purity and blue, blinding fire. The waves shone steel-bright in their frozen light, rising in liquid metal arches, crumpling like silver paper as they hit the stones.

Was he really going to back down out of compassion for Emily's murderer?

Dorian waited for the water to roll back, then ran down the beach and jumped onto a rock. He didn't want his fragile missive to get swamped. When the water tumbled in below him, he waited a moment and dropped the little boat on the outracing foam. As soon as he let go of it, something tightened in his stomach. He fought down a sense of queasy apprehension.

The boat sped away, becoming no more than a pale triangle skating up the dark surging water, spinning down again. He hadn't given much thought to the timing, but now he could see it had been perfect. The tide was going out, taking the folded drawing away with it. He found himself lingering on the rock in the irrational hope that the drawing would drift close enough again that he could reach down and snatch it back from the sea.

It was far away now. A white blinking eye on the wild water.

"Hey," Dorian said softly. He didn't know how he'd gotten in the dubious habit of talking out loud to her all the time. "Hey, girlfriend." That was a pretty sick joke, really. He suppressed an unwanted memory of her arm holding his waist, her glossy, almost luminous shoulders, that bare chest. His lips twisted into something between a smirk and a grimace. "I really don't want to cause trouble for you, but you're forcing me to. I have to do *something* . . ."

Of course there was no answer. There never was. It seemed like all he ever did these days was talk to the unresponding night.

4

The Diver

She could stay away from him, Luce told herself. After all, she'd had the self-discipline to develop the power of her singing in ways the other mermaids had never even imagined, practicing hour after hour. And she'd managed to overcome the cold desire to sing humans to their deaths, bind them in enchantment, even as she'd felt the dark, addictive thrill of controlling so many people. With her singing Luce could force anyone to love her to the point of self-obliteration, but she'd refused to continue doing it. Compared to that, ignoring one pathetic human boy should be easy.

It was dangerous, of course, to have him howling her song on the cliffs at night. If any of the other mermaids heard him, they'd probably figure out that Luce was guilty of letting him survive; her song was so recognizable that it would almost certainly give her away. But as Luce thought it over, she decided it was a risk she could take. Her old tribe almost never swam that far from their own cave, and as long as the boy didn't see her again, he'd get tired of calling her and give up before long. Humans were cowardly and weak-minded. They got bored easily. There was no reason to believe he'd be any more determined than the rest of them. For the next few days Luce deliberately swam in the opposite direction, toward the Aleutians, even though there were more orcas that way.

On the fourth night, though, her curiosity got the better of her. Was he really still showing up at that spot on the cliffs, singing his ugly parody of her song? She skimmed through water that glowed blue with dusk and shivered with whale song, stopping at a rock heaped with drowsy seals. They were used to her and didn't startle, though a few of them looked up with dreamy black-glass eyes and snuffled.

She'd made up her mind to see if the bronze-haired boy was still singing to her. Why was she so reluctant, then, to discover the truth? Luce imagined arriving below the cliffs and hearing nothing but the rasp of surf and wind and suddenly felt almost nauseous with loneliness.

If that was it, though—if she actually *wanted* him to keep coming to the cliffs and singing for her—then that was worse than insanity. Hearing him would be all the pretext Anais would need to persuade the other mermaids to attack her, for one thing. She should want the human boy to forget about her as soon as possible. Talking with him would be pointless even if he didn't hate her so much, and Luce had to admit, so deservedly . . . It suddenly occurred to her that he might be trying to lure her close enough that he could murder her in revenge. Maybe he was carrying a knife, even a gun.

She slid quickly along under the surface, not bothering with any singing games this time, and popped up fifty yards from the cliffs. She was careful to hold her face lowered toward the water, to keep him from seeing a telltale patch of pale skin out on the dark waves. Luce hovered in place with just a slight rippling of her fins, comfortable with the steep lift and fall as her body rode the swells.

His voice was very faint at this distance, a melodic scratching on the wind, but he was there. Luce was incredulous, again, at just how terrible human singing was, but he was clearly doing his best to reproduce the song Luce had used back when she'd lured humans to their deaths. Really, he sounded even worse than last time, as if he'd sung his throat raw. The notes croaked and sputtered, flapping awkwardly over the sea like wounded crows. She didn't know whether to think it was funny—or horribly, wrenchingly sad.

His voice was thick with heartsickness, Luce realized, with icy grief and loneliness as blue-black as the Alaskan sky in deep winter. And all that suffering was her fault. As she kept listening, she noticed a new emotion seeping from that voice as well: frustration and the beginnings of rage. He was getting furious with her for failing to appear. He wouldn't just give up, Luce suddenly realized. Instead he'd only turn crazier, more extreme . . .

Didn't he understand that she *couldn't* talk to him? The timahk stood between them, of course, along with the risk that her old tribe would discover them together, but there was also the whole untamed vastness of the sea. Luce remembered reading somewhere that the sea covered two-thirds of the earth. To humans the sea was only an afterthought, but in reality it was the dominant force, the roiling mind of the planet, and she was a part of it now. As far as the sea was concerned, human life—*his* life— was filthy and insignificant. Just a source of leaking poisons.

Luce dove down again, giving herself up to the glassy dimness of the water. It was an impossible situation, and any choice she made would be wrong one way or another. She couldn't talk to him, but she could hardly leave him in so much pain either. He was maddened by a song that had pierced into him and stayed there, barbed deep into his flesh. Luce twisted in the water, her chest tight with worry. Torment would drive him to do something crazy . . . Luce fought down a sudden, vivid image of his body snapped and bleeding on the rocks. Maybe the simplest solution would be to talk with him, just once, but it was hard to see how that could resolve anything. Schools of shimmering fish fanned through the greenish black water while the brilliant stars refracted into pale writhing blobs on the restless surface overhead.

Only the rare occasions when she skimmed up for a breath gave her any sense of passing time; she swam along in a blur of night and the liquid movements of the animals that shared the depths with her. Luce was so absorbed in her thoughts that she didn't notice how long she'd been swimming, or how quickly. She recoiled in surprise when the coastline suddenly bent into familiar shapes: a deep cove dipped away on her right, and she noticed a certain odd, sofa-shaped rock now almost completely submerged by the tide. She was at her old tribe's dining beach already; that rock was the one where Catarina always used to sit. It loomed in front of her, a lonely slab of darkness interrupting the rippling starlight. But the strange thing was that the rock wasn't the only patch of black standing out against the shining water. A shape pitched up and down five yards away from Luce to the left. It took her a moment to recognize what it was: a small boat, painted jet black, and anchored in the inlet's mouth with its engine cut. Luce darted deeper underwater and curled behind Catarina's rock, peering around the edge at the boat in total perplexity. The moving water made the image curve and ripple, but she could still see it clearly enough. It was so bizarre, Luce thought. Humans *never* came to this place.

Whoever they were, they were being extremely quiet. Luce had almost decided that the crew must be asleep when she saw two figures slip out of the cabin. Both of them were as pitch black and sleek as the boat itself. One helped the other adjust what Luce guessed was some kind of oxygen tank. The glossy blackness enveloping them was their diving suits, then. Were they marine biologists, here to study creatures that only emerged at night? Luce froze behind the rock, keeping her head under the water and her body deep in the shadow thrown by the burning moon. Strange helmets with attachments Luce couldn't identify covered the two figures' heads; if they were seriously planning on diving this late they were probably wearing some kind of night-vision goggles. Any movement might attract their attention. She couldn't even risk slipping to the surface to breathe, but with any luck they'd finish whatever they were doing here and go away before her air ran out. Luce could stay underwater for a long time if she had to.

One diver plopped overboard: a careful, vertical drop as if it was important to minimize the splash. Luce could just see the black body slicing down through the water, the flippers stirring as the diver began kicking deeper into the cove, angling toward the rough shelf of rock that walled one side. The other figure remained on deck, peering intently into the night away from Luce. Something about the moody, anxious tension of the figure on board began to worry Luce, and it suddenly occurred to her that these people were acting more like criminals than scientists. It didn't make any sense, though. There was nothing in this desolate spot that any thief could possibly want.

The swimming diver had reached the rocks and seemed to be fiddling with them somehow, pulling back swags of seaweed and jamming or twisting an object that Luce couldn't make out. The spot was deep enough that it would probably be underwater, though barely, at even the lowest tide.

A square patch of light suddenly gleaming off to the left made Luce swing her eyes back toward the boat. The figure on board had some kind of device out, bigger than a cell phone but smaller than a computer, with an oblong, glowing screen. Like that of all mermaids, Luce's hearing was much sharper than a human's. She could hear a quick tapping at some controls, see the figure nod in apparent relief. "We're good, okay, we're doing all right here . . ." a man's voice mumbled, but something in the helmet distorted it into a staticky growl.

The diver was already kicking back to the boat with nervous speed, clambering up the side. The suited man still onboard stared fixedly at the screen, which was now giving out a darker glow, and didn't move to help.

"It's already transmitting," the man growled, still nodding. The diver jumped down onto the deck and reached up to unfasten that dark, complicated helmet. "*Do not* remove that! You know the protocol. Do not remove your hood under any circumstances until we're back on land!"

"There's nothing here," a woman's voice objected. Feedback whined from the helmet. "I was underwater for ten minutes, and I didn't see anything worth worrying about. I'm sweating like a dog in this thing."

"Take it off, and I guarantee I'll write you up." The man's voice was curt, and his companion hunched her shoulders resentfully but didn't answer. They were already moving into the cabin, and Luce could just make out a few more voices coming from inside. A quiet motor had started, and Luce could see the chain running down to the anchor slowly spooling up. A few minutes later the boat was creeping out of the cove, its engines velvet-soft. The wake was so low and smooth that it didn't even foam.

Luce squeezed her hands against the rock to calm the trembling, and her tail began to thrash. Something was very wrong.

It's already transmitting, the man had said. Had the woman diver attached something to the rock? The worst possibility was that they'd installed some kind of underwater camera. Given the way the man had stared down at the screen in his hands, that even seemed likely. But if a camera was already transmitting images, Luce couldn't very well disable it without revealing herself. She had a sudden, disquieting memory of the first time Catarina had warned her of what would happen if the humans ever learned mermaids existed. *They'd poison the whole sea if they had to*, Catarina had told her, *just to kill all of us . . .* Humans had every reason to want the mermaids dead. Leaving an under-water camera where it might capture images of mermaids—well, that was unthinkable. It simply couldn't be allowed.

Did the intrusion of that quiet black boat mean the humans *already* suspected there were mermaids darting through their coastal waters, mermaids hunting their ships? It did seem peculiar that a diver was intruding on their territory not long after other ships had almost completely stopped navigating anywhere near them. Luce tried to shake the thought away. They were just scientists, she told herself, biologists or oceanographers, and the fact that they'd chosen to monitor this particular cove was purely coincidental.

Luce flicked away from the sofa-shaped rock, careful to give a wide berth to the area the diver had tampered with. Maybe if she stayed pressed to the rock wall above that spot she could approach the camera without putting herself in range of its lens. She swept far out, then squeezed up to the rock face and began wriggling carefully along, dislodging a few tiny crabs from their hiding places. They skittered away from her in annoyance, cling-ing to the slanting wall. It was an uncomfortable way to swim and the sharp crags scraped at her scales as she bellied along. The gray wall with its twisted kelp and feathery, pale green weeds slid by, only a fraction of an inch from her cheek. The diver had been somewhere over here, but for a long time Luce couldn't find anything unusual. She had a sudden awful sense that she might have dragged herself at full length across the camera without noticing it.

No. Something dark and very small poked between two broad brown leaves. Its lens reminded Luce of the wet darkness inside a snail shell. Luce paused a foot away from the camera and considered what to do. It was tiny and well-concealed enough that she never would have seen it there if she hadn't been searching carefully.

She broke a rubbery leaf free and lined the palm of her hand with it. If a human hand suddenly appeared on screen it would certainly attract attention. Then she found a sharp rock, crept a bit closer, and slammed the rock down hard into that lifeless, staring eye. She heard the glass shatter, and brought the rock down again, grinding deeper. This time there was an electrical fizzling as something in the camera's insides shorted out.

That was easy, Luce told herself as she began the long swim back to her own cave. She'd protected the mermaids from discovery. Everything was going to be fine.

Of course those people were scientists. Humans were so convinced they owned the planet, sea and all. Luce could slap them right in their faces with her tail and the existence of mermaids would still be more than they could comprehend.

* * *

Luce's cave was the same one where she'd taken Catarina to recover after the tribe had assaulted her. Luce could never slip through the entrance without remembering the time she'd come back bringing dinner for the two of them and found Catarina gone, the cave somehow colder from abandonment. It felt even worse tonight. Luce had thought she was used to being on her own, but now she squeezed tightly against one wall of her cave and gazed into shadows that seemed suddenly malignant. It wasn't a particularly cold night, especially not for a mermaid, but Luce still felt horribly chilled. She curled there shivering, remembering the song from the cliffs, until the bronze-haired boy's voice turned into hundreds of black sinuous eels. The eels emitted terrible music, shrill as electrical feedback, as they squirmed up the side of a soot-colored boat. Soon there were so many eels that the boat was just a black, glossy, wriggling mass, tugged gradually downward into water so black and slimy that it might not be water at all. And suddenly Luce knew that the boy was in the center of that mass. He was going under . . .

Luce's tail convulsed. She felt the splash hit her face, heard her own small scream, and opened her eyes to the twilight glow that filled her cave even on the brightest days. It took her a moment to understand where she was and that it was already morning.

And she wasn't alone. Dana was there, sitting with her back against the opposite side of the cave. Her tail was flicking, and Luce couldn't help noticing the hard, strained look on that beautiful face. Dana had been angry with her before, of course, but this look was different: cold and skeptical and, Luce thought after a second, disappointed. Coming up from anxious dreams, Luce felt instantly worried.

"Dana? What happened? Is something wrong?"

Dana smirked. "Are you *expecting* something to be wrong?" It was a strange thing to say, Luce thought. "Actually, I just came to visit you. Violet wanted to come, too, but then—" Dana broke off sharply. There were so many different emotions moving in her satiny brown face that Luce couldn't keep track of them. "But I sent her home. I thought it would be better if I talked to you alone."

Luce sat up facing Dana. Anxiety twisted inside her like the slippery eels from her dream. It was so out of character for Dana to take this cool, abrupt tone; her personality was usually warm and relaxed.

"What did you want to talk to me about?" It took all of Luce's courage to ask the question. She wanted to stare down at her hands, at the wall, and she fought to keep her gaze steady on Dana's eyes.

"Well . . ." Now Dana seemed embarrassed, too. Her voice switched abruptly from curt to oddly shy. "Luce, I mean, last time I saw you, you said something? And I just wanted to ask what you meant by it." Luce began to have a sense of what was coming. She braced herself. Suddenly Dana was the one who couldn't hold her gaze on Luce's face, and she stared off. "You said you weren't sure you *believed* in the timahk anymore. What was that about?"

Luce cringed. She had to say something. "I just meant that I don't want to sink ships anymore. I told Catarina that, too. I mean—I don't actually believe that it's good to kill humans, so I decided not to do it again." Luce's voice faltered. It was an outrageous thing for a mermaid to say. It must sound practically insane to Dana, and Luce started to hope that Dana would decide Luce was a hopeless case and go away. Then she knew from the unyielding look Dana suddenly flashed at her that what she'd said wasn't going to be enough. Dana *knew* something. She was too smart and sensitive to let Luce put her off that easily.

Luce started desperately trying to think up excuses. If Dana had heard the bronze-haired boy singing Luce's song, couldn't Luce insist that he must have listened to her secretly when she'd been sure she was completely alone? Maybe kayaked to the entrance of her cave without her knowing it? Did the fact that he knew her song *necessarily* prove she'd saved his life?

"But, Luce . . ." Dana sounded like she was forcing herself to stay calm, to speak carefully. "You know that's not what the timahk says. I mean, you know it doesn't mention anything about *having* to sink ships just for fun or something. So if that was all you were talking about, you wouldn't have felt like you needed to *say* that." Luce was absolutely certain now that Dana had heard the boy singing. "There are really only two rules about humans. You can't talk to them or touch them or have anything to do with them. And you *have* to kill them, but only . . ." Dana paused and stared at Luce. "But only if they've heard mermaids singing. So they can't go around telling other humans about us."

Luce took a deep breath. She'd just have to deny everything. There was no actual proof.

"I know what the timahk says, Dana."

"Then which is the part you don't *believe* in? Because I know you weren't talking about the rules for how we have to treat other mermaids. It's got to be one of the human rules."

They stared at each other. Both their tails had been swishing involuntarily as they talked, stirring up a froth. The water was cloudy with bubbles, dabbed here and there with foam. Luce couldn't answer.

"Luce, do you think—I mean—if some human finds out about us, do you really believe it's *okay* to let them live?" Dana couldn't maintain her forced calm anymore. Her voice was getting shrill, rising with outrage. "Even though if *any* of us did something that *stupid*, it would guarantee that we would *all* get killed? Not just the mermaid who broke the timahk but everybody. It's one thing if you want to throw your own life away. Crawl onshore, then. But how could you *do* something like this to the rest of us?" Dana's face was streaked with tears. "You hate us all that much because of Catarina? Is that it? You want to see me with my *head* blown off?"

Luce knew she should lie. She should play dumb, get indignant, say she had no idea what Dana was talking about. But seeing Dana's huge brown eyes staring at her in wounded disbelief, tears flooding down her cheeks, Luce couldn't do it.

"I would never want you to get hurt, Dana. I *promise*. Even if I did break the timahk somehow . . ."

"*If* you broke it?" Dana was yelling between fierce sobs, leaning over. She was reaching behind her back where it was pressed to the wall, pulling something out. "Luce, *if* you did? You know what you did! You know, and even if I don't know *exactly* what went on, I do know you're even worse than Anais!"

The shape in Dana's hand was a white triangle. Paper, wet and floppy in places. She started unfolding it.

Luce was shocked into speechlessness by the savagery of what Dana had just said. Her face felt hot and thick, and her heart was pounding. Then as the paper began to spread out and reveal an image, she thought she might faint, and pressed back hard against the rocks to steady herself.

It was a drawing done in heavy lines of black ink, like a very skillful panel from a comic book. A giant, sharply peaked wave blocked out most of the sky, and centered in the wave there was a girl's face. Hers. Obviously it was meant to be hers. Her tail was curled behind her as she swooped downward, so that her fins fanned out of the water above her head. And it looked like there was some writing up near the paper's top edge.

Wordlessly Luce stretched out her hand for the drawing, but Dana jerked it out of reach.

"You want to know what it *says*, Luce? You want to know what—whoever this is—this human who's writing you *notes* wants to tell you?" The bitterness in Dana's voice was terrible. Her sobs were tinged with outraged laughter. "Just that he's going to keep putting drawings of you in the sea unless you talk to him. That you'd better show up if you don't want your *friends* to find out what you did. He doesn't say what that was, but I can guess. Which ship was it, Luce? Where you just decided that the timahk didn't *apply* to you anymore?"

Luce choked. There was no way out of this. Dana had the proof right there in her hand. "The one right after Miriam died."

"Oh, now you admit it! What, was he incredibly hot or something? This is from a guy, right?" Dana's tone was shifting again, taut with sadness. "You seriously think you're the only mermaid who wishes she could have a boyfriend?"

"It wasn't like that," Luce objected. She was half whispering. One thing Luce knew for certain. She definitely couldn't tell Dana her real reasons for saving the boy: that he'd had the same dark shimmering around him the mermaids did and that he was the first human who had ever resisted her enchantment. That he was the only one who'd ever been brave enough to sing *back* to her. All that would just sound like a bunch of lame excuses, and it would only make Dana angrier. "It is a guy, but I wasn't—it wasn't like I was planning to ever see him again, Dana."

Dana stared at her. "You don't know how lucky you are that I'm the one who found this. Anybody else would have shown it to Anais. Then she'd have a *great* reason to kill you. Everyone would agree that you were asking for it."

Luce nodded, slowly. "I know."

"But I'm going to give you another chance." Dana shook her head in disbelief, but at least she wasn't sobbing anymore. "God, Luce, I *trusted* you! I really thought you were something special—like everything would get better if you were queen. And now, I mean, I just can't understand. How *could* you? How could you risk all our lives—not only of our tribe, even, but of all the mermaids everywhere? After all the horrible things the humans did to us, too? Just because you liked some *guy*?"

"I didn't think anyone would believe him." It was a pathetic excuse, Luce knew. "Dana, I'm *sorry*. Just—we'd drowned so many people, and then Miriam killed herself, and I couldn't stand it anymore. There'd been so much death, and . . . I just wanted *somebody* to live." She was only making things worse, Luce realized. Dana gaped at her with a kind of dull horror. "But really, I really, truly swear it, Dana. I'm never going to talk to him again. I'll obey the timahk from now on!"

"Oh, you are so *going* to talk to him!" Luce stared at Dana in amazement; what was she saying? "You are absolutely, definitely going to go talk to him! And I mean *today*, Luce!"

"What are you *talking* about?" Even as Luce gasped out the question, she already had a miserable realization of what the answer would be. Dana laughed caustically.

"I'm talking about the fact that you're going to go meet him, just like he wants you to. And this time," Dana snapped, "*this* time you're going to make sure he dies!"

5

The Rowboat

The day seemed bleak and endless. Luce was buffeted by waking nightmares, by memories that pressed in on her mind and wouldn't stop. A black boat, then Miriam shuddering with agony as her tail dried out, then her father smiling at her the last time he'd said goodbye and sailed off on the *High and Mighty*, not imagining that it would never return to shore. Miriam's voice whispered on and on in her mind, telling Luce about a dark recurring dream: human soldiers invading their cave, raising guns. If that ever happened in reality, though, couldn't the mermaids simply overcome them by singing? Luce couldn't remember why, but in Miriam's nightmares the mermaids' songs had been useless to defend them. It bothered Luce that she couldn't reconstruct exactly what Miriam had said about that. But then, what Miriam had told her had been just a dream. It didn't make any sense to wonder why their songs were rendered powerless: of course in a dream things wouldn't work the same way they did in waking life.

Still, Luce couldn't stop remembering that boat, the sleek black diver, those distorted voices.

She hadn't mentioned the boat to Dana. And she'd kept quiet about that, Luce realized, because she'd known exactly what Dana would think. Those black-suited divers were no scientists. They'd come hunting for solid evidence of the reality of the mermaids. And if they wanted evidence it must be because they already had an idea.

And if that was true, well, probably someone had tipped them off. Someone had told the authorities a story that seemed too incredible to be real—but if it *did* turn out to be true, it would really explain a lot. Who had a better explanation for why so many ships crashed in this area, even in good weather?

Luce didn't want to believe that the bronze-haired boy had talked about them. But that was clearly irrational, and she knew it. He had every reason to hate the mermaids desperately. As far as he was concerned, mermaids were vermin that had to be eliminated in order to protect human beings, and human beings were the only creatures who counted. When Luce tried to imagine things from his point of view, she knew that he simply couldn't feel any different. It didn't matter that she'd broken the timahk for him and carried him to safety, not when her tribe had murdered his family. It would be insane to hope that he could feel any gratitude for what she'd done. Any *loyalty* . . .

Then why did she feel so betrayed?

Dana was absolutely right, Luce realized. Luce had endangered the mermaids by saving that boy, and that meant it was her responsibility to undo the damage. She'd been a fool to trust him. A sucker, even, for caring what happened to someone who didn't hesitate to inform on her. As long as he lived he'd keep talking, insisting to anyone who would listen that there were mermaids living right there at the edge of the Bering Sea, that they had to *do* something . . .

She'd promised herself that she'd never kill a human again. But she was going to have to make an exception, just this once. The prospect of drowning him appalled her, knotted her insides with sorrow and disgust, but there was no alternative. If she didn't, Miriam's nightmares might very well come true.

There was no choice. However, there *was* one enormous problem.

Unlike all the other humans Luce had encountered, the boy had the ability to resist the power of her song.

* * *

With any other human it would have been ridiculously easy. Luce could have gone to the cliffs and gently uncurled her song of enchantment: the death song, wilder and lovelier than any music on Earth. The melody would insinuate its way into the victim's mind, promising that all the sorrows and wounds of his whole life would be healed, promising that every bad or cruel thing he'd ever done would be forgiven completely. A human who heard that music would *want* to die. They'd dive into the water under the spell of her fantastical song, even swim straight for the bottom of the sea. And, just as long as Luce kept singing to them, they'd die without any pain or fear. More than that, they'd die with their minds flooded with sweet, silky bliss, with a sense of rapturous homecoming.

But that wouldn't work on the bronze-haired boy. As much as Luce hated the idea of killing him, what was even worse was that she'd have no way to protect him from torment while he died.

Dusk fell over the sea like a judgment. Luce knew she couldn't turn back, but it occurred to her that it might be best if she died along with him. Much as she wanted to hate him, Luce couldn't help feeling a soft but definite bond with the boy she was about to murder. It would be by far the ugliest thing she'd ever done. She would live through it physically, but she knew beyond all doubt that her spirit could never survive an act like that.

She swam slowly along the surface, looking at a world turned a thousand shades of blue by the twilight. Then she noticed how the northern horizon was melting, its contours softening into a purple vapor, and forced herself to swim a bit faster. The fog was rolling in. The boy had to be able to see her for her plan to work. She curved away from the harbor in front of the village, then passed the pebble beach. The memory was so potent that it came over her like a vision: she watched her former self lashing frantically through the surf with the bronze-haired boy caught in one arm. She could see her dark jagged hair emerging from waves where they collided with the beach, her pale back straining as she pushed the boy as far onto land as she could. She watched his weakened crawl up the shore, and saw how he turned to stare back at her as she rose and fell in the heart of a wave . . .

The cliffs were next. Luce closed her eyes, trying to shut out the impending horror, but she still kept swimming.

His voice came into the darkness of her closed eyes. The same mangled version of her song, but this time the voice was sad and the melody moved like something half asleep. Luce swam directly below him and stopped, stirring her fins to hold herself in place a short distance from the shore. She could hear the song break off with a sharp cry.

"You did show up! Did you find my drawing?"

Luce made herself look up and meet his gaze. He was leaning eagerly from his perch on the cliff, his hair gusting across his cheeks. She saw the same wide-set ochre eyes and strong cheekbones, the same big, slightly crooked nose, all blue-dusted with evening glow. But there was something that Luce wasn't prepared for at all. She'd pictured him glaring down at her, his eyes slick with venomous hatred.

Instead he was smiling. Warm and relieved. He actually seemed happy to see her.

Luce didn't say anything; she only gazed at him. If she got into a conversation with him, she was sure she wouldn't be able to go through with it.

"Okay. I know you must think I was trying to mess with you. I *really* wasn't. I'm even glad you didn't get in trouble. I know it doesn't make a lot of sense, but I kind of felt bad about doing that." How could he behave so familiarly? From his casual, open tone, anyone would have thought he talked to her all the time. Tears blurred Luce's eyes, and she tried to fight them down. She shifted her position in the water. Just a few feet to start, being careful to keep herself where he could look into her face. She had to draw him back in the direction of the village.

He came along a few steps. Confusion creased his forehead.

"Why won't you say anything? I know you speak English,

remember? You talked to me that time. You told me to take a deep breath." Luce began swimming very slowly as the trees came between them. He kept weaving away from the path and leaning out between the trunks to look at her. "Is somebody watching you? Like, one of your friends? Is that why you won't talk?" He was suddenly speaking far more quietly, and he stopped pushing his way out of the cover of the trees. "I thought I'd figured out that you aren't supposed to talk to me. I got that right, didn't I? Okay. At our beach there's this giant boulder at—for you it would be the left side. If we stay behind it they won't be able to see us."

Luce couldn't see him anymore, but she heard his steps as he took off running.

It was a start, but she had to lure him past that beach. If she could draw him close enough to the village, he'd probably get the idea of filching a boat and rowing out to her. As long as he stayed on land there wasn't much she could do, but in the water she was far stronger than any human.

Our beach, he'd said.

When she'd seen him before, he'd called her evil and sick. A monster. And much as it had hurt her to hear him say that, Luce found herself wishing urgently that he would lash her with insults again.

It would be so much better than the way he was acting now. Almost as if they were friends.

* * *

She was there way ahead of him, waiting. She didn't slip behind the boulder he'd mentioned, though. Instead she floated in place offshore where he would see her as soon as he came out from the woods but far enough out that he wouldn't be able to speak to her without shouting. The fog was pressing in on the coast and a midnight-colored haze swallowed the cliffs where he'd stood minutes before. She could barely hear the crunch and scuffle of his steps as he leaped out from the shadow of the trees, almost falling as the stones skidded away beneath him, and gazed wildly around the beach.

Luce forced herself to wave, once and then again. The second time he saw her. She could see the sweep of his arm as he beckoned to her, but she stayed where she was, riding the swell of the sea.

He looked in the direction of the village, toward her again, then toward the encroaching fog. She could almost see the thoughts forming in his head: he could steal a boat, but would he be able to find her in the mist? Luce gathered her voice and let out a long, sweet note, music that sounded like shimmering light, like a gliding wing. It wasn't the beginning of the death song, but a musical beacon, just loud enough for him to hear. Would he understand?

Luce was just able to see him stare at her and nod before a swirl of dim blue cloud erased him from her view. She could hear his footsteps grating hard against the stones as he took off running again, and Luce drifted along parallel to the shore. She'd go as close to his village as she dared; she couldn't make it too hard for him to find her. The long note trembled and coiled in her throat, becoming a hovering lullaby. Luce closed her eyes as she pitched alone in the fog and sang to comfort herself. Anything to soothe the dreadful chill in her heart, to hold off the sense of creeping evil. Her heart raced as she tried to lull it with unearthly music, but even the beauty of her own song wasn't enough to protect her from the brutality of what she was planning.

There's no other way, Luce told herself, letting the thought sway with her song. *There's no choice, but tomorrow* . . . She finished with an image: floating on her back through Bristol Bay, eyes closed, until the water surged below her and sharp teeth snapped shut around her sides. She stayed suspended in her song and that awful vision for what seemed like a very long time, before she caught the steady beat of oars coming closer. The waves out here were too rough for a small rowboat, and its hull slapped down hard with each passing swell. When she opened her eyes again and looked around, the fog was so thick that the world seemed engulfed in deep blue velvet, and she could barely make out the slightly sharper form of the rowboat first approaching and then gliding past her, the boy's body tipping forward as he spotted her. His oars thumped as he pulled them in, and Luce swam close enough that they could see each other clearly. The lift and fall of her face wasn't quite matched to his, so that they stared at each other in a kind of vertiginous dance. Of course, she remembered, his night vision wouldn't be nearly as good as hers, but the subtle light of her skin would help. She noticed a strange look on his face, awkward and bitter and, she suddenly thought, resigned.

Did he guess what she was planning? Suddenly her heart doubled its speed, and dizziness rushed through her.

"Hi," he said flatly. "Going to talk to me now? Or you can't be bothered with that?"

It would be so much better for both of them, Luce thought, if he would only succumb to the death song. Tentatively, she tried it out, letting her voice slide up into the soaring note where it began. It was disturbing to hear that fierce, haunting song sound so choked and shy.

The boy clenched the edge of the boat and gave a single gasping laugh. Then he poured out the melody in return. Now that he was so close, Luce could actually feel how he seized her song with his voice, bent it, and twisted it back at her. It felt like a physical movement, as if her voice were caught in a hard grip and wrenched. Trying to enchant him was pointless. He could deflect her as long as he had to.

Luce let the music drop abruptly, and they stared at each other again. She could see the golden brown tint of his eyes even in the blue darkness, see the harsh skepticism on his face. A cloud of dark sparkling flickered around his head. With a human girl that shimmer would have been a sign that she was on the verge of turning into a mermaid herself. But as a boy he couldn't possibly change, even though he was marked the same way Luce was.

The wind sighed around them. He laughed again, with the same hurt, sarcastic suddenness.

"You think I'm surprised? I know what this is about. I knew it as soon as you didn't come to the beach." His voice was low, taunting. Luce shuddered, wishing she could pull her gaze away from his. "I just wanted you to talk. I need to understand— what *happened* to me. But I guess you're never going to give me that. What's it to you, what I need, right? You really won't say anything to me? One word?" Luce heard herself sob. He stared hard for a moment, as if he wanted to give her time. "Then get it over with, already."

Why did you have to tell the police about us? Luce wanted to ask, but the words seemed too difficult. Instead she bit her lip, and let her body drop straight down into the water. Catarina's voice whispered on in her mind, telling a story about her previous tribe on the Russian coast, about Marina, who'd been queen there. *One man—I don't know how he managed to resist her. Marina was a singer like no one I've ever heard; her voice could swallow a ship whole. But he held out, so three of us shot up from beneath his lifeboat and capsized it. Marina pulled him under . . .*

Luce sank down until the rowboat was nothing more than an inkblot on the blue-gray darkness above her, squeezed her eyes tight, and aimed. A violent spiral of her tail sent her rocketing upward, and she felt the bruising thud on her shoulder as it slammed into the hull, knocking the boat clear of the surface. She just had time to see him reaching out into nothing as he was thrown through the air, to hear him cry out in shock. She dipped through the blue and caught hold of him, and his arms reached back and grappled with her. All she had to do was keep her grip while she used her tail to drive them deep under the waves. No human could hope to overcome a mermaid out in the water.

Luce closed her eyes tight again. She didn't want to watch his face as he died. She heard his sudden inhalation as the water lapped over their heads.

Then they were struggling with each other, his legs flailing as her tail lashed, his hands gripping her shoulders. Her arms were around his back, and she clung to the drenched fabric of his parka. It should have been so simple for her to overpower him, but somehow her body felt weaker than usual. Her tail refused to move the right way. Even with her eyelids squeezed shut, Luce could feel by the lightness of the water above that they weren't far from the surface at all. She could feel his hair swirling against her cheeks, the rolling motion of his back as he twisted. She willed herself to drag him deeper . . .

The surface of the water shattered like a window, and the wild air billowed against Luce's face. She could hear breath rake into his lungs. It was all wrong. He would only suffer more this way. Luce tensed herself to plunge under again, when the chill, pulsating wind was interrupted by something inexplicably warm and soft. A silky pressure took hold of her mouth.

Luce gasped in disbelief. He was *kissing* her, his full lips slow and smooth on hers. One of his arms squeezed her waist, while his other hand cupped her cheek. It felt like all the sensual wavering of the sea against her skin but so much warmer, the sweetness unbearably concentrated where they touched.

Her tail wasn't spiraling to drive them under. Instead there was only a subtle rippling of her fins, just enough movement to support both their heads above the surface, and she could feel the recoil of the water as he started to kick. They were sliding across the ocean's skin together, and the kiss wouldn't break. It only turned hungrier, and even the bitter waters of the Bering Sea prickled with a soft, unsettling heat.

She wasn't fighting him anymore. If anything, she was helping to propel them back toward the shore. Luce didn't know how long it was before there was a light scraping and a few pebbles rolled away beneath her back. She looked up and saw his face above hers, the mist so close that all the world beyond was canceled out.

He pulled away from her, and Luce let her head fall back against the stones. Her thoughts rocked dizzily in blue darkness.

She'd failed abjectly. He was still alive, and Luce realized with despair that she would never find the willpower to attempt his murder again. He was half crawling and half thrashing up onto the beach, dragging himself upright until he sat cross-legged just beside her, bent over so that his face was only a foot above hers. Salt water streamed from his slicked hair and coursed like tears around his cheeks.

"Jesus, that's cold!" He almost barked the words, and Luce let out a sound halfway between a laugh and a sob. He was looking straight at her with the same lack of surprise he'd shown the first time she'd seen him, when he'd gazed at the mermaids as if he'd known about them all his life. "Can you come sit under the trees? At least that way we'd be out of the wind."

Luce sat up, still waist deep in the water, and shook her head. "I can't take my tail out for more than a few seconds. None of us can."

"Why not?"

"It's incredibly painful. When they start to dry out. And if we can't get back to the water pretty soon it kills us." It was strange to hear her own voice addressing a human being. She sounded shaky and her hands were trembling. He leaned back and grimaced at her.

"You just tried to *drown* me. And now you're seriously coming out and telling me the best way to kill you?" He snorted. "What makes you think I won't do it? Are you really dumb enough to *trust* me? I could drag you onshore right now."

Luce considered the question. The waves dashed against her back. "I could get away. I can outswim an orca. Getting away from you would be practically nothing." His expression stayed rough, sardonic. "And I didn't try to drown you that hard, anyway. Not hard enough. I'm supposed to make sure you die tonight. And I just blew it *completely*."

For a second his face froze in astonishment, and then he cracked up laughing. Luce found herself laughing, too, though her laughter had a desperate sound, and she knew it wouldn't take much for her to burst into tears instead.

"*Supposed* to? So it wasn't even your idea? Somebody told you to? Another mermaid, I mean." Luce was still laughing, or gasping, too hard to answer. She just nodded. "So how come you didn't do it? It's not like you give a shit about killing people. You murdered my whole family. Or at least you *helped*."

"I don't want to kill anyone," Luce objected, but her voice was feeble. The boy just glared at her, suddenly vicious, and his eyes went blank and desolate.

"But you don't even know what that means, do you? A *family*? Do you—whatever you are—do monsters like you even *have* parents?" Luce's insides clenched with pain, and she looked down. Getting drawn into this conversation was obviously a horrible mistake. Mermaids and humans couldn't possibly have anything good to say to each other. How could she have forgotten that? "*Got* it. You don't."

Luce made herself look back at him. "I don't anymore. My parents are both dead." She still half hoped that he would soften again, but instead he gave a bitter laugh.

"Yeah, but for you that's normal, right? I bet your parents swim upstream to spawn and then die. You were hatched from an egg or something. Like a salmon with . . ." He hesitated and pitched a rock into the waves. His whole body was trembling.

"Whatever. You look beautiful, but that doesn't mean anything. You don't have any real emotions at all."

Luce fought down an angry impulse to point out that, if he really thought she was a talking salmon, maybe he shouldn't have kissed her. That wasn't what mattered, and he could say he'd only done it to stop her from killing him. It didn't matter that she'd once been human herself either, though it was becoming obvious he didn't know about that. The sadism in his voice reminded her of Catarina.

"You know you sound exactly the way mermaids do when they talk about humans. They say the same kinds of things. Like having legs makes somebody automatically worthless."

He was still glowering. "I *bet* they do!"

"Well, if you think we're monsters with no emotions, why do you want to act the same way we do?"

His expression changed, and he sat back. Luce was surprised. She'd expected a blast of hostility or defensiveness; instead he seemed to be seriously thinking over what she'd just said.

"So *you* don't agree with that? That humans are all trash?"

"If I did, why would I even be talking to you?" She *shouldn't* be talking to him, Luce thought. She should just race south before Dana found out that she'd let him live a second time. He nodded, and now Luce could see that he was trembling harder, wrapping his knees against his chest for warmth.

"Then maybe you shouldn't have tried to kill me."

"What about what you did when I *didn't* kill you!" Luce snapped it out in exasperation. "I broke our law to save you, and you just went and told the police about us!"

If he had denied it, Luce would have been sure he was lying. Instead she watched his expression turn utterly flummoxed, watched him obviously struggling to understand what she was talking about.

"Told . . . Is this about the drawing? But I didn't even put my name on it . . ." Luce stared, wanting urgently to believe that he'd kept her secret. She wanted it so much that she knew she couldn't trust herself.

"You really didn't tell anyone?" Luce asked, and he looked at her too hard. Suddenly Luce realized that he was having trouble keeping his gaze from sliding down to her chest. She'd been living with other mermaids for so long that she'd completely forgotten how the sight of her naked torso would affect a human male, and she flushed and wrapped her arms across her breasts. His stare flicked down, taking in the gesture. He looked as embarrassed as she felt.

"I mean, I put that drawing in the water. To force you to talk to me. But I'd have to be insane to go around talking about seeing mermaids!" He gave a raspy laugh, and his teeth chattered. "You thought I ratted you out to the *cops?*"

Luce let herself believe him, then. It was like a sudden rush of warmth in her heart, a deep release.

"I thought I had to drown you, to protect everyone. And then Dana found the drawing and realized I'd saved you, after that boat . . ." The words bubbled out too fast in her relief. She turned and splashed water on her face to stop herself from crying.

"I mean . . ." He was being careful now, but there was also an incomprehensible gentleness in his voice. "I feel like I'd have a right to tell the police if that wouldn't sound totally nuts to them. After what you guys did. It's actually sick that I don't hate you more than this. I *should* want to kill you. I'm, like, a fucked-up person for *not* wanting to kill you. Do you—I mean, does that make sense to you at all?"

Luce couldn't answer, not without letting her tears loose, and she didn't want him to see that. She just nodded. The wind lifted damp strands of his hair and slapped them against his cheek. He hunched his shoulders and stared around at the beach. His teeth clicked more loudly.

"You're going to get sick," Luce said. It came out broken, whispering. "You should go home." He twisted where he sat, grating the rocks together.

"And you care about that? You're just trying to get rid of me."

Luce's voice halted in her throat. She shouldn't care, of course. She shouldn't even be there. The thud of trampling hooves sounded from the woods, maybe an elk running nearby, followed by the snap of branches, and somewhere a seal moaned. Suddenly she was aware of how isolated the two of them were together, buried in the core of the vast dim fog. He stared at her with fierce concentration.

"You're talking to me now, is the thing. If I let you go you're never going to come back. So I'm going to sit here and freeze." He was shaking so hard that the pebbles rattled faintly under his sneakers. "Are you really not cold at all?"

"It's against the law for me to talk to you. We're not supposed to have any contact with humans." She didn't know how to explain that the timahk was much more than just the law, at least in the way humans thought of it.

"So?"

"So Anais will kill me if she finds out. *Literally* kill me. She wants me dead anyway." She watched him suppress an impulse to ask who Anais was. "And I can't let Dana find out you're still alive. You don't get— For us this is really serious."

"Dana's the one who found the drawing?"

Luce nodded. "She's actually—she's one of the nicest girls in the tribe. But there's no way she'll understand how I could do this. Let you get away twice. She'll feel like I let her down." His eyes took on the same expression of intense consideration she'd noticed earlier. She couldn't stop herself from liking that look.

He reached up and pulled down the long zipper of his drenched parka, shrugging it off his shaking arms. His long-sleeved T-shirt was still soaked, clinging to him. Luce was ready to snap at him for doing something so stupid when he grinned and leaned closer, holding the parka out to her. It was olive wool, with a lot of pockets and a quilted orange lining; even soaking wet it felt warm in her hands.

"Give it to Dana. She'll think I'm dead. That way you'll get enough space to hang out with me."

"Enough . . ." Luce wanted to refuse, to tell him to forget he'd ever seen her. Instead she said, "Why would she believe me? That it's yours?"

He smiled brilliantly. "There are five more of my drawings folded up in the pocket. She'll totally buy it. You'll see."

Luce cradled the jacket, and noticed a name written in black marker down one sleeve. "Dorian."

"You *can* read. Crazy." He was still smiling. "Are you going to tell me your name?"

She hesitated. It seemed wrong to tell him, but then everything else she was doing was wrong, too. "Luce."

For some reason that made him laugh. "But I guess since you're a mermaid that isn't short for Lucille or anything?"

The question made Luce snort in annoyance. "It's short for Lucette! I *hate* Lucille; it's like the worst name ever." He laughed harder. Now that he didn't have his parka he was almost doubled up with tremors. "What's so funny?"

"You . . . sound so *human* . . ."

"I . . ." Luce started, and then caught herself, dismayed at what she'd been about to say. *I am human.* How could she even think something like that?

While she was consumed by the disturbing implications of that thought, Dorian got up on his knees, leaned across the narrow span of sea between them, and kissed her again. The kiss was so soft that it could have been part of the night, a single drop of blue darkness spilled on her lips. Foggy heat gathered inside her, reminding her of her lost human body. *This* was what Catarina had felt, Luce thought, the reason she'd kept up her forbidden encounters with drowning boys . . .

"You're going to come back?" It wasn't really a question.

"Yes," Luce told him, and instantly regretted it. She watched as he staggered to his feet, then realized that she didn't want to see him leave. She slashed away fast into deepening waters, trying to obliterate her thoughts with movement.

6

A Glass of Water

The wave faced him, swaying slightly. It was enormously tall and hunched over so far that the foam dribbling like spittle from its crest dripped onto Dorian's upturned face. Huge as it was, it leaned pathetically, stretching out its hands like a beggar. There was even something piteous in its roar. Dorian backed slowly away, pushing through a dense gray substance that was neither air nor water, but the wave shambled stubbornly after him, pressing closer and licking him with cold tentacles. Its breath stank of seal carcasses and weeds; it exhaled chill mist until Dorian's moistened hair clung to his face. It wanted something, and if he didn't find a way to placate it the wave would turn from fawning to savage in a heartbeat. It would lash down and crush him. The trouble was that he had no idea what to give it. A drawing? He groped through the pockets of his parka, searching for one, but somehow the fabric disintegrated at his touch and his hands kept reaching endlessly through cavernous space.

The wave stretched itself, its watery chest inches from Dorian's eyes, and then he saw a little girl's curled arm and hand suspended in its core. The hand was green with decay. Tiny fishes nibbled the loose skin from its fingertips, but as Dorian gaped the forefinger crooked twice, beckoning him inside.

He was still trying to back away, but his path was blocked by a cloudy wall, his legs snarled in warm weeds. In the murky depths of the wave, he could just see a girl's face beginning to form. Dorian knew that he couldn't let himself see that face, and with a frantic effort he flung himself around, straining to run. Something fleshy hit his mouth, and he heard himself screaming, and screaming again.

He had a mouthful of cloth. It was his pillowcase. He was banging his head into the pillow, and that awful yielding wall was only the mattress. He lurched up onto his knees, gasping, with his sweat-slicked hair cloying around his face, and found himself staring at a baby koala perched on its mother's back, gray light sifting through the frilly curtains.

"I hope you had a nice restful sleep," the man in the suit said. He was sitting in the rocking chair where Lindy did her knitting. His blue eyes were as blank as gobs of flattened chewing gum on a sidewalk. "A nice, deep, soothing sleep really makes all your troubles seem to melt away, doesn't it?"

Dorian wasn't sure if this was another dream. Irrationally he thought his clock might be able to tell him whether or not he was asleep. All the red digits said, though, was that it was already twelve minutes past eight. Why hadn't the alarm gone off?

"I'm going to be late for school," Dorian announced reflexively to the man, who suddenly appeared far more substantial.

"You won't be attending school today, Mr. Hurst." The man stood up. He was tall, and his blue eyes were small and so close-set that they seemed to be about to merge together. He had freshly shaved, sticky-looking cheeks and a long, flat nose with broad pink nostrils.

"I have a test today. In English." Dorian was finally awake enough to wonder what the man was doing there. He was awake enough to remember the night before, when he'd skimmed along the pitching sea with a mermaid's lips soft and cool against his own. How could anything in his normal life seem real compared to that? *Luce.* And she would come back to the beach tonight . . .

The tall man smirked. "I believe Mrs. Muggeridge will accept a note from the FBI, Mr. Hurst. You can take your test after you get back from Anchorage."

"From . . . I'm not going to Anchorage!" Dorian heard a soft shuffling out in the hall and looked up in time to catch Lindy's frightened eyes blinking in at him. She hurried out of view.

"You aren't? You know, I've mentioned to your nice relations here that we suspect some unpleasant things about the *Dear Melissa.* Foul play, maybe. Criminals, maybe. Extortion, you see, aimed at the cruise line. We'll keep popping your ships if you don't cough up." The man bent down and jerked open Dorian's dresser: not just any drawer but the bottom one. Dorian was suddenly very still. *The drawings . . .*

The man threw a pair of jeans onto the bed. Dorian forced himself to be casual, even obnoxious.

"So?"

"Well, I've explained to them that these extortionists are smart people. They recruit someone on board to help out. Someone impressionable, like a teenager. Naturally, I told them, young Mr. Hurst will want to do whatever he can to help us bring these fiends to justice." A gray sweater flew after the jeans, landing on Dorian's knees. That freckled hand couldn't be more than half an inch away from grazing the stacks of paper.

"Wait!" Dorian yelped the word, and the agent straightened and raised his eyebrows, his pink lips puckering. "Of course I want to help. I just didn't see why it had to be Anchorage."

"Can't stand the thought of getting out of this dump for a day or two?"

Dorian stared him down. "Can I get dressed, please?"

"You hadn't exactly studied for that test, anyway, had you? I'm doing you a favor."

"Are you trying to see me with my clothes off?"

"You think you're the first person to come up with that line?" The agent was sneering, but he still backed off, slapping the pale lavender door shut behind him.

Dorian wasn't about to put on the clothes the agent had flung at him. He picked out an outfit that was as obviously different as possible: a red hoodie over a ragged Mr. Bubble T-shirt marked all over with his own sketches, a pair of black cargo pants. Then he reached through the tangled clothes in the bottom drawer and stroked the paper. Even without looking he was painfully aware that he was touching an image of Luce's face. He stared around the room, but there was really no better place to hide the drawings. Not from someone who might search, anyway.

After a minute's thought, he pulled the drawings out and slipped them under a pile of Lindy's knitting magazines. He didn't think she ever looked at them.

A day or *two*? What would Luce think if he wasn't at the beach tonight?

He walked out into the kitchen and found Lindy nervously flipping pancakes while the tall agent leaned on the counter. He gave Dorian's outfit a sharp once-over but didn't say anything. Lindy caught the look, though, and turned to Dorian reproachfully.

"Dorian, couldn't you wear something nicer? For your trip with Agent Smitt?"

"Oh, that doesn't matter, Mrs. Basel. We don't care how our young man here looks. External appearances are so unimportant." He gave Dorian a wide, sickly smile. "Don't you agree, Dorian? What matters is what's on the *inside*."

* * *

After the first shock of Smitt's arrival Dorian's thoughts began to drift again. As he went through the motions of stuffing an overnight bag and layering on extra sweaters in place of his missing parka, he was thinking of Luce, imagining how he'd explain: *I thought if I didn't go along with it maybe they'd start following me or something. I had to throw them off* . . . She was already worried about the police. She would understand that he had to act in a way that would keep them from getting suspicious. At least, she'd understand if she ever gave him a chance to explain. Maybe she'd get so angry at waiting around for him tonight that she'd never come back. The idea sat inside Dorian like something cold and gelatinous clogging his heart. Real life was wherever she was, in her face where every curve held a kind of shudder-ing brilliance, in her disarming bursts of honesty. *I'm supposed to make sure you die tonight. And I just blew it* completely. Maybe it was crazy, but Dorian couldn't help grinning at the memory of those words.

Everything else in his life was just something other people expected from him. He kissed Lindy on the cheek, carried his bag to the car, and sat silent next to Smitt as they drove to the airfield. Whatever happened, Dorian thought, it shouldn't be too hard to convince them he was totally ignorant. The FBI thought a criminal gang had brought down the *Dear Melissa*, Smitt had said. Dorian could truthfully claim he didn't know anything about that. Once they'd boarded the small propeller plane Dorian stared out the window. Instead of the clouds he saw her face with its soft internal glow, her eyes shut tight, in the moment before he'd covered her mouth with his. Once again he'd known exactly what to do.

He'd outsmarted death a second time. It was impossible to repress the thrill of that, the sense it gave him of his own outra-geous specialness. If he could make a mermaid like him too much to kill him, how ordinary could he be?

* * *

In Anchorage there was another car waiting. Smitt took the front seat while Dorian slumped into the back. He'd spent a day here with his family just before they'd left on their fatal cruise, and he remembered the drive into town, the freeway curving beside a blue waterway, a handful of white office buildings set against whiter mountains, the blue-green luxuriance of trees. They pulled into an underground parking lot beneath one of those white buildings and took an elevator up to a floor where anonymous beige hallways mazed away in all directions.

Smitt led Dorian around several turns. His eyes were still empty, but his smirk kept getting tighter, as if someone were steadily pulling on a drawstring threaded through his mouth. After a few minutes he opened a door onto a small room where a brown plastic table sat surrounded by blue plastic chairs. An older, thickset man looked up at them expectantly. He had tan skin—maybe he was Italian or Hispanic—gray hair, and large sympathetic eyes. His smile struck Dorian as genuine and even reassuring.

"Thank you, Agent Smitt. And this is Dorian, of course. I've seen your picture. I'm Ben Ellison."

"Hi." Dorian smiled back awkwardly and shook the proffered hand. Ben Ellison waved him to a chair, and Dorian sat down while Smitt leaned against the door. Ellison pulled a file folder out of a laptop bag and opened it, and Dorian caught his breath.

"Your mother really liked to post pictures online, didn't she? It's wonderful to see a strong relationship like this between a boy your age and his little sister. I wish my kids could get along half this well."

The picture in the folder showed Emily sitting on his shoulders. They were in a park, the pale sky laced by bare black branches. She was wearing a bright polka-dotted jacket and mittens made to look like duck faces. She held her hands up menacingly on either side of Dorian's face, thumbs flared to show that the ducks were quacking furiously. His own gloved hands wrapped her legs, and he was laughing so hard that he couldn't quite stand up straight.

Dorian turned his eyes away, only to find himself confronting Smitt's contorted smile.

"You must miss her very much," Ben Ellison said. Now his voice sounded too warm, almost gluey.

"Of course I miss her," Dorian said. It came out harsh, rasping. He didn't know where to look; definitely not into Emily's giddy face.

"I know you do. I spent a great deal of time studying these pictures." He turned over the photo of Dorian and Emily in the park. From the corner of his eye Dorian could see more images of himself: roughhousing with his sister, reading to her, jumping with her in a pile of leaves. "Seeing them, I couldn't doubt that you were telling us absolutely everything you know that might help us to understand why she died."

Dorian didn't know what to say to that. "Sure."

"The little jerk's been doing nothing but lying his ass off from the first time we talked to him," Agent Smitt snarled from behind Dorian's left shoulder. Dorian couldn't help twisting around at the words, and Agent Smitt's blue eyes met his with a slick, repellent look of self-satisfaction.

"Please, Agent Smitt." Ellison was warmly reproachful. "That's not at all constructive. We have no reason to believe that Dorian is actually lying."

Dorian was aware that he was being played with, but

awareness didn't stop any of it from affecting him. He felt the repulsive slap of Agent Smitt's words, his queasy smirk, and then the soft comfort of Ellison's reply.

"From everything we've learned, it sounds as if Dorian had a truly enviable life before the tragedy. Mother a professor of Russian history, father in medical research. Beautiful home, top schools. Everyone who knew them describes a very cultured, happy, loving family." Ben Ellison was watching Dorian too intensely as he spoke those last words. Dorian was careful to keep his face completely frozen. "Dorian would have more reason than anyone—anyone at all—to want to get to the bottom of this."

Dorian sneezed, loudly. Smitt snickered and said, "That's what you'd think, all right."

"That's what we *all* thought," Ellison agreed. He focused his attention on Dorian again. "Your story doesn't explain anything, of course. 'Everything went dark'?" Was there a note of sarcasm in his voice? "But considering how little we know about the effect an occurrence like that might have on the human mind . . . Well, let's just say that I was prepared to accept your version of events. It did leave open the question of how you reached the shore, though. We can definitely rule out the possibility that you *swam*."

"I never said I swam." Dorian felt his throat getting rough. "I said I didn't know how it happened." Ellison nodded, fixing his serious gaze on Dorian's face.

"You don't know how it happened. Of course. But how do you *think* you made it to land? What's your theory?" Dorian stared blankly. "Just speculate. I'd like to see what ideas we can come up with together. Anything at all."

"I mean . . ." Dorian had found a spot of carpet to stare at. "Maybe I took a lifeboat or something part of the way? And I just repressed it?"

"Maybe." Ellison nodded. "But if you took a boat, you did it long before the *Dear Melissa* crashed. You were discovered on the beach exactly fifty-three minutes after the time of impact, but by my estimate it would have taken you at least four hours to paddle that distance alone. And that"—for the first time his mouth bent like Smitt's—"that would suggest you had some advance knowledge."

They were getting back to the whole criminal conspiracy idea, then. In a way it was a relief. "I didn't know anything."

"Then you didn't take a boat."

Dorian met Ellison's brown eyes as Smitt burst out laughing behind them. The gaze Dorian shared with Ellison went on for too long but it was also somehow unstable, disorienting.

"We know how the brat got to shore!" Smitt yapped. "Stop pretending we don't."

"Agent Smitt . . ."

"He knows it, too. He just keeps spewing lies."

"Withholding information isn't the same thing as lying."

There was a lull. Ben Ellison started flipping through the stack of photos again, and Dorian clung to the edges of his chair. He was feeling terribly unbalanced, as if ocean waves were pushing up beneath the dull beige floor and tilting it subtly from side to side. Something cold and vast and seething was coming too close.

"Dorian . . ." Ellison seemed genuinely concerned. "At a certain point I was forced to entertain the idea that there were some things you weren't telling us. But I couldn't believe you would have willingly participated in anything that might hurt Emily. I had to try to come up with other explanations for why you might be choosing to keep quiet, even though you must realize what's at stake here. We're trying to make sure no other little girls have to die the way Emily did. You do understand that, don't you?"

"Yes." Dorian thought of Luce insisting that she didn't want to kill humans. Even if she'd been telling the truth, though, it was pretty clear the other mermaids didn't feel the same way. They'd just go on murdering as many people as they could until someone stopped them. The floor kept pitching dizzily, and he could feel the blood drain away from his face. Ellison was watching him closely again.

"I can think of two very good reasons why you might not have told us everything you know. The first one is that you were convinced nobody would accept the truth." Dorian swayed. "Agent Smitt, would you please get Dorian a glass of water? He's looking a bit peaked."

Smitt was sneering so hard that Dorian thought his face must ache, but at least he left the room.

"Reality is far, far more complicated—and much richer and more amazing—than the vast majority of people could ever imagine. Would you agree with that? Dorian?"

"Yes," Dorian said again. At least he hadn't lied to Luce. He'd told her straight out that he thought he had every right to expose the mermaids if he could just find someone who would believe him.

"Then let's just assume that, in this room at least, there is nothing whatsoever too incredible to be believed. I'll accept absolutely anything you tell me. Does that change your story?"

Dorian opened his mouth to tell Ben Ellison everything, and stopped. His breath hissed abruptly. They wouldn't understand that Luce was different from the others, and he'd have no way to make sure she didn't get hurt. He pictured her dead body, back arched and fins dragging, floating in a giant tank of formaldehyde. Luce, short for Lucette. Dorian felt a sudden surge of desire to bury his face in her hair.

Ellison waited patiently, his deep eyes studying Dorian as if this choked silence was remarkably interesting.

"I see," Ellison said at last. "You want to tell the truth. There's something stopping you."

Dorian was having trouble breathing. The ocean followed him everywhere.

"That brings me to my second theory, then. The other reason why you'd refuse to talk. It might sound a bit far-fetched, but personally I'm convinced that it's the right explanation." Ellison started nodding to himself. "Dorian, I think you've been subjected to a form of mind control. You're not telling me what you know because the ability to do so has been *stolen* from you."

Subjected to mind control, Dorian thought. Wasn't that just a fancy way of saying he was enchanted? When he considered the way Luce's song stayed with him, traced like razor cuts all over his thoughts, he had to admit that made a lot of sense. He had been so arrogant, thinking he was somehow totally immune to a power that was strong enough to kill practically anyone.

Luce seemed too sweet and straightforward to control

someone's feelings with magic that way. But that could be an act, or just another way her spell was working through him, warping and reshaping his perceptions. Dorian still didn't want to accept the idea, but if Luce had deliberately enchanted him—*if* she had—then that would definitely explain why he couldn't make himself hate her. It would explain why he thought about her constantly and why he was starting to have feelings for her that weren't hatred at all.

"Dorian?"

Dorian looked up. Even the walls seemed to ebb and swell.

"What if somebody saved me?" His voice sounded terrible, the words torn off like shreds of old paper.

Ellison nodded his enthusiasm. "That seems very plausible."

Smitt opened the door, a dark blue glass in his hand, and passed it to Dorian. Dorian clutched the smooth surface desperately. There was a pause while Ellison shot a warning look at Smitt, who backed out of the room again with obvious reluctance. "Dorian. I know this isn't easy, but you need to make the effort. *Who* saved you?"

Dorian took a gulp of the water, gagged, and sent it spewing out of his mouth. The glass dropped onto his lap, sending a soaking tide across his knees, then rolled unbroken along the carpeted floor. He heard his own panicked cry. *Sea*water. The taste of drowning, the taste of squeezing death, thick with salt, weedy, airless—

"That *bastard!*" It came out in a shriek; even Ellison's composure seemed shaken.

"Dorian, what—"

"That bastard Smitt! He did that! He— It was salt wa-ter . . . just to mess me up." Even as Dorian yelled, he realized how strange it was: the night before, when Luce was actually trying to drown him, when the Bering Sea had licked between his lips, he hadn't really been afraid at all. Just cold, and angry, and brilliantly excited.

Apparently he was only afraid of drowning on dry land, in classrooms or office buildings. He almost started laughing from the irony of it all. But hadn't he heard somewhere that sailors got seasick when they left their ships and tried to walk instead through calm, leafy streets?

Ben Ellison, meanwhile, had gotten up and gone to the door. Of course Smitt was standing right there, Dorian thought; he'd probably been listening.

"Hello, Agent Smitt. Would you mind telling me where you got the water you gave Dorian just now?"

Smitt's stare looked impudent. "The drinking fountain down the hall, there."

"And did you add anything to the water?"

"Of course I didn't." The voice oozed contempt.

"I see." Ellison picked up the glass and shook one of the lingering drops out onto his finger, then put it in his mouth. "It tastes fine to me, Dorian."

Dorian gaped in total disbelief. Salt still hung heavy in his throat. Were they lying, or was he actually losing his mind?

Ellison was nodding again. "Maybe this is another of your symptoms. If anything it just confirms what I already thought." He sat back down, setting the glass on the wood-grained plastic of the table. "Anyway, Dorian, you were saying?"

"I don't remember." The familiar words came back, steady as a rolling wheel.

"You were saying someone saved you after the *Dear Melissa* crashed."

"I said someone *might* have saved me."

They stared at each other, neither of them breaking, until Ellison grimaced and glanced up irritably at Smitt. "Would you mind not hanging around like that?" Smitt and his bland blue eyes left the room, and Ellison sighed. "Are we really back to this, Dorian?" He sounded genuinely sorrowful.

Maybe Luce had put some kind of spell on him, Dorian thought. But maybe she hadn't. It was only fair to give her a chance to explain, wasn't it? "Back to what?"

"I believe a psychologist might describe what you're suffering from as Stockholm syndrome. A disorder in which the victim becomes emotionally attached to his torturer. But in your case it's probably even more complex than that."

"You think I'm getting attached to you?"

Ellison flashed him a hard look but didn't take the bait. "You have heard the mermaids singing, Dorian Hurst. Each to each. Maybe they even sang to you. And it severely damaged your mind."

* * *

Dorian went completely silent after that. Dead still and dead faced, waiting for it all to be over.

Once he'd recovered from the initial horror of Ellison's words, Dorian began putting things together. Obviously they'd talked to Mrs. Muggeridge, and she'd told them how he'd flipped out when he read those lines in class. Ellison didn't mean what he'd said *literally*, obviously. He couldn't. Instead he'd just decided to use that poem as a weapon, because he knew Dorian would find it upsetting. It was another trick, like the salt water.

After a while they gave up. A new agent, a woman this time, came and drove Dorian to a hotel and left him in a drab room with a takeout cheeseburger and a milk shake. Those things didn't taste horribly salty. Clearly, then, he hadn't hallucinated that awful taste in the water. After he ate he flicked on the TV and took out his sketchpad. All he wanted was to draw a new portrait of Luce. He had the feeling he'd been drawing her wrong all this time, but now that he'd seen her up close again maybe he'd finally be able to capture that weird, dark brilliance of hers.

They might take his bag, of course. Look through it. After thinking for a minute, Dorian decided it was safer to draw Luce as a human being, sitting on the beach and just looking at the sea. Nothing could be less suspicious, could it, than a teenage boy drawing pictures of a hot girl? He drew her wearing jeans and a striped T-shirt—the clothes looked really out of place, but he couldn't help that—with a book on her knees. She seemed like, if she were human, she'd probably be the kind of girl who read a lot. Where had she learned to read, anyway? Did the mermaids like to kidnap English teachers and hold them in captivity?

The thought of asking her that made him smile to himself as he drew.

* * *

The woman agent's name was Emily James. Probably they'd done that on purpose, too. Probably Emily wasn't even her real name. She came back at nine the next morning and took him to a diner for breakfast. Unlike Ben Ellison she didn't ask him anything about the *Dear Melissa*. Instead she just made friendly conversation about school, his interests: the kinds of things a dentist might ask to distract you from the fact that you were about to get your teeth drilled. Still, Dorian talked: he'd played basketball but not that well. He wanted to be a comic book artist. Back in Chicago he'd been in a band, but they were kind of half-assed and didn't practice much. She told him all about her brother, who was an illustrator. He kept sneezing. It wasn't too surprising that getting dragged through the Bering Sea had given him a cold.

Then Emily James took him back to the same room in the same white building. Dorian felt the tension all over his back and shoulders. He wasn't going to even consider telling them anything, at least not until he had a chance to talk things over with Luce more. He'd be calm this time. Friendly but quiet. And he wouldn't take anything to eat or drink unless he knew where it came from.

Ben Ellison seemed completely together again, too. He looked up at Dorian with a smile that was oddly warm, considering how things had gone the day before. "Hello, Dorian." He was opening a laptop, and the movements of his lumpy brown fingers were surprisingly deft and graceful. He looked somehow older today, and his heavy body sprawled wearily in its chair. "I thought you could use a break from all the questions today. It seemed like it might be a better idea to go over some of the background behind this investigation instead."

"Okay," Dorian said. That was definitely an improvement. He wouldn't have to talk too much. He was pleased to see that Smitt was nowhere around, too. He sat at a right angle to

Ellison, who turned the laptop so they could both see the screen.

"I realized that you might have a mistaken idea. You might think that what happened to the *Dear Melissa* was somehow new or anomalous. But the fact is that there have been similar ship-wrecks through all recorded history. Have you read the *Odyssey* yet?"

"Last year," Dorian said. The screen showed a map, but it wasn't of Alaska. He thought it might be the coast of Africa. In a few places there were patches of red dots.

"Then you'll realize where I'm going with this. These clusters of unexplained shipwrecks have been occurring for thousands of years. In certain areas ships will start spontaneously slamming into cliffs or occasionally into each other, even in very good weather. And a feature of these shipwrecks is that there are almost never any survivors. You sometimes find the lifeboats lowered but without anyone in them or life jackets drifting around empty. And in most of these cases dry land should be quite easy to reach. That island the *Dear Melissa* crashed against, for example. No one made it ashore. And the same thing was true for a Coast Guard boat that smashed into the same island several weeks prior."

Dorian began to think he'd prefer being grilled after all. He didn't want to think about the number of deaths Luce might be responsible for. "Okay," he said.

"You'll admit it was strange? Almost nine hundred people on board, an island right there, and not one person swam to safety? You have to ask yourself if they actually wanted to drown. And our sole survivor turned up a dozen miles away." He smiled at Dorian as if that was somehow a compliment.

"It's totally strange," Dorian agreed.

"So strange that people have come up with all kinds of wild explanations. The Greeks, of course, attributed these wrecks to the sirens, calling mariners into the rocks with irresistibly beautiful voices. You probably remember the episode in the *Odyssey* where Odysseus plugs his sailors' ears with beeswax so they won't hear the songs . . ." Dorian made his face as still and empty as possible while Ben Ellison gazed at him with blatant curiosity. Sirens: wasn't that really just another name for mermaids? There was a disturbingly long pause. Dorian made a point of studying the map.

"That's Africa?" Anything to keep the conversation away from sea-girls with magical voices. Ben Ellison only smiled.

"Of course," he said, just as if Dorian hadn't spoken, "in a more rational age people turned away from myths as a way of making sense of strange phenomena. In recent years these sinkings have usually been attributed to collective hysteria or mass hallucinations. A sudden fit of insanity that overwhelms the crew and passengers all at once. Sometimes referred to as 'mad ship disease.' That's the black-humor term for it, at least."

This didn't add up with what they'd told him earlier. "Smitt—Agent Smitt—he said the *Dear Melissa* got sunk by extortionists. Like, some kind of gang . . ."

Ellison smiled, but he looked sad.

"Nobody here believes *that*, Dorian."

"But Agent Smitt told my guardian—"

"Surely you of all people can appreciate our position, Dorian. It's not so different from the problem you've been struggling with. We have to tell people *something*. Ideally something that they might possibly believe."

Ellison stared at Dorian, obviously waiting for him to ask what the FBI *did* believe. Dorian just gazed into the screen. How many lost lives did those hovering dots represent?

"And to answer your question, yes, that's the west coast of Africa. Let's look at a map of shipwrecks in Alaska now." Ellison clicked a button. "Keep in mind that the Bering Sea is notoriously dangerous. Terrible storms. There's a high incidence of wrecks there in any case." A new map came up, and as Ellison had suggested red dots were loosely scattered across it. But in two places they were thicker. One was at the bottom of the image, well south of the Aleutians. There were definitely more dots down there but not really *so* many. But up near where Dorian was living, around Kuskokwim Bay and a bit farther north, red dots swarmed angrily: so many that whole patches of shore were blotted out. And one of those dots covered Emily's body.

"Why don't people just stay away, then?" Dorian could hear that his voice was getting harsher.

"They do now. There's been an official warning to avoid that section of the coast since early July. The number of sinkings around there escalated so abruptly that people were simply caught off-guard at first."

"But then . . ." Dorian stopped himself.

"*But then it doesn't matter?* Is that what you were going to say?"

"No!"

"Dorian, I know I said we'd take it easy on questions today. But this person, or this entity, that might have saved you from drowning—"

"That's not even real—"

"This unreal entity, in that case." Ellison paused. "Have you seen it again?"

7

The Queen

It served her right for trusting a human, even once. Even after the big deal he'd made about wanting to see her again, even after that bewilderingly tender good-night kiss, Dorian hadn't shown up the next evening. Luce had swum back and forth for over an hour between the beach and the cliffs where he'd sung before she finally accepted that he wasn't going to come.

A few hours after he'd given her his parka she'd even fought down her aversion to going near human towns, just to bring the rowboat back. She'd towed the boat as far as the village's main dock—it had taken her a while to find both oars, but to her surprise the boat's hull was undamaged—and tied it to a strag-gling rope. Incredible as it seemed to her now in the cold blue light of a new day, she'd actually been worried that Dorian might get in trouble for stealing it. He must have seen what she'd done for him, Luce thought, but even so he didn't care enough to keep his word to her.

There was only one explanation for his absence that seemed at all likely to her. It must be that he enjoyed playing with her emotions. Maybe this was his way of getting revenge. And to make matters worse Dana was going to show up sometime, and Luce would have to show her Dorian's jacket and rattle off a whole series of lies straight in her old friend's face. Luce had never felt so stupid before, so demeaned. Obviously Dana had been right. Obviously Dorian was treacherous and cold-hearted, and the smart thing would have been to drown him without caring at all. Luce couldn't remember the last time she'd been in such a foul mood. The day seemed mockingly bright and beautiful, with an azure sky and satiny breezes, with water that thrummed to the distant, booming calls of whales, their pitch so deep that it made her scales vibrate.

She hadn't been working enough on her singing, Luce decided. She'd let herself get distracted by some human boy instead. She couldn't do anything about Dorian or about the fact that she'd acted like an idiot. But she could at least develop the one power that was absolutely hers.

She swam out into deeper waters. Even when she had practiced singing recently, Luce thought with disgust, she'd just been playing pretty little games, sculpting blobs of water in midair, making tiny pirouetting fountains and arches. Clearly it was time to get back to using the full force of her voice. Time to remind the waves who their queen *really* was . . .

The waves were rough and high, the currents so strong that she had to flick and dance her way between them, slicing back with her tail each time the water grasped at her. Did the sea really think it could push her around like that? Luce dove down and gathered her voice into a long, driving note, slamming it right back into the face of one especially fierce current. Her voice fused with the water. It became a creature of living sound. Luce held the current where it was for a moment, then her unwavering pitch pulsed higher, shoving the immense pressure of the flow back on itself. She blasted the note until it was almost a scream, and for an instant the water in front of her surged in crisscrossing directions. Just above her head Luce saw the surface of the sea starting to bulge in a glassy dome, a swelling tumor of sound. A few porpoises approached, stared at Luce and the misshapen water forced up by her high, pounding outcry, and then rushed off in fright. Luce didn't care. The swell made by the two battling currents rose higher, and Luce was lifted inside it. For a few moments she hovered in tremulous space, gazing down through water like a huge curving window onto an unsettled sea.

Then the bulge erupted. Luce went flying up on an explosive jet of foam, surrounded by airborne waves that curved like wings. She twisted in space at least thirty feet above the surface, screaming now from pure exultation, and crashed back down so hard that it knocked all the air out of her. She fell through waves where the bubbles frothed in such dense clouds that all she could see was moving streams of whiteness, letting her tail spin. Her body rolled with no sense of direction. When Luce finally surfaced again her side stung from the impact, but she was laughing too hard to sing.

She'd raised the water before, used her voice to lift curling waves or straight towers of water. But she'd never controlled such a huge volume of water as that, never made the sea leap so high. If only Catarina could have seen it, or Dorian—

Ugh. Why did she have to spoil the exhilaration she felt by thinking of him now? Luce circled wildly in the murky sea until her body lashed the waves into a ring of froth. Vaguely she noticed the island where Dorian's cruise ship had crashed looming up on her left. Normally the sight of it would have depressed her. Normally she would have worried about slipping into her old tribe's territory, too. But today she didn't care about any of that.

She was gasping from swimming so crazily. Luce made herself calm down enough to drift along the surface, pulling in deep inhalations. Seabirds with bright red feet spiraled in the air above her, as free in their breathing medium as she was in her fluid one. Luce wanted to try mastering that much water again, maybe raise it in a single high wall this time, but she couldn't do that unless she had enough breath to sing with her strongest voice.

She really was getting too close to the old cave, though. She'd thought those were seals popping up for air fifty feet away from her, but now she realized that one had a mushy baby's face and stick-up tufts of hair. There were a few larval mermaids mixed in with the seals, then, and larvae didn't usually swim out this far unless they were tagging along after the older girls. Maybe she should slip back down the coast a bit.

"Samantha? You see that? Is that like a rotting porpoise or something?" The voice was chirpy and cold; it would have sounded completely emotionless if it weren't just a bit too shrill. "I'd say we should drag it out of our territory. Except then we'd have to touch it."

Anais and Samantha bobbed up and down in the waves, both pearl-skinned and almost shining with beauty, both lacquered with mist and the dizzy pale sunlight. Luce noticed that they were keeping their distance, though, and that Samantha couldn't hide the apprehension in her sea green eyes. It made her want to laugh. "Hi, Anais. Hey, Samantha." Luce wondered if they'd seen the wild burst of water carrying her up into the air. She smiled to herself. There was no reason not to be polite to the two blondes, not when she could send a vertical wave slashing up beneath them anytime she felt like it. "How's everything been going?"

As Luce had expected, her friendly tone annoyed Anais more than any display of hostility could have done. Luce could feel the hardness of her own smile as she watched Anais's sharp blue eyes start to flicker back in the direction of the tribe's cave. Her golden hair rayed out around her, curling gorgeously with each loft of the water.

"Let's just go," Samantha muttered weakly, tugging at her queen's arm. "Why should we even talk to her?" Anais ignored her.

"Oh, wait." Anais made a show of suddenly recalling something, rolling her eyes upward. "Isn't this thing some kind of trashy, broken-down mermaid? I know it's kind of hard to believe, Samantha. But don't you remember there was a mermaid with dark, ratty hair like that? We threw her out of the tribe. Remember?"

Luce felt a little ill, like there was something clammy and

thick in her stomach. But what really surprised her was how little Anais's words upset her. Mostly they seemed funny, in a disgusting kind of way. There she was, the perfect blond pseudo-queen, the heartless usurper, pretending that insults could change what they both knew perfectly well: the best singer was the rightful ruler. And while Anais might be very good, she wasn't even close to equaling Luce. Catarina had said so before she'd vanished, and suddenly Luce found that she believed it absolutely.

"Threw her out?" Of course that wasn't really what had happened, but still Samantha was being pretty slow on the uptake. She was clearly too nervous to think straight. "Anais, please! Let's just get out of here before she tries something."

Lazily Luce began to hum a little, stretching backwards on the waves. Even as she did it, Luce was aware that she was acting in a way her old self wouldn't have recognized. Even when she'd been furiously angry before, she'd never been deliberately cruel, never enjoyed taunting someone. Now, though, the rising anxiety in Samantha's gaping face filled her with hard sparks of delight. She wasn't entirely comfortable with what she was doing, but she was too excited to stop. And anyway, didn't these two deserve whatever they got?

Luce lifted her voice a bit higher, and a tiny wave no bigger than a sparrow edged up out of the sea. Luce caressed the delicate thing with a long, soft stroke of music until the wave was glass-thin and elegantly curved, a scimitar of water glinting in the sun. Samantha goggled in tense disbelief, and Anais tried to smirk. Dreamily Luce sent her voice in a sweeping trill, and the wave spun quickly around her once before it collapsed. One of the larvae splashed closer, twittering with joy, and pawed at the air where the wave had pranced a second before. The red-headed little thing warbled eagerly, trying to beg Luce to raise another wave.

"Anais? Oh, *why* did she have to come here? What does she *want*?" Samantha was practically squeaking. Luce laughed outright, but something about Samantha's questions also sent a rush of sadness through her heart. Wasn't all of this showing-off basically silly? What was the point of it?

It wasn't like she even wanted to be queen. Not of a tribe like this one, anyway.

"I was wondering that, too, Samantha. After all, she knows we said we'd kill her if she ever showed up again." Anais was trying to stare Luce down, but it wasn't working. Samantha kept her eyes on Luce and jerked hard on Anais's arm. "What, Samantha? Are you worried about her stupid little singing tricks? What's she going to do?" Now Anais's sneer looked more genuine. "Get you *wet*?"

Maybe she didn't need a point, Luce thought. Maybe it was enough that they'd brutally attacked Catarina. Maybe it was enough that . . .

Suddenly Luce realized why she was playing around this way, trying to intimidate mermaids she didn't even respect. It was all because she'd been foolish enough to believe a human's kisses meant something. All at once Luce felt ashamed of herself, and she stared around at endless waves, the sunlight winking on all sides like a sarcastic audience.

"I'll see you around," Luce told them vaguely, and turned to leave.

A moment later a sharp squeal pierced the air at Luce's back, followed by a kind of high-pitched chattering. Luce swung back around and saw that Anais had the redheaded larva gripped in both hands. Smiling straight at Luce, Anais flipped the thrashing little thing upside down and held it by its tail. She held it far enough under that, no matter how desperately the larva twisted its babyish torso, it couldn't bring its head up into the air. The other larvae—there were three of them—clung to each other and stared, chirping out half-musical cries of alarm.

"I guess it'll take too long to drown this thing, huh, Samantha?" Anais delivered the line with icy cheerfulness. "What does it take, like half an hour? I'll get totally bored if I have to hold it that long."

"Let it go," Luce snapped. "What's *wrong* with you, anyway?"

Of course that was exactly what Anais had been waiting for. Smiling her loveliest golden smile, she hoisted the larva slightly higher. Just high enough that a few inches of its stubby lilac fins protruded from the water, exposed to the soft breeze, the butter-colored sun. Even Samantha looked appalled. Her mouth hung open, but she didn't say anything. The larva's fins had started twitching.

"This way will be a lot faster, though. Hey, Samantha? How *much* of its tail has to dry out for this to work?"

The larva's thin scream reverberated through the water. The vibrations shivered all over Luce's fins, crawled over her like chilled fingers.

"Anais, *please* . . ." Samantha was whimpering. "Luce will

do something crazy." Anais just lifted the larva slightly higher. Droplets bright with sunshine flew from its writhing tail.

Luce dove. The gray-green water was shaky with the larva's screams, but even so Luce could hear Anais's distorted voice: "See, Samantha? Luce can't actually do anything. All she ever does is run away." Anais's sky blue tail with its overlay of pink iridescence flicked in the water above Luce's head, and Luce tensed herself. Those awful pulsating screams made it hard to concentrate. For a moment Luce couldn't find her voice, couldn't gather power behind it. The first note she tried came out broken, scared, and the two blond mermaids heard it. Samantha's shrill, relieved laughter mixed with the larva's shrieks.

Luce closed her eyes, water all around her like cool, rippling space, and felt the deep hum of the darkness. The sea had its own voice, even far in the depths where the crash of waves became no more than a web of echoes. She had to listen to that voice and not the clamor of that poor little larva's suffering. Luce felt something pulling into her body, a fathomless tide of whispers, a smooth upwelling harmony. And then she felt it begin to rise, right through the center of her chest.

It didn't even feel like she was singing. Instead the sea sang *through* her. Why had she wanted to fight the water before? It was a new music, different, older and deeper than any song that had poured from her before, and as Luce surrendered to it the sound began to spin like a hurricane. Notes rose and whipped through space, gliding up and down the scale.

Dimly Luce heard the scream rolling on through the water. It didn't sound the same as before, though. Luce looked up, still caught in the trance of that astonishing music, and saw the red-haired larva's tiny silhouette as it threw itself across a glowing stretch of water. If the larva was free, though, where was the scream coming from?

A bright cone shape stabbed down through the green-shining waves just ahead of Luce. She couldn't make sense of it at first, but then she realized what it was: a whirlpool made of merged voice and water propelled by the song endlessly tearing from her throat.

Anais was caught in it, flung around in desperate circles, her hands grappling empty space as she struggled to escape. The scream was hers. A few silver fishes spun with her, too stunned even to fight.

Luce gasped in astonishment, letting out a final burst of music. Then everything went utterly quiet. Luce couldn't tell where the music that had filled her had gone, but the sudden silence left a hollow ache in her chest. The whirlpool fell apart, its force scattered in random swirls. Anais splashed a few feet in confusion and then flopped into Samantha's arms.

Singing that way had wrenched all the air from Luce's chest. She needed to breathe. As she surfaced, the first thing she saw was Samantha crying wildly, clutching Anais and stroking her golden hair.

"Is she okay?" Luce felt disturbed by the thought that her singing might have injured another mermaid, even if that mermaid was Anais. She should at least help Samantha pull Anais back to their cave.

"Just get away!" Samantha gagged the words through her sobs. "Luce, just get away from us! No one here wants you! Go back to whatever hole . . ." She couldn't finish the sentence.

"Samantha! You know I had to do that. She was torturing that larva; I *had* to make her stop." Somehow Luce hoped the other mermaid would see reason. Even Samantha knew that the timahk protected larvae, after all. She knew how wrong it was to hurt them.

"Anais is our *queen*, Luce!" Samantha yelled it in hysterics. Anais looked like she'd fainted, but Luce wouldn't have been surprised to find she was faking it. "She can do whatever she wants! What do you even know about *anything* we do? We got rid of you and Catarina, and now—"

"Now you just torture larvae for fun?" Luce snarled the words, but even so she expected Samantha to get defensive, to say that Anais had just been freaking out, and nothing like that had ever happened before.

"No one *cares* about larvae! Luce, no one cares!"

Luce opened her mouth to protest, but then Samantha yelled something that shocked her into silence. "Anais has killed like *four* of them!"

* * *

Luce watched in numb silence as Samantha swam off, towing Anais in one arm. The queen's golden head rested on Samantha's shoulder. It reminded Luce of another time, when she'd pulled Catarina along the surface, away from the frenzied tribe.

Anais had started *killing* larvae? It was so sick that Luce had trouble believing it, even after what she'd just witnessed. She drifted under the waves with a strange, hopeless pain in her heart. What had her old friends become if they allowed something like that to happen? Did they know what was going on?

If things were really so bad, it seemed obvious that she had a responsibility to challenge Anais. She should take over as queen and put a stop to the horror. But then, it wasn't clear that Dana would support her anymore, not now that she'd learned Luce's secret. Maybe no one would. Luce knew that Anais would never give up power without a battle. Luce would need the help of as many mermaids as possible, and who would even want her to be queen? Especially, who would want her enough to *fight* for her?

And even if Dana kept quiet, even if no one ever discovered that Luce had broken the timahk, Luce would never be able to erase the shame of what she'd done from her own heart. She'd know she had disgraced herself and that she was unworthy to rule. Knowing the truth, how could she possibly find the strength to confront Anais and her followers?

Luce found herself at a complete loss. The problem seemed insoluble. She swam back and forth through water banded with pale autumn sunlight; she stopped at random beaches, drifted on again. She kept swimming, sad and distracted, even as the day began to fail and the water dimmed. Strokes of reddish sunset filtered through the waves and curved around her arms. Some-times she sang quietly to herself, caressing the sea's profound voice with her own.

Caressing another voice: a voice that was coarse and desperate-sounding, coming from somewhere above the surface. Luce stopped where she was even as a huge school of small sinu-ous fish sleeked around her so thickly that all she could see was the weaving silver of their bodies. *Dorian.* How dare he think he could trick her again? He wasn't singing Luce's song this time, but something else: a human pop song, probably.

She wasn't going to have anything to do with him, Luce

told herself. Then she swam a bit closer to the shore. He sounded so upset, she thought, so *unhappy*. She barely felt the water sliding open around her head.

"Luce! I was afraid you were going to be too mad to come back! Wait, I'll meet you at the beach, okay?" She caught just one quick glimpse of him, one flash of gold between the trees, before he was running. It was typical, Luce thought, that he was too full of himself to even give her a chance to say she didn't want to see him again. Still, she dipped under and swirled toward the spot he'd mentioned before, the one tucked behind a boulder protruding steeply from the waves. Maybe, just maybe, he had something important to say to her? Even swimming slowly she'd been much faster than he was, and she waited with a nervous irritation, her tail curled against the pebble seafloor and her arms wrapped tight around her chest. The sky was a glassy violet sparked by the burning pallor of the stars.

Dorian broke through the branches, sliding so quickly that he fell onto his rear, and yanked off his shoes. Then, to Luce's confusion, he splashed out to her and threw himself onto his knees, not caring how cold the water was or that his pants were getting soaked. But he didn't kiss her. Instead he wrapped her head in both hands and pulled her cheek against his. She was saturated with the warmth of his skin, the sweetness of his touch, and all he did was hold her. His breath came rough in her ear as if he were struggling not to cry.

"Oh my God, Luce! I didn't do it! I almost did, he almost talked me into it, and then I knew I couldn't!"

She felt a single tear glide down where their faces pressed together and impulsively slipped her arms around him. All her fury at him was abruptly gone, but nothing he was saying made any sense.

"Dorian?" His fingers slid through her wet hair. "I don't actually know what you're talking about." He tipped his head back a little and looked into her eyes.

"They took me to Anchorage. That's why I wasn't here last night. I didn't have any choice, but at least . . ." He saw the confusion on her face. "Anchorage—that's this human city, farther south—"

"I know what Anchorage is!" Now it was Dorian's turn to look confused. "What I don't understand is the part about someone *taking* you there. Why?"

"How *can* you? I mean, how can you know about—all this human stuff?" He gave a short laugh, and Luce didn't answer. His wide ochre eyes stared at her; he still seemed half frantic, though he was starting to calm down. "Do you know about the FBI, too? They took me. I had to sit through getting questioned for two days, and I just got back."

"What would the FBI want with you?" Luce asked. But even as the question was leaving her mouth, she already understood. "They were asking you about"—she could barely make herself say it, but then avoiding the words wouldn't cancel out the truth of what her tribe had done, what *she* had done—"about the ship you were on?"

Just as she'd feared, his eyes hardened. He let her go and shuffled the few feet back out of the water, then sat facing her with his chin on his knees. Luce hid her breasts with her arms again. It felt awkward, and for once she wished she had some human clothing.

"About the *Dear Melissa*, yeah. Are you ever going to explain why the hell you *did* that? And they showed me a map with all the ships you guys have been sinking, too. You're all totally out of control. And I still didn't tell them anything! Luce, *why*?"

Luce wasn't sure what the "why" applied to. Was he asking her to tell him why he hadn't talked or why the mermaids destroyed ships? Both questions seemed like more than she could answer.

"I'm never going to hurt another human, Dorian. I really promise. At least, not unless they attack one of us first."

"Maybe *you* won't! Maybe. But your friends will, Luce! Like, can you promise me that the other mermaids won't go around killing people? Because if you *can't*—"

"I'm not even in the tribe anymore!" Luce felt desperate. "Dorian, I mean— Anais will even kill other *mermaids*. I just learned today, she's been doing horrible things, and there's no way I can stop her. So how am I supposed to promise that she won't kill humans?"

"You said that name before." Dorian thought for a second. He was breathing too hard from agitation. "So why shouldn't I tell the FBI about this Anais if she's the problem? Why shouldn't I do whatever I can to stop them—your old tribe? I just didn't want anything bad to happen to *you*. That was the only reason I kept my mouth shut, Luce! And even that might be because"—he looked at her with an awful, searching ache in his eyes—"because you did something to my mind. I don't even know."

Luce stared. "What do you think I did?"

"I don't *know*." Dorian suddenly seemed embarrassed. "They

said something about—they said I'd been subjected to mind control. That was how the FBI guy put it. That guy Ben Ellison."

Luce looked down at the water swishing gently around her fins. It was a miserable thought, but maybe it made sense. After all, her song had forced dozens of humans to love her more than they'd ever loved anything in their lives. Even if Dorian was able to fight off her magic to some degree, still, maybe he only liked her because her singing had messed up his head. What other reason could he have?

After all, he seemed like someone who never would have noticed her when she was still human.

"I hope not! I mean, I really hope I didn't do anything like that." Her voice sounded pathetic even to her; she could hear the note of pain breaking through it. Luce began to wonder if she should just leave. Dorian was staring, his forehead creased with the effort to understand. "Dorian—I'll go away, you don't ever have to talk to me again—but if I did do something permanent to your mind it wasn't on purpose!"

"How can you not *know*?"

"I mean, you sing *back*! You're the only person who knows how to fight off getting enchanted by us. But people who've heard us sing aren't ever supposed to live, and I don't know, maybe that did something bad to you."

"But you *hope* it didn't? You hope you didn't, like, do something to make me have—" Dorian broke off abruptly, raking his fingers through the stones. Even as he stared down Luce could see the struggle on his face. She watched him brace himself and gaze up at her again. "Something to make me have feelings for you?"

Luce felt like crying. "If I did, then that's seriously depressing."

"Why?"

"Because I only want you to like me if it's real." Luce was surprised she'd found the courage to say that. Being so honest with him soothed her heartache, and she didn't feel on the edge of tears anymore.

"Because you like me?"

"Yes." Luce considered for a second and then suddenly grinned at him. "Does that mean you used some kind of mind control on me?"

Dorian smiled back, and slid a little closer to her. "Totally. With my incredible singing. I fried all your neurons."

Luce snorted. "Your singing sounds like somebody beating up a frog. Humans really shouldn't even try."

"Just because you're magic doesn't mean you have to be such a *snob*." His voice was playful now, and he reached out to stroke her hair, then gently tugged her until her upper body tipped back onto the beach. "I used to sing in a band and everything."

Even as he kissed her with melting softness, Luce was uncomfortably aware that they hadn't actually resolved anything. He was still threatening to talk to the FBI, and she still had no idea what to do about Anais. She hadn't yet tried to explain why the mermaids had destroyed the *Dear Melissa*, and Luce couldn't help but realize how empty her reasons would sound to him. She hadn't answered his questions about her knowledge of things on land, either. Somehow she felt an intense reluctance to let him know she'd once been human herself, but how could she avoid that forever? And it wasn't even clear if his tenderness toward her was only a lingering effect of enchantment.

Dorian had the indication around him, the same dark shimmer as the mermaids, and she'd assumed that it helped protect him from their power. Luce hoped that his shimmering didn't mean he could also see the sparkling around her. If he could, he'd be able to see that she'd been just as human as he was. Worse, if he just looked at her from the corners of his eyes, he might be able to see the events that had *changed* her.

His own cloudy shimmering proved that someone had once done something terrible to him: terrible enough to leave a lasting crack in his very identity as a human. So far, though, a kind of shyness or politeness had kept Luce from looking to see what that heartbreak was. But as his lips flowed on hers like a velvet wave Luce stole a single sideways glance. She couldn't stifle a cry at what she saw there. A younger Dorian lay pretending to be asleep, straining to control his terrified breathing, while his mother—

"Luce?" Dorian pulled away slightly. "Did I hurt you?"

"I'm okay," Luce whispered back. She slipped one hand up and lightly brushed his cheeks. "You don't have to stop." She wanted to kiss him until she forgot everything else: her own overwhelming problems, yes, but also the cruelty that made being human insupportable for so many others like her.

She wasn't nearly as sorry now that Dorian's parents were dead.

8

The Jacket

When Luce woke up the next day she stretched and rolled
where she was, acutely aware of the subtle wavering of the
water against her scales. The sensation of Dorian's cheek pressed
to hers lingered on in her skin. She felt imprinted by his warmth,
and the softness of his touch still breathed through her hair.
Luce had been too shy and withdrawn as a human girl to talk to
boys at all, much less kiss them. She was still in shock from the
sweetness of it all. The timahk, she decided, must simply be
wrong. There was no good reason, not really, why she shouldn't
have a boyfriend onshore, at least as long as she could persuade
him to keep the existence of mermaids a secret. She remembered
how passionately Catarina had warned her against falling for a
human, but then Catarina hated humans so much, and so indis-
criminately, that it simply made her unreasonable. A lot of hu-

mans might be evil and destructive, Luce knew. But there were others, like Dorian, who were warm and brave and open-hearted and who understood how infinite the world really was.

She slipped out to look for breakfast and found the sea blanketed in a dense, sullen fog. Every time she came above water it was as if she were enclosed in a soft gray egg, and even her outstretched hands vanished from sight. Only the rattling of a high wind in the spruce trees told her the direction of the shore. Winter was coming fast. It was going to get colder very quickly now, and there would be ferocious storms. She should look for a better spot where she and Dorian could meet; even if he was exceptionally brave, Luce thought, he was still fragile like all humans, terribly vulnerable to the cold.

Luce swam underwater so that she could see the way to her dining beach; that was the only way she could make out the shape of the coast and spot the familiar rocks going by. When she came up she heard a windy half-song. It wasn't wind, she knew at once, but another mermaid disguising her voice with the airy call they used to beckon each other when they were afraid of being overheard by humans. The fog was so thick and pillowing that it muffled the sound, and Luce dipped again to try and find the source of it. Whoever it was sounded nervous, she thought, and then the voice began to seem a bit familiar. By the time she caught sight of a distant, coppery flash, Luce had already recognized it: Dana, resting on a sandbar not far from shore. She'd finally come to demand an accounting, then. Luce hurried over to her, rehearsing lies as she swam, and came up ready to pour out the story of how she'd murdered Dorian.

"Oh, thank God! I couldn't tell where I was, and I thought

maybe I'd gone way past your cave." As Dana spoke she still scanned the sea anxiously, though there was nothing to see but the pearly gray blindness of the mist. "I got too scared to keep going. You remember Regan?" Luce had hardly ever talked to Regan, but she nodded. "An orca almost got her, Luce. A few of us were just swimming over to get dinner yesterday, and we weren't paying attention. It came up so *fast*, and she actually managed to leap sideways right before its teeth snapped closed, but her fin got torn. They're really . . . Kayley says there aren't as many seals as there used to be, so the orcas are getting really hungry. They keep acting crazier all the time." Dana was so agitated that Luce didn't have any time to react to this. "And Samantha sure can't keep her mouth shut, but I don't know what to believe. But you did *something* to Anais, right? She was being a total screaming bitch last night. She didn't seem to care about Regan at all, and the rest of us were freaking *out*, we were so worried."

Luce had been so ready to start reciting her story— slamming up into Dorian's rowboat, dragging him under—that she was almost disappointed to find that Dana didn't seem interested anymore. "I ran into Anais and Samantha yesterday."

Dana flashed her a skeptical look. "You *ran* into them?"

"No, really. It was really by accident, Dana! I wasn't trying to start anything with them. It just—things got weird really quickly."

"Okay. They *would* get weird. You're going to tell me everything, right?"

It wasn't the story Luce had expected to tell, but maybe it was better this way. "Let's go to the beach first, okay? I haven't had anything to eat yet."

Sprawling next to Dana on a beach, cracking oysters and talking while their tails swished side by side along the seafloor, felt almost like being back in her old tribe. Much as she felt drawn to Dorian, powerfully as she wanted to feel his hands on her face again, Luce realized that his company was never going to stop her from missing being with other mermaids, too.

Dana listened wide-eyed while Luce described her encounter with Anais, stopping her every few moments to ask questions. When Luce got to the part about Anais torturing the larva, Dana gasped and put her hands over her eyes for a moment.

"She held its tail *out*? Luce, really?"

Luce was relieved. It wasn't just that Dana had chosen to ignore what Anais was doing, then.

"Really, Dana. I saw her do it, and the larva started *screaming . . .*" Luce told the whole thing, including the moment when Samantha blurted out that Anais had been murdering larvae. When Dana heard that, she choked, then went quiet for a while.

"I'd wondered about that. It seemed like too many of them were getting washed up on the beach, way back from the water, too. But, Luce, I didn't actually *know*! I would have at least tried to stop her . . . and I would have told you what was going on."

"It's way too sick to believe," Luce agreed, then considered for a moment. "I still don't want to believe it! Dana, you think she's been throwing them *onshore*?" They both knew what that meant. The larval mermaids had all died in unspeakable pain, writhing and juddering until their hearts stopped. Then tiny human legs lay on the beach where their tails had been before.

For a few minutes they sat silent together, clouded in cold fog and a few spatters of rain. Wind sawed at the trees until they moaned like violins.

When Dana finally spoke again, it was to ask Luce about the whirlpool that had caught Anais.

"How did you *do* that, anyway? Have you gotten that insanely powerful?" Luce shook her head, remembering the deep trancelike feeling that had possessed her as she'd sung those unearthly scales.

"I'm—I'm pretty sure I couldn't do that again, actually. I've gotten more control over the water and everything, but that—it didn't even feel like the song was coming from me, Dana. It was more like I was so upset that I called to a bigger song, and it came *through* me somehow . . ." Luce realized from Dana's expression that this sounded utterly crazy to her.

"It was *completely* you. It was just you and them there, right?"

"And the larvae."

"Whatever. You know larvae can't sing at all."

"I'm not saying there was another *mermaid* singing, though!" Luce didn't know how to explain it, and Dana's gaze was mocking, even if she also looked impressed. "I'm saying I don't actually have as much power as it sounds like, from what happened. I heard something singing with my voice, but it wasn't exactly me."

Dana smiled at Luce with a funny, disbelieving look on

her lovely brown face, and lifted both arms over her head to stretch. Luce was just cracking another oyster when Dana brought her hands down into the water so suddenly that the splash soaked both of them, and as Luce yelped in surprise Dana twisted her tail around Luce's and flipped her sideways. When she came up with sheets of water tumbling over her face, Dana was already ten feet back and barely visible through the fog, laughing, but with her hands raised to ask for a truce.

Luce lunged through the water to tackle her anyway, but Dana spun to one side and caught Luce's shoulders between her cool hands. "Wait, wait, Luce! Wait, okay? I'm trying to tell you something, but you're not listening to me. I had to get your attention somehow!"

Luce drew back, wary, half expecting Dana to flip her again. "What's so important, then? That you need to tell me?"

"That you've always been scared to death of how powerful you are." Dana suddenly sounded completely serious. Luce gaped.

"What makes you think I'm scared? I'm just—I'm trying to be honest about it, Dana!"

"Because! Because even if you were, like, calling up some bigger force, you were still the one who was doing the calling! No one else was there, Luce. And I'd be scared, too, if I could do that, but sooner or later you're going to have to deal with it!"

"I bet you could learn how to do it. I don't think there's anything I can do that you couldn't."

Dana just shook her head. "You just don't want to face up to it. You . . . I don't want to say you don't have an ego because you do. But sometimes I think you're basically hiding from yourself. That's the real reason you don't want to be queen!"

Luce was astonished. "How can you even *talk* about me being queen? I mean, now that you know . . ."

"About that guy?" Dana ran one glossy hand over her face. "It still kind of blows my mind that you did that, Luce. I wish you hadn't, I mean, so I could still think of you as being—I don't know, the one who's always so serious about the timahk and all intense about what it means to be a mermaid. Even if I told you off for being uptight about it before . . . I really liked believing I could *count* on you that way. But our tribe hasn't done such a good job of sticking to the timahk anyway. We've all kind of screwed up. So it's not really fair for me to hold that against you, right?"

Luce sat silent for a moment, resting her fingertips on the milky gray whorls of out-rushing foam. Someone had to stop Anais. On the other hand, living on her own made it a lot easier to slip off without anyone noticing. As queen of a tribe, sneaking away every evening wouldn't really be an option. Before too long she'd get caught in Dorian's arms.

"Luce?" Dana's voice was suddenly shy.

"What?" Luce's thoughts were far away, and it took her a moment to focus on Dana again. When she did Dana's brown doe eyes looked tentative and sad.

"You *did* drown that boy, right?"

"Yes," Luce said. The lie was like a cold stone jammed in her throat. "I took his jacket. Just in case you wanted to see."

"I don't want you to think I don't trust you or anything . . ." Why did Dana's voice sound so mournful? "But I guess, sure, I should look at it. Like, for the record."

Luce noticed that Dana stayed nearby as they made their way back to her cave and that she kept almost herding Luce so that they hugged the shore as closely as possible. Luce had to maneuver carefully to keep her scales from getting grazed on the rocks. That orca attack had really rattled Dana, then. Luce couldn't blame her. She'd seen orcas leap herself, seen the sea tint red with blood.

Luce had left the jacket wadded up in a corner of her cave in a deliberate show of indifference. Dana smoothed it out with delicate movements, turning it from side to side in the dimness. She caught sight of the writing on the sleeve.

"Dorian. You think that was his name?" Luce was amazed to hear Dana's voice cracking.

"Maybe. That or it was some band he liked."

"Have you checked the pockets or anything?" Luce hadn't. She'd wanted to make sure everything looked perfectly untouched. She tensed as Dana's graceful fingers began sliding through the many pockets, pulling out bits and pieces of Dorian's life: a pencil stub, some gum, coins, a thick black marker. Then something shifted in Dana's face, and Luce knew she'd found the drawings. They were folded in a white square, stiff with salt. There was something strangely gentle in Dana's movements as she unfolded them. Luce was shocked to see a single gleaming tear curve down Dana's cheek then land with a tiny splash on the pebbled shore.

"Look, Luce. They're all pictures of you!" Luce tried to keep her expression calm as she slipped closer to Dana. It had never occurred to her that Dana might cry over the death of a strange human, and for some reason the sight of it made her nauseous with guilt. What would happen if she told Dana the truth? "Wow, he could draw! And he must have been so obsessed with you . . ." Luce appeared again and again on the sharply creased pages: her body curled inside a wave, her face and shoulders as she towed a dazed-looking Dorian in one arm.

"He had the indication around him. The sparkling." Luce knew it was a mistake to tell Dana too much, but somehow the words escaped her anyway. Dana looked up sharply, tears streaking her full glossy cheeks. "He was a metaskaza, Dana, except that he was a boy. You remember how Catarina told us it was impossible for them to change?"

"*That's* why you saved him?" Dana didn't seem angry about that anymore.

"Maybe." Luce was suddenly close to tears herself. It almost felt like Dorian was really dead. "I don't completely know why I did it, but . . . that was probably the reason." She still didn't want to talk about Dorian singing her song, not to anyone. It seemed too personal. Dana looked down.

"I mean . . . did you really like him, Luce? Like, seriously?"

"Yes." Was it wrong to admit that?

"Then do you hate me for making you do that? You . . . you know I had to, right? If we let him live . . ."

"I don't hate you," Luce insisted. Dana was crying harder now. She buried her face in her arms. "Dana, you were right! I don't hate you at all." Luce could barely keep going. It was monstrous to lie to her sobbing friend this way. "You forced me to do the right thing, Dana, okay? *Please* don't blame yourself for that!"

Dana looked up, her eyes blurred by tears, and pulled Luce into a long hug.

* * *

Luce came back from accompanying Dana almost as far as the tribe's cave that afternoon. The fog had pulled back, and a sluggish, clammy rain had started falling; the fresh water felt slick and repugnant wherever it touched her skin, and Luce realized, a human wouldn't like it any more than she did. Dana's nervousness had gotten to her, and Luce hugged the coast much more closely than usual. More than once when she surfaced, dim scythelike shapes were faintly visible through the silvery strands of rain: almost certainly the dorsal fins of orcas. Luce began to wonder if they were shadowing her, just waiting for her to drift a bit farther out. She hadn't bothered exploring the coast much recently, and there were bends and shelves of splitting stratified rock that she'd forgotten. At one point she noticed a shallow cave, not much more than a deep dent in the cliff with a peaked overhang of rock reaching into space above it. It was squeezed between low points of rock capped by wind-thrashed spruce. Erosion had ripped the ground partly away from beneath the spruce trees, and a snarl of bare roots protruded overhead, clawing at the empty air. A fallen tree spanned the shallow water, its bark worn away and its stripped branches as pale and smooth as a skeleton.

Luce kept thinking of Dana. Mermaids never talked about their human lives, so Luce had been surprised that afternoon to hear her murmuring, between her sobs, about her early childhood. Dana and Jenna had still lived with their mother then, and Dana had told how their mother had sewn matching purple velvet dresses for their sixth birthday, how she'd sung them songs in a language Dana didn't know so that the words seemed to melt into the music. Luce had listened in silence, stroking Dana's hair, until she'd finally calmed down.

Back in her own cave she fidgeted. She tried singing for a while, but the fluid beauty of her song didn't absorb her attention the way it always had before. She raised a wave with one thrumming, endless note and sent it winging in circles through the shadows, but somehow her heart wasn't in it and after a minute she let the wave collapse with a disconsolate splash. Evening seemed so far away, and with the weather so dismal Dorian probably wouldn't show up anyway. Knowing that didn't stop the twisting sensation in her chest every time she thought of him. She gave up trying to practice and sprawled on the stones, gazing at Dorian's drawings. Dana had smoothed them all out, and they lay in a row just above the tide line. The paper was warped and buckled from its long submersion in the sea, crisped by dried salt, but other than that, the drawings were undamaged. The images were so beautiful, so dimensional; Luce especially admired the way Dorian had drawn dozens of broad curving strokes that followed the contours of each wave. It gave an amazing sense of depth, and it added to the surprising effect of her own pale face breaking through. It was impressive that he'd captured her so well from memory, too, as if her face had burned its way into him and these drawings were the scar . . .

Luce kissed the paper, soft and slow, glad that no one was there to see her do it. After she'd stared at the pictures for another hour she dug a shallow pit in the loose pebbles of the shore, as far above the tide line as she could reach, and carefully tucked the folded jacket and the drawings inside. Then she covered everything with a flat stone. There was no guarantee, after all, that Anais or one of her followers wouldn't find the cave sometime.

* * *

Before she went to look for Dorian, Luce tied wide leaves of brown seaweed across her breasts in a kind of improvised bikini top so that she wouldn't have to feel self-conscious around him. Then she started wondering if the seaweed looked ridiculous. It felt a little foolish to be worrying about that, though, when she was almost certain he wouldn't be there.

As she'd expected, the beach was gray, dull, and empty, the failing daylight the color of slate. Rain slashed down like millions of tiny silvery fish, then burst into gray stars on the rocks. For an instant Luce had the strange idea that the endless rain might somehow erase her from the world, as if she were no more substantial than one of those hurtling drops. She tried to stifle her disappointment. Wouldn't it be unfair to expect Dorian to come out in this weather? But on the other hand, *she'd* come out, and it wasn't like Dorian was the one who had to worry about getting snapped in half by an orca either. Her tail swung out of the water in a sullen flip, sending up a high cascade of water. She turned to leave.

"Luce!" Hard steps came rattling down the beach. "Hey, wait! Oh, I almost didn't see you." He had a new jacket, Luce saw, a navy blue one this time, and he was holding a flag-sized slab of tattered tarp up over his head. His eyes were wide and darkly golden, and for the first time Luce saw something hesitant in his expression, as if it had only occurred to him now that she might be some kind of mirage. He glanced at the bikini and smiled strangely. "'Sea-girls wreathed with seaweed red and brown . . .'" Luce didn't know what to say to that. She was somehow too sad to respond, but he didn't seem to notice. "So. How's the being mythological going?"

It was uncomfortable to hear him sound so clownish, so awkward. He seemed to be trying to hide a spasm of embarrassment, and Luce noticed, he didn't splash out to hug her the way he had the day before.

"I don't feel any more *mythological* than ever," Luce snapped. It came out more sharply than she'd intended; for some reason she was annoyed with him; even as he stood bedraggled and gawky under his dripping tarp. The slope of the beach was steep, and since Luce was sprawled stomach-down against the shore his face seemed much too far above hers. "Just grossed out by all this stupid rain." Why was that what she said when there were so many more important things she wanted to tell him?

"*Water* bothers you?"

"Rain is *fresh* water. It's different." Suddenly she had an idea. "Dorian? Can you swipe that rowboat again?"

"Want to take another crack at me?" Dorian was almost sneering, and Luce stared at him, too hurt to react at all. He saw the shocked look on her face, and for a moment they just gazed at each other, his ochre eyes wary and hard.

Luce tensed with the urge to turn away, and suddenly the tightness in Dorian's face unraveled and he fell to his knees, leaning over so far that he lost his balance and one hand splashed down into the water. "Oh, Luce, I don't actually mean it! I've been freaking out all day. I keep thinking the same shit over and over, and none of it makes any sense." He reached to touch her face, and Luce stiffened but didn't pull away. Dorian's eyes went wide and bright, almost desperate-looking. "I'm really, really glad you came. I've been going crazy waiting to see you all day! Don't get mad at me."

"Don't say stuff like that to me anymore, then!" The words burst out of her, raspy and wild, even as it occurred to her that she couldn't really justify her fury. He might truly be worried that she'd try to kill him again. "Dorian, I'm *sorry* I . . . helped sink your ship. I can't take it back, though. So if you hate me just don't talk to me anymore!"

Her face burned even through the streaks of slippery rain, and Dorian caught her wrist and held it tightly. She'd known that he would, really. In her heart she'd known perfectly well how dismayed he would be at the thought that she might disappear from his life.

"I *need* to keep talking to you, though! Luce, I really . . . I need it more than anything. Like, you're the one who isn't supposed to be real, right? But you just make it seem like everything else is fake instead." From something in his voice Luce could tell he'd thought those words over and over, maybe even whispered them to himself in private. His face was much closer to hers now, and the tarp was slipping back from his shoulders. Rain twisted in long streams from the tips of his trailing hair.

"It's only humans who go around thinking they're *supposed* to be realer than everything else," Luce said. The words were still angry, but her tone was softening, and in spite of herself she reached to stroke the rain from his face.

"So, where do you want to go?" Dorian asked.

Luce looked into his eyes, disoriented. He was so close she could feel the faint cloud of warmth that breathed from his skin.

"You said to get the boat, right? Doesn't that mean you want to go somewhere? I can probably get away with borrowing it whenever we want. It belongs to my—to the people I'm staying with, and they never use it."

"Oh." His cheeks were bright from the cold, his breath misty and scented with coffee. He had such a beautiful mouth, Luce thought, especially when he smiled the way he was right now. "I was just going to take you somewhere out of the rain."

Suddenly his lips were on hers, hovering so lightly that it was barely a kiss. Why couldn't he just make up his mind how he felt about her, once and for all?

"I'll meet you." Then he was up and running again, the tarp flapping above his head, flinging loose streamers of water. Everything about him seemed so quick, so fluid, at least by human standards.

Luce was possessed by a sudden impulse, and she slashed deep underwater. There might be humans around the dock at this time of day, even in the rain, so she swept along in the low green regions where the light graded away and she could hide in the dimness. She didn't start to slip closer to the surface until she sighted the gray blot of the rowboat just above her. Too many boats jostled overhead, and she could hear faint human voices; she wished Dorian would hurry. After several minutes his steps came urgently pounding along the planks, beats of vibration transmitting through the water and around Luce's skin.

She had trouble stifling a laugh as he caught the rope and the rowboat jarred closer to the dock; of course he never suspected that she was lurking just below.

Dorian thudded down into the boat, off-balance and out of breath, and untied the rope, absently letting it slide down into the sea. He started carefully turning around to settle in without tipping over. The next second the boat was whipping away from the dock so quickly that he almost tumbled backwards off the seat. Luce heard him yelp with surprise and laughed loudly enough for him to hear her. The rope was in her hand and her tail spiraled out, driving her through gray-green shade, through long pale streaks of bubbles, past pollock and the glassy reddish blots of jellyfish, and Luce noticed with sudden delight a sea otter that briefly tried to keep pace with her then danced away.

Behind her, Dorian whooped. They were going faster than any motorboat now, and Luce drove her tail harder, smiling at Dorian's breathless laughter. He must be watching the cliffs jumbling by, the trees blurring blue-green, while his hands clenched hard on the boat's rim. She rolled onto her back and streaked up to the surface just long enough to grin into his half-frightened, half-thrilled face, water slicing around her shoulders like a trailing dress. Then she vaulted herself up in a backwards arc, her long tail breaching and twisting in the air, brash with silvery lights. She just had time to hear Dorian crying out before she was under the waves and racing on again.

Just before they reached the shallow cave Luce began to slow, sending pulses of water backwards with her tail to counter the boat's momentum. At least here they'd have some shelter from the wind, the rain. Stands of rock broke the waves so that the sea only flicked gently at the stones. Water dripped from the tangled roots overhead, and a curtain of rain cut off the world beyond. Dorian clambered out of the rowboat and flopped onto the shore while Luce tied the rope to a spiky branch of the fallen spruce tree. "Jesus, you scared me!" The words gasped out, but he was smiling at her.

"It kind of serves you right." Swimming so quickly had streaked the tension out of her, though. Dorian stretched out near the edge of the water, and she swam close to him and let him slide his hands into her hair. After a moment she rested her head on the beach, her face inches away from his.

"If I keep kissing you all the time we're never going to talk." His voice was warm and already going throaty. "But it's hard not to."

"I don't even *want* to kiss you now." Luce was surprised to hear herself say it, especially in such a strong tone.

"Because I said *one* stupid thing? And it might not even have been that stupid, anyway. Luce, I mean, how am I supposed to *know*—"

"No. Because it's too hard for me that you're always changing how you feel about me." His fingers were still curling back and forth across her cheeks, brushing against her neck. Almost against her will she found herself leaning into his touch. The warmth of each caress washed through her skin.

"That's not *true*." He sounded so serious that Luce let her hand drift up to touch him back. "Luce, I mean . . . I've been getting freaked out because it *doesn't* change. I'm way too into you, and it doesn't ever stop. You don't know that? And I hardly even know you. I don't even know what you *are*, really."

"You hate what I am." *Even though you're one of us,* Luce thought. *You just don't know it.* "You think we're all evil, and you're *still* talking about going to the FBI, even though that would make them start coming after us—"

"Most of you *are* evil! You said your friend Dana is one of the nicest ones, and *she* tried to get you to kill me." Dorian halfway laughed. "You can't say that's not—some pretty warped shit."

"I showed her your jacket." *This* was what she had to tell him, Luce realized. He needed to understand. "You were right. She completely believed me that you were dead. She was even embarrassed to be asking me about it at all."

"Good. We fooled the bitch."

"She couldn't stop crying. For hours. Dorian, she never even met you, but she couldn't stop crying thinking about it, and I had to sit there and keep *lying* to her . . ."

Dorian's eyes went wide and uncertain. He was too startled to answer her at first, but his quick breath fluttered on her mouth. "Why do you guys keep *doing* it, then? Killing people? Luce, I don't want you to think I'm, like, rubbing it *in* . . ." He gave a sick, airy laugh. "But what the fuck?"

She had to face it, Luce realized. They'd just keep going in circles until she did. "You mean, why did we sink the ship your family was on? The *Dear Melissa?*"

"Oh, for *example* . . ."

"My friend Miriam had just killed herself. The *Dear Melissa* ran into—" Luce tried think of a way to explain it. "It was Miriam's funeral. We were all singing for her, and then the ship was almost on top of us. And our law is that humans aren't allowed to live after—"

"After they've heard you." Dorian was biting his lip, and his hand had stopped stroking her face. It was almost completely dark now. The only lights were a few faint sparks of green phosphorescence where the water licked the shore, the dim luminosity of Luce's skin.

"Yes."

"It *still* doesn't make any sense, though. I mean, who gave you that law to start with?"

As soon as he said it, Luce couldn't understand why she'd never asked herself that question. "It's supposed to be . . . They told me it's the same for all the mermaids in the world. That we all have the same laws."

"But do you actually know where it came from? Like, who the boss is?" Dorian asked. Luce was flummoxed by the idea that there might actually *be* a boss. The mermaids were so free, the timahk so impersonal and strong. But, she realized, he had a point. The timahk must have come from somewhere. It must have a beginning, and she had no idea what that beginning might be. Dorian sat up abruptly and coaxed her head up onto his knee. "Luce, okay, this is going to sound crazy. But I have this theory, and I can't stop wondering if maybe I'm onto something . . ."

"What *theory?*"

"I mean . . ." Dorian seemed embarrassed, but he pushed ahead. "What if you used to be human, and you just don't know it? Because I realized there are all these things that don't make sense, like you knowing how to read, but they would if . . . like, if the mermaids are the ones who are really enchanted? If, okay, if somebody is *using* all of you." Luce was glad that she was lying down. The words swam through her, bright and swarming and unmanageable. He was so close to the truth, but also so wrong . . .

"What makes you think I'm enchanted?"

"Well, I mean . . ." He was definitely embarrassed now. He looked away, deep blue shadows and the dim reflections of the water curling around his face. "It's exactly like a story, right? The boy who falls in love with a mermaid?" Luce felt her heart start to race. What was he *saying*? "So in a story—if you were, like, under a spell . . ." Dorian suddenly stared down at her, his face wild with longing.

"What then?" It was awful, Luce thought, but maybe she couldn't avoid telling him the whole thing much longer.

"Well, then it would be my job to break it, right? Like, kill whoever enchanted you?" Dorian looked so hopeful as he asked this that Luce ached inside.

"There's a big problem with that." Luce shuddered a little as she remembered that terrible night on the cliffs when her uncle had tried to rape her, then left her alone and howling. When the change had started to come over her, she knew, she *did* have a choice, even if she didn't understand what that choice was going to mean.

"What *problem*?" Dorian was getting too excited, and Luce cringed. "You know who did it, don't you? And you think he's too, like, powerful for me to fight—"

"No! Dorian, it's not *like* that!" They were gaping at each other, and Dorian's hands squeezed her shoulders convulsively. "I *did* used to be human, Dorian. But the trouble is—"

"But if you were human *before*, then—"

Luce cut him off. "But nobody enchanted me! Or maybe I did it. I enchanted *myself!*"

Luce had never seen anyone look so completely astonished. Dorian gaped and seemed as if he was trying to say twenty things at once. Crosscurrents of emotion surged in his face, and his nails sank into her shoulder.

"Luce!" It was the best he could do.

"I didn't know I was going to turn into a mermaid or anything. I didn't know what was happening to me, but I still let it happen . . ."

"Oh my *God!*"

"I didn't want to tell you. That I was ever human. Because I knew you'd flip out . . ."

"But how can you be sure there's nobody else behind it, Luce? Behind whatever did this to you? Because if there is then maybe we could . . ." Luce knew what he'd been about to say: *"Maybe we could turn you back."* How could she tell him that she didn't think she would want to turn human again, even if it were somehow possible? It was terrible to realize what he'd imagined: stabbing some wizard or demon, the enchantment vaporizing as it died and the mermaids all miraculously restored to human form. And in his daydreams she was so grateful to have legs again, to be rescued from her life in the sea . . .

To be stuck in foster care somewhere, to lose her freedom and her wildness. Even worse, to open her mouth and hear those thin, clacking squeaks humans called "singing" coming out of it.

Luce sat up and wrapped her arms around him, scattering soft kisses around his face. He was trying to be heroic, to risk death out of love for her. It was just a kind of heroism she didn't want.

"Is it okay if you're out late? Because I think I'd better tell you what happened, and it's a really long story . . ."

"I don't *care* about getting in trouble." His breathing was labored, and Luce felt a tremor in his back. She desperately wished there was some way she could make it all easier for him.

Luce sighed. There were so many things she didn't want him to know about, and she was going to have to start with some of the worst of them: her father's death, her uncle's beatings, and the attempted rape. Oddly, one of the things that worried her most was what he'd think of her father. Dorian gave the impression of being one of those kids from a big, elegant house, the kind with packed bookcases and a rose garden and art objects brought back from distant countries. And boys like that didn't have anything to do with girls whose fathers were petty thieves, girls whose bedrooms were just a sleeping bag thrown in the back of a red van.

Maybe *that* was the real reason she hadn't wanted to tell him the truth?

Luce kissed his mouth, and he tipped back to gaze at her with frantic eyes. Then she began at the beginning.

* * *

As hard as it was for Luce to tell him, it was even harder for Dorian to hear it. He wanted to hurt her uncle somehow, so Luce refused to tell him what town she'd lived in or what her last name had been. Dorian had too many emotions that he didn't know what to do with, and Luce was afraid they'd goad him to do something crazy. As the story went on she felt him falling into it, as if they were both sharing the same dream. How she'd sunk her first ship completely by accident, how Catarina had found her and saved her life, the living magic of tall gray waves and ferocious music . . .

The rain died down until there was no sound beyond the sullen drip of water from the roots above, but still the story went on. He interrupted her a few times; he seemed especially interested in what Luce told him about the dark shimmer around each mermaid and how it revealed the private horrors that had turned each one of them from human girls. He asked her more than once about Catarina, who had always refused to let anyone look into the nightmare images of her own transformation. Something about the topic seemed to make him uncomfortable.

When she described how she had come to help Catarina with the sinking of the Coast Guard boat, Dorian made a rough, strangled noise, and snapped, "Are you saying you murdered people because of *peer pressure?*"

"Partly. But it was more like if they were going to die anyway, I didn't want them to die with so much pain. Not when I could take it away just by singing . . ." It was hard to overcome the impulse to justify herself, but at the same time she didn't want to sound like she was making excuses.

She told him about the coming of Anais, her own fights with Catarina, the terrible moments that had led up to Miriam's death. Dorian became very still and so quiet that Luce was momentarily afraid he'd stopped breathing. Her own voice quieted, too, into a numbed chant. They both knew what was coming next, and Luce thought this might be the end for them. Dorian had said he was in love with her, but that didn't mean he'd be able to forgive her once he knew the whole truth. Probably nobody in his position could forgive something so awful; probably she didn't deserve that much generosity from anyone. Luce tried not to think about how he'd react, to keep the story coming as steadily as falling rain. It was his life, too, and he had a right to understand as much of it as possible.

She came to the first moment when she'd seen him, his bronze hair flicking in the golden dawn glow. She described it all: how he'd sung back to her and then she'd seen something sparkling in the air around him. Like a cloud of black mica or like tiny glittering insects . . .

"No," Dorian said. His voice was cold.

"But you do. You have the indication, so I thought in a way you were one of us."

"I'm *not* one of you. There wasn't anything like—like with your uncle. There wasn't anything that sick at all! My parents were really great people, Luce. Like, maybe you just *want* to believe they deserved it, but . . ."

But I've seen what they did, Luce wanted to say. *You know I've seen the whole thing!* Then she noticed the way Dorian's face was shutting down, closing like a door, and stopped herself just in time.

"I mean, I know all the other mermaids, like, even Anais, can just look over at me and see my uncle—everything he did. I was afraid at first that you'd be able to see it too . . ." Luce said it as gently as she could.

"I can't see anything. I just know what you've told me." He sounded very stiff, and he wasn't looking at her anymore.

"But you know everything now, and you're going to keep thinking about it—"

"I know because you *told* me. You didn't have to. You could have made up a different story and I never would have known."

Luce was quiet for a minute. She wanted Dorian to say that of *course* he was like her, that he was basically a merman stuck on land. But he couldn't give her that, she realized. The idea hurt him too much. Just like Catarina, he couldn't stand to have anyone know the truth.

"We don't need to talk about it again, Dorian," Luce said softly. He kissed her, and each kiss was as lush and slow and thrilling as a flower opening inside her skin.

She was amazed to find that he could touch her so tenderly—that he could stand to touch her at all, really—even now that he knew her story. Although whenever they paused for an instant, she noticed that he seemed to be having trouble meeting her eyes.

Maybe he did really love her, then, even though he knew he was supposed to hate her . . . Dorian had even more reason to despise mermaids than the rest of humanity did. If he could truly forgive her for everything, even for his little sister who'd been left to decay at the bottom the sea . . .

If he could yield up his heart like this, it must mean that she was actually *forgivable*, and that all her fellow mermaids were, too.

Maybe other humans would also see the situation that way, someday. And maybe the mermaids could even forgive them in return.

His hands stroked through her hair like waves of possibility. Like hope.

The broken world might yet be whole again. She twisted closer, kissing him more deeply still, and softly bit his lower lip.

9

Little Ditties

Ben Ellison had been sitting in the waiting room for over an
hour, sometimes pulling his briefcase onto his knees for no apparent reason and sometimes shoving it irritably to the floor. He'd
had time to memorize the room's stuffy, hard-edged mahogany
furniture, the upholstery and wallpaper in various shades of
drab mauve and pinkish tan. He'd also had time to take a piece
of glossy white paper out of his briefcase and stare at it grimly
before putting it away, only to reach for it again minutes later.
He had it in his hand now. It was a drawing done in densely
curving lines of thick black marker, and it showed a girl's face in
the sweep of a wave. A stroke of corkscrewing seafoam bowed
just above her head and fell to either side of her shoulders like a
mantle. The girl had short, jagged dark hair that fell in points
across her broad forehead, and long, deep, expressive eyes.

There was, Ben Ellison thought, a wrenching sense of solitude in that face, as well as a profound humanity. He knew perfectly well, though, that the face in the drawing didn't belong to anything *human*. And that, he supposed, was why the image bothered him so much.

He'd looked at dozens of these drawings, sitting on the floor of the boy's room, but he'd taken only one before he'd slipped the stack back into its hiding place. Now he wondered why he'd chosen a picture where no glimpse of the mermaid's tail was visible. Did he want to forget that he was dealing with monsters and not with little girls?

"Agent Ellison?" He looked up at the slender receptionist in her crisp gray skirt and glossy blouse. "The Secretary of Defense is ready to see you." As professional as she was, Ben Ellison noticed the half-concealed amusement in her face. She'd heard people talking about him, then: the high-ranked FBI operative—in charge of a special unit on maritime security, no less—who'd developed a ludicrous obsession with the idea that *mermaids* were routinely killing thousands of people worldwide and who'd somehow managed to persuade a contingent of other agents, and maybe even the Director, that he was right. He grimaced and stood up.

People wouldn't find it amusing for much longer. That much seemed certain.

* * *

Ten minutes later Ellison was playing a video file on a giant monitor while half a dozen men in business clothes and a single woman with frosted gray-blond hair and a neat burgundy suit all stared into the screen. The image was green and murky: the waters of the Bering Sea tended to be somewhat cloudy from all the plankton. Light fell from behind, casting the figure as a dim silhouette. It was impossible to make out the color of the girl's long scrolling hair or the features of her face. But the important part was clear enough: this was a girl's head and torso, shifting at the hips into a sinuous, whiplashing tail with broad, sensitively curling fins. She appeared for only an instant, and Ellison tapped a few keys on his laptop. Now the video played again and again, slowed down to a twentieth of its original speed. The whiplash of the tail became a dreamlike snaking, and the girl turned her head to the surface before vanishing upward. Then she was back in the bottom corner of the frame: her tail snaked again, her head turned again, and again she flicked away . . . Ellison had watched this tape a thousand times, but once again he was mesmerized by the strange beauty of the image, the heartbreaking grace of the mermaid's movements.

It was appalling to think that Dorian Hurst was—there was no other word for it—*dating* one of these creatures. But Ellison had to admit to himself that the mermaid on the screen was completely irresistible. If he were in Dorian's place . . .

"Be simple enough to fake something like this," the Secretary of Defense snarled. It made his jowls quiver. His stiff white hair looked like cake frosting, and there was an unpleasant dullness, an obvious absence of feeling, in the hard glint of his eyes.

"We've already checked for signs of digital manipulation, Mr. Secretary," a young, fidgety man with a sky blue tie objected. "It appears to be legitimate."

"You don't need digital manipulation to pay some girl to tie on a fake tail and go swimming. They have these girls in Florida, as a tourist attraction. Babes in tanks." The Secretary of Defense sounded somewhere between snide and impatient. "This all you got, Agent Ellison?"

Ellison tapped again, zeroing in on the section of the footage that showed the tail, blowing it up so that it filled the whole screen. "With all due respect, Secretary Moreland," Ellison said, trying to stay calm, "a girl wearing a mermaid costume still has *knees.*"

"And your point is?" Secretary Moreland droned. The woman in the burgundy suit was quicker on the uptake, though. She let out a sudden cry and jumped from her chair, eyes round with shock, pointing at the screen.

"He's right!" Now the complex, hundred-jointed, three-dimensional flux of that tail was apparent to everyone. Shock spread through the room in a palpable wave. "Secretary Moreland . . . it would be anatomically impossible for a human being to move that way. And the fins . . ." She pointed again, and Ellison tapped, magnifying the image even more. The fins rippled on the screen, as sensuous and agile as the fingers of a concert pianist. The woman turned to the young man with the sky blue tie, a look of desperate appeal on her face. "Are you *sure* this wasn't created by a computer?"

"I'm *reasonably* sure—" the young man started, but Secretary Moreland waved him to silence.

"Think what we're dealing with, people. Agent Ellison here gets hold of *one* photo that just looks like a bunch of seaweed to me, and he goes off on this rampage. Says he has audio files, but he's been shouting all over the place that these record-

ings are *somehow*, for some big fat mystery of a reason, too dangerous for anyone to hear. That's the best reason he can give for
hiding his alleged evidence. And then he talks the Director into
sending out teams to install video cameras, and they all come up
blank for weeks. All of them except one, which just *happens* to
get smashed a few minutes after they turn it on. Now this."
Moreland cocked his head at the screen. "*Reasonably sure* doesn't
cut it. Not when this video is coming from a known fanatic. No
offense meant, of course, Agent Ellison."

The men in the room were glancing around at one another,
obviously doing their best to be persuaded. The woman in burgundy still gaped helplessly into the screen as if she hadn't heard
Moreland speaking, and for some reason the boy with the blue
tie was staring at the woman, a look of inexplicable compassion on his face. An excruciating sense of futility choked Ben
Ellison as he sat with his hands stiffly folded on the conference table. There would never be any stronger evidence than
this; they would never manage to capture one of these creatures alive. He felt sure of that. These idiots were stubbornly
determined to avoid a truth too big to fit in their tiny minds,
and every day, somewhere in the world, another ship was
lured to its destruction. It was all he could do not to explode
with rage.

"Of course," Secretary Moreland went on, "if these audio
recordings were actually produced, *maybe* we'd get somewhere."

Ellison looked up. "We've done an analysis of the sound
waves, Secretary Moreland. I sent you the report."

"Bunch of squiggly lines. What am I supposed to do with
that?"

"Those *squiggly lines* massacred the entire crew of the *Integrity*, Mr. Secretary. When we recovered the black box, we found it had captured a full eight minutes of these sounds. The crew members never speak . . ." Ellison's frustration had started sharpening his voice, and he struggled to control it.

"But Agent Ellison . . ." A gray man in a beige suit was speaking, a very important gray man, Ellison knew. "I think Secretary Moreland's point is well taken. Correlation doesn't imply causation, after all. You tell us that the *Integrity*'s black box recorded some unidentified music. But for all we know this music could be something the captain was playing on the stereo." Agent Ellison almost gagged. "This claim you make, that this sound file is so dangerous . . . What basis do you have for that belief? Has *anyone* listened to it?"

"I have." Ellison knew that admitting this would only lead to more problems, but . . . "Immediately after we found the black box. I played exactly one second of the file."

"And?" the gray man pursued.

"And what I experienced convinced me that this recording poses a severe hazard to anyone who hears it." Ben Ellison tried to keep his expression steady. He couldn't tell these people how that momentary burst of music had affected him, not when they already suspected he was at least half insane.

Secretary Moreland got up from his chair and started pacing, brushing past the woman in burgundy, who remained fixated on the screen, her eyes consumed by the dark, rippling form. "Agent Ellison . . ." The Secretary's tone was scolding; he even waved a finger. "Still not good enough."

"Mr. Secretary—"

"Still just your personal claims of this, that, and the other. Do you have this little ditty on your laptop now?"

Ellison felt a rush of nausea at hearing mermaid song described this way. "I do."

"Play it for me. I'd like to hear it." Secretary Moreland smiled and spread his hands in invitation.

"Mr. Secretary, I can't take any responsibility—"

"I've served in two wars, Agent Ellison. I've had my best friend's blood spray across my face, and I picked his severed head up off the dirt with my bare hands." Moreland was still smiling broadly as he said this. "I think I can handle it."

Ellison looked around the room, and the gathered faces gazed back at him. It was horrible to think of what might happen to these people. "Please listen through earphones, then, Secretary Moreland."

"Oh, certainly." Moreland's smile turned predatory.

"Will a one-second excerpt be sufficient?"

"Try thirty. Thirty seconds, and then I'll tell you what kind of career you can expect after today. I don't think even the FBI tolerates this kind of time-wasting."

Ellison clicked on a different program, opened the file, and set the in and out points. He plugged in the earbuds and passed them to Moreland, who sat down again and shoved them aggressively into his ears, still smiling horribly. There was no telling what this music would do to the country's Secretary of Defense, but it didn't seem likely that the man would emerge with his mind intact. As far as Ellison was concerned, the most remarkable thing about young Dorian wasn't that he was still alive; it was that he was even partly sane. Ellison's thick brown hand hung over the keys. Arrogant as Secretary Moreland was, hitting Play was clearly unethical. No one, Ellison thought, deserved that.

"I thought I made myself clear. I've had *enough* of your self-indulgent, crackpot bull—"

Ellison's finger snapped down, hard.

The room became deeply quiet. The woman in burgundy walked forward and gently spread both palms on the screen, then leaned close so that her cheek rested in the image's center. Now the mermaid's fins flowed again and again through her outstretched fingers. Everyone else turned to stare at Secretary Moreland. A sloppy, vacuous grin spread across his face, his jowls swayed, and a thread of drool spilled over his chin. He bobbed slightly in his chair and then let out a kind of shrill, ecstatic whimpering.

An almost subliminal flutter of music leaked from the earbuds. It was so quiet that they all felt it rather than heard it: a soft sonic mist that moistened their fingertips, altered the patterns of their breathing. Ben Ellison felt an urge to do something, but he couldn't be sure what that something was. Vaguely he thought that the unbearable pressure swelling inside him might be relieved if he licked the walls, or took that young man's head in his hands and planted bites as soft as kisses all over his cheeks, or dug out his own eyes so that the light could shine straight into his brain . . .

At the twenty-eighth second Secretary Moreland suddenly stood up. The cord for the earphones wasn't long enough and they popped out of his head and thudded onto the conference table. The music drifted a bit louder then stopped. Ellison felt a whirl of unspeakable promises passing through him: promises of sensual pleasure and power and tenderness. They were all so *close*, so ready to burst in his mouth like grapes.

"Secretary Moreland?" The gray man's voice was pitched so high that Ellison didn't recognize it at first. Ellison thought the man might be trying to sing opera, and he made a confused effort to smile encouragingly. Beauty was universal, immediate, cataclysmic; of course the man should sing if he felt like it.

"Excuse me," Moreland murmured absently. "A touch indisposed . . . something I ate . . ." He was already shambling across the room, bumping against chairs. The door opened onto a luxurious sitting room. Ellison watched Moreland's ink blue back receding, saw the bathroom door on the far side open and close.

Indisposed, Ellison thought. That happened. He pictured Moreland huddled on the cold tiles of the bathroom floor; those tiles would be so white, so *gleaming*. It was hard not to feel envious.

Dimly he heard the water running.

Dimly he heard the presence of air, the outrageous splendor of electricity passing through the wires, the soft kittenish meows of the woman in the burgundy suit. The young man with the sky blue tie was embracing her from behind, his face nuzzling hard against her shoulder.

The water was still running. Maybe, Ellison thought, the water had been running for a long time. Wasn't there some reason why you shouldn't leave the tap open like that? Maybe someone should go and turn it off.

Maybe . . . The gray man in beige jumped up and let out a

warbling scream. That seemed uncalled for. "My God! People, snap out of it!" Then the gray man was bolting through the door and across the sitting room; Ellison heard a lamp topple and smash.

He was running, too. Something was very wrong. Something in the bathroom. He reached the bathroom door a fraction of a second behind the gray man, who was banging it wildly with both fists. Ellison felt himself pull the man away, but his own movements seemed floaty and sluggish, as if he were suspended in a cloud of feathers. He barely felt his own steps on the floor as he jumped back to get a running start, kicking the door as hard as he could. The wooden door frame split, and the door smashed open.

The first thing Ellison noticed was the sheet of water glossing over the side of the sink. That water looked so lovely, so inviting. Secretary Moreland's thick, bent figure interrupted his view of it, though. The back of his inky suit was ripping down the center seam as he hunched forward, his hands clutching both sides of the sink while his face disappeared into the basin. Ellison heard peculiar gurgling sounds, and it occurred to him that Secretary Moreland might be drowning. Was that important? He reached to seize the inky shoulder, to haul it back, while the gray man appeared and tugged the Secretary from his other side. A crimson face burbled up from the basin and squealed, gray eyes slopping around in a way that reminded Ellison of ice cubes on a hot sidewalk. The Secretary's dark, lumpy shape began to writhe, trying to throw them off. It looked like he was crying in frustration, though the trails of water dribbling all over his face and down his suit made it hard to tell. The bathroom was crowded with human bodies now, all of them scrabbling to get a hold on Secretary Moreland. The inky jacket tore again as they dragged him out of the bathroom and dumped him on the floor. A few of the men sat on him.

Moreland lay on the Persian carpet like some hideous primeval fish on a beach, weeping loudly. His face was blobby and scarlet, capped with twists of drenched white hair. He vomited a watery soup down his own front, still sobbing.

"Why don't you ever let me do what I *want?*" Moreland whined. "Why can't I . . ." He snuffled and stopped. "Why don't I get to be *happy?*"

Ellison felt terribly sorry for him. Maybe it was unfair to keep the poor, sweet man from getting to experience true happiness, just this once.

Maybe it would have been nicer to let him drown.

10

The Beckoning Wind

"Luce? Would you do something for me?" It was two weeks later, back in the same cave in early afternoon. A Sunday, so Dorian didn't have school. Things had been wonderful between them recently and getting constantly better as they learned to understand each other. Still, there were some subjects they'd silently agreed not to talk about anymore.

"Probably." He'd been kissing her and stroking her hair for hours, and Luce was flushed and blissful, softly sliding her cheek against his. "What is it?"

"I want you to sing for me." He saw the shocked look on her face. "Not, I mean, not to try to kill me or anything! But you said you can sing in other ways . . ."

Luce tried not to mention singing around him, though she'd slipped up once or twice. She was back to practicing a lot, and sometimes she was simply too excited about the discoveries she was making *not* to say something. Still, she was always afraid when she did, always glancing nervously to see how he reacted. It might remind him of the *Dear Melissa*, or of his idea that her song had affected his brain somehow.

"You said hearing me sing messed you up," Luce objected. "It seems like a *horrible* idea to try that again!"

"It *did* mess me up. It's getting easier now that I'm seeing you and everything, but I still hear you singing the whole time I'm asleep. Even when it's not like I'm dreaming. I mean, it's all dark, but I still keep hearing that song."

"So, I mean, I don't want to risk hurting you, Dorian. Or of course I would."

"I *need* you to." Luce didn't understand. "It's like your song went into me and shoved a lot of stuff around, and I still . . . I'm never scared when I'm with you, Luce, but the rest of the time I can suddenly start feeling like I'm drowning, out of nowhere, just sitting in a chair or whatever, and my head starts filling up with your voice. It's really crazy."

"Then why? Why would you want me to?"

"Because maybe . . ." He seemed to be searching for the right words. "I've been thinking about it all the time, and I feel like hearing you—but hearing you sing something else—maybe that would be the one thing that could help?" His voice kept getting higher as he spoke until by the end it had a thin, desperate ringing. He stroked her, looking wildly into her doubtful eyes. "Just show me that thing you can do. Move the water for me. One wave?"

"You promise you'll tell me right away? If it hurts you?

Dorian, humans really aren't strong enough to deal with it. I've seen them go totally insane . . ."

"Try it. Even a few seconds. *Please.*"

Luce sighed. Then, watching him carefully, she let out a slow, spinning note. Dorian squeezed her hand, hard, and even though he'd said he wanted to watch her raise the water his eyelids closed tight.

Her song stroked into his mind, throbbed around his thoughts. She could feel it happening, and she completely forgot any idea of sculpting a wave for him. Her voice spiraled in a long strand, three separate notes that wove over and through one another, and the music waltzed through the mind of the boy she loved. It lifted his memories, breathed in the crevices of daydreams he could barely even admit he had . . . Dorian let out a sound halfway between a gasp and a moan, and Luce abruptly broke off.

"Are you *sure* you're okay? Dorian . . ." She didn't want to stop, though. She wanted to feel her song moving inside him, her voice like a flock of birds that soared endlessly even while they were fast asleep, like biting stars, like a strangely brilliant world where no one had ever walked before.

"Please, Luce!" He opened his eyes just a slit, so that their dark gold showed between the soft brown fringe of his lashes.

She still felt worried, but the desire to sing, and to sing *into* him, to caress his living thoughts with music, got the better of her. The song came back, and the cold wind spiraled strands of Dorian's long bronze hair just as the notes spiraled in his dreams. Luce watched his closed eyes, heard the quick pulsations of his breathing. He reached to pull her tight against his chest.

The song smoothed across thoughts like a rippling landscape—then abruptly Luce hit a jagged place, an area of fissures and misalignments. Even in his arms she experienced a sensation of stumbling, falling. He *was* damaged, and this was part of the problem . . .

She had to concentrate. She had to sing very precisely, very delicately, to set the broken planes back in order, smooth the cracks. Dorian's breath was quick and raw, and he was trembling. Luce wrapped one splintered thought in a note like binding silk, then when she was sure she'd sensed everything correctly she gave a quick push, swishing up the scale, and felt something snap back into place. He moaned and kissed her randomly, his mouth landing just below her ear. Luce found another trouble spot, something like a field of rubble, and she gently rolled the fragments over and over, looking for the matching edges . . . This broken area wasn't her fault, Luce realized. This was the result of all those sleepless nights when Dorian had waited in icy dread for the noise of his mother's footsteps.

Ten minutes later Dorian's face was streaked with silent tears. He still hadn't opened his eyes, and Luce was suddenly afraid that she'd pushed him too far. This time, though, she was careful to lower her voice very slowly, to hold him in the last wisps of music for a softly sustained moment, so that he wouldn't be too shocked when it stopped.

"Dorian? Are you okay?"

He looked at her through lashes diamond-flecked with teardrops, his eyes like molten gold. But there was something crazy in his look, an inhuman glow, a wavering exaltation. Did he even know where he was?

"Dorian?"

"I don't know how anyone can stand to be alive. The world is *way* too beautiful to live in, Luce! Just being me is—it's so amazing I can't begin to deal with it. And the sea, and the light. It's so beautiful I want to stab it with daggers, or I want to blow up into those *colors* . . ."

This didn't exactly make Luce any less worried. "Tell me you're okay! Before I get completely freaked out."

"You are the most beautiful thing in the world. If you were the sea I'd walk right in, and I'd be so *happy*."

"*Dorian!*"

"Of *course* I'm okay, Luce! I'm so, so much better now. More than I've ever been." There was still something manic in his smile, but he seemed to be slightly more grounded. "I wish my mom was alive. I wish you could sing to her that way. Maybe you could have fixed—whatever it was that made her *do* those things. Luce, I was so scared of her, but even more than that I was so, so, so sorry . . ." Luce held his face in both hands, watching his eyes. Their gold looked a little more solid now. Even though she could see for herself what he'd been through with his parents, she knew it would be much better for him, and for their relationship, if he could tell her the truth of his own free will. Was he about to? "I'm really in love with you, Luce. You know that, right?"

"I'm in love with you, too . . . ." She couldn't help smiling, even as she watched him intensely, hoping for signs that he was truly sane.

"If you can't be human again then I want to be like you," Dorian announced. The melted craziness came back in his eyes.

"I don't think it's *possible*—"

"You said I am, though, that I have the . . . that you can see it . . ."

"You do. I can see the sparkling around you right now. But Catarina said boys can't change, and I'll hurt you if I try."

"What did Catarina know? It's not like she'd seen everything. Her saying it's impossible—that doesn't prove *anything*."

"Dorian, I mean . . ." She hated to remind him of it, but he still seemed deranged by joy. He just wasn't being rational. "The mermaids killed your family. Mermaids, including me. You really want to be a merman?"

"They killed your father, too, though. Probably Catarina killed him, right? But if you ever saw somebody try to hurt Catarina you'd drown them, like, *boom*. Instant death."

Luce couldn't actually deny it. "That's the only way I'd ever kill a human again. If I had to, to protect another mermaid."

"*Exactly.*"

"I loved Catarina. It was too hard for me *not* to forgive her."

"Yeah, well, it's too hard for me not to forgive you. I've always told you that. I couldn't help forgiving you, not even when I used to try to make myself hate you."

As important as Dorian's words felt to Luce and as hungry as she was for the forgiveness he was offering her, she was suddenly distracted by a distant sound. The wind was whistling, but there was something unusual in the tone of it. A kind of musical accent, an urgent intonation. Luce's skin prickled, all her nerves rising to meet the cry.

"Luce?"

"Dorian, I'm sorry, but . . . do you hear that?"

"You mean the wind? It does sound kind of strange."

"That's not wind!" Luce couldn't see past the crags that walled them in, but it sounded like the source of that sound was getting steadily farther away. It was a terrible moment to leave Dorian, but . . . "I have to go. Now."

"Did I do something? Luce, I mean, at least take me back! It'll probably take me hours to row."

"I can't. It—she sounds wrong somehow, like she might be in trouble . . ."

"Another mermaid?" Luce didn't answer, just flashed him a blind, frantic smile and dove. That voice in the wind didn't exactly sound like any mermaid she'd heard before, but it didn't sound like anything else either. And it had a dreadful quality, a crawling alarm, that made Luce's heart race and sent cold, trickling sensations running through her skin.

The voice was louder under the water. The waves transmitted its silvery, whispering resonance; Luce was more certain now that it was another mermaid and that she was calling for help, but from farther out in the sea: out in those deepening waters where Luce had avoided swimming lately. Too many orcas. There didn't seem to be much choice about that now, though, if only she could figure out exactly where the call was coming from. It fractured in the deep water, shivered into her ears, and she couldn't pinpoint its direction. Luce broke the surface in confusion, staring wildly around. A huge fishing trawler was just starting its swing out to sea, heading away from the mermaids' territory. Not that it would have interested them much in any case. Luce could remember Catarina saying that most of those ships were double-hulled to protect against collisions with sea ice. Trying to sink them was too chancy, not worth the risk, and Luce reflexively looked away from its rust-colored bulk, still scanning from one horizon to the next. There was only the ship, a few bobbing seals, the far-off spouts of whales. Nothing to indicate where that strange voice might be coming from.

Then Luce looked again and felt a cold flash of certainty. The ship edged by, hideous and monolithic, a floating mountain. Deep below the water its vast net sieved endless volumes of water, catching and entangling hundreds of animals. The net was hungry and undiscriminating, and any mermaid unlucky enough to be snared in it would surely drown.

Unless . . . It was barely possible, but if she swam faster than she ever had before, there might be time. Luce's tail was already spiraling, whipping her through the gray-green water in a corolla of streaming bubbles, blurring her vision. She was going so fast that she had to slow momentarily to make sure she was heading in the right direction. The smallest mistake would surely result in that strange mermaid's death.

Luce oriented herself, trying to stay calm. Then she lashed out her tail again, but she didn't rush toward the ship. Instead she was headed north, and as she swam that distant voice whispered steadily through her mind, begging her to hurry.

Back to her old tribe's cave.

* * *

Fifteen minutes later Luce was streaking through the familiar tunnel, her lungs aching for air, dizzy and sore from the violent speed of her swimming. Even deep underwater she could hear a babble of voices; it sounded like the whole tribe was there. All Luce could do was hope that they wouldn't put up a fight. "I don't care what we have to do!" The voice was probably Jenna's. "I don't care if we swim for hours as long as we finally find a ship somewhere. I can't stand not having anything to do all the time. If I can't sing to someone soon, I don't know, I'm going to go to a human town and get right up near them and get to *work*—"

"Just because you're bored doesn't mean you should act like an idiot," Dana snapped back. Then Luce's head broke through the water.

Samantha looked right at her and screamed. Dana stared, her expression both alarmed and hopeful. Mermaids dashed back and forth across the cave, obviously unsure what to do. Luce noticed the confusion of the cave, the piles of ripped clothing, the empty liquor bottles and broken jewelry. There was a complicated stink of stale perfume and spilled beer and mold. Anais's obsession with collecting human objects had resulted in this awful trash heap crowding the cave. Maybe she could take advantage of the chaos here, Luce thought, and get what she needed before they decided to attack her.

"You get out of here right this second!" Anais was shrieking somewhere behind her. Luce ignored it.

"I need a knife, quick! There has to be one here somewhere . . ." Luce begged. She stared desperately around the piles of debris. Even if they left her alone, there was no time to search. That trawler must be far out to sea by now.

"Like anyone would give a *weapon* to a psycho like you!" Anais shrieked. Luce glanced around at Anais, her lovely golden hair contrasting horribly with the infuriated smirk that contorted her face. Then Anais thought of something. "Everyone, pin her down! We'll gag her before she tries any of her stupid tricks." Several mermaids shifted uncertainly forward, but most of the tribe just hung back around the walls, clinging to one another and whispering nervously. The water frothed from the twitching of their tails. Luce stared from face to face, noticing Rachel and Kayley gawking at her weakly. These were the same girls she had laughed and swum with, and her head had rested beside theirs as they slept, but now they met her eyes with the unfeeling gaze of strangers. She found herself wondering if any of them were on her side at all.

"Some of you still care about the timahk! There's a strange mermaid caught in a net; we have to save her! I need a knife. Now!" Luce heard her voice crack with urgency.

Jenna had fetched a pile of scarves. She was edging closer to Luce, working up the nerve to lunge at her. And Anais was still behind her somewhere, moving, closing in.

"Why are you all such cowards?" Jenna raged. "Aren't all of you sick of worrying about her? Let's get this *over* with!" A few more of the girls swam slowly forward, and Luce realized that she was almost surrounded. Mermaids were digging through the random trash heaped up all over the shore, probably gathering pantyhose and ropes that they could use to tie her up.

Suddenly Luce saw Dana's face. Her brown eyes were wide in warning and her mouth sagged wordlessly. The truth flashed in front of Luce: once they had her gagged and helpless Anais would order them to throw her on shore, just like she'd done to those larvae. Instead of saving the strange mermaid all she'd managed to do was set herself up to be murdered. Something silvery gleamed in the shadows behind Jenna, and Luce felt a flash of primal terror at the thought of metal violating her flesh. A slim hand held a curved, sinister-looking hunting knife up where Luce could see it, and for an instant fear almost overcame her. She was ready to dive blindly into the crowd of mermaids around her when she noticed the hand with the knife wasn't poised to threaten her. Instead it was held out in a furtive offering, and Violet smiled shy and proud from the dimness behind Jenna's back. Then Violet's glossy brown head licked under the surface, so smoothly that no one but Luce saw her go. Deep below the water a soft hand gently tugged Luce's fins, urging her to follow.

"I can send a wave to throw all of you on shore," Luce announced. She tried to sound cold and determined. "Let me go now, and I won't have to hurt you." A few mermaids stopped where they were, gaping in sudden doubt, but Jenna gave a piercing cry and leaped.

Luce didn't have a chance to gather her breath or to think about what she should do. Instead the music that burst from her was shrill and spontaneous and uncontrolled, yanking a vertical pillar of water straight up under Jenna. Jenna suddenly flailed at the peak of a steep-sided wave ten feet high, towering in the tightly confined space of the cave, and then Luce realized with dismay that the wave *was* about to throw Jenna far onshore. Luce barely mastered her voice in time to send the wave swinging sideways, slamming Jenna against a rocky outcropping instead.

Jenna howled in shock from the impact and then dropped into the water, stunned and keening. Dozens of voices were jabbering, and tails flashed randomly through the cave's continual dusk.

Luce dove. She might have hurt Jenna seriously, maybe even broken some bones, but there was no time to think about that. Luce whipped her way back out of the cave and angled toward the surface at the sight of wavering fins. Violet was there, a feverish glow in her eyes, her smile somehow sad and eager at the same time. And the distant, windy voice still beckoned them, though now it was so faint Luce's heart burned with desperation at the hopelessness of reaching it in time.

Violet's head dipped toward the water. It took Luce a moment to understand that Violet was bowing to her.

"Queen Luce," Violet whispered, "you saved me before. I know you'll save her, too!" Luce felt the handle of the knife pressing into her hand and tried to focus. She could just see the fishing trawler, a rusty dot propped in front of the dim blue shelf of Russia far away. In the instant before she dove, it occurred to Luce that the ship was farther from the safety of the coast than she had ever swum before.

The water became an endless gray-green tunnel. Luce drove herself relentlessly, the water whipping out behind her until it no longer seemed to be water but only an unceasing road. The pain in her body streaked like bubbles, like falling light, and more than once she slapped against startled animals, her speed throwing them aside. The baby faces of beluga whales winked at her, and she parted walls of fish with the currents that rushed off her body. She couldn't hear the silvery voice anymore, only the storm of ripped water striking her cheeks like millions of torn flags. Every now and then she surfaced to catch a quick, panting breath, and also to make sure she was still heading for that distant fishing boat. Was she even getting any closer? And even if the strange mermaid was exceptionally strong, wasn't it crazy to imagine she could survive so long without air? Luce saw the black and white smears of orcas dash by below her. They seemed to realize she was going too quickly for them to catch her, but sooner or later her exhaustion would become over-whelming and she'd have to slow down.

The fishing boat *was* closer, suddenly. The water shivered with the roar of its engines. Luce was so tired that her head swayed, and the boat seemed to become a stained metal cloud. But, very softly, she heard a last exhalation of windy song, a fi-nal call. Whoever it was in the net was still alive, then, if only barely. Luce dove again, the spiraling of her tail harsh and auto-matic. She could see the boat through the water now, the swell of the enormous net behind it like some vast, pulsating tumor. Luce raced on, and soon the silver mass of thousands of strug-gling fish was all she could see, spreading for dozens of yards on both sides. She clenched the knife and threw herself against the net, her free hand digging through its strands and against the cold, squirming bodies of a nation of pollock.

Then she raised the knife and slashed, cutting the clustered fish in her desperation. Blood began to spiral through the water and red gouts striped the gleaming scales, but the net didn't give. Luce tried to calm herself and began to cut through one strand at a time, still gripping the net like a mountain climber. Bit by bit a gash began to form in the net, the first few wounded fish slithering through it. Luce cut steadily on, and a bulge of fighting silver bodies began to squeeze toward the opening, shoving at her hands and sometimes slapping straight into her face as they burst free. Luce began to hear the moan of straining fibers, the popping sounds of breaking strands.

Suddenly there was a loud ripping noise, and the piece of net Luce was clutching swung far back, almost throwing her. An avalanche of shining fish tumbled out, pummeling Luce's arms and head. The knife flew from her right hand, and she managed to reach through the beating silver forms and lace her fingers through the net's holes while her body pitched wildly back and forth among the scrape of scales and round black eyes. All she could see was the constant flash of fish, disgorged so thickly that they became a desperate, living flood. Then came other creatures: a family of drowned porpoises, pulped jellyfish, a small shark, all crushed together. Clinging like this there was the risk that she would be pounded into unconsciousness and drown before she came to. But if she let go, the torrent would sweep her far away. Luce pictured the strange mermaid sinking deeper all alone. Where *was* she?

Then, in the endless repetition of silver shapes, Luce caught a glimpse of something hopeful. It was a single elegant hand, its skin the somber green-gold-brown of a bronze statue left for centuries in the ocean. The hand hung limp, its owner still wedged between fish close-packed into a bowed wall. Luce tried to reach it, but the rushing animals beat her back. Then something gave, and a girl's form swept toward her in the middle of a tumbling mass of scales and fins and fur. A mermaid, dark-skinned and with a deep emerald tail. Luce barely managed to catch her in one outstretched arm. The fish were thinning out now, and with an involuntary groan Luce lashed her tail, tugging the strange mermaid toward the surface. Her greenish eyelids were closed and she didn't move, but somehow Luce thought she could feel an almost imperceptible flutter of life deep inside her.

They came up just below the hard, rust-colored wall of the ship. There was an outcry of voices above as angry sailors noticed the ruptured net, the escaping haul of fish. Under normal conditions Luce would have never taken the risk of surfacing where humans might see her, but the situation was too urgent for her to worry about that. She embraced the strange mermaid from behind and leaned steeply so that the unconscious face dangled out over the rocking sea. Then Luce squeezed under her ribs to bring the water up from the girl's lungs. It spattered out, and Luce squeezed again, then turned the girl and caught her face, blowing air between her still lips. Again, and then again. The girl didn't move, and Luce thought of Miriam. Once again she'd come too late to save a mermaid from death, and Luce thrashed in fury, ready to fling the dragging body away from her.

Then the dark girl coughed and another stream of salt water gushed down her chin. Luce hurriedly grabbed her head and held it angled down. Then, for what must have been the first time in an hour, the mermaid inhaled freely, with a drawn-out, rasping sound. Luce heard her sigh. She had a crow's nose and a thick cloud of black, savage, looping hair; she was beautiful, Luce thought, in the way a thunderstorm at midnight is beautiful.

A pair of greenish black eyes turned sidelong to look into Luce's, calm and curious. Seeing those eyes was like gazing far into the past, into ancient memories and impossible distance. It took Luce a moment to recover from that glance and remember that they were still far from safety. If only there was a nearby island, even an outcropping of rock, they could rest before they attempted the journey back to shore. Luce scanned from one horizon to the next, seeing only the repeating peaks of tall gray waves. The cliffs of her own coast were strangely shrunken, no more than a zigzagging band of gray and green. Now that her frantic race for the fishing trawler was over, Luce's muscles seized up with pain. Reaching that distant land seemed impossible, especially with the addition of this strange girl's weight dragging on her arm.

The mermaid said a few words in a low, singsong language Luce didn't recognize, and laughed. She was probably in shock, Luce thought. She didn't understand how awful the situation really was.

Then Luce thought of something. Her tail was gripped by cramps, her body was trembling from weariness, but she still had her voice. It seemed like too much to hope for, but once they were far enough from the ship she could at least try. Slowly Luce began towing her strange companion along the surface, and to her surprise the other mermaid inhaled sharply, then began driving her own tail as well, although from the heaviness of her movements it was obvious that her strength was almost gone. But at least, Luce thought, she wouldn't have to fight all alone to get them back to shore.

When they were half a mile from the trawler, Luce released a long, sustained note, lifting a smooth arch of water below them. They hovered together up above the beating of the wild waves, and the strange mermaid turned her head to examine Luce with calm interest. Luce ignored her. Instead she focused on the music that poured from her, expanding her voice to call the wave onward. The stone-colored twilight was rapidly deepening, and the clouds above them sagged like a dim blue tent. Now that she was singing Luce felt a sudden thrill of serenity, and the darkening world became bright and vital with music. The sea sang through her, and the low clouds cast down harmonies like shadows. They weren't traveling as quickly as Luce had before, but they still sailed along much faster than they could have hoped to swim in their weakened state. Once an orca leaped at them, but the wave swirled them on and the huge jaws snapped on empty air.

The strange mermaid laughed again, then raised her own voice in an undercurrent below Luce's. That voice, Luce thought, seemed to carry an impossible weight of dreams with it; it was foreign-sounding and mournful and so beautiful that even Luce could barely stand to hear it.

11

Nausicaa

"I thought this would be the time," the strange mermaid said. She had an unrecognizable accent that seemed to flare up suddenly and then vanish again. They had stopped to rest on the shore of the same craggy island where Dorian's family had met their deaths, and the night was thick and starless. "What are the Fates to do when there is one like you waiting to snap their thread?" Luce didn't know what the dark girl was talking about, and the slow, unrelenting curiosity in those greenish eyes made her feel shy and uncertain. "And is it even right, I wonder? This thing you've done?"

Luce felt herself flush. But why should she feel ashamed of saving someone?

"I heard you calling. I couldn't just leave you to die there!" Luce protested. The strange mermaid rolled back against the shore, stretching her back and twisting her emerald green tail. It gave off complicated lights, blue and amber mixed with flashes of deep purple.

"It doesn't matter at all that I did not die today." The dark girl's voice was cold and lazy as she said this, and her words rang like heavy bells.

Luce was appalled. "Of *course* it matters!"

"What matters is that you made the choice to save me as you did. Who are you?"

Luce couldn't understand why such a simple question had the power to embarrass her so much. "I'm Luce."

"Queen Luce . . ."

"I'm not Queen anything!"

"My name is Nausicaa. But if you are not queen, then you must be alone here?"

"Oh, Luce!" Another voice broke in on them. "Oh, I *knew* you'd get her! I tried to follow, but you were going too fast." Luce turned in the direction of this new voice to see Violet's sweet, gray-green eyes staring at them. Violet was so excited that she seemed to forget her usual shyness. "I bet Luce would *never* tell you this," Violet went on breathlessly, beaming at Nausicaa, "but she saved my life, too! My very first day as a mermaid I was so dumb I tried to leave the water, and Luce came after me. She almost died! And she is *so* the greatest singer."

Nausicaa gave Violet one of her oddly peaceful smiles. "I have heard your queen sing. Though she denies her rule here. But none of what you tell me now surprises me."

"She's *supposed* to be our queen," Violet explained with an audible note of resentment. "She just won't do it. Maybe she'll listen to you, if you tell her? I mean they did try to kill Luce just now, when she raided our cave to get the knife, so now she probably hates us even more than she did already . . ."

Nausicaa was glancing back and forth between them, a quizzical smile on her face. Luce thought she should say something. "It's a really long story, Nausicaa. You're probably way too exhausted to want to hear it now."

"All the stories are long," Nausicaa observed dryly.

"Once you've had a rest I'll take you back to my cave, and if you want I'll tell you about it tomorrow . . ." Luce went on.

"All the stories are so long that they"—Nausicaa paused, and her hand drew a circle on the air—"that in the end, they become the *same* story. So I may already know yours, Queen Luce."

Luce didn't quite know what to say to that.

"Just Luce. Okay? And this is Violet." Luce suddenly noticed other shining heads popping up in the water around them. "Um, Nausicaa? We should probably get out of here."

Nausicaa shook her head and held up one hand with a casually majestic gesture. "We will wait, please. I will speak to them." Anais's golden head emerged directly face to face with Nausicaa, her expression savage. They were no more than five feet apart, and Luce thought how bizarre they looked together; this close to Nausicaa's dark patina, Anais's brash blond beauty seemed phony and brittle, like something made of tinsel and plastic. After a moment Anais registered Nausicaa's devastating calm, and something wavered in her eyes. She glanced around for her followers; Luce noticed then that Jenna was missing and that Samantha was cowering pitifully behind a rock. Nausicaa waited in silence for so long that Luce could hear the blood surging in her veins.

"It is your cave, where Luce stole the knife?" Nausicaa said at last. "You think this is a cause for an argument?" Luce was glad to notice that Anais was visibly flustered. There was something about Nausicaa that she simply didn't know how to deal with.

"Like anything around here is any of your business!" Anais tried sneering, but it sounded false and whiny. "I don't think I owe you an *explanation*. Just get out of our way now, okay?"

"She stole the knife so that she could save me from the net. She has only done what you should have done. She has *timay*." It took Luce a moment to understand that this was Nausicaa's way of saying that Luce had only been obeying the timahk; three seconds later Anais seemed to realize the same thing.

"Oh my God! Did everybody hear that? She can't even say *timahk* right, and she thinks she can tell us what to do!" Anais's sneer sounded more genuine now, and a few mermaids laughed.

Nausicaa wasn't fazed at all. "To say *timahk* is a corruption. A change that has come over the word from many hundreds of years. The Greek word is said '*timay*.'"

"Like you know Greek!" Anais almost squealed it. Luce saw Nausicaa's slow, unending smile, a smile that seemed to cross whole oceans, and suddenly felt sure that Nausicaa knew Greek as well as she knew the sea itself.

Everyone seemed to be waiting, with inexplicable anxiety, for Nausicaa to answer back. She didn't bother, just gazed at them all with the same merciless calm, the slightly ironic smile.

"Anyway, *retard*," Anais snapped at last in a tone that suggested she was desperately trying to cover the silence, "I'm queen here! And I say you've got to get lost, like you *and* Luce had better get out of Alaska right now and never come back, or I'll make sure you're both sorry!"

"You are queen?" Nausicaa didn't even sound sarcastic, just coolly disbelieving. "If you can outrank Luce, you must be a singer such as our world has never heard before." Anais opened her mouth, then shut it again, and to Luce's surprise a handful of mermaids laughed openly. Luce wanted to warn them to stop. Anais would definitely find a way to get back at them later. "Luce? You will come with me?" Luce saw Nausicaa's outstretched hand, and took it. No one tried to stop them as they swam away.

* * *

Luce wanted to be sure Dorian had made it safely home, but there was no way she could do that with Nausicaa right beside her. For the first time in weeks Luce found herself feeling a little ashamed of her forbidden romance. Nausicaa believed that Luce was honorable, after all, worthy of deep respect; somehow it would be unbearable to disappoint her. They stopped at Luce's dining beach and ate, both of them too tired out to talk much, and Luce was pleased to see that Nausicaa didn't mind the two little larvae at all. Instead she crooned to them and fed them oysters and petted their hair. They warbled around her, splashing and giggling at the attention.

It wasn't just exhaustion that kept her from talking to Nausicaa, Luce realized. She felt shy around this dark, powerful mermaid in a way that she hadn't felt with anyone since the days when she was just a helpless human girl.

"That *queen*," Nausicaa said after a while. Her tone made it clear how ridiculous she thought it was to call Anais that. "Why do they not drive her away? Anyone can see that she is *sika*."

Luce was confused. "Are you saying—I mean—are you calling Anais a psycho?"

Nausicaa looked blank for a second, then cracked up laughing. It was the first time Luce had heard her sound *young*, although she had the face and body of an exquisite fifteen-year-old girl.

"Not *psycho*. How strange, I always think, that the English for 'crazy' is almost the same as '*psyche*,' the Greek name for soul. Do you all believe here that to have a soul at all is to be insane? She has no soul. *Sika*: a cold one. You must see it when you look at her, so." And here Nausicaa gave Luce the sidelong glance that would reveal the secret past that had changed her. Luce flinched at having Nausicaa gaze at her that way, but Nausicaa's face remained so impassive that after a moment Luce relaxed. And then she understood what Nausicaa was trying to tell her.

The dark shimmering of the indication always hung thickly around Anais's head. But unlike every other mermaid in the tribe, with Anais that sparkling didn't seem to contain a story. You could gaze at her sideways until your head throbbed from the effort and not see anything more than a few hazy winks of boring, everyday events. She had the mark, it seemed, but not the deep emotional wounds that the mark implied. Luce had always wondered why that was and what it meant.

"You mean because you can't see anything *happening* to her?

I never understood that. Do you—I mean—you know what that's about?"

Nausicaa looked surprised. "You don't know this, Luce? This tribe does not know? Have the mermaids truly forgotten so much? That would explain why they allow her to stay here, like a poisonous snake sleeping beside them. A wiser tribe would never permit it."

"I thought you could only throw a mermaid out if she broke the timahk! Anais has broken it a bunch of times now, actually, but at first—"

"Not *sika*. No one should allow *sika* to remain. They will always cause terrible dangers. They will destroy any tribe that welcomes them . . ."

"But I don't understand . . ." Luce fell silent, wondering. Nausicaa looked deep into her eyes. Her gaze had a green and black brilliance that reminded Luce of a field of fireflies.

"You must remember this feeling, Luce? Of your time of changing? You lay on the cliff, just as the Unnamed Twins once did, and you felt . . ." Luce didn't know what twins Nausicaa was talking about, but she remembered the feeling perfectly.

"I felt like I was turning cold. At first it was just my body, but then it was my heart and everything—My body changed into water. I could feel the moonlight shining *through* me."

"Yes." Nausicaa nodded, her snaky black hair surging with the wind. "You *turned* cold. All the way to the quick. And yet in such a cold sea as this you have recovered so much warmth of spirit."

"But then . . ."

"A *sika*, like this Anais, she does not *turn* cold. She is cold to start with. Cold to the quick from birth. So there can be no vision to see of her *turning* cold. It is her essence, and her danger. She can care for nothing," Nausicaa added with calm finality.

Luce was quiet for a minute, and Nausicaa went back to nibbling seaweed. Would it make any difference if Nausicaa explained this to the tribe? Luce had a depressing intuition that it wouldn't.

"Nausicaa?" Luce asked suddenly. "Do you come from Greece?"

Nausicaa glanced up, smiling. There was such deep acceptance in that smile that Luce thrilled at the sight of it.

"I do. It was long ago."

"How long ago?" Luce felt oddly embarrassed as she asked this, as if it was somehow a terribly personal question.

"Oh, Luce," Nausicaa sighed. "How can I know? Why should I look for numbers in the sky? Long ago. But if I guess for you, I will say, perhaps three thousand years."

Luce had been prepared, though barely, to hear Nausicaa mention *hundreds* of years. This was almost too much for her.

"Three *thousand*?" It came out high and frantic.

"It might be less," Nausicaa conceded. She looked amused. "But it was a time of few men on the earth, and there were many fewer ships then, all with oars. There were places where the whales swam so thick that it could be hard to find enough room between them to reach the surface, and everything was clean. I cannot believe, sometimes, that the world has not yet crumbled to dust from so much time passing by."

"But how have you *survived*? I mean, all that time . . ." As

Luce said this she noticed that Nausicaa's smile had turned strained.

"Death does not like the taste of me, I suppose." Nausicaa looked away, and Luce saw something almost grim in her eyes. "I have taken enough risks. I have traveled the world around and again around, more times than I can remember. I know so many languages that I could tell you a story speaking only one word from each. And on many occasions I have come very close to dying, but something always interferes. Today it was you. A new mermaid, but with the courage of one so long in the sea that death has become an empty threat, and with the rare power of singing so that the water will understand her. Yet she will not be called queen. Very little can still make me wonder, Luce. But with you I admit I am curious."

Luce looked down at the bright crescents of seafoam, the subtle glow of her own hands refracting through the night black water. "You can ask me whatever you want, if you're curious about me. But I don't think it'll be very interesting for you, Nausicaa. I mean, I've only been a mermaid since April, and anyway you said you probably already know my story. Remember? You said all the stories turn out to be the same."

Nausicaa laughed. Her deep olive-bronze skin gave off a richer light than Luce's, a strong greenish gold. "Perhaps someday someone will change that story. Perhaps *you* will, Luce. Then the story will be new, even for me. I would be very pleased if that were so."

Luce looked up at her, intrigued. "Change it how?"

"If I could guess that," Nausicaa observed sardonically, "I might be the one to do the changing." She suddenly looked bored, and Luce winced at the idea that Nausicaa was already getting tired of her. Still, the conversation made Luce think of another moment several months before, another mermaid murmuring to her in the darkness.

"What you're saying—it reminds me of my friend Miriam. She thought it was pointless to kill humans, when there were always more of them anyway. She couldn't understand why we had to keep doing the same things over and over." Luce felt her stomach seize up. She was painfully anxious to hear what Nausicaa thought about sinking human ships.

"I long ago came to that view myself. Humans are repulsive and senseless, and they work restlessly to destroy the world that carries them. But singing them to their deaths, though we are charged to do it . . ." Nausicaa shrugged. "A game for the newer ones, and I feel I have done my share. But no doubt you enjoy it."

"I don't, actually." Luce heard her voice break a little, and Nausicaa's glance sparked at her again.

"From the beginning? You felt this way? Do you think, even, that it is wrong, the vengeance mermaids bring?"

Luce paused and considered this. She couldn't help being aware that the conversation was veering into dangerous territory, but the impulse to trust Nausicaa was overwhelming. "I mean, I helped sink ships at first, once or twice. But I always felt horrible about it. I kept remembering humans I'd loved."

Nausicaa was nodding in a slightly impatient way, and Luce realized that this was just another story Nausicaa already knew. "It happens so, sometimes. There are those who still feel with their human hearts, and they cannot bear the task that is given to them."

Luce was simultaneously bewildered and fascinated. *The task that is given to them?* Who gave it, then? Even more exciting, though, was the information that there were other mermaids somewhere who felt the way she did. If they could all live together . . .

"Where *are* they?" Luce asked, too eagerly, and Nausicaa looked blank. "I mean, the mermaids who don't kill. Do they have their own tribe?" Now that, Luce thought, would be a tribe where it would be a tremendous honor to be queen, if they only thought she was good enough. Maybe she could persuade Dorian to run away, and they could start a new life together. Maybe mermaids like that would even accept him.

"Oh." Now that Nausicaa understood what Luce was asking, she looked a little sad. "There is no such tribe, Luce. Mermaids who feel as you do—they do not choose to live as we must. All that I have ever known or heard of, they pull themselves soon enough from the water and die in the air."

Luce stared at Nausicaa in horror, and suddenly remembered something Catarina had said when Luce had just changed and had barely escaped from an encounter with orcas: *Luce, were you trying to die? Tell me the truth!* So Catarina had known mermaids who preferred suicide to a life of murder in the sea. And Miriam . . .

"That's what Miriam did," Luce said; she could hardly restrain her tears.

"Of course. I knew that instantly from what you said of her."

"But I haven't! Maybe I thought about it, but I never tried . . ."

"You may yet." Nausicaa said this with terrible indifference. "But maybe you will make a different choice and live with what you are now, knowing that the longing to kill belongs to all of us."

"But I want to *change* it. I mean, I want to completely change what it means to be a mermaid and start a new tribe someday. That's why I taught myself how to sing to the water. I was looking for a way I could do that . . ." Luce broke off when she saw the way Nausicaa was staring at her; her gaze was suddenly glinting with fascination, even with longing and other emotions Luce couldn't identify. Was that *pity*?

"It is our father, Proteus, who has given us this task, Luce. The price of our being is that we must avenge all the girls who are broken and outcast as we are. A mermaid may neglect her work, as I do, but all of us are charged with it. The urge moves in our hearts and in our voices."

"Our father *who*?"

"Proteus is a god. If you try to alter the destiny of the mermaids, you will not merely be defying their nature. You will be defying the will of the gods themselves!"

Luce considered this in silence, staring out at the white rippling trails of foam sliding over the black sea. It was the first time she had ever revealed her secret ambition to anyone, and she was grateful to find that Nausicaa didn't hate her for it. But Nausicaa clearly knew much more than Luce did, and from what she'd said—about *defying the gods*—it sounded like she thought Luce's hopes were utterly impossible.

"So are you saying it's crazy? To defy Proteus? I mean, are you saying I *shouldn't* try to do that?" Luce couldn't suppress her anxiety as she asked this, and she gazed urgently into Nausicaa's eyes. If she had to surrender her deepest hope, Luce thought, then maybe life as a mermaid *would* become unbearable, even now that she had Dorian. And what if he outgrew her someday?

"Oh, Luce." Nausicaa smiled with ferocious brilliance. "I am not saying this. Not at all."

Luce felt so disoriented that for an instant the sea and sky seemed to reverse their places, rocking her between two immense black fields. "But you said . . ."

Nausicaa reached out and lightly rested her hand on Luce's forehead. It was a strange gesture but somehow also profoundly sweet.

"Defy whom you will, little queen," Nausicaa said firmly. And then Luce saw the tears welling in her night-deep eyes.

12

Enough

Luce was worried at first that having Nausicaa around would make it impossible for her to visit Dorian. But immediately it became apparent that, even if Nausicaa regarded Luce as a friend, she tended to be restless and to prefer her own company most of the time. She was used to traveling alone. Nausicaa told Luce about her trick for hitching rides on huge ships: she'd either steal or find a life preserver and lash it to a ship's hull at the waterline in a spot where the curve of the ship would hide her from anyone who happened to peer overboard. By tying her body into the life preserver she could keep her tail submerged and her head above water, watching through the days and sleeping through the nights. She'd crossed entire oceans that way, back and forth, freeing herself from the coast-bound life of the other mermaids. It all sounded insanely dangerous to Luce: what if a shark or an orca came at her while she was sleeping? What if someone in a passing boat saw her there? But it was clear that Nausicaa simply didn't care much about danger, and Luce didn't want to annoy her by arguing.

The day after Luce rescued her, Nausicaa began to fidget, then announced that she was going exploring. It was getting to be the middle of the afternoon, almost time to meet Dorian, so Luce only smiled, trying to disguise her relief. "Are you going to come back tonight?"

"I may." Nausicaa glanced over at her with moody interest. "Perhaps where you are is a place something will happen." Luce didn't know whether to be flattered or hurt. She couldn't escape the sense that Nausicaa regarded her as a kind of experiment, something that might or might not turn out well. Luce watched Nausicaa swim slowly out through the purple bands of oncoming dusk; evening came so *early* now. She was heading into deep waters, completely ignoring Luce's warnings about orcas.

Dorian might be angry with her for leaving him so abruptly the day before. But once she explained what had happened, he'd have to understand. Wouldn't he?

The daylight lasted for a noticeably briefer period every day, and the dusk dragged on for what seemed like hours, descending a slow scale of darkening tones. Luce arrived at their beach in the deep blue slur of fading afternoon. The beach looked empty, but Dorian often waited back under the trees. Luce gazed around and let out a quick windy call before she remembered that he might not understand it.

"Hey." He wasn't concealed in the forest margin at all. Instead he was perched eight feet up on the tall boulder to her right where she hadn't noticed him. "Thanks for making time for me. I know you have a lot of more important things to deal with. You know I didn't make it back until almost eleven? And my arms were *killing* me, and I nearly capsized like twenty times. I had to talk an incredible amount of shit to keep from getting grounded, too."

Luce stared up at him, uncomfortable with the distance between them. Had he climbed up there because he knew she wouldn't be able to reach him? "I saved her *life*."

"You did what?"

"That mermaid we heard calling. She'd gotten swept up by one of those huge nets, and I realized I'd have to go back to my old tribe's cave to get a knife to cut through it. Dorian, I barely got to her in time . . ." Hurt as she felt, Luce couldn't hold back the story. She launched into it too quickly, so that her nervousness was obvious to both of them. Dorian sat on his rock, leaning out so that his head seemed to float over her in the darkness, his face stiff with resentment.

By the time Luce reached the part about the fight in the cave, though, he suddenly let out an exclamation. Luce looked up, surprised. "Oh my God, Luce! You did that for someone you don't even know? They could have killed you!"

"Yes, but Dorian, Nausicaa's seriously incredible. I can't wait for you to meet her!" Dorian laughed a little nastily, and suddenly Luce realized the absurdity of what she'd said. "I mean, I *wish* you could."

"Did you think at all about what would happen to me if you died? Like, did you ever think that you're all I have left?" Dorian asked in an overly calm voice that made Luce's skin prickle. She hadn't thought about that, in fact; the situation had seemed so imperative that she hadn't stopped to think about anything. But maybe Dorian was right and it had been insensitive to put a stranger's needs first. Especially after she'd helped kill his family. Dorian stared down, his dark blond hair hanging in tendrils all around his face. "Okay. I get it. You didn't give a shit about that." Luce started to protest, but he interrupted her. "Just tell me the rest of the story. Okay? You used this insane power you have to throw Jenna into a wall . . ."

She'd been so excited to tell him everything, but now as Luce went on she felt close to tears. He was so angry at the risks she'd taken when she'd secretly hoped he would be proud of her, thrilled with how brave she'd been. It was hard to keep going. "The trawler had swung way out, and I had to chase it. I was swimming so fast I could barely see where I was going."

"You told me it's too dangerous to swim out now. Because of the orcas." Dorian's voice was still flat, and Luce found herself flushing.

"I was going too fast for them, though. I mean, I saw a few of them, but . . ." Luce felt a powerful impulse to understate the danger she'd gone through, but she could tell by Dorian's expression that he wasn't fooled. He listened to her with his lips set in a grim line, not saying anything, until Luce reached Nausicaa's confrontation with Anais.

"That all sounds completely amazing." He said it coldly, still glowering down at her. Luce wished he'd climb off the rock at least, even if he was too angry to touch her.

"Dorian, I—" Why couldn't he understand that she'd only done what she had to do? "I couldn't have left her to die that way. Really. I had to at least try."

"My life must seem so boring to you, compared to that. I can see why you don't want to be human again. Even though that's the only way we could really be together."

You probably wouldn't love me anymore if I was human, Luce thought. But out loud she said, "You know I can't, though! Dorian, I can't ever turn back."

"You don't *know* that." He almost snarled the words.

"Anyway, you said you wanted to be the one to change. Into a merman." If anyone knew a way to make that happen, Luce thought, it would be Nausicaa. But then she'd have to tell Nausicaa the truth.

"But that's just because—" Dorian hesitated. "I mean, I'm fifteen now, Luce. But what about when I'm seventeen, or twenty, and you're still only fourteen, and we *still* can't be together? I'll go crazy." Suddenly Luce understood what he meant by the words "be together" and flinched. Why remind her of that when he knew she'd never be able to be with him in that way? It was hard enough for her to know that she would never experience that kind of closeness, while her body still retained its human cravings. "So I thought, if I became a merman, it would be the one way I could deal with it. Like, it might not bother me then. That you can't even grow up or anything—"

"Who wants to grow up?" Luce heard her voice going sharp and high-pitched.

"Jesus, Luce." Dorian had never sounded so snide before. "I do."

For a few moments they just stared at each other, deep blue light cradling them on all sides. Luce felt the first tear gliding across her cheek. Was he actually breaking up with her?

Dorian sighed, loudly, and started clambering off the boulder, his toes scrambling for the few jags on its side. He thudded down onto the pebbles as Luce watched miserably, wondering if he'd simply turn and leave. Instead he sat down cross-legged near the water's edge. "I really love you, Luce." He sounded more resigned than tender, though.

"Then why are you doing this to me?" Her voice broke, and she fought to hold back tears. She couldn't escape the feeling that he was just looking for excuses to resent her, and that proved he'd never truly forgiven her at all.

"Doing what to you? You're the one who ran off and abandoned me in the middle of nowhere. You're the one who almost went and got killed in like three different ways yesterday, and you expect me to be *okay* with that? I'm not. And now you're so excited about this new mermaid that you don't care how I feel at all, and you haven't asked me one question about anything in my life."

That was so unfair, Luce thought, when he'd kept insisting that she had to finish the story. But still . . .

"What happened with you, then? Besides having to row back, I mean."

"That guy Ben Ellison came to see me," Dorian announced, and Luce gazed at him in confusion. "The FBI guy, remember? From Anchorage. He had breakfast today at our house. I saw him for a while after school, too. And Lindy started talking about how I'm always going off on these long walks alone, staying out late, and how she *worries* about me."

Luce couldn't believe what she was hearing. "You talked to the FBI?"

"What do you think I *did*? I didn't tell him anything about you. We just talked about other stuff. Like, he knows a lot about art, way more than anybody else around here, anyway. He's actually really nice, Luce." He grinned at her in an awful, pinched way. *"I can't wait for you to meet him."*

"Dorian!" Somehow everything he was saying today felt unbelievably cruel to her, even if it was mostly reasonable enough on the surface.

"And I'm thinking of starting a band. There's this guy in my school who plays keyboards, and he's kind of not terrible. He says he knows some other people around here, too."

"What are you going to do, then?" Luce was overcome by bitterness, and she couldn't keep the sarcasm out of her voice. "Sing?"

"Well, do *you* want to be our singer? We could get some kind of tank for you, or like a wading pool or something." Dorian halfway leered at her. "I bet you'd be pretty good."

Luce stared at the mass of his body sitting hunched in the violet-gray darkness. He probably wouldn't be able to see it if she did cry, but still, maybe it would be simpler just to leave. "This is *horrible.*" The words leaped out of her unexpectedly.

"What's horrible? That I'm starting a band?"

"That we're fighting like this. Dorian, I don't want to feel angry with you. And there's still so much I haven't told you, and maybe it's important." Dorian reached out for her for the first time, curling his fingers around her shoulder, pulling her close. Luce didn't resist, but she didn't go to him either.

"Tell me everything later." He had her tight in his arms now, tugging her far enough onto the beach that her tail was barely covered by each new wave rolling in; intermittent breaths of icy air prickled on her scales. Luce felt herself go tense, ready to fight. "Just kiss me now. Okay?"

"Let me get a little deeper in the water, then." Luce squirmed in his arms, trying to work her way down the beach's slope.

"Is the air hurting you?"

"It isn't really hurting. There's still enough water hitting my tail that it just stings a little." The real problem was that it made her nervous, not that it hurt. She couldn't completely rid herself of the fear that he might suddenly wrench around and send her flopping up onto the shore. He might imagine he could turn her human that way and wind up killing her by accident. But how could she say that to him? Luce thrashed hard enough that his grip loosened, and she was able to slide three feet down. Immediately she felt better, her tail cool and secure in the rocking sea.

"I don't see what the big deal is, then," Dorian said. He was still sulking, but he kissed her anyway. After a moment Luce lost herself in the endless warmth of his mouth, the drifting tremor of his hands exploring her skin.

Something crunched back in the woods. At first Luce didn't react. There were so many wild animals here; something was always crackling through the branches. Then an unsettling thought flashed through Luce's mind: maybe Ben Ellison had followed Dorian down here? She listened for a while longer, but there was only the hiss of wind in the spruce trees.

Then heat and softness consumed her completely. Again there was that disturbing concentration of smoky warmth in her core, an eager feeling that wouldn't go away no matter how she squirmed. Her fins rippled over the stones, and her blood grew so warm that she felt almost human again. She began and ended in that kiss. What else could matter?

After they parted for the evening Luce realized she still hadn't told him everything Nausicaa had said. She was sure he'd be interested, especially in the things Nausicaa had told her about the god Proteus and how he was the "father" of the mermaids. In a way it turned out Dorian had been right all along: the mermaids *did* have a kind of boss, even if a lot of them didn't know it.

She needed to find out more, Luce realized. If there was a solution to her impasse with Dorian, Nausicaa would know what it was.

Her argument with Dorian had made everything unavoidably clear, after all. They couldn't go on like this forever. Sooner or later one of them would have to change. It was either that or . . .

But Luce couldn't bear to finish the thought. If they loved each other, why shouldn't that be enough for both of them?

Luce waited impatiently through the rest of that evening for Nausicaa to return while a rising wind whistled savagely, sometimes blowing a long, hollow musical tone through a chink low in the cave's wall. A storm must be coming, howling up from the direction of the Aleutians. After a while she stopped feeling annoyed and instead became worried that Nausicaa was in some kind of trouble. When she finally started drifting off to sleep Nausicaa still hadn't appeared, and Luce began to wonder if she'd ever see her again. The idea depressed her, and the wind lashed through her dreams.

She woke to a noise like an explosion and jolted upright before she understood that lightning must have struck a nearby tree. "Such violence to this storm and to the currents," Nausicaa said. She was leaning back against the cave's wall, the glow of her face filtering through the maze of wild hair that obscured one eye, and Luce noticed that she'd brought back a haul of oysters in a rag of torn net. "The struggle of swimming through them is too much. So you can tell me your long story if you like."

Luce gazed around the cave. It was as dark as midnight, and the air pulsed and reverberated with the intensity of the waves slamming just outside. For a moment she didn't even care that Nausicaa was back safe. With the storm this powerful it would probably be impossible for her and Dorian to see each other, and the memory of their fight lingered on inside her like a chill. She thought for the first time of him walking through the halls of his school, joking with other kids his age. He'd told her that part of his life didn't seem real to him, but he obviously didn't mean it. Not if he was starting a band.

"Luce? Has something disturbed you? Would you prefer if I was gone?" Luce looked back at Nausicaa's gold-green glow; she looked serene but a little concerned.

"Oh—no. Of course I'm glad you're here, Nausicaa." Luce knew she didn't sound glad and cast around for an excuse. "I just had a really bad dream."

Nausicaa didn't ask what that dream had been. Instead she cracked an oyster on the wall, still gazing speculatively into Luce's eyes. "Eat something. It will help you leave your dream behind." Luce moved closer to take the oyster Nausicaa held out to her.

Nausicaa had told her to defy whatever she chose; Luce wondered if that included the timahk's prohibition on contact with humans. Maybe, just maybe, Nausicaa wouldn't think badly of her for loving someone on land. And there was still so much Nausicaa could teach her. "Nausicaa? Instead of me telling *you* stories—" Luce stopped, suddenly overcome by shyness, and Nausicaa waited. "I mean, maybe you could tell me about your life instead. And what you said yesterday, about Proteus being our father . . ."

Nausicaa looked disgusted. "*No one* has told you this?"

"I'd never heard anything like that before. About Proteus, or what you said about twins," Luce said.

Nausicaa was shaking her head as if she wanted to make Luce's words go away.

"I wish I could say that I have never before met mermaids so forgetful of our history. I have met many. It is like the mind erasing itself. If the mind becomes erased, where can the world live?" Luce thought she almost understood. "You have never heard the story of the first mermaids? The Unnamed Twins?"

The first mermaids, Luce thought. Somehow it hadn't occurred to her before, but of course someone must have been the first to experience the change, to feel her body becoming a cold spill of liquid flowing into the unknown. "Who *were* they?"

"They were no one. That is, they were the daughters of a poor shepherd. Born sickly, and as daughters not worth saving. Not worth the granting of names. He left the infants on a cliff beside the sea, intending they would die there. But Proteus, the herder of seals, found them and carried them back to his cave. They nursed on seal's milk, and he raised them as his own."

Luce was fascinated. "But if they changed when they were babies weren't they stuck being larvae?"

"They had not yet changed. They were still human girls. Girls raised half in the water and half onshore, their father a sea god, but human."

"But then . . ."

"Proteus raised them until they were adolescents and then gave them a choice. They could return to the human world and marry, or they could remain as creatures of the sea, both gifted and tasked. The Twins had pride, being the adopted daughters of a god. They refused to return to the people who had treated them as filth to be cast away. The sea was enough."

Luce wondered if that meant there was something wrong with her. She couldn't honestly say that the sea was enough for her, not when she longed for Dorian's love as well. Even her singing wasn't truly enough. "So that was when they changed?"

"Yes. Proteus is a shape-shifter, and he chose for them a form that embodied their history: half human and half of another world, needing both air and salt water to survive. He gave them their voices and their beauty as his gifts, their enduring youth, and the promise that other girls turned cold by human cruelty would have the same chance of finding the sea. He described the *timay* they would live by. Along with these gifts he gave them the task of avenging their own wounds and also all those girls who are not saved in time."

"So they didn't mind?" Luce asked a little breathlessly. "Killing people?"

"They were delighted. Why would they pity humans? When I knew them, they were fierce with the hunger for ships. We let none escape. Only once did a ship elude us, when a captain stuffed wax into the ears of his crew while he stayed bound tight to the mast."

It took Luce a second to process the implications of what Nausicaa had just said. "When you *knew* them?" Luce shrieked. She couldn't doubt that Nausicaa was telling her the truth. "Nausicaa, you *knew* them? Like, you were in the same tribe?"

Nausicaa smiled—a little distantly, Luce thought. "Where else would I be but with them? I too was among the first. When I came to their tribe it held only five of us, but it grew very soon." So many questions were whirling through Luce's head that she couldn't speak for a moment. Nausicaa's eyes sparked green, gazing into space, and the crackle of distant lightning thrilled through Luce's skin.

"Did they ever get names?" There were more important things to ask, but somehow that seemed like the easiest question to start with. Everything else was just too overwhelming. Nausicaa laughed, clearly pleased by this, and swished her tail a little.

"They had more names than you can count. Remember, their father was a shape-shifter: an old man one day and on another day a giant serpent. They were accustomed to change, to things with no settled form. We used to call them different words for hours, as a game, waiting to see when they might choose to answer. One of them might reply only to 'Fish Hook,' the other one to 'Bread,' and it would be so until they decided those names no longer suited them. It was hard to keep track, of course. But they enjoyed that."

They were quiet for a while. Nausicaa cracked oysters and stared around as if she could barely tolerate the confinement of the walls. Luce was too agitated to eat. She kept trying to think of some way that she could ask the next question without it sounding suspicious, but she couldn't come up with anything. "Uh, Nausicaa? Can I ask you something else?" She tried to keep her tone relaxed, but her anxiety was painfully audible.

"Of course." Nausicaa was still calm, but there was a subtle flash deep in her eyes.

"You said Proteus promised them that other *girls* who got hurt and . . . and outcast would be able to change into mermaids." Nausicaa didn't say anything, but her lips pursed slightly. "So, well, I was wondering. Is that why there aren't any boys with us? Like, mermen?"

"That is why." Nausicaa's tone was caustic. "Proteus thought of his daughters. He had no sons. And the Unnamed Twins were discarded *because* they were girls. Why would Proteus give the same consideration to male children, then?"

"So, well . . ." Luce tried to go on, but Nausicaa looked so irritated that Luce could hardly force the words out. "Does that mean there's *never* been a boy who changed? Somebody where there was an exception? Have you ever heard of that?"

"I wished this would not be your question, Luce." Nausicaa's voice was suddenly much lower, almost growling, and her face changed to a heavy, contemptuous mask. "There are no exceptions. Do not waste such hopes on your human lover, even if you are wasting yourself!"

"Nausicaa . . ."

"Now I know why you leave your tribe to the mercy of a

sika! You, who are their true queen. Once again, a mermaid of great talent turns from all responsibility, from *timay*, from her own potential, for the worthless love of a human male!" Nausicaa shook her head, black hair gusting in the drafts that leaked through the cave, the glow of her skin reflecting in harsh glints on the water. Luce gazed at her and knew that denying it wouldn't help. "I know this story, Luce."

"So what if you do!" The words lashed from Luce before she could stop them. "So *what* if you think you know everything already, and all the stories are the same, and you're mad because it *bores* you?"

Oddly, Luce's outburst seemed to soothe Nausicaa's fury. She was even smiling, though there was something morose about it. "Perhaps this boy has the shimmering around him, and you thought of how he had suffered and how in justice he might be considered one of us?" Nausicaa watched steadily as Luce jerked with surprise. They gazed bleakly at each other. "You see, Luce? I can relate those things that occurred as well as you can."

Stunned as she was by Nausicaa's words, Luce still thought the older mermaid was missing the real point. She scrambled to find a way to explain her feelings. "But Nausicaa? That doesn't *matter*. If you can tell me how it happened, I mean."

"It doesn't prove to you that I have witnessed this story too many times already? And that since I know how it starts, I may also know how it ends?"

"But I *don't* know this story," Luce objected. The words came out in a feverish rush. "It's new to me! And it's not some story, anyway. It's my *life*."

"Your life. Of course. Your pardon, Luce." There was still

something deadly crawling through that low voice, even as Nausicaa's smile became a taut grin. "Though I have seen the same thing happen three hundred times at least and seen every time the mermaid destroyed by her forbidden passion, I should assume that your case will be different. Because with you it is not a story."

Luce was ready to rage back at her, but something in what Nausicaa said stopped the words in her throat. *Every time* the mermaid was *destroyed*? Nausicaa gazed hard at Luce and nodded as if to acknowledge her stunned silence.

"Should I tell you, then, Queen Luce? What your story would be, if it were a story and not a *life*?" Nausicaa spat the word. "Though he loves you for your magic and your beauty, for your voice and your strangeness, those are the very things he will want to take away from you. He will ask you to become again a human girl, no different from the girls he might have with far less trouble. You will resist at first, but in the end, in fear of losing him, you will try to make the change."

Luce's hands flew out randomly and grasped at the loose rocks of the shore, but it wasn't enough to keep her from feeling like she was falling. How did Nausicaa know so *much*?

Nausicaa watched her swaying and went on relentlessly. "You will let him carry you ashore, then. And you will die. Forgive me, Luce, that I am not happy in such a future for you."

Luce let herself fall back onto the beach and threw her arms over her face. She could feel pinpoints of electricity in the water, a breathing sharpness to the air, and there was the strong blue smell of ozone mingling with the familiar reek of salt and wet stones. The darkness moved inside her closed eyes like a private sea, trying to carry her away from everything Nausicaa was saying to her. It all sounded so *true*. Sooner or later, Dorian would persuade himself that Luce could change back without dying. And then he'd try to persuade her, too, and she loved him so much that she'd start to believe he was right . . .

"It is not only because I'm *bored*, Luce." Nausicaa's anger was entirely gone now. Her voice was soft and endlessly sad. "It is not only because I have great hopes of you, or because you saved a life that I can hardly find the will to value. I am not so entirely selfish. I don't want you lost as others have been because . . ." Suddenly Nausicaa seemed to be at a loss for words. "So bright a spirit," Nausicaa went on at last, sounding uncharacteristically hesitant. "The world cannot afford to let you go. Not when so many ills threaten it."

Luce wasn't in any mood to care what the world could afford. "Nausicaa?"

"Yes, Luce?"

"Is that *always* what happens? I mean, that the mermaid tries to change back and dies?"

"Oh." Nausicaa sounded tired. "For a few things have not turned out this way. Only a very few, Luce. Twice I have known the mermaid to live through the suffering and stand up on human legs again. Though I can't truly consider that the better fate. One of my earliest friends survived and went back into the human world. She told me later that it was her deepest regret." *Two*, Luce thought. Out of three hundred. It wasn't encouraging.

"Those were the only times?"

"More commonly the exception is that the male betrays the

mermaid who loves him for a human girl. Then the mermaid remains in the water. Alive for the moment, but with her honor gone, her life newly broken."

That almost sounded worse. The thought of Dorian lying beside some *human* was intolerable: her bare legs wrapping like pink tentacles around his body, her tinny, empty voice squawking along with some song on the radio.

"In such cases," Nausicaa observed coolly, "it is the man who will not survive. The mermaid will kill him. Then die of grief herself."

13

The Grays

The storm thrashed against the cliffs for three days. When Luce darted out for food, she found for the first time that the force of the water almost overpowered the quick dancing flow of her swimming, and she hardly had the strength to fight her way back into the cave. The currents jerked her back and forth, and waves caught her and threw her into the air before she had a chance to compensate for their aggression. Even if she used the full power of her singing, Luce realized, the storm would be even stronger. Its roar was enough to drown out her voice. Trying to reach Dorian was hopeless, and then he'd certainly be shut up indoors himself. Nausicaa repeatedly made quick forays out of the cave, only to return in frustration minutes later. She listened while Luce practiced singing or else swam in circles like a shark trapped in a tank.

On the fourth day Luce woke to waves that suddenly beat a drowsy cadence, and she slipped out into the open sea. The late, lazy dawn smeared the eastern sky with peach and crimson and pale bluish lilac, and the waves rose and fell as if they could hardly be bothered to make the effort. Even after the terrible things Nausicaa had told her, the change in the weather meant one thing to Luce: later that day she'd be able to see Dorian again. He'd run his hands through her hair, then down around her throat; kisses would settle on her shoulders like soft, tiny, loving animals. It would be obvious that all their problems were insignificant compared to what they felt together, and maybe she'd sing for him again . . .

"Do you see them, Luce?" Nausicaa was suddenly beside her, and Luce glanced over sharply, annoyed at having her daydream disrupted. "Look there. To the north." Luce looked. A kind of pale disturbance traced the distance. It reminded Luce of a scene in a movie she'd once seen, where a far-off cloud of dust revealed the approach of a vast army. What could that mean out here in the sea? Nausicaa's eyes flared with green exultation. And, Luce realized, the water popped, trilled, and hummed with sounds, still far away but all coming from the same direction.

"What *is* that?" Luce stared at the oncoming froth; only Nausicaa's obvious joy kept her from feeling alarmed by the sight.

"The *grays*, Luce! The gray whales are migrating! They were nearly all slaughtered not so long ago, like so many other animals have been. I've seen blue whales killed in their hundreds by harpoons made to explode inside their brains, and countless other nightmares brought to this earth by humans."

Luce had trouble believing that those enormous billows of mist were being thrown into the air by a species that was nearly extinct. "But if they were almost all killed, then . . ."

"They've come back! Luce, so many things are gone forever. Creatures that once ran so thick they were like a second ocean rolling through the first . . . But the grays, the grays are coming back! It is one reason I can still have hope." Nausicaa spiraled her tail in the water and leaped straight up, pirouetting in naked space, the emerald flash of her tail answering the dawn. She dove deep and came up with gold-lit droplets flinging out around her hair. "I must go to them, Luce. Would you like to come with me? There are some I've known before. They should remember me . . ."

"Maybe I'll . . . come find you later." Luce could hear the embarrassment in her voice, and Nausicaa glanced at her sharply but didn't say anything. There was the possibility that Dorian would cut school and wait for her at their beach. The gray whales barely seemed interesting compared to the prospect of touching his face again.

Nausicaa was already gone.

* * *

Luce knew that there were other things she should do besides go to find Dorian. She hadn't seen Dana since the day of the fight with Anais. And, while Luce didn't know what she could have done differently, the fact was that she'd thrown Dana's twin sister into a wall. Jenna might be seriously injured, and Luce should at least try to find out how she was doing. And then there was the question of Violet: would Anais figure out that Violet had betrayed her to help Luce? Maybe it wasn't completely safe for Violet to stay in the tribe any longer.

But what was she supposed to *do?* Luce asked herself resentfully. Going back to the tribe's territory to look for Dana and Violet would only mean another fight, wouldn't it? The last thing Luce wanted was to find herself in a situation where she'd be forced to hurt another mermaid again, and then Dana was probably furious with her over Jenna. Luce slid through the gold-streaked water, listening to the high, silky moans of the gray whales. She was almost to the beach where Dorian might be waiting for her, and she quickly peered above the surface to see if she could catch a glimpse of him.

He was thirty yards away, sitting with his arms around his knees and scanning the waves hungrily. But for once he wasn't alone on the beach. A strange woman was walking her dog along the shore and Luce darted under the waves again, her tail almost whisking from impatience. It looked like the woman was on her way back to the forest trail, but still . . . Luce couldn't completely repress a sudden fantasy of letting a few notes uncoil from her mouth, just a few, and luring the woman out into the ocean. Then she'd be out of their way more quickly.

"Come on, Biscuit!" Luce heard the pebbles grind far to her right. They were almost gone, at least. And there was a slight disturbance in front of her, Luce realized: somebody wading in the icy water. So Dorian had seen her, and he couldn't wait either!

Luce skimmed along the seafloor until she could see Dorian's bare feet, blue-white from the cold, then slipped close enough to kiss his ankle. "Wait till she's farther away, okay?" Dorian murmured. Luce rolled onto her back so that a rippling pane of water covered her face and smiled up at him, his image split and curled by the unresting sea. He didn't exactly look happy, staring away in the direction the woman had taken. "Maybe we're . . . I think we're good now. God, I missed you. I even came down here two days ago, just in case. The wind was blowing so hard I could barely walk."

Luce came up and wrapped her arms around his knees. She leaned her face against his thigh and breathed in his warm smell; it was all beautiful to her, even the faint trace of mildew in his unwashed jeans. "It was the first time the water's ever been too strong for me. Swimming was almost scary." The dog was barking again, not really far enough away, and Dorian tensed a little.

"But you missed me, too?" Dorian asked; he sounded a little sad, Luce thought.

"You know I did. I missed you so much!" But Nausicaa's words still rebounded through her mind in a stream of bitter echoes. "Dorian, Nausicaa *knows*. About us. I don't think she'll do anything to hurt us, though."

Dorian staggered back out of the water and sat down hard on the beach. "You *told* her that? That you're breaking those big-deal laws? Luce, I mean—what makes you think we can *trust* her?"

"I didn't tell her! She— Dorian, she's been a mermaid for like three thousand years, and I thought she might know more than Catarina. I asked her if there was any way a boy could change, and she realized right away why I wanted to know that." There was no way she'd ever tell him all the other things

Nausicaa had said, Luce thought. Repeating those words out loud would give them too much power. Even remembering them seemed destructive, as if delicate fibers between her and Dorian were being torn. And while she couldn't quite put her finger on why, she had the impression that Dorian looked a little different somehow.

"Are you saying she wasn't mad?" Dorian pulled her closer so that she was leaning back against him and wrapped her in his arms. Everything was fine between them, Luce decided. Doubting him before had been unfair of her, and Nausicaa was just being pessimistic. Mermaids always believed the worst where humans were concerned.

"She was totally mad, actually. But it wasn't like it would be with another mermaid. It was more like she thinks I should try to become queen. Challenge Anais for the tribe. She thinks I'm being irresponsible because I want to be with you instead." Luce snuggled into him. It was hard to believe she'd felt this absolute warmth only a few days before.

"I can see her point," Dorian said. Luce tipped her head back to look at him, her eyes wide with disbelief. "I've thought about it a lot, Luce. If you took the tribe away from Anais, you could keep them all from killing any more people, right? And, seriously, 'queen of the fucking mermaids' does sound like kind of a no-brainer." He laughed.

"I'd just be queen of this one messed-up tribe, though!" Luce gazed up at his wide gold-brown eyes, his crooked nose, thinking that he had no idea what he was talking about. "And if I did, I'd have to stop seeing you. I wouldn't be able to keep it a secret."

"If you were *queen*, though . . . couldn't you just tell everybody that you have a human boyfriend, and too bad for them if they don't like it?"

"You mean, just make up my own timahk?" Luce delivered the words with heavy sarcasm. She suddenly realized that Dorian hadn't asked the most important question: if Nausicaa knew about some way he could change. Why wasn't he at least curious?

"*Yeah.* I do mean that. Why shouldn't you make your own version? Like, why should we care at *all* about these random laws that come out of nowhere? Especially when they screw us over? Luce, think about it, you could just take the good parts . . ."

Luce had imagined doing exactly that a thousand times, but now she felt a stubborn impulse to argue with him. "The timahk doesn't come out of nowhere, actually. Nausicaa told me the whole story."

"She also told you she's three thousand years old," Dorian observed roughly.

"And you're kind of right, about somebody making us into mermaids. Except he was trying to help us by *letting* us change."

"Some *help*, making you all into murderers," Dorian hissed. Luce felt Dorian's body shift as he pulled himself straighter, and she looked up to see the dark smolder gathering in his eyes. "Who is this scumbag?"

Luce suddenly remembered what Dorian had said before, about wanting to kill whoever was responsible. He wouldn't be crazy enough to think he could fight a *god*, would he? A little nervously she told him the story of Proteus and the Unnamed Twins, and how the mermaids had first come into the world. "And that's why it's just a thing that happens to girls. That's what Nausicaa said. She said there aren't any exceptions for boys, ever. But, Dorian, maybe if we asked him . . ."

"Forget it," Dorian snarled. Luce gazed up at him in dismay. "Not because I don't want to be with you, Luce. I do. But because— Think about it. This *story*. It sounds like Proteus is just another asshole dad who doesn't want his daughters to grow up. Of course he wouldn't let any boys change. Because then his daughters would just leave him." Luce was surprised and also a little impressed. None of this had occurred to her, but now that she heard Dorian say it she thought he might have a point.

"I don't think my dad would have been like that," Luce objected, but her voice was suddenly uncertain.

"Yeah, well. Too bad your real dad is dead. Just because he ran into this, like, project Proteus had of making a bunch of girls into total killers. Luce, I don't know how you can even think about asking this creep of a god for a *favor*." They were both gazing out at the narrow band of sea that showed beyond the boulder, and Dorian had started lightly stroking her body. Platinum ribbons of sunlight stretched in sleek layers on the water. "Look at that! Luce, do you *see* . . ." An arch of dark gray flesh like a living cathedral split the surface, not that far away.

"The gray whales," Luce said. "They're migrating now."

"They were talking about that in school yesterday . . ." Luce began to feel Dorian's sudden excitement running through her own body, and she twisted around to face him. "Oh my God, Luce. Let's get the boat! We can go out there—"

"Nausicaa is swimming with them, though!"

"So?" Dorian was grinning now, with the hard, defiant courage Luce loved so much. "You said you want me to meet her."

"But . . . I don't know how she'd react to that! I mean, she knows and everything, but if she actually *saw* you . . . She keeps talking about how much humans have messed up the world." Nausicaa *probably* wouldn't try to kill him unprovoked, Luce thought. But it didn't seem likely that Dorian and Nausicaa would get along too well, and there was no telling what Nausicaa might do if some human made her angry.

"Let her say that stuff to my face, then." Dorian's smile had a cast of grim determination now. "I'll tell her she's right about humans sucking. Fine. And I'll tell her that my being *human* doesn't mean I shouldn't love you!"

Maybe he was being reckless, Luce thought. But she couldn't say no to him, not when his recklessness was so strong and beautiful. She found herself grinning back at him.

"Let's go."

* * *

Half an hour later they were skimming out across the unstable sea, the water brushed pale green and milky blue by the glowing sky. White seabirds flocked in strange, continually shifting patterns against the delicate blue above, all of them rushing south. The rowboat knocked rhythmically against the low swells, and the water hummed around Luce's scales and trembled on her bare skin. The haunting soprano moans of the gray whales echoed inside her skull. Now closer and now farther away, their spouts rose in frost-colored plumes, V-shaped, spanning the blue air. Dorian kept twisting in his seat, his face luminous with excitement. All at once Luce had an idea and started laughing.

"I want to try something. Okay? Wait right here." Luce had almost forgotten that Dorian didn't have any choice about waiting, until he cracked up laughing, too. She smiled at him and slipped just below the surface, watching the golden light weave through the green around her. She gathered her voice into two narrow, soaring notes, sweet and as focused as twin beams of light, then sent them vaulting into the air above her. Two jets of water leaped skyward in sympathy, and Luce heard Dorian's shout of astonishment. They weren't quite as tall or diffused as the spouts of the whales, and they arched as they fell; the result looked more like a fountain in a park, Luce thought. Still, it wasn't bad for a first try.

She came up thirty feet from the rowboat and grinned at him. "God, Luce!" Dorian shouted; he was out of breath, leaning so far toward her that the boat tipped dangerously. "I know you told me you could do that, but actually *seeing* it, and the way you *sounded* . . ."

"I didn't get it right, though," Luce told him.

"What wasn't right about that? It was *fantastic!*"

"But I'm trying to imitate the whale spouts. Wait, I'm going to do it again. Tell me if I'm close . . ." She dipped back under, rolling again and again in the green glass brilliance of the sea, then let those bright expansive notes burst up again and spill out through the water. This time the plumes were airier, broader, full of froth and the resonance of mist. She held the song while the jets of water fanned up above her, white and fresh as the clouds of geese flying in formation. She thought the effect was almost perfect, and she let herself float gently to the surface, face-up, watching the far-off shimmer of a million wings.

"*Luce!*" She swung around, and her heart stopped when she realized she couldn't see the rowboat anywhere. Bizarrely, she couldn't really see anything in that direction: only a gray rolling wall, crusted white with barnacles, like something in a dream. Trying to understand it was like trying to read a book as the paper suddenly darkened and the letters crawled away. And, Luce realized with horror, Dorian was somehow behind this thing, or inside it . . .

The broad gray flukes cleft the air, lofting a shower of sunlit water with them, and Luce heard her own cry of relief. Why hadn't she understood that it was only one of the gray whales, maybe coming over to investigate the peculiar music she'd been making? The rowboat was rocking wildly just behind the place where the whale had disappeared, and Luce rushed over. Dorian was gripping the edge of the boat so hard that his hands looked like knotted rope. His face was white with shock, and he gazed at Luce and then past her as if he could barely comprehend what he was seeing. His breath jerked out, fast and uneven. Luce covered his hands with hers, squeezing gently, and then he finally looked into her eyes.

"Dorian, what *happened*? I couldn't see you for a minute."

"It just—" He seemed to be searching for words. "Luce, the

way it *looked* at me . . . The whale was suddenly right there, and I saw its eye come up, and it looked at me so hard. I mean, I've never had a *person* look at me like that. And then your voice was in my head, and it felt like I was exploding . . ." Dorian shook himself and laughed a little, but he sounded shaky.

"I shouldn't have left you alone . . ."

"No, it was fine. It— You know how you said that time that only humans think they're realer than everything else? The way that whale looked at me, I felt like it was a lot realer than I am." Golden strands of light reflected off the water and wobbled on the curves of his face; his full lips were parted.

"And that comes as a surprise to you, of course." Nausicaa's deep, thrumming voice came from behind Luce's shoulder. Luce twisted around to see the dark flash of Nausicaa's eyes—while a few feet farther back another immense gray presence came surging up. Its head was long and tapered, patched with barnacles like pale scabs; its eyelids were thick, lemon-shaped, and as rough as rinds. One glossy black eye pivoted to inspect them with fathomless awareness. Luce gasped a little, suddenly understanding what Dorian had felt. She forced herself to look away so that she could meet Nausicaa's ironic stare, and all the while she kept her hold on Dorian's left hand where it gripped the boat. Just in case . . .

"Nausicaa . . ." Luce struggled to sound normal, to remember what she was supposed to say. "This is Dorian. Dorian, meet Nausicaa."

Luce watched Nausicaa calmly twist her head sideways to inspect the indication that flickered around Dorian. Luce hoped Dorian hadn't noticed.

"Hey, Nausicaa." Dorian's gaze was challenging and, to Luce, impressively steady. He actually leaned from the boat to extend his free hand in Nausicaa's direction. "Luce has told me a lot about you."

Nausicaa gave the outreached hand a single brooding glance, but didn't approach. "She has said nothing of you, however," Nausicaa growled. "Except that she does not consider you a story."

It occurred to Luce with a jolt that, even if Nausicaa wasn't exactly being friendly, she was still violating the timahk by speaking to Dorian at all.

The gray whale stayed where it was, gazing into each of them in turn, while another surfaced on the opposite side of the boat. The boat looked so vulnerable between the whales, no stronger than an eggshell. The three of them were drifting inside a huge building with living walls.

"I get that a lot." Dorian smiled, lowering his hand as if he hadn't noticed Nausicaa's rudeness. The boat pitched, and he doubled over, grasping at the seat before he was able to right himself. "Look. You care about Luce, right?" All the flippancy had abruptly disappeared from Dorian's voice.

"I do," Nausicaa acknowledged, but she sounded cold. Luce could see the churning pallor of the water where Nausicaa's tail was stirring. Still, there was a focused brightness in those glittering dark eyes that suggested Nausicaa was more intrigued than she wanted to admit.

"Then why don't you want her to be happy?" Dorian asked seriously. "She's going to live for maybe hundreds of years. You really think she should never get to be in love?"

Nausicaa's stare was acerbic, but Luce noticed that she didn't even try to answer the question. "I suppose you claim to care for her, *Dorian*?"

"I love her." Dorian said it so fervently that Luce's heart skipped. His love had never felt so definite to her before, so *real*. She wanted to pull herself into the boat and drown in the warmth of his skin. Meanwhile Nausicaa was skimming closer to them, her bronze-dark face rising and falling with the water in a smooth, hypnotic dance, her black hair cresting over her head in heavy whorls.

"You love her, and yet you promise her a thing you cannot give." Nausicaa's voice turned low, meditative; the air seemed to vibrate in time with it. "Why?"

Luce didn't know what Nausicaa was talking about, but still she started to feel alarmed. What if Nausicaa started telling Dorian about all the other mermaids she'd seen fall in love with humans? From the fierce way Dorian and Nausicaa were staring at each other, it was clear that there was nothing she could do to put a stop to the conversation. They were both determined to have it out.

"I haven't promised her anything, actually," Dorian announced; his cool tone sounded a little strained. "But when I do make her a promise I'll definitely keep it."

"You give her your promise *now*. With every breath you promise her that she has found a home for her heart. You promise her that she is no longer one of the lost. And that promise is an unending lie, *human*."

Dorian sat back in the boat, and Luce felt the startled pain in his face reflecting in her own. For the first time she almost hated Nausicaa for being so sure she was right—and for being so merciless. "She *isn't* lost. I found her." Dorian's forced bravado was obvious now. "Or she found me. Has Luce told you how we met? Because it wasn't *online* . . ."

Nausicaa didn't deign to respond to this, just scowled away into the distance. Several gray whales crowded around them now, silently staring, jostling one another so that the patch of open sea around the boat grew constantly smaller.

"I care for Luce enough to offer her the truth," Nausicaa pronounced at last. She hadn't so much as glanced at Luce through the whole conversation with Dorian, but now she swung her head and shot her a quick, cutting stare. "She can do with it what she likes."

Nausicaa dove, but not quickly. Instead her movements seemed deliberately lethargic, her tail swinging in midair long enough that Luce knew it must burn. "Like I haven't seen any damn mermaids before . . ." Dorian hissed. Then Nausicaa was gone, with a last hard slap of emerald fins. The gray whales squeezed in so close now that Luce began to feel a little panicked, staring around at the stony banks of their hides. *She* could easily dive and escape, after all, but Dorian?

Luce saw the same idea occur to Dorian; his brows lowered and his eyes flashed around, searching for a way out. There wasn't one. Luce began wondering if she could possibly raise a wave big enough to carry the boat safely over the back of a whale, steady enough that Dorian wouldn't be thrown out. But if the whale chose that moment to dive, lashing its enormous muscular flukes into the air, the boat would certainly be crushed and Dorian with it.

A hovering soprano call moved in the water, welling up from the shadowy green below. It was like whale song, but also, Luce instantly realized, utterly different. The black eye closest to her seemed to glow with recognition, and the long head leaned deeper into the sea. Suddenly Luce and Dorian sailed up on a huge billow of displaced water as the whale dipped away, and Luce's whole body shook to the high pulse of its answering song.

The voice from the deep cried again, in a long, alluring vibrato. *Nausicaa*, Luce realized with amazed gratitude. Nausicaa was calling the whales away so that Luce could get Dorian out of there. And one by one the enormous bodies curved downward, sweeping away in dark arches, plunging like waterfalls. The boat lurched up rising slopes of water, and Luce dipped underneath, supporting the hull with both arms to stop Dorian from being flung overboard. The dim space around her began to brighten as the whales dove away, their huge shapes sailing below her like the shadows of clouds on a hillside. As soon as everything was calmer, Luce surfaced again. Dorian's face shone with sweet amazement, and Luce felt a kind of joy as acute as grief. And then Dorian was pointing again, out behind her.

Thirty feet away from them one of the grays threw itself high above the surface, its whole streamlined form in one long balletic curve, fins sweeping by its sides. Sunlight sharp as shining wounds flashed in the ruffs of water flying from its tail. Then it curled in space, racing downward into the vanishing green of the deep.

14

Darkness

By late November the sun barely had the strength to heave itself in a low arc above the horizon. Even at midday the light looked bluish and tired. The endless, somnolent dusk set in by early afternoon and slowly fell into the yawning nights. It was hard not to get depressed, to feel starved for scraps of daylight. Dorian got used to meeting Luce after dusk, to watching the dim glow of her body parting the smoke-dark water. It was a beautiful sight but also lonely somehow. And it made his time with her seem even more remote from the rest of his life. The rooms of his school and house seemed like brightly lit boxes sealed to keep out the darkness where dangerous secrets leaped and swam.

Today he'd lingered in the village's tiny library, and now he was running late. All the tenth-graders had been assigned a research paper on an environmental challenge of their choice, but Dorian hadn't been able to stop with one. He'd begun with problems that affected whales and gone on from there to a whole list of threats to the world's oceans: acidification, dead zones, global warming . . . Already he had almost fifty pages of notes and he couldn't seem to stop collecting more information. When he glanced up from the computer it was already after four, and he hurried to stuff his books away, bundle himself into his hat and parka, and run to meet Luce.

Luckily she could read in the dark without any trouble, and he talked over his research with her. He'd started to bring her stacks of library books, too, tightly wrapped in layers of plastic so that they wouldn't get soaked as she carried them home. Even so he'd had some pretty serious fines for water damage, and the librarian had told him to stop reading in the bathtub. A little to Dorian's surprise, Luce wanted to read his school textbooks, too. But it was a good idea, he realized. That way if she ever turned human again she wouldn't be too far behind.

Maybe next year she'd even be in high school with him.

All they needed was someone they could trust and who could help them figure out how to change her back without killing her. Someone smart, like a scientist. Out in the street the air itself seemed to be tinted with bruise blue ink, and the cold bit into his face and bare hands. Stretches of dead grass separated the small brown-shingled houses. The printed red roses and blue plaids of the curtains glowed like lanterns, and at the bottom of the street the lights of a few boats tossed gently up and down. Dorian thought the dusk even had a smell; it was like the scent of clay, musty and dank.

"Dorian. Lindy said you might be here, so I thought I'd see if I could catch you."

Dorian had already recognized the voice before he turned to look. It was Ben Ellison. Dorian hadn't heard from him for a few weeks. Seeing that broad brown face in the blue dimness provoked a mixture of feelings in Dorian: anxiety that he couldn't get to Luce right away but also a strange sense of comfort. He couldn't tell Ellison about the mermaids, of course. But unlike everyone else Dorian knew, Ellison would believe him if he *did* tell the truth. He felt sure of that, and it almost made him think of Ellison as a kind of fellow conspirator. This was someone who understood about secrets. "Hey."

Ellison looked at Dorian with his usual expression of fatherly concern. Dorian had hated it at first, but now he felt himself softening a little. Not that Ellison needed to worry about him, but still it was nice that somebody gave a fuck. "Can I take you for something to eat?" Ellison asked; he was somber, unsmiling. "We haven't had a chance to catch up for a while."

Dorian shook his head. "I'm . . . kind of supposed to be somewhere."

"Band practice? Did you find a drummer yet?"

"No. Well, Steve says his cousin knows this girl who plays the drums, so maybe. But she lives like fifty miles away, and we haven't even met her. They're supposed to drive up here sometime." As Dorian spoke he found himself wondering what would happen if he said something completely different: *"Look, I really need your help. It's about my girlfriend . . ."* If only Ellison weren't in the FBI, Dorian thought, it might be worth taking the chance.

"It sounds like it might be difficult to schedule practice

times, then. If your drummer lives that far away." Ben Ellison sounded distracted, and Dorian suspected that he was only going through the motions of having a normal conversation, just the way Dorian was doing himself.

Somehow they'd started walking together in the direction of the dock. Between the buildings the sea appeared as a huge dark blot where all the ordinary human things, houses and cars, were simply canceled out. But in a way, Dorian thought, that darkness was his real home, at least as long as Luce was living there. How was he going to shake Ellison? "Steve's about to get his driver's license, though, so we'll be able to go there for practice. It could work out all right."

"Not if you—" Ellison's voice leaped higher and then broke off abruptly, and he shook his head hard. They had stopped in a place with no streetlights, and Ellison's broad body appeared as a black silhouette against the charcoal sea.

Dorian was confused. "Not if I what?"

"Dorian, I'm . . . facing a dilemma." There was an unmistakable ring of sincerity, even desperation, in that low voice, and Dorian started. "There's something that I know I need to say, and soon. Someone I care about is putting himself in a position of extraordinary danger, and I'm the only one who can warn him."

The sudden shift in their conversation was too weird, Dorian thought. Warn someone? What was the guy *talking* about? "Then why don't you?"

"Because the young man I need to warn is frankly untrustworthy. And I don't know whether I can make him understand the danger he's facing without revealing information that could be . . . quite sensitive."

They were walking again, but Dorian still couldn't see Ben Ellison well enough to make out the expression of his face. "If you're talking about me, I'm totally fine." Dorian impatiently snapped the words out but then realized that his heart was racing. The hill sloped steeply away at their feet and he felt a rush of vertigo.

Ellison seemed not to have heard him. He was staring at the sea as if he half expected it to come rushing up the hill and engulf them. "Maybe you remember something I told you that time you came to Anchorage. I mentioned then that there have been very few recorded survivors of shipwrecks like the one you were on."

"So?" Dorian's voice wavered audibly. They were passing in front of a tiny gray house with brightly shining windows, its curtains drawn back, and golden light spilled over them both.

Ellison abruptly stopped and wheeled toward him, taking him by the shoulders. His broad fingers squeezed in so hard it hurt. "Dorian, you're frightened. I can hear that you are. And you *should* be. You still have some instinct for self-preservation, and if you'll only listen to what your instincts are telling you . . . you might grow up to be a very interesting person."

Dorian reeled a little in Ellison's grip, unsure if he should try to pull away. Wasn't there something skittish, even a little crazy, in the older man's eyes?

Ellison kept on, his voice hard but also somehow distracted. "I realized that I needed to investigate. To find out what happened to the other people who went through experiences similar to yours. It wasn't easy. But I did discover— unsurprisingly, I suppose—that most of your fellow survivors have also been young males." Ellison made a sound that was almost like laughter, but his mouth was twisted downward. He was staring into Dorian's face without actually meeting his eyes.

It was all so strange that Dorian had trouble processing what Ellison was saying to him. Then it hit him: *unsurprisingly* the survivors were young men? For some reason Dorian felt offended by the statement.

Ellison let go of Dorian's shoulders, but he didn't move out of his path. "In two of the cases where I was able to track down records, the young men in question went permanently insane. Institutionalized. There was a case like that twenty-five years ago, outside Anadyr, Russia—"

"*You're* calling *me* crazy?" As soon as Dorian said it, he realized it was the wrong approach. He should try to reassure Ellison, not provoke him. "It's nice of you to worry about me, but I'm a lot better now. I've pretty much stopped having nightmares and everything." It was true. Every time Luce sang to him he felt a little stronger, not as broken inside. The sea had stopped following him around like some huge watery ghost, a heaving shadow. It mostly stayed where it belonged.

"Three others drowned within two years of escaping from their shipwrecks, Dorian. It appears that for many people in your position, survival is only a temporary reprieve."

Dorian stared. "I'm not planning on *drowning* myself. Like I told you, I'm feeling way better—"

"I'm not worried about suicide. At least, that's not my primary concern. I believe that you do indeed . . . have something to live for." Ellison's tone didn't make any sense, Dorian thought. Was he actually envious?

Just for a second Dorian considered running. But what good would that do when Ellison could find him anytime he wanted? "Then what's the *problem?* If you know I'm not going to kill myself—"

"Something else might kill you. You may have placed your trust in something . . . extremely capricious, and lacking any conscience as we understand it. You may be naïvely putting yourself in harm's way, day after day, with no idea of the risk."

Dorian's knees suddenly buckled, and he barely stopped himself from falling. The cold wind whistled between the houses, and his hair snapped hard around his face. Was Ellison talking about *Luce?* But how could he know anything about her?

If the FBI was after Luce, Dorian knew, he had to find out. But it was hard to see how he could ask the right questions without giving too much away.

"Are you talking about my girlfriend?" Dorian struggled to keep his voice as flat and noncommittal as possible. He waited anxiously for Ellison to react with surprise: the older man should smile at him and say something like, *"Oh, you have a girl-friend now, Dorian? I didn't know."*

"Of course I'm talking about your *girlfriend.*" Ellison growled. Somehow hearing him say this out loud made it worse. "I suppose the term applies."

Could Ellison really know that Luce was a mermaid? Dorian had trouble believing it. But either way . . . "Well, it's not fair for you to say shit like that about her, then. You don't *know* her."

"That's true. I don't. But I doubt I'd make it through an introduction intact."

"She's not like that." There was a strange timbre in the rising wind, Dorian realized, a haunted musical beckoning. It was a sound he'd learned to recognize. Luce was upset that he hadn't come, and she was calling him from the dimness below. They were only a block from the harbor, and by the intensity of the sound Dorian guessed that Luce had come recklessly close to the village dock.

Ellison seemed to be listening to the wind, too hard for Dorian's comfort. He turned away from Dorian to gaze down into the bluish darkness. "She's 'not like that'? Are you sure about that? Because in that case, Dorian, I'd . . . like to meet her very much. Maybe you'd be willing to pass on the message?" Ellison paused and seemed to think of something. "How does she communicate?"

So the guy was still fishing for information, Dorian thought sarcastically. At least that showed that the FBI didn't know everything. "She won't want to meet *you*."

"Why not?"

"She doesn't like cops much." Dorian's tone was deliberately insulting.

"I can see that she might have her reasons for feeling that way." Ellison delivered this in a snide voice that clearly implied Luce was a criminal, and Dorian glared at him. "But I'd actually like to meet her on a personal level. Not as part of my job, but simply—"

"Simply to *what*?" Dorian couldn't have explained why he suddenly felt so furious. He fought down an impulse to lash out, shove Ellison in the chest, punch him.

"Simply to know, I suppose. What she is. What she wants. Maybe there are other approaches . . ."

"You need to leave us alone!" Dorian couldn't keep his voice down. It was stupid of him to yell in the street like this. It was a tiny town, and at any moment people would come to find out what was going on. "I'm not in any *danger*. My girlfriend's not . . . a bad person." As Dorian said this Ellison grinned strangely. "I just want you to leave me *alone* from now on, okay? I don't want to talk to you again."

"I doubt that avoiding each other will be an option for us, Dorian."

"I'm going to *make* it an option . . ."

"I tend to think of you as a kind of hostage. An innocent mixed up in things he can't possibly understand. But other people won't see the situation that way, of course, and I've taken a considerable risk by coming here to warn you. At the worst my actions could be construed as treasonous."

Dorian began to think he might have some leverage. "I *promise* I won't tell anybody about this, then. As long as you don't come back here."

"The two of us belong to a very select society, Dorian. There are only a handful of people in the world who have heard what we've heard. Whether we like it or not, that binds us to one another."

Dorian gaped. He simply couldn't accept that this meant what it sounded like. The idea that Ellison could have his own share in the most powerful experiences of Dorian's life—it was revolting, impossible. He braced himself and looked up, glowering straight into Ellison's sad brown face. "You're *insane*. What do you think I've heard?"

Ellison smiled, but there was something shattered and terribly distant in his eyes. "Haven't we already discussed this once? In Anchorage?"

Dorian's stomach lurched, and his legs seemed to be crumbling under him, but he did his best to stay brazen. "I don't know what—"

"Say hello to your girlfriend for me. I expect I've made you late for your meeting with her, haven't I?"

"I'm not—"

"Make sure you give her my message. It's . . . in her best interest if you do."

Dorian watched as Ellison turned away and walked back up the hill, his dark body half vanishing in the shadows and then winking into view again as he passed through the rare patches of light. Luce was still calling, but instead of running to her Dorian slumped down abruptly on the brittle grass of a nearby lawn and leaned his head against his knees. He knew he had to tell her what had happened, but as he thought it over he realized that Ellison hadn't quite said anything that *proved* the FBI knew about the mermaids. And now Dorian wasn't sure if he'd be able to remember exactly what Ellison had said to him, much less convey just how threatening and disorienting their conversation had felt.

The wind shrilled through his hair, but now the sound of it was empty of magic. Luce had given up waiting for him, then. He'd just have to find her tomorrow.

It seemed so unfair. Ever since the day of the gray whales, he and Luce had been so happy together. She'd stopped worrying about her old tribe and about the police, and Dorian finally felt like he had her almost completely to himself. He had stopped telling her to become queen, too—he didn't actually want to share her with the tribe. Even Nausicaa's hanging around didn't seem to be much of a problem anymore, though Dorian still would have been glad to hear that she was going away. And now he was supposed to tell Luce—what, exactly? That some FBI agent had dropped a lot of hints that *might* mean she and all the other mermaids were in serious trouble—or that might just as well mean something totally different?

Capricious, Ellison had said. *Lacking any conscience*. Luce wasn't like that at all, actually. But weren't there plenty of human beings you could describe that way?

Even worse: what if Luce became convinced that Dorian had betrayed her? After all, how else could Ellison know so much? Dorian had never really promised Luce that he wouldn't talk to the FBI. So what was she supposed to think?

The cold seeped through his parka until he shivered, and the wind came rushing faster from the wild black sea. A few drops of sleet spattered against Dorian's face.

People kept saying it would be a bad winter.

* * *

When Luce and Nausicaa slipped out late that evening to look for dinner, snow was falling in thick plumes that dissolved the instant they hit the coal black sea. Luce felt like she was swimming through an endless maze stitched from pale lace and crisp billowing silks. Even Nausicaa stopped and spun in circles, gazing around at the white frills drifting down the black sky. It was all magnificently beautiful. The snow pranced in each gust of wind, and Luce could just make out the subtle tinkling sound of the huge flakes crumpling into water. Luce and Nausicaa floated slowly together to the beach, where they ate, both of them silent from wonder.

"Soon enough the ice will come," Nausicaa observed at last. She was nibbling seaweed, and the green-gold shine of her skin reflected in each snowflake that swirled past her. "We will have to swim south, far past the peninsula. Some years ago I knew the queen of a tribe that lived there—"

"It didn't get that bad last winter," Luce objected. She had cracked her first oyster, but she was too perturbed by what Nausicaa had just said to eat it. "I mean, I wasn't a mermaid yet then, but everybody told me there wasn't too much ice. They all just stayed here."

Nausicaa glanced at Luce with sardonic affection. Of course she knew why Luce didn't want to think about migrating. "This winter will be worse. I can almost feel the breath coming off the pack ice already. And we have not even reached the darkest days." Nausicaa paused. Snow clung to the fringes of her black wild hair in a kind of icy halo, the flakes sparked with gold here and there by her soft brilliance. "I may think of leaving soon, Luce. And you should come with me."

Luce's heart jarred in her chest. Nausicaa's words felt almost like a threat. "I'm not going to *leave* here. And I wish you'd stay, too. I don't care about the ice."

Nausicaa had given up arguing with Luce about her love for Dorian. Instead she smiled, and her green-black eyes flashed with sly amusement. "I knew a mermaid once, gone utterly mad, who kidnapped an entire human family: a boy perhaps six years old, his mother and father. She plucked them one by one from the lifeboat where she found them drifting and dragged them to a cave. The cave had a deep underwater entrance, and the humans could not hope to swim through it without her help. She kept them there for years, making them pretend that she was their beloved daughter, the boy's sister. The family had to play games with her, comb her hair, and invent imaginary memories of her childhood with them, all in endless darkness. If they tried to resist or if they confused their 'memories' too much, she would cease to bring them food for a day or two . . ."

Luce knew Nausicaa well enough by now to understand why she was telling this story: it was a way of implying that Luce's sense of belonging with Dorian was just as delusional as the crazy mermaid's pretending to have a family. Luce tensed with annoyance, but at the same time she was intrigued by the thought of this human family held captive in a cave like dolls kept in a box. "So what happened?"

"Well, the mermaid—her name was Kumiko—I was told that she died very strangely. That she was lured by a spirit in the water and followed it to a depth where she drowned. Maybe she died another way, but one day she did not come back. Then there was no one to feed these humans she had kept as her pets, of course."

"But . . . if you know all this . . . the other mermaids around there must have known, too?" Luce couldn't stop herself from hoping that someone might have rescued the family after Kumiko's disappearance.

"They all knew. Kumiko was so insane that her tribe felt sorry for her. No one interfered with her games, but they hardly wished to deal with the humans she left behind. I passed by that way again some years after, and I stopped at the cave. The family's bones were all scattered at the water's edge. As if they had kept trying to find the courage to attempt an escape, right up to their last moments."

Luce lost her appetite completely as she imagined the three

humans exploring the margin of the water with their hands, never quite daring to dive, and gradually falling into complete despair. The perfect blackness all around them must have crept into their brains like a parasite, devouring what was left of their sanity. And the other mermaids hadn't even cared enough to drown them out of pity . . .

"Did Dorian bring you any new books today?" Nausicaa went on dreamily.

Luce looked up, uncomfortable at the sudden change of subject. She almost wondered if Nausicaa was playing with her somehow. "He . . . didn't actually show up," Luce admitted, and then tried to cover her embarrassment. "I guess something must have happened so that he couldn't get away."

Of course it was ridiculous to try to bluff Nausicaa this way; Luce felt twice as embarrassed as she realized that. Luce watched a quick glimmer of irony pass over Nausicaa's face before it blinked out again.

"Unfortunate," Nausicaa observed dryly after a moment. "I've been learning so much from the books and from everything he tells you. I would like to see more of what he discovers about the damage humans have done to our oceans . . ."

Luce was still upset by the story about Kumiko and also irritated with Nausicaa for telling it so calmly. "If you'd talk to him yourself, I guess you could ask him to bring you more stuff about the ocean."

"I thought you preferred to see him alone." Nausicaa wasn't bothering to keep the sarcasm out of her voice anymore. "But of course I can speak to him directly if you like."

Luce jumped a little from sheer surprise. Nausicaa had

talked to Dorian once before, though just long enough to insult him, on the day of the gray whales' migration. But Luce assumed that Nausicaa had been making an exception, doing something she actually considered wrong. "But don't you care about . . ."

"About timahk, as you call it?" Nausicaa's sarcasm was gone; she was staring out at the waves rising to meet the seething snow, and there was something wistful in her gaze. "You know I do, Luce."

"But then . . ."

"You have not seen what I've seen. The humans are multiplying wildly. What I thought were terrible crowds of them five hundred years ago, or even fifty . . . that can't be compared to their numbers now. They are choking the shores, and there are ever fewer places where we can live hidden from them."

Luce didn't understand what humans multiplying had to do with talking to Dorian, but she couldn't help seeing the awful sadness welling in Nausicaa's eyes. Impulsively Luce took Nausicaa's dark olive-bronze hand in her own. "Nausicaa . . ."

"And as there are more humans there are also more of us, of course: their cast-off daughters. There are many more mermaid tribes, and larger ones, most full of mermaids too new and too bitterly angry to have any wisdom. Humans' numbers grow and so do ours, but the world remains the same small tumbling stone."

Suddenly Luce thought she knew what Nausicaa was getting at. "You're saying—we might *have* to talk to them? If the world gets so crowded that humans and mermaids can't help running into each other?"

"For years now I've wondered how much longer we can keep ourselves entirely secret from them. It seems inevitable that they will start to notice. Too many ships will vanish; too many people will hear a strange sound in the far distance. And then"—Nausicaa looked hard at Luce—"too many mermaids will spare the lives of human boys. They will think that this *one* boy can do no harm. Who would believe his story when no one else has *ever* seen what he has seen?"

Luce stared out at the lush, heavy snowfall, a wild tangle of emotions in her heart. What Nausicaa said made her afraid and ashamed—she *had* been foolish to believe, as she'd carried Dorian to safety, that no other mermaid had ever made the same choice. But she couldn't accept either that it would have been better to let him die. The snowflakes fell in such huge clusters that they looked like cupped pale hands begging in the dark.

Besides, if Nausicaa was right, humans would find out about them soon enough anyway. The problem wouldn't be Luce and Dorian, but something bigger than that: a world too packed and busy to allow for secrets. Luce suddenly pictured the earth as a prison yard restlessly crisscrossed by floodlights. No patch of darkness would be allowed to rest undisturbed.

"But Nausicaa?"

Nausicaa's eyes were fixed on the snow. Luce had never seen her look so depressed. "Yes, Luce?"

"If the humans do find out about us—do you think talking to them might help? Is there something we could say . . ." Luce broke off as she saw the expression on Nausicaa's dark face. It was utterly bleak, so heartsick that Luce felt almost desperate at the sight of it. "You think they'll still want to kill us, Nausicaa? No matter what we do?"

"I'm sure they'll *try*," Nausicaa said, and Luce realized there was more than despair in her friend's face. Beneath the pain there was a steely ferocity, determined and calm. "We would hardly be the first creatures they've driven to extinction. But there will always be new mermaids arriving in the sea, and we won't cease to fight."

"But if we promised to stop killing *them*, then . . ."

Nausicaa's look was scathing. "No doubt you would like to believe it could be as simple as that, Luce. But humans have wiped out hundreds of species that posed no threat to them. They find happiness in their power to destroy."

"Not all of them do!" Luce insisted. "Anyway, what does this have to do with you talking to Dorian?"

"It remains dishonorable, certainly, for me to have a discussion with your human lover." Nausicaa sounded so thoughtful that Luce suddenly understood she'd been brooding over the question for a long time. "But what will honor of such a kind finally matter, Luce? In a world where so many things are changing?"

Luce didn't try to answer. For some reason she wondered again how Dana was doing and why she never came to visit anymore. Probably Dana was furious that Luce had hurt Jenna, even in self-defense. Still, Luce thought, she should try to make up with Dana sometime.

She kept meaning to head over to Anais's territory to look for Dana and Violet. And she kept putting it off. Why risk a fight when it was so much easier to dream in Dorian's arms?

15

Prisoners

Violet was lying on the sloping white leather couch of the submerged cabin, her arms behind her head and her straight brown hair weaving around her with each tiny fluctuation of the water. Her tail flopped across the armrest. She looked over at Dana, who was asleep on the floor ten feet away, a steady stream of bubbles seeping out where her full lips met the trailing hose that was the cabin's only source of air. Violet knew she couldn't take the hose away without waking Dana, so she did her best to endure the painful craving growing in her own lungs. As long as she stayed very still, Violet found, she could go without air for longer than she would have imagined possible. It was hard to know exactly, but Violet guessed she'd held out already for almost an hour. It helped that they weren't more than a dozen yards below the surface, so the pressure wasn't too overpowering. Most of the yacht had remained lodged between two under-water crags when it sank, though parts of it had broken free and tumbled much deeper.

When Violet couldn't stand it anymore she slipped over the edge of the sofa and swam across the electric blue carpet. In the water-warped bluish glow Dana's full mouth took on a pur-ple tint; she gasped and half opened her eyes as Violet gently tugged the hose free. A stream of bubbles surged upward, danc-ing with blue light. "Sorry," Violet whispered, then inhaled urgently. The hungry ache in her chest subsided and she thought she could feel the oxygen tingling in her blood and lighting up her cells. It felt like electricity sweeping back through a city gone dark, golden light bursting from all its windows with a movement like an oncoming wave.

"'Sokay . . ." Dana murmured drowsily. "Take your time, Vi." With only one air hose between the two of them they were forced to take turns sleeping, and the one who remained awake would draw on the air as rarely as possible. Even so they were both constantly exhausted from being woken at regular intervals as the other came for her ration of breath.

Anais could pull the hose up anytime she felt like it, of course, and drown them both. But there was no point in dwell-ing on that. Dana kept insisting that Jenna would never allow that to happen anyway. Violet didn't say so, but she wasn't so sure, though it was only Jenna's intervention that had persuaded Anais to lock Dana and Violet up instead of murdering them outright.

It was Rachel who'd spied on Dana and who'd reported that Violet had slipped away to bring Luce the knife; Rachel, who'd always seemed so sweet and fragile, and who'd been one of Violet's few friends. She couldn't think of Rachel as a cruel person, but Violet knew the little nervous blonde was terrified of Anais. If Rachel did bad things sometimes, Violet told herself, then she did them out of cowardice rather than meanness. Who knew what Anais had said to pressure Rachel or to threaten her?

Violet sighed, pulled in a final inhalation, and gave the air back to Dana, who took the hose sleepily and rolled onto her side. The movement set off a small current in the confined space, and the curtains waved lethargically. At the bottom of the room the man's skeleton seemed to shake its head as the current brushed against it.

That skeleton had once been Anais's father, Violet knew. But she tried not to think about that too much.

She also tried not to look too closely. The tiny fishes and strange accordionlike orange worms had devoured most of the flesh, but in places gray-pink shreds still clung to the bones. Small sharp-toothed animals came to gnaw on them. Ribbons of what had once been a large green polo shirt and a pair of khakis hovered like awful plants around the rib cage and pelvis. Violet had seen human corpses before, of course. But she'd never spent so much time with one, and the longer she went on with this dead man as her cellmate the more she began to think about him: how he'd felt as he died and what serpentine dreams might still be wriggling through his empty skull. Sometimes she had to fight down an impulse to talk to him, maybe even to apologize.

Violet made herself look away, up and around the cabin. Most of the yacht's rooms had been thoroughly plundered, but even Anais had been a little squeamish about entering the cabin where her father's bloated corpse rocked with each new current. A collection of framed photographs of sea animals had remained untouched, including one of a leaping orca that Violet had turned toward the wall. The walls were white, and the bright blue ceiling echoed the color of the carpet. There was a chrome desk clogged by warped papers and photographs, a shelf of rotting books with dreadful titles like *The Financial Warrior*, and a glass cabinet full of brightly colored crystal dolphins and brandy decanters long since flooded with salt water. There was a single door, barred on the other side, and three shattered portholes much too small for Violet or Dana to squeeze through. An early attempt to get out through the vents had proved to both of them that that was impossible, too.

Violet never doubted that Luce was looking for them. The yacht where Violet and Dana were imprisoned was north of the tribe's usual territory; Luce just hadn't thought of checking it yet, that was all. But, smart as Luce was, Violet was surprised that she was taking so long to figure it out. It definitely made a kind of perverse sense that Anais would use her family's sunken yacht as a prison. She still thought of it as her personal property, almost as her home.

A warty, banana-colored starfish oozed out of a large purple vase, its legs groping at the aquatic emptiness. It flopped onto the desk and lay there upside down. There was something hopeless in the feeble way it squirmed, Violet thought, as if it didn't actually believe it could ever right itself.

No one was there with her except for the sleeping Dana, the skeleton, and the starfish. But somehow Violet felt exactly as if somebody had just accused Luce of not caring what happened to them. Luce hadn't found them, the invisible presence suggested, because she wasn't bothering to search. Maybe she hadn't even noticed that Dana didn't come to visit her anymore or thought about it enough to realize that Dana's disappearance must mean something bad had happened. All Luce cared about was herself and her singing . . .

"That's not *true*," Violet whispered. It seemed important to answer out loud, to make sure whatever it was heard her, but on the other hand she definitely didn't want to wake Dana. "Luce is coming to get us out of here. I *know* it. She would anyway, but especially since—since we're only in here because we were loyal to her."

The presence didn't seem to be convinced. Violet felt something like a contemptuous shrug close by.

It was her own shoulders.

Some queen, Violet thought, then shook her head wildly to make the words go away.

The brief interlude of blue daylight was already fading. Dana's beautiful brown skin took on a midnight shading outlined by her dim golden glow, and her coppery tail thrashed in sympathy with some unseen dream.

As far back as she could remember Violet had suffered from a sense that magic was everywhere: that dreams might grow like vines in empty skulls: that the air might take on a voice of its own or suddenly feather itself into a pulsing wing. From the wing a hawk would sprout, then dive at her and claw out her eyes. She'd felt the stirring of enchantment under her fingertips, and it had horrified her. With her transformation into a mermaid that creeping magic had suddenly, violently, invaded her body and taken it over, *without asking her*. Violet still couldn't feel the involuntary force and grace of her own tail without a shiver of aversion. Changing was simply the most devastating thing that had ever happened to her. It was even worse than watching her older brother being molested when she was still a small girl. And as for singing, well, Violet liked listening to the other mermaids, especially to Luce. But her own singing was stiff and uncomfortable, barely mediocre, and she usually tried to keep her voice as quiet as possible. She didn't want power, and most of all she didn't want the magic to think she'd *accepted* it.

But now Violet felt an inexplicable desire to sing, maybe even to try copying the odd, smooth tone—smooth even when it rose to a scream—that Luce's voice took on when she controlled the water. She glanced at Dana again. It would be too inconsiderate to wake her, Violet thought, and she stared around the room in frustration. The starfish didn't have the same shape as before. Now it was weirdly bundled in on itself like a squashed lemon.

Violet looked again and realized that the starfish was halfway through the laborious process of flipping itself right side up.

* * *

Miles down the coast later that night Luce stretched out on the beach of the shallow cave where she usually took Dorian, glancing around at the geometry of the broken rocks and the complicated snaking shapes of the roots that dangled overhead. A froth of gleaming snow covered everything. Somber clouds and mist choked out the sky almost all the time now, but this was a rare clear night. The stars were fierce and razor-bright, surrounded by radiating fangs of white brilliance, and an icy wind whirled down from the far north. Luce was a little bored. Dorian and Nausicaa had been talking so intensely—for what felt like hours now—that Luce was starting to feel sorry she'd suggested it.

And Dorian had looked upset when Luce had shown up with Nausicaa, too. Luce had the feeling he'd been waiting to talk to her alone, maybe about something important, though now it seemed like he'd forgotten about that. He was too absorbed in the conversation, not even reaching to brush away the snow that dropped from the roots overhead and landed on his neck. He was sitting cross-legged right at the edge of the softly lapping sea, leaning forward while the incoming tide soaked the frayed edges of his jeans. Nausicaa was close to him, her tail coiled in a circle around her and her emerald fins occasionally flicking above the glassy, star-streaked water.

Everything Dorian told Nausicaa provoked a stream of questions. "Okay, so the oceans soak up like a third of the carbon dioxide from the air, and that's making the water get way more acidic. If it keeps up the acid's going to kill all the coral reefs and maybe a lot of the plankton." Dorian was excited and he kept going too fast, forgetting how many things Nausicaa wouldn't know after her three thousand years apart from the life humans lived on land.

"Carbon dioxide? I've heard these words before, but the exact meaning . . ." Nausicaa's brow was creased with concentration.

"It's pollution, basically. It's in the air naturally, but we're putting tons more in the atmosphere all the time. From people burning fossil fuels. So we're screwing up the balance, and that's also why we're getting global warming."

"Then why do they burn these fossil fuels?"

"Well, that's how they make all the cars go. And they make most of the electricity that way."

"Electricity? That means all the lights at night?"

"Electricity makes the lights, but it also powers all the factories and everything. Where people make stuff."

Nausicaa looked genuinely puzzled, even overwhelmed. Much as Luce loved her she couldn't help enjoying it a little. For once Nausicaa couldn't just say she'd heard it all before. "Humans can't make things with their hands? They did so once."

"They can make a lot *more* stuff, though, by using machinery and robots. And they can make it a lot more quickly. But that takes electricity." Dorian obviously liked his new role as a teacher. "Okay, but the scariest thing about the acidification . . ."

"Yes?" Nausicaa asked; her voice was strained.

"Plankton makes a lot of the planet's oxygen. And if the plankton dies, like, maybe extra algae or something will make the oxygen instead. But the scientists are all still arguing about whether or not that would happen."

Luce looked up, ready to burst in with a question of her own—humans needed oxygen, too, after all—but Nausicaa was already speaking: "But the *whales* eat plankton? The whales with screens instead of teeth? Like the grays?"

"The baleen whales, yeah. Those screen things are baleen. Nausicaa, I hate to break it to you, but the whales are in pretty serious trouble anyway. There are these insane levels of like mercury in their bodies—"

"But they've been coming back!" Nausicaa's voice was suddenly so frantic that Dorian softened visibly. He looked like he wanted to give his old enemy a hug. Then Luce saw him glance down nervously at Nausicaa's magnificent bare chest, only partly hidden by the dense tangles of her hair.

Luce was ready to be irritated when Dorian turned his gaze deliberately on Nausicaa's eyes instead of her body. "I love them, too, Nausicaa. The way that gray whale *looked* at me . . ."

"What you humans call *love*, though . . ." A little of Nausicaa's contempt was coming back.

"But I'm not totally human!" Dorian blurted. Luce smiled to herself. It was wonderful to hear him defend himself that way. "I mean, Nausicaa, if Luce can see it you must be able to, too, right? I'm like"—Dorian laughed—"a *land* merperson."

Luce stretched her tail, feeling the cold silky wavering of the sea against her scales. The brilliance of the stars filled her eyes, and she wished again that Nausicaa would leave so she could wind her fingers through Dorian's hair. It was strange and uncomfortable to be so near him without touching him, without feeling his breath on her shoulders, tasting his mouth . . .

"You mean, can I see how you waited on many nights for your mother to decide—"

It took Luce a moment to realize what Nausicaa was about to say, and she jolted out of her daydreaming in alarm. "Nausicaa!"

Nausicaa only glanced at Luce curiously and went on. "To decide to kill you, as she stood above you with the pillow in her hands? And how your father insisted that you were insane and that he'd have you sent away to the asylum if you spoke of this to anyone?" Nausicaa asked all this in the same cool, almost scientific tone she'd once used to suggest that Luce might someday commit suicide. "I've seen this, yes."

"Nausicaa, *stop it!*" Luce cried out breathlessly. She was almost in tears, and she looked at Dorian with helpless anxiety, wondering what he would do. His face was bone white around his stunned, vacant eyes, and his hands were clenched. He tilted his head and gazed vaguely into the darkness, and a crescent of reflected starlight gleamed on his wet lower lip. He might start screaming, lashing out, calling Nausicaa a liar . . .

Instead Luce watched him exhale deeply, once and then again, and then slowly start to uncurl his trembling fingers. He shot Luce a quick, reassuring look, then turned with an obvious effort to face Nausicaa again. "I guess I shouldn't have *asked* that," Dorian murmured wryly. "Not if I didn't want an answer." He flashed a contorted smile.

Nausicaa was confused, staring from Dorian to Luce and back again. "But, Luce, what have I done wrong? Of course he would *know* . . . There's no reason not to speak of the truth."

"Luce tried to talk to me about it once," Dorian explained. He sounded almost calm; only the quickened rhythm of his breathing gave his emotions away at all. "And I just freaked out at her. That's why she's worried. But the thing is, I'm way better now, and I can stand to hear it. It *is* the truth."

Luce stared at him with a tumult of conflicting emotions.

She was relieved and amazed to hear him deal so well with Nausicaa's bluntness, but she was also hurt that he was saying these things for the first time to Nausicaa rather than to her.

"You are better because Luce has been singing to close your wounds, shaping your psyche as she shapes the water. Hasn't she?" Nausicaa agreed. Dorian opened his mouth as if he wanted to say something, then bit his lip and looked down. His dark blond hair hadn't been cut in months, and it tumbled over his eyes. It reminded Luce of the fact that her hair hadn't grown since her transformation. "As with the water, it is not that she changes what is there, but that she caresses it into new forms. This is what interests me about Luce, that she finds so many unexpected ways to use her gifts. She goes exploring inside her own voice."

Luce was bewildered. She hadn't told Nausicaa anything about the dreamy afternoons and thrilling nights that she'd spent singing her way through Dorian's mind. It was too private to talk about, and she could tell by Dorian's wounded expression that he thought so, too. Nausicaa had a way of knowing more than she was supposed to, but how could Luce explain that to Dorian?

"I haven't . . . Dorian, I mean . . . I haven't actually been talking to Nausicaa about this," Luce murmured uncomfortably. Nausicaa looked back and forth between them again, unsure what the matter was. For someone so wise about so many things, Luce thought bitterly, Nausicaa could be oddly clueless about people's inner lives. Thinking that made Luce miss Dana's sensitivity; it was so sad that Dana didn't seem to want to talk to her anymore.

"No," Nausicaa said after a moment. "You don't need to talk to me about this, Luce. I can tell."

Dorian looked up again, and Luce saw tears in his eyes. This wasn't fair to him, Luce thought. She was used to dealing with Nausicaa's brutal honesty, but there was no reason Dorian should be forced to listen to all this.

"How can you *tell* something like that?" Dorian asked. "I mean, I guess I never *asked* Luce . . . not to talk to anyone about that, but . . ."

Luce had never imagined that she would see Nausicaa surprised so many times in a single night. "The images are fading! The sparkling around you, Dorian. It's starting to dim. I know what that must mean. I've heard before of mermaids who could use their voices in this way. Why would I need Luce to *tell* me when I can read the signs for myself?"

Luce had wondered before, once or twice, if the indication around Dorian might be getting just a little weaker. Now, hearing Nausicaa say so, she knew it was true. She stared into the night above his head and saw the shimmer, still there but guttering like a candle. When she looked sideways Dorian's mother winked in and out of focus, a powerless ghost, uncertainly waving the pillow that was still clutched in her hands.

Dorian met Luce's eyes, and a wave of unspoken sorrow flowed between them. Luce's heart felt raw and somehow bright, beaming with a vital pain that she couldn't explain to herself. Of course, she told herself, all she'd *wanted* was for Dorian's heartbreak to heal. Why should the knowledge that he was truly recovering hurt her so much?

"I don't understand humans," Nausicaa muttered. "Why should such simple truths cause so much distress?"

"You don't understand more stuff than you realize, Nausicaa," Dorian answered. But his voice was alive with tenderness as he said it, and Luce thought that he suddenly seemed much older than he ever had before. Even Nausicaa's three thousand years clearly hadn't taught her what Dorian seemed to have learned in the last few minutes. "Do you mind letting me and Luce have some time alone together now?"

"I'm glad it's you Luce loves, I suppose," Nausicaa said abruptly. "If she must . . ." But, Luce saw, her friend's face was grim and sad as she torqued herself and swam away.

Then Luce was finally alone with Dorian in the star-streaked darkness. The rivulets of snow outlining all the roots above seemed to glow with a vehement diamond shine, blue-white and somehow terribly alert, as if all the world was watching them.

"Oh my God, Luce!" Dorian whispered. "There's all this serious shit happening, and I *need* to tell you about it, but it's been . . . it's just been such a crazy night."

Luce was already in his arms. His hands slid over her body, sensation moved in her skin like breath, and her tail began to thrash. For the first time he reached to pull the band of seaweed away from her breasts, and Luce writhed to press herself against his fingers. The kiss took her like a wave as warm as blood, and she felt as if she were tumbling inside it. Dorian fell back onto the beach, pulling her partway on top of him, and kissed her until her mouth filled with a strange, almost shivering heat.

Whatever it was he had to tell her, Luce didn't want to know. Not just now.

* * *

Dana was awake. She and Violet sat on the floor, their tails coiled around them, eating the mussels that one of the smallest mermaids had thrown through a porthole. The room was entirely dark but they could still see each other. Dana looked moody and didn't seem to feel like talking. The tide swelled around them, and Violet could hear the skeleton's head gently knocking on the carpeted floor.

"Do you think—" Violet began, and then stopped abruptly. She was afraid her idea would sound stupid.

Dana had managed to keep up her optimism so well that Violet was shocked to see the desolation in her huge brown eyes. "What now, Vi?"

This didn't exactly make Violet feel any less self-conscious. "If Luce was in here with us . . . I was thinking . . . maybe she could control the water well enough to push that bolt up? Even from this side of the door?"

Dana's lovely face went hard. "I don't want to talk about *Luce*, Violet." She glowered off into empty space. "We're on our own. What's the point of pretending that anybody's going to help us?"

Violet was overwhelmed with embarrassment. Her idea was obviously idiotic. It was childish, even pathetic, for her to pretend any escape was possible. She should just keep quiet. "But . . . I mean, I know *I'm* a terrible singer and everything . . ." Violet didn't know what force was making her keep blathering on this way. *Shut up shut up shut up, Violet.* Now the voice in her head was screaming, and it wasn't even hers but her stepfather's. He'd had his own kind of dark magic; that was clear. Violet's mother had been too enchanted to do anything to protect her children. *Shut up, you little moron, or I swear you're next!*

Dana sighed loudly, and Violet cringed as if Dana might be about to hit her. "What are you going *on* about, Violet? If you actually have some kind of plan, you might want to come out and tell me already."

"Maybe . . ." Violet whispered. Why couldn't she *control* herself? All she was doing was annoying Dana. "You're such a great singer, Dana. Maybe you could sing the way Luce does? Like, move the water? And if you got good at it . . ." Violet didn't finish the sentence, but suddenly to her own amazement she didn't feel nearly as ashamed of herself. She felt the same awareness of unexpected courage that she'd experienced when she'd stolen the knife for Luce.

Violet looked expectantly at Dana, ready now to argue with her if she refused to try. It wasn't a stupid idea at *all*. For a few seconds Dana looked impatient, even angry, then Violet watched something shift in the older mermaid's face. Dana's eyes got wider, and her full mouth narrowed with concentration.

"Luce *did* say one time that she thought I could do it, too!" Dana exclaimed. She sat up higher, and her eyes flashed with golden intensity. "She said I could learn! I thought she was just embarrassed about being the only one, but maybe . . . but she's not even here to teach us, Violet." Dana's excitement was already collapsing. "I don't know, actually. It's nice to think it would be possible, but Luce—she doesn't want to admit it, but probably she just has powers the rest of us don't."

"But Dana . . ." Violet had never felt so strong before. She was even smiling secretly to herself. "Do you remember how Luce sounds? When she sings that way?"

"Pretty much, I guess. It's kind of a weird sound. It's really different from her other singing."

"Try it."

Dana flashed a skeptical look at Violet, but then she grinned. Some of Dana's old warmth and hopefulness was coming back, Violet thought, feeling her tail starting to switch a little with enthusiasm. As awful as everything was, Violet suddenly felt a kind of exhilaration that went deeper than mere happiness.

"I guess we've got plenty of time on our hands," Dana admitted. "Okay. Let me get a jolt of that air, and I'll see if I can get close." Violet passed Dana the hose and watched her breathe in again and again, a sparkling veil of bubbles racing across her brown eyes. Dana was stalling for time, Violet realized. She was scared of failing, scared of letting them both down.

Finally Dana dropped the hose and sat stiffly with her eyes closed tight. She looked so nervous that Violet glanced around, half imagining a vast and highly critical audience jostling in the corners. Then Dana let out a slow, sustained, velvety note, as soft as summer air.

It was wonderfully beautiful, Violet thought as she listened. So beautiful that her skin shivered and her heart seemed to blossom into flowers with the shapes of castles, with petals curving into high turrets. Dana's singing was splendid and strange, but the sound she was making was also unmistakably wrong.

Dana opened her eyes, and Violet could see at once that she knew perfectly well how far she'd been from getting the song right. "Not even close," Dana said sadly, shaking her head. "It's got to be some kind of magic only Luce has, Violet."

"But you didn't—" Violet didn't want to be rude, but she didn't want Dana to give up either. "I think Luce sounds a little different than that when she does it. Like, she gets this weird, *smooth* kind of tone . . ." Violet concentrated on remembering, and Dana stared at her. Violet gestured, a mussel shell still in one hand. "It sounds almost like she's feeling the water with her voice. Like . . . I don't know how to describe it, but . . ."

Dana tried again. Her voice was full of rippling magic. It was a living miracle that poured through Violet's skin, though her mind, dancing with delirious surprise. It just wasn't the *right* magic. Too bumpy, Violet thought. Pushing too hard. Luce didn't push; instead she joined her voice to the water, *sympathized* with the water, then coaxed the water to follow the notes as they ran up the scale or leaped skyward. Violet could hear it in her mind so precisely that she almost felt like Luce was there with her after all.

Dana fell silent and flopped back onto the floor, despair plain on her face. "Oh my God, Violet. What if . . ." Dana didn't let herself finish the sentence, but still Violet knew what she'd been about to say: *"What if we die here?"*

"I think . . . I know you're so much better at singing than I am, and I don't want to try to tell you, but . . . doesn't Luce sound more like . . ." Violet let out a tentative note. The timbre was odd and smooth, and Violet could actually feel her voice reaching out to the water, as if her song held the ocean's hand and they were racing together to a place where no one could ever hurt them again.

Violet wasn't gripping the mussel shell anymore.

Instead the blue-purple shell was bouncing in place a foot

in front of her eyes, supported by a current that definitely hadn't been there a moment before. The white glow of its mother-of-pearl winked joyfully, and then Dana looked up and saw it, and screamed.

16

Departures

The sea looked very dark around the floating block of milk white ice. The block bobbed and spun with each pulse of the waves, a slick of meltwater gleaming bright blue on its sides. Nausicaa and Luce both stopped to look at it, neither of them speaking. Nausicaa had her usual look of detached curiosity, but Luce felt sick at the sight of the ice, her body buckling at the waist as if she'd just received a blow to the stomach.

It didn't help that they were at the dining beach and that only one larva, the Inuit one, was still living there. The fair-skinned one had vanished the day before and her little black-eyed companion couldn't seem to stop keening wordlessly as she lay hidden behind a jag of rock. As Luce and Nausicaa arrived at the beach the endless whimpering formed a kind of plaintive harmony running under the sound of the sea. The poor little

Inuit larva had probably seen her friend swallowed alive. They'd tried repeatedly to comfort her and brought her oysters, but she refused to eat anything.

Luce and Nausicaa settled in a relatively sheltered spot, leaning back against low crags. Although they'd come there for breakfast Luce didn't feel like eating, and she got the feeling that Nausicaa didn't either.

"Luce?" Nausicaa's voice was unusually gentle. "I will be leaving here. Perhaps today." Heavy snow felted the beach, vibrant blue in the endless twilight, and the snow-laden trees looked like melting blue candles. It was probably ten o'clock in the morning, but time seemed to blur into meaninglessness in this light, as if the old distinctions of days and hours no longer applied. Nausicaa's billows of midnight hair appeared even darker than usual, and her greenish bronze face was sad and determined.

Don't leave me! Luce thought, but she didn't say it out loud. Nausicaa would know what Luce was feeling without the words being voiced. They stared at each other in silence for a moment. Luce had known this moment might come sooner or later, but she still couldn't quite believe that Nausicaa would truly abandon her.

"Come with me," Nausicaa said in reply to Luce's unspoken words. "Luce, I do not like to beg, but please. Go and gather your tribe, whoever will agree to come with you. We will lead them away from here together. I cannot escape the feeling that some evil is coming to this place."

You know I can't leave Dorian, Luce thought. She deliberately closed her mind to the possibility that the approaching ice might force her to leave him, at least for a while. In any case the ice wouldn't get that bad for weeks, and there was no reason to worry about it yet. *Nausicaa, don't make me choose between Dorian and you!*

"Your romance will end, Luce." Nausicaa's voice was softer than Luce had ever heard it. "It will be so much better for you if you can accept that, and keep Dorian only as a beloved memory. Come with me, and I will help you found a new tribe. We will live by our own *timay*, breaking Proteus's thrall, and hunt humans no more. You will be queen in a new way, leading your mermaids on journeys never yet imagined. It will be exactly as you've dreamed . . ."

Luce felt such an overpowering rush of longing that she wondered if Nausicaa was enchanting her. But no: the magic was all in Nausicaa's words. It was in her promise of a new and passionate life, a life in which the mermaids would finally be truly free to create their own future. Luce looked at the soft gold-green shine trembling on Nausicaa's skin. Luce understood how urgently her friend wanted to make this vision come true. Together they would certainly succeed, Luce knew, and for an instant she pictured herself fervently kissing Dorian goodbye. His lips devoured hers, and the trickling salt of their merged tears flooded her tongue . . .

No. It was a horrible idea. She and Dorian *needed* each other.

"Nausicaa . . ." Luce spoke aloud for the first time. The words stung her mouth, clawed at her throat; how could she keep going? "I *can't*. You're my best friend ever in my life, and I'd give almost anything to start a tribe with you, but I can't leave. And I don't see why you have to, either!"

The larval mermaid's whimpering got louder. A long, shrill cry spiraled under the wind. The little creature was maddened by loneliness that nothing would ever heal.

"I have to leave, because—" Nausicaa stopped abruptly. "Ah, Luce. You are very dear to me. I would even call Dorian my true friend now, human or not. And I cannot bear to stay and see you destroyed by your love for him. Already yesterday I could sense that things between you two will not last much longer. However this ends—"

"It's not *going* to end!" Luce insisted, too loudly. Just because Dorian's brutalized heart was finally healing, did Nausicaa think he wouldn't need Luce anymore?

Nausicaa didn't argue, but the look on her face wasn't calm at all now. A dark fire seemed to lick and needle at the inside of her skin. She gazed at Luce and then away into distances Luce could hardly imagine, as if centuries were scrolling along the far horizon. It was at least a minute before Nausicaa sighed and turned her stare back toward Luce. Luce could feel the gleam of those eyes entering her mind. She wanted to throw her arms around Nausicaa's neck and stop her from going, but somehow she couldn't move.

"I hope you will defy more than the gods," Nausicaa said at last. "Queen Luce."

Luce wasn't sure what Nausicaa meant by that, but she didn't seem to have enough strength to ask her. There was some kind of awful acrid smoke in her throat where her voice should have been. Nausicaa reached out and stroked Luce's face.

"I hope you will defy, not only Proteus, but everything I know of the world. Everything I've seen in my three thousand years. I hope you will be the one who discovers the strength to make a different choice. Then someday, dearest Luce, I will find you again . . ."

All Luce could see through her tears were bright webs of blue glow. Her cheek was suddenly cold where Nausicaa's hand had been, and the icy wind buffeted her shoulders, tossed her short hair. She didn't hear a splash, but even so she knew that Nausicaa was gone, and gone forever.

Her parents couldn't help dying, Luce told herself. They'd left her for somber regions she knew nothing about, but they hadn't *wanted* to go. But Nausicaa had abandoned her here on this cold beach voluntarily, purely because Luce wasn't doing what Nausicaa wanted her to do. Luce heard her own sobs merging with the larva's wails.

* * *

Later that day Dorian met her in the rowboat, and she towed him through the daytime night to their secret shallow cave under the overhanging roots. But it hurt Luce to be there. It was incredible to think that only yesterday she'd sat on these stones listening to Dorian and Nausicaa talking, feeling annoyed and left out of the conversation. Now, of course, she would have given anything to have Nausicaa appear and interrupt their privacy. The sea seemed so brutal, so infinite in its rough indifference, like a monster that would only talk to itself. Dorian held Luce tight—she could hardly feel the shape of his body through all the winter layers—and stroked her hair while she cried.

"I was just getting to like her," Dorian observed wryly. "At first I thought she was such a *bitch*. But, Luce, listen—"

"Why didn't she understand that I can't leave you? It seems so *unfair* . . ." Luce was dimly aware that she was being a little childish, but she couldn't help it. She felt as if her father's ship had just vanished, as if she'd watched her mother dying a second time, as if Catarina had run away from her again, all at once. She just couldn't stand to *lose* people anymore.

"Luce? Baby? Listen. I know you don't want to hear it, but I swear it's better this way."

Luce looked up at him, outraged. Was he still resentful of the time she'd rushed off to save Nausicaa's life? "Just because you had to row home that night, and you got, like, *jealous*—"

"Not because of that," Dorian sighed. He was still gently caressing Luce's back and hair as he spoke, and her face rested on his shoulder. "I admit I was a jerk about that. Okay? But Luce, Nausicaa didn't mean to, but she's kind of been holding you back."

Luce couldn't believe what she was hearing. No one had ever taught her as much as Nausicaa had. How could Dorian not realize that? "She's so brilliant, Dorian. And she knows so much . . ."

"She is, she is, she is. Brilliant. But Luce, Nausicaa's also, like"—Dorian laughed—"*old-fashioned*. She just doesn't get how different everything is now. Because, I mean, from everything I've been reading the ocean is really in danger. And I know you'd like to help, right? If you could. But the thing is, there's not a whole lot you can do about it if you're stuck living in some cave somewhere, and you can't even let anyone know you *exist*."

Luce had a sudden queasy sense of where this was going. He hadn't mentioned his idea of trying to turn Luce human in weeks. Why did he have to bring it up now? "Dorian, it's crazy to keep *talking* about this!"

"It's not crazy! You could do so much *more* if you were human again, Luce. I've been thinking, we could both become like marine biologists or climate scientists, and I'll be an artist, too. Then we could work together to *change* things! It would be a lot smarter than splashing around getting chased by orcas. But Nausicaa would never be able to see that, and as long as she was hanging around . . ."

Luce understood. Dorian hadn't bothered to mention his project of turning Luce human recently because he'd known he'd never be able to persuade her to attempt it. Not while Nausicaa was there urging Luce not to listen to him. But now . . .

"Nausicaa knew a bunch of mermaids who tried it. Changing back. She said she's known *hundreds* of mermaids who left the water, and only two of them survived." Luce tried to keep her voice calm and reasonable. Why couldn't she make Dorian understand this? "So, Dorian, you really shouldn't keep asking me this! Not unless you want me to die."

"But those—" Dorian began. Luce looked up to see his eyes staring into the darkness. The indigo sky was crystalline with falling snow and with icicles that spiked from the roots above them. He took a deep breath. "Luce, those mermaids didn't have any help, right? They just let their boyfriends carry them onshore."

Luce was bewildered. What kind of help could a mermaid have in that situation? The best she could hope for was that someone would hold her while the pain lanced in from all directions, while she screamed in a blur of white, burning agony. Luce had felt that impossible suffering when she'd left the water to save Violet, and even the memory of it made her shiver. But if Dorian *did* have a better idea, well, then she might at least consider . . . "*Help?* Dorian, what are you talking about?"

"We can't do this on our own, Luce. I know that. You'll die if we try it. And I don't ever want to live without you." His voice was grim and settled. This wasn't some sudden impulse, Luce realized, but an idea he'd been mulling over for weeks. But there was only one entity she could think of who might be able to do what Dorian wanted.

"But . . . you said you didn't want to ask Proteus for any favors. Even if we could find him." *And what if Proteus agreed?* Luce thought. Would she really give up the sea, the wild free sky, and her own astounding voice for the tedium of a normal human life? Even a life with Dorian?

Maybe. Maybe she would. Since he was warm and kind and brave enough to accept her, forgive her, even after Emily . . . Luce owed him something for that. She owed him so much . . .

And he was right, anyway. It was the only way they'd ever be able to sleep beside each other; the only way that nagging heat could ever flare high enough to quiet again. Maybe. If she was really positive he'd still love her . . .

Dorian twisted to look into her face. "I wasn't thinking of asking Proteus."

"Then who?"

Dorian's eyes fixed on hers. They were full of secretive glimmers, passing shades. For the first time it occurred to Luce that there was something he wasn't telling her. He hesitated for a few more moments, his hands sliding through her jagged hair. "Ben Ellison."

"WHAT?" Luce screamed. Ben Ellison the FBI agent, Ben

Ellison the enemy, always out to break Dorian's will. Luce felt the sudden panicked certainty that Dorian must have betrayed her and she began thrashing violently, wrenching her body out of his arms. She splashed back a few yards and slumped with her tail coiled tight, ready to whip away into the distance. Dorian was leaning toward her with his legs folded under him, his hands spread on the stones.

"He's not a bad guy, Luce! I swear to God if we just talked to him . . . he'd do whatever he could to help us. I *know* he would. And he's really smart, and he has to know, like, scientists and people who could figure this out. He just doesn't understand what it's like for you, but if you *told* him—"

"Told him *about the mermaids?*" Luce's voice was so bitter she thought she might choke on it.

"Well, I guess you'd have to, yeah." Dorian almost sounded like he thought this was funny. "He'd probably notice the tail. But Luce, I'm pretty sure he already knows. He said some things . . . I can't explain exactly, but I think the FBI knows you guys are out here. He said something about—that him and me are both in a *select society*, that almost nobody alive has heard what we've heard—"

"If they know," Luce snarled, "then it's probably because somebody *told* them."

"I knew you'd think that." Dorian sighed. "But it's totally unfair. I didn't tell them shit."

"But then—"

"Jesus, Luce. It's not like I'm the only person who ever got saved by a mermaid! Maybe there aren't a lot of us, but . . . And the FBI might have other ways to find stuff out, anyway. I mean, all those *ships* your tribe sank. Did any of you ever think that they might have surveillance cameras or something?"

The camera, Luce thought. The words were like a slow-motion explosion that obliterated the world around her. Dorian was still talking, but she couldn't make out what he was saying. That black, furtive boat and the black-suited diver planting the camera she'd smashed. How could she have been stupid enough to believe it was the only one?

"They'll try to kill all of us," Luce said breathlessly. Her own voice was part of the white burst still spreading through her mind.

And if the mermaids were threatened, how could she even consider changing into one of the creatures that wanted them dead? She'd have to do her best to defend her own kind. Not that Dorian would be too happy with her if she announced her intention of fighting on the mermaids' side.

Some evil is coming to this place, Nausicaa had said.

War.

"That's exactly why you should talk to Ben Ellison," Dorian answered coolly, and Luce struggled to focus on him again. "Look, Luce. He needs to know that you're not all the same. You'll be a lot safer that way. And if we can figure out some way to turn mermaids back without killing them . . ."

Luce had never felt so angry with him. Did Dorian actually believe that she would abandon her fellow mermaids, even give the FBI information about them, simply in order to save herself? "*No.*"

"He said he wants to meet you, Luce. I think he might be pretty . . . open-minded about the whole thing. If you just gave him a chance."

Luce was leaning back propped on her hands, trying to think through everything Dorian was telling her. Her fingers curled over the pebbles of the seafloor, and she felt a subtle disturbance in the water. Maybe there were seals playing nearby?

Suddenly Dorian was scrambling to his knees, throwing himself behind a snarl of roots and jumbled shards of rock. Luce gaped after him, confused. He wasn't completely hidden, just huddled back in a gloomy corner, but he was obviously trying to get out of sight as best he could.

"*Luce!*" Violet screamed behind her, and Luce swung around in shock. Violet's sleek brown hair was streaming, her gray-green eyes bright and wild with some combination of exhilaration and terror. "Oh, God, Luce, she tried to *kill* us! I guess she heard the way we were practicing singing and got worried, because she actually pulled the air hose away! But I . . . but we . . . we'd gotten good enough at moving the water, and we managed to sing so that we shoved the bolt up just in time! Dana! Dana, she's here! I *found* her!"

Luce was so overwhelmed that she could barely understand what Violet was saying to her, but one thing seemed clear. The *she* who'd tried to kill Violet could only have been Anais.

And Violet was so beside herself that she hadn't spotted Dorian yet. But that couldn't last. "Let's go talk somewhere else," Luce hazarded. If she could just coax Violet out of this shallow cave, around the bend of the cliffs, then she could come back for Dorian later.

"We've got to get away *now*, Luce! When Anais finds out we've escaped . . . we're swimming south before they start searching for us, and you *have* to be our queen now! You can't say no anymore!" Even in her bewilderment, Luce couldn't help but notice how different Violet suddenly seemed. The shy, cringing little mermaid who never even made a suggestion was actually ordering Luce around. "And, Luce, I can move the water by singing! Just like you! I'm not as good yet, but I will be! But you'll always be my queen because I learned it from you!"

Luce had Violet's hand, and she was gently tugging her farther out. They were just moving beyond the jags that enclosed the cave and into the rough, high waves of the open sea. The darkness was speckled white with fine eddies of snow, and Dorian was behind them. As long as he stayed quiet Luce might be able to stop the other mermaids from discovering him.

Dana's luminous brown face burst out of the water, blocking their way. Her hair was loose and matted and, Luce saw, she looked utterly drained. However giddy Violet might be, she and Dana had clearly been through a terrible ordeal. Dana glared at Luce as the three of them pitched in the darkness. Through the black glass waves Luce could see that Dana actually had her hands on her hips.

"Why didn't you do anything to *help* us?" Dana demanded fiercely. "Why didn't you even *try*? Okay, we're alive, but it was way too close."

"I didn't know you were in trouble," Luce objected. It sounded horribly lame. "I just thought you didn't want to talk to me anymore because of Jenna . . ." Was Dorian visible from this angle? It took all of Luce's willpower to keep from glancing over her shoulder to check. Dana stopped glowering at Luce, and her eyes fixed on something back in the direction of the cave.

"What's that rowboat doing here?" Dana's voice was suddenly much quieter, stunned and airy.

Luce's heart stopped, and she struggled to hold her voice steady. "Probably it just drifted here."

"It didn't drift! I can see the rope, it's tied up to that fallen tree!" Violet was whispering, too. She'd spun in place to stare back the way they'd come, and her sleek brown hair gleamed in the darkness. "There's got to be a human here, Luce! And they've been listening to us, and maybe they've even *seen* us . . ."

Dana's face took on a weary, incredulous look, as if she just couldn't believe that there was one more problem she had to wrestle with. "Luce has this thing about not killing humans," Dana explained to Violet, loudly enough that Dorian could almost certainly hear her. "I'll take care of this. Luce, sorry, I know you don't like it, but you're just going to have to deal." Dana and Violet were swimming back toward the cave now and Luce followed along beside them. She wasn't about to let Dana hurt Dorian, and she knew she had to at least try to explain, but she had no idea where to start. Dana would be so *hurt* . . .

Dorian stepped out from behind the roots and walked calmly to the edge of the water, stopping five yards away from them. He looked strangely beautiful standing there, almost princely, with the golden tint of his wide, high-boned cheeks and his tangled brown-gold hair framed by the shadows behind him. "Hey," he said. "That's not going to work."

Dana's eyes went wide. She was shocked into answering him. "What's not going to work?"

"Killing me. I'm not as easy to kill as most people," Dorian announced. He sat down with his legs folded insolently close to the water's edge; close enough that Violet and Dana could simply grab him and drag him under, Luce realized. She was dismayed at the thought that she might have to fight the mermaids she cared about most.

Dana was beginning to get over her astonishment at being spoken to by a human, and a wicked look came into her eyes. She was clearly eager to prove this presumptuous boy wrong, and she smiled as she started to hum very faintly. Dorian could defend himself perfectly well against mermaid song, Luce knew, but still . . .

"Stop it!" Luce yelled.

Dana wheeled around to confront her. "Luce, if this upsets you then you don't have to watch. Head south and we'll catch up with you in a few minutes, okay?"

"It's not going to work," Dorian repeated coolly, and the three mermaids spun to stare at him again. "Singing to me. I know how to keep from getting enchanted. And anyway, Dana, I'm not your enemy. Killing me would be totally stupid."

Dana and Violet both started speaking at the same instant. "Dana, I mean, he hasn't actually *heard* us sing yet," Violet objected shyly, just as Dana snapped, "How do you know my *name*?"

Dorian looked back and forth between the two of them, then grinned blatantly at Luce. He clearly found the situation entertaining, but Luce's insides were ice cold and her heart thrummed painfully. Much as Luce loved Dorian's courage, this seemed like a horrible moment for him to make a display of it. "Don't you know who I am, Dana?" Dorian asked.

Dana's face turned green. "The boy Luce killed. The boy she *said* she killed . . ."

"She tried. Twice. Like I said, I'm not that easy." Dorian smiled with unconcealed amusement. "Now we've settled that, maybe we can be friends. I'm Dorian."

"Dorian," Dana said. Her voice was as empty as the charred remains of a burned-out house. She turned to look at Luce, and her blank, violated face was the most horrible thing Luce had ever seen. "You lied to me." She sounded much too calm.

"I . . ." Luce began, but she couldn't keep going, and she couldn't look away from those ruined eyes. "Dana, I . . ."

"You *lied* to my *face* while I was *crying!*" Dana's voice was rising to a shriek now. Her beautiful face was contorted into a crumpled mask, and with her rising scream serpents of seawater pulled themselves from the waves and writhed in the gusting air. Luce had never seen another mermaid control the sea with her voice before, and she stared mesmerized. "And we almost *died* because of you! You filthy, worthless, lying . . ." A twisted length of seawater ripped forward with insane speed, slashing Luce in the face so hard that she could feel her skin break. The blow threw her sideways, and she wobbled for a moment below the surface. Everything was green-black, warped, and shaken, and she could still hear Dana shrieking, her voice tearing at the sea as if it were made of thin fabric. Strange fissures of air like living wounds opened in the water around Luce, and she tasted her own blood.

Luce came up screaming a note as harsh as stone, pain throbbing in her face. A rolling wave picked Dana up and twirled her over and over at full length, her long body a blur of caramel and ruby, until Luce gasped and Dana crashed back down. Her coppery tail kicked up white arcs of foam. For an instant they were silent, glaring at each other while Violet and Dorian looked on in shock, hands clenched over their ears. *Stop this, Lucette!* "Dana, this is wrong . . ." Luce tried. The welt burned from her forehead all the way to her chin.

"You're the one who's wrong!" Dana was still screaming, but the magic had fallen out of her voice. The ocean crashed indifferently again, following its own cold rhythms.

"But what was I supposed to do? Dana, please, *think* about it . . ." Luce gasped the words out desperately. Maybe it was too much to hope that Dana would ever forgive her, but at least she might be able to understand.

"What were you supposed to *do?*" Dana was half sobbing now, her arms stretched out on the pitching waves as if she was searching for support. "God, Luce, how can you ask me that?"

But I couldn't do what you wanted, Luce thought. *I couldn't kill him!* She was just starting to say this when Dana interrupted, her voice like a sustained moan. "Luce, you were supposed to *trust* me! You should have trusted me enough to tell me the truth!"

Somehow this was the last thing Luce had expected Dana to say.

It was *worse* than anything she could have imagined Dana would say. And it was impossible to answer, because she knew that Dana was right. Luce was knocked into silence and darkness. Her thoughts billowed like smoky clouds, and she stared helplessly at the rocks and the icy, domineering sea. The unforgivable thing wasn't that she'd let Dorian live, but rather that she'd treated one of her few real friends as if she were an enemy, as someone who deserved to be fooled.

Apologizing wouldn't help, Luce realized. Dana's face

was buckling in pain, smeared with tears. For a full minute no one spoke.

"Violet," Dana murmured at last, "let's get out of here. We're never coming back. We'll never even *think* about this . . ."

"I still want Luce to come with us," Violet whispered. "She's still my queen." Despite the words there was something horribly raw in Violet's face, Luce saw: the dull grief of disillusionment.

"*That* is no one's queen," Dana replied coldly. She wouldn't look at Luce anymore.

"But . . ." Violet gazed at Luce in urgent appeal, her childish gray-green eyes washed by tides of heartache. "Luce, don't you want to be with us?"

"Luce isn't going anywhere," Dorian suddenly put in loudly. There was something disruptive about the sound of his voice, as if they'd all forgotten he was still there or that he was capable of speech. "She belongs with me."

For the first time Luce wasn't so sure. Hadn't Dorian asked her to talk to the FBI? If Dana felt this betrayed now, what on earth would she think if Luce became an informant for the humans?

Violet was crying as she swam up and kissed Luce on the seeping welt that striped her cheek. The kiss stung, and Luce knew that the taste of her blood would linger on Violet's lips through her long journey south.

Then Violet and Dana were gone. The waves closed behind them. Luce gazed out beyond the spot where they'd vanished, and the sea appeared like a vast field crowded with the black silk tents of a lost army.

Luce swirled over to the shore and stretched out face-up, her fins dragging weakly across the stones of the seabed. Dorian drew close and softly washed the blood from her face. "Luce?" he said. "You know they had to find out sometime, right?"

Luce didn't answer, and Dorian gave up trying to talk to her and wrapped his arms around his knees, staring out to sea. Luce turned her head until she couldn't see even a sliver of his clothing. Nothing but the racing snow. She knew Dorian was still sitting silent beside her, and she knew she had to take him home, but it was hours before she moved or spoke.

17

Ice

The pack ice began to float in from the north. It came sparsely at first, a broken white parade dancing over the surface of the water, and it didn't take Luce long to realize she'd underestimated how dangerous it might be. The blocks were big and heavy enough that if the waves threw one against her head, maybe in a storm, the blow would surely knock her unconscious or possibly even break her neck. The world became a waltz of ice and darkness, the pale crags of far snowy mountains traced on a black sky far taller than any mountain. And the cold was fierce enough now to bother even a mermaid a little. Luce dug Dorian's olive parka out of its hiding place every night and slept with it wrapped around her upper body, breathing his warm, earthy smell.

Dorian had said she was all he had left. Now with Nausicaa and Dana gone he was all she had, too. She couldn't escape the suspicion that he might be secretly glad about that, but she couldn't stop loving him either. In the days following their confrontation with Dana, Luce and Dorian seemed to be living in the center of an infinite castle carved from black glass and white snow. Their voices echoed in each other's minds as if through winding corridors and abandoned ballrooms. Every afternoon they sprawled together on the beach, Dorian's breath emerging in a series of pale clouds. Sometimes Luce would drag the rowboat along the shore under crystal overhangs that dripped from the cliffs, accumulated icicles so thick that they became monstrous slabs of rippling light in the darkness. The aurora borealis hovered like shining green rain or like scarlet plumes, the colored glow caught and distorted by the ice.

It was all so beautiful and so dreamlike that it could be hard to remember how *real* the world was and how serious their problems were. Once or twice Dorian tried again to bring up his idea of asking Ben Ellison to find a way to turn Luce back.

"I'd rather try it without him," Luce finally said. "Just you and me. It might kill me, maybe, but I wouldn't be betraying anyone else that way. Even if I died at least I wouldn't hate myself!"

Even in the dimness Luce could see that Dorian's face had turned ashy white. "I *will not* let that happen! Luce, we're not going to do this unless . . . unless it's at least kind of safe. I mean, I'd go insane if you died because of me!"

Safe, Luce thought a little contemptuously. The word was ridiculous considering what they were talking about. "Then don't ask me anymore, or . . . Dorian, can't we just be together like this?"

She might have to do what she could to protect the other mermaids someday, but she couldn't tell him that. He'd only get angry if he knew she was considering doing anything as danger-ous as throwing herself into battle.

She couldn't realistically hope ever to change back, of course. Almost certainly not. But even so she pictured herself walking barefoot up to his door, his old olive parka hanging to her thighs; how astonished he would look as he realized it was *her* standing there . . . Would he still love her as much if she had an ordinary human face again, though, and if she lost the power in her singing?

They were lying on their secret beach. Dorian was stretched out parallel to the shore while Luce's head rested on his stom-ach. On one side a motionless fountain of dripping ice hung in permanent suspense from a jumble of high roots, and on the other the pale fallen tree sprawled in the water like the diamond-crusted spine of a murdered giant. The rowboat jerked in the grip of its stripped, ivory branches. "This is *amazing*," Dorian admitted. "It's all more gorgeous than anything I ever thought would happen to me. Except it's so damn cold." He laughed.

"And anyway," Luce pursued doubtfully, "if I got to be hu-man I wouldn't be able to sing to you anymore. Not, like, *real* singing anyway . . ." She was surprised at how anxious she felt to hear what he would say about that.

"That would suck," Dorian agreed. "I've kind of imagined that maybe you'd get to keep your voice. But if you didn't I'd really miss it." He was quiet for a moment, his fingers brushing across Luce's naked shoulders. "Sing to me now?"

Luce was a little disappointed by his answer, but she sang anyway. She sang a cluster of delicate notes as pointed as the light of stars, then idly used her voice to pull a sphere of water free of the ocean's surface. Dorian let out a faint cry, and Luce began carefully shifting the tone of her song. She sang several notes at once and gathered some of them into tense bundles, let others blow and belly outward, all to sculpt the blob of water that was trembling in midair. It looked ebony black and gleaming in the dimness, but a few hints of crimson glow slipped from the far-off aurora and curled in the watery head. She gave it broad high cheekbones, wide-set eyes, and then with some difficulty managed a large, slightly crooked nose. Shaping the sculpture with her voice felt almost like caressing Dorian's head with her fingers, tracing the familiar curves and planes.

"Oh my God!" Dorian whispered after a minute. "That's me! Luce, how can you . . . I mean, it's so incredible . . ."

Luce didn't answer. She was still concentrating on her portrait of Dorian, trying to get the slope of his forehead exactly right. The hair was going to be tricky. She divided her voice into more notes than she had ever managed before, all weaving together, and thick sinuous strands of water began to spin from the floating head. The red light of the aurora curved like rose petals in its core. Her voice was soft yet still piercing; it felt like they were listening to the night's own secret thoughts cast in music.

Dorian had started crying silently from the power of that music, and Luce softly lowered the water-sculpture, letting it flow back into the sea. She was amazed herself by how much the sculpture had looked like him and by how graceful it was. Her earlier attempts had been crude by comparison.

"God, Luce! I wish there was some way we could have kept that! I mean, I think I'm a good artist and everything, but that was *so* beautiful!"

"Thanks," Luce said shyly. "I don't know if I could do that again, though."

"Maybe we could, I don't know, like freeze one of those heads while you were singing? I guess it would be hard for you to keep it up that long, though. Or at least I could take a photo next time . . ."

"You can take a picture if you want," Luce said, but for some reason she didn't like the idea. "But I don't see why you should, actually. Dorian, it's just something for you to remember." They were quiet for a while, and Dorian wiped his tears with his sleeve.

"I'm going to have to start leaving early on Wednesdays," Dorian said abruptly. He sounded slightly embarrassed, but Luce couldn't tell why. "We finally met that girl Zoe? The drummer? And we're going to try to have band practice regularly twice a week. Wednesday nights and Saturday mornings."

Luce felt a quick rush of jealousy and just as quickly repressed it. Of course Dorian would meet human girls sometimes; it didn't mean he was going to fall in love with them. "What's she like?" Luce asked with deliberate lightness. "Is she a good drummer?"

"She's not a *bad* drummer, anyway. Pink hair and like three nose rings. Maybe kind of a poser punk, and a little bratty sometimes? But she's funny. She might be smart, too. It's kind of hard to say."

"Is she pretty?" Luce couldn't completely keep the edge out of her voice this time.

Dorian rolled over so that Luce's head slipped off his stomach and then reached to pull her close. For a few moments he just stared at her, his gloved fingers softly exploring her face. "I really can't tell. If Zoe's pretty or not," Dorian said at last. His voice was very low and his breath feathered against Luce's cheek.

"You can't tell?" Luce was suddenly intensely happy and so in love she almost felt like crying.

"I can't tell. I mean," Dorian added, "maybe some guys would think she was. Cute, anyway. But that would only be because they've never seen *you*."

At another time Luce might have pointed out to him that the astounding beauty of her own face was just a part of her magic—that the beauty of the mermaids was, in some sense, not real. But she didn't feel like saying that now.

There were advantages to staying a mermaid, after all; in some ways a human couldn't hope to compete.

* * *

As she towed Dorian home that night they could both feel the swelling aggression in the wind. The waves started to chop and jar below them, and white rafts of ice pitched perilously close to the boat. As he clambered out onto the dock they both looked back at the high slopes of water beyond the tiny harbor. The waves appeared to be getting taller by the minute, and Luce felt her stomach tighten a little at the thought of swimming back to her cave. She should try to collect a supply of food in case the storm lasted for days; she might be trapped inside for some time. Dorian looked worried, too. "Is it going to be safe for you? Getting home?"

"I'll try to stay underwater," Luce told him. "So I don't get slammed by an ice floe." She didn't mention the possibility that she might be overpowered by the currents. Dorian's hair whipped in the icy spray now blowing off the harbor. "Dorian, I might not be able to see you for a few days . . ."

Dorian answered Luce by throwing himself face-down on the dock and leaning out to take her face between his hands. He kissed her with such intensity her lips ached, and then he reached to squeeze her shoulders.

"I'll wait for you." He struggled to his feet and ran up the dock, his body doubled against the thrust of the storm.

Luce fought her way through the violently swaying currents. Black nets of water swept her far away from the coast, dragged her deeper, then rolled her through streaking foam. She would escape from one watery fist only to be seized by the next, slamming her away from the air, then just as suddenly find herself thrown free of the surface. Veils of snow spiraled above waves at least twenty feet high, but she could just make out the jags of the coast that sheltered her own small cave. Luce stared back that way, her view broken by each new wall of water, and realized that exhaustion might overwhelm her before she could reach the coast again.

Luce screamed a long note, bright and urgent with the will to live. Her song was no match for the ferocity of the storm, but as she called to the water she found she had enough power to create a slight countercurrent, an eddy immediately around her body. She tried to drive it with her voice and found that at least it was strong enough to keep her from being swept farther out to sea. She drove with her tail and her song at the same time, dodging ice floes that appeared as suddenly as ghosts, and slowly, painfully, saw the coast sliding nearer. It was at least two more hours before she grasped the stone walls of her small cave, her weary muscles relaxing in the sudden stillness of its sheltered water. Luce flopped to the shore and fell into a long, profound sleep.

* * *

It had been impossible, of course, for her to stop and collect shellfish on her way back to her cave. She woke to darkness and cold, hungry and just as suddenly aware that she might not eat for days. The storm screamed and whistled, and even enclosed as she was in solid rock, Luce could hear the groan and snap of shattering trees. At least she had a pile of books Dorian had brought her, though there was something a little ironic about reading Jane Austen to distract herself from hunger as she lay on the stones in a cave as dark as soot. The women in the novel worried about their romances and about how many servants they could afford, and Luce read on and listened to the storm's vast orchestra of crunching ice cellos and yowling brass. No matter how long she read, no trace of light seeped through the entrance, though she could still see the pages and the stone vault above her. The clouds must be thick enough to erase the few brief hours of bluish daylight whenever they came.

After a while Luce put down the book. The darkness made it impossible to fight off the images that crowded her mind. The black diver slipped from the boat again and plopped down into midnight water, Dana's wounded eyes stared at Luce, and Nausicaa touched Luce's cheek as she readied herself to swim away. The pictures jumbled and merged with one another until Dana's eyes became the winking lens of the camera, until Violet spoke with Luce's father's voice.

Luce nestled her cheek against Dorian's olive jacket, trying not to think about the long months of winter still ahead of her. It was only December now. The worst was still to come.

* * *

"Why don't they turn on the lights?" Luce asked. She couldn't see anything, but somehow she knew that she was standing in a slick corridor with walls and floors of polished gray marble; maybe it was some kind of museum or a huge bank. *Standing,* Luce thought. That seemed peculiar, but then as she thought about it she couldn't understand why it should seem strange to her. Her sneakered feet squeaked against the slippery tiles.

"They must have all burned out," her father answered from somewhere beside her. "Lights burn out as quick as matches in these places. But I don't know how you're going to help me if we can't see where we're going."

Luce squeezed her eyes tight and then opened them again. Now there was a faint dusk glow coming from somewhere up ahead. "Are they in there?" Luce asked. The glow revealed the hard, glossy planes of the hallway, but for some reason it didn't allow her to see her father. She knew he was right there, though.

She could feel him as a kind of warm shadow, invisible but some-how more powerfully alive than a normal person would be.

"That would be the place," her father agreed. "I'm so glad you could come, Lucette. I've been trying and trying, but I can't get them out."

They were moving down the corridor, and Luce was vaguely relieved to find that she could hear his footsteps as well as her own. The glow ahead got gradually brighter, more sil-very, and then they turned a corner and entered a large window-less room. Blocks of ice much taller than she was were lined up around its gleaming walls, and each clear mass seemed to have a flaw at its core: a milky impurity. Those flaws were the source of the light, each of them dully luminous. Luce stepped closer, her heart pounding savagely, and saw that there was a mermaid frozen inside each block. And, Luce realized, she knew all of them: there were Rachel and Jenna, Regan and Kayley, Saman-tha and the red-haired larva Anais had tortured, along with other girls from the tribe. Luce spread her hands on the cold glassy blocks, leaning close to see. The mermaids' eyes were closed, their mouths open around knots of ice they could never swallow, but Luce felt sure they were still alive. She had to find the block with Anais, Luce thought. It was important to make sure that Anais was in here somewhere; if she wasn't she might cause terrible trouble.

"I can't get them *out*, Lucette," her father said. Luce forgot her search for Anais and turned to stare at him. He was visible now, oddly hunched and much older than he should have been. His curly hair looked dusty and brittle. "I've tried everything I can think of, but I just can't break through that ice . . ."

Luce looked at her pale blue sneakers on the gray marble floor. She understood what her father was trying to tell her, and shame overwhelmed her until she could barely stand. Her old tribe was trapped in frozen suspense as payment for the legs she was walking on, and there was only one way to free the mermaids. Her legs would have to be cut off, Luce realized, and her father was holding the saw . . .

Luce screamed in terror. Something was holding her fast, and the blade was coming closer. Her body twisted and whatever was gripping her middle bent like rubber and then ripped, and she screamed again as her eyes opened wide.

* * *

More darkness was around her, but now it was darkness she could see through. It took her a few moments to understand that she was back in her own small cave, and she lifted her hands to confirm their faint inhuman shine: she was still a mermaid. The wind moaned, and the clamor of her heart beat through it. Had that really been only a nightmare? There was still something catching at her middle and keeping her from moving freely. Luce looked.

A layer of ice covered the water in her cave. It was only an inch or so thick and peculiarly flexible in the way of freshly frozen salt water. Nilas, Luce remembered. That was what this weird elastic ice was called. Her struggle had wrenched part of it free of the water's surface so that a giant whitish air pocket shaped almost like an uneven skirt extended from Luce's rib cage and concealed most of her tail. Luce reached down and tore the nilas open, then slid deeper into the water. The ice layer wasn't that strong, she told herself; it hadn't even come close to trapping her for real. And horrible as her dream had been, it was torn like the ice now. There was nothing to be afraid of.

At least not just yet.

* * *

When the storm finally passed Luce swam weakly from her cave into a vague haze of blue daylight. It was a little warmer, and the film of ice had melted, much to her relief, but there was no way she could tell how many days she'd gone without eating anything. She was so hungry that her body veered sloppily through the water. It would be crazy to let herself get stuck without food like that again, Luce realized. She needed to plan ahead. Once she made it to her dining beach she looked for the little Inuit larva but there was no trace of her. Luce sat disconsolately cracking shellfish, trying to gather her strength.

Much as she wanted to find Dorian, there was something else she needed to do first. Luce gazed to the north. Pack ice came from there in a steady procession like a herd of pale animals. As soon as she could swim steadily again she'd head that way.

Two hours later Luce was skimming through her old tribe's territory, keeping underwater to avoid the ice but also to make it less likely that she'd be seen. She had to wait until she could catch one of the girls from the tribe out on her own, and that might take some time. Luce slipped behind a jag between the tribe's cave and their dining beach and waited. They were probably all still frightened enough of the orcas to stick near the cliffs.

It wasn't long before she heard the voices of the tribe as they swam back to their cave. Even from a distance they sounded shrill and irritable, all bickering at once. "If Anais says we're staying," Luce heard Jenna snap, "then we're staying! If you don't like it you can go look for a new queen!"

"Stop shoving me!" Kayley yelped just as someone else whose voice Luce couldn't place said, "But Jenna, that storm was so *horrible* . . ."

"Like they don't get storms in the winter south of here! Even if we went all the way to, like, Canada! What, you want to swim to Hawaii?" Jenna's tone was contemptuous, and she wasn't far at all from Luce now. "Go right ahead. Maybe you'll pass Violet's corpse on the way."

"I'm still . . . kind of worried about Dana," Kayley murmured, but everyone ignored her.

"Besides," Samantha added as the tribe flowed past Luce, "like Anais says, it would suck big-time if we ran into some other tribe. They'd probably be all hung up on the timahk, and we'd have to deal with all their stupid *issues*. And Anais thinks the ships are going to come back this way in the spring, so it really makes more sense to just wait here . . ."

Then they were gone, except for what sounded like a single straggler. It was just what Luce had been hoping for. She could hear the half-stifled whimpering of someone trying to keep the others from noticing that she was crying. Cautiously Luce skimmed around her crag and peered out. It was Rachel, dragging against the rocks with her head lowered so far that the strands of her pale blond hair formed a kind of cage around her face.

"Rachel!" Luce whispered. "Keep quiet, okay?"

Rachel recoiled as if the water was grabbing at her. Her head swung wildly around before she spotted Luce and jerked again, her pale eyes bright with fear. Even the magical beauty that all mermaids possessed couldn't save Rachel from looking a little mousy, Luce thought, and she felt an impulse to comfort her. Rachel was such a sad, scared, broken little thing. Tears gleamed on her cheeks, and her nose was running.

"Rachel! Don't be scared. It's just me, Luce."

"Are you going to kill me?" Rachel squeaked. But she was whispering, too.

Luce was shocked. "Of course not! Rachel, I would *never* hurt you. How could you think that?" When Luce had still lived with the tribe she'd given Rachel singing lessons, held her when she woke from nightmares. Why should Rachel look at her with that frantic, hunted expression?

"Because I . . ." Rachel started in surprise, then shook herself. "No reason. Except that you hate all of us, Luce."

Luce tried to calm her rising impatience. "I was mad at all of you because of Catarina. But that doesn't mean I *hate* you, Rachel! And I only hurt Jenna that time because she was trying to kill me." Rachel wobbled from side to side as if she couldn't make up her mind whether or not to dash away. "But you need to come with me for a few minutes," Luce added sharply, staring hard into Rachel's eyes. "There's something I have to show you, okay? It's really important."

Rachel was still wavering and gazing nervously around when Luce took hold of her wrist. She couldn't allow Rachel's neuroses to ruin her chance of getting a warning to her old tribe. Luce's nightmare of the ice blocks still had a terrible grip on her mind, and she knew it wouldn't let go until she'd made sure the other girls were safe.

Luce kept a firm hold on Rachel's wrist as she led her back to the tribe's dining beach. There was Catarina's sofa-shaped rock half-submerged as always in the lapping waves; there was the place where the black boat had bobbed with silent engines; there was the dense, rubbery seaweed matting the cliff wall, though now the leaves above the waterline were sleeved in brilliant ice. As long as the camera was still here and she could find it again . . .

Rachel kept twitching fearfully in Luce's grip, but Luce ignored her as she dove to search among the brown leaves below the tide line. Kelp swirled into their faces as they squeezed close to the wall, Luce ransacking the leaves and fronds. After a few minutes Rachel stopped struggling. "Luce? What are you looking for?"

"A camera," Luce told her absently. "I smashed it."

"A *camera*?" Luce couldn't have said if Rachel sounded more confused or more terrified. "Why would . . . what would . . . Luce, a camera here?"

After another minute Luce found it, its shattered lens still peeking blindly between two thick leaves, its black body wedged securely into a chink in the wall. Luce began wrenching leaves away until she'd cleared a pale circle of stone around it. "We need to make it easy to find again. So you can show everyone," Luce explained. "But you have to tell them you're the one who smashed it, Rachel, okay? You can't let them know I was here." If Anais thought the warning was coming from Luce she'd be sure to ignore it.

The two of them rose to the surface again. Cold wind licked their faces, and ice floes bucked on the lead-colored water.

"But Luce . . ." Rachel squealed. "Why would somebody put a camera here? What does it *mean*?"

Maybe it would have been better to find a different mermaid, Luce thought. Rachel was already close to panic. Luce hesitated for an instant and then decided that she couldn't afford to beat around the bush. She had to make sure Rachel understood exactly how serious the situation was.

"It means the humans know about us, Rachel," Luce said levelly. "It means they're watching us. It's lucky that I found this camera, but I'm sure it's not the only one."

Rachel opened her mouth wide as if she couldn't decide whether to argue or scream. In the dull blue-gray light she looked sickly, almost decaying. "But then . . ." Rachel gasped and stopped abruptly.

"The humans are going to come after us. I don't know when, but it could start anytime. They're going to hunt down the tribe," Luce announced, then waited a second for this to sink in. "You have to show *everyone*, Rachel. It's your job to make sure they understand. Do you hear me?" At first Rachel only gaped, but after a moment she pulled herself together just enough to nod. "You all have to get away from here. Find someplace where the humans aren't looking and stay hidden . . ." Luce heard how her voice was rising now, getting harder and more urgent. "No matter *what* Anais tells you, you all have to run away!"

* * *

When Luce came close to Dorian's village she saw that almost all the boats, including his rowboat, had been hauled out of the water and lined up on a bank dense with brown grass. The boats were all set upside down on trestles, probably to keep them from getting damaged by the ice. She and Dorian wouldn't be able to go to their secret cave anymore, Luce realized. Not until the spring. She doubled back and found him sitting on the snow-covered beach, almost exactly in the spot where she'd thrown him ashore six months earlier. He was doing homework and didn't notice her at first, and Luce watched him in silence. *Only six months ago*, Luce thought. How could so much have happened in such a short time? Dorian looked up and straight into her eyes.

"Hey, baby," he said sadly, and leaned out to kiss her. "Looks like we've lost the boat for a while."

She hadn't thought Dorian was beautiful when she'd first seen him, but she did now. He seemed gorgeous to her sitting there in the dusk with his dark blond-bronze hair and full pale lips, his amber-tinted skin, his air of tattered nobility. And, she realized, the dark sparkling of the indication was almost completely gone from around him. Luce felt oddly shy. She didn't want to tell him how she'd gone to warn the tribe, in case he was angry with her for risking another fight. After a second she decided not to mention the slick of ice covering the water in her cave either. But keeping quiet about all the important things left her with nothing to say. They were too close to his village here for her to sing to him.

Instead she kissed him. She kissed him fervently for hours, clinging to his shoulders as if something was trying to tear her away.

On her way home that evening Luce noticed a series of

dots in the water ahead of her. They appeared to be moving south, and her heart skipped hopefully. As quickly and quietly as she could Luce sped along below the surface, passing her own cave, until she was just close enough to confirm that what she'd hoped was true. Through the dim green water she could see the rapid, graceful flash of mermaid tails all swimming away together. Rachel had done her job well, Luce thought. The tribe was as safe as it could be now. If the humans found their old cave it would be nothing more than a vacant, garbage-strewn hole.

She stopped to gather a supply of oysters, then turned to go home. Once she was back in her own cave Luce realized that she was now truly the only mermaid living on this stretch of the Alaskan coast. She felt more alone than she ever had before, but she told herself it didn't make sense to feel that way. Not when she had Dorian.

* * *

A few days later Luce woke to find a fresh skin of ice covering the water of her cave. It was thicker than the time before, stretchy and as dark as the water below it. She tore through it easily enough, but she couldn't help imagining that soon it might be harder to break free. When she went to meet Dorian later that day she found that the water near the shore was covered by an elastic veil of nilas some three inches thick. It bellied and fell with the waves, tearing in places, so that sheets of soft ice over-lapped one another in ridges. Luce rounded the boulder that sheltered their meetings from view and looked at Dorian stand-ing on the far side of the bending ice. He was about twenty feet away from her.

"I could try to walk out on it," Dorian called doubtfully.

Luce felt sure it wouldn't support his weight. "Stay there, okay? I'll break through from the bottom." Luce swam along the seafloor until the ice ceiling pressed claustrophobically against her head, then drove herself upward. The ice sheet swelled above her while she drove up with her fists, finally bursting through at Dorian's feet. He knelt down, and his hands slid tenderly around her shoulders.

"Luce," Dorian said immediately, "I'm really getting worried." He was gazing out anxiously at the shuffling white blots of pack ice on the distant waves. "What if you got trapped under the ice somewhere and it was too thick for you to break and you couldn't breathe in time—"

"It wasn't like this last winter," Luce told him, as if that could change anything. "The tribe stayed here, and they said the ice wasn't bad at all . . ."

"Everyone says last winter was pretty unusual, though, like it was some kind of global-warming thing. But this year is already so cold, and the pack ice is coming like a whole month early . . ." Dorian's face was against hers as he spoke. His cheeks felt burning hot after the bitter chill of the Bering Sea.

"My cave's been freezing over," Luce admitted, and Dorian flinched as if she'd smacked him. She hadn't meant to tell him that, at least not yet, but somehow the words slipped from her.

"You're going to have to leave, Luce! You should really go *now*, today, before it gets any worse. And it might be months before you can get back here, and we can't even *e-mail* . . ." Dorian sounded despairing now. "Lindy says sometimes the ice doesn't start melting until March. Even April. Luce!"

He was right, of course. Luce didn't answer at first, just held him in her arms and tried to think of something she could do, some way she could keep reality at bay for a little longer. Nothing occurred to her. "I love you so much, Dorian," she whispered at last. She fought to hold back her rising tears and failed.

"I love you so much, too. You're really all I want, Luce. In the whole world . . ."

"What if . . ." Luce hesitated. "Dorian, what if I can never turn human again? Would it be better . . ." *Would it be better for you if I just stayed gone?* Luce thought. But she couldn't say the words out loud.

"I love you anyway. I *want* you to be human, Luce. I want to make a real life with you and grow up with you. But I'm in love with you no matter what you are." He pulled back just far enough to look at her. "You *promise* me you're going to come back? As soon as the ice breaks up?"

"I promise," Luce told him. His lips were brushing across hers, and his ochre eyes swayed across her vision like satellites.

"No matter what?" Dorian whispered. "You won't abandon me again?"

"No matter what. I'll be back as soon as I can."

"And you promise you'll be careful, Luce? You won't try any more of your crazy heroic stuff?"

"I'll be careful. But Dorian . . ." She squirmed in his hands, trying to pull back enough to look at him straight. She wasn't sure if she could say this.

"Baby?" He was trying to tug her close again, and Luce knew that once he did she wouldn't talk for a long time.

"Do you want me anyway? Even though I can't be with you the way a human girl could?" She'd almost choked on the words, but now they were out. Dorian's face was buried in her hair; she couldn't tell how he was reacting.

"Hearing you sing is better than that," Dorian murmured. His hands brushed every inch of her exposed skin from her fingertips up to her ears, and then his mouth found hers and kept it.

18

The Lost Island

Luce swam blindly away that night, barely conscious of the need to stay near the shore. Her sense of the geography was a bit hazy, but she knew she'd have to swim through Bristol Bay and then around the Alaskan Peninsula and through the Aleutian Islands. That might take a few days. On the far side she'd soon be beyond the reach of the worst sea ice, but she'd also be in areas that would probably have too many humans for comfort. But Luce had a vague memory of someone telling her that there were vast forests and wild cliffs along the coast south of Anchorage. There'd probably be caves along the waterline, and she'd find one and pass the winter in solitude. It would be lonely and maybe kind of boring, but she'd have plenty of time to practice her singing, and in a few months she'd swim home again.

Dorian would wait for her. He loved her no matter what.

The fact that they could love each other in spite of everything that stood between them proved that anything was possible. The important thing was to remember that so that she could face the long, dark months ahead bravely and not crack up somehow.

She skimmed along below the surface with the dark shore to her left. Her thoughts were so full of Dorian that she barely saw the clouds of silvery fish or the dipping seals, and hours passed in darkness. She felt nothing but the sinuous movements of her own swimming. It must have been morning when she finally stopped to rest somewhere along the peninsula. The coast was low and grassy and she couldn't find a cave, but the beach where she finally stretched out seemed isolated enough that humans probably wouldn't discover her there. Her tail fanned through the water, and her head rested on a patch of grayish sand.

Luce slept and woke with her whole body aching, convinced in the first few moments that Dorian was sleeping beside her and that he was somehow perfectly comfortable half-submerged in the Bering Sea. Then she realized how alone she was, and she shivered. She didn't even have his jacket to nestle in.

And, she suddenly remembered, there were still half a dozen of his library books stacked on a rock in her cave.

* * *

The constant bluish dimness made it hard to guess the time. Luce looked out on an inky sky and thrashing waves as she ate mussels and braced herself for the onward journey. The pack ice was thinner down here at least, and there was no nilas clinging to the shoreline. Her muscles were so sore that she was reluctant to face another long night of swimming, but this beach obviously wasn't a good place to stay for long. It was too open. If she hadn't been so exhausted she never would have stopped here at all.

The wind yowled and battered the stunted trees behind her. Luce pulled herself together and swam on, forcing herself to keep a steady pace for hours through the growing twist and push of the water. At first she tried to hug the shore, but as she went on the increasingly powerful currents threatened to overwhelm her. One towering wave caught her off-guard, swinging her high up through a blur of gray mist and then hurling her against the stone beach. For a few seconds she rolled, battered and confused, with her tail exposed and blasted by the stinging wind. She was only bruised, and she slipped back to sea on the next breaker that rolled in, but she couldn't escape the realization that she could easily be stranded beyond the reach of the water next time.

Luce drove herself through the heavy currents, heading into deeper waters. She didn't want to accept the possibility that a severe storm was gathering, but by the time the Alaskan Peninsula began to break into distinct, sharply peaked islands with huge slablike breakers rolling between them, it was becoming unmistakable. The only islands she could see had low, flat shores buffeted by the violent waves; there were no crags or caves where she could wait out the storm in safety.

She looked around hopelessly. At the bottom of each swell she could see nothing but sculpted walls of black water and whorls of bright foam. It was only as each wave lifted her that she could even glimpse those unwelcoming islands and the dark vacancy between them that might offer a way through to the other side. A few ice floes darted and pitched around her, and she had to dive abruptly to keep from being brained.

Luce sighed wearily and went on. There was no telling how long it would be before she could rest, though her tail muscles burned and her head swung heavily with the urge to sleep. The wind screamed as she surfaced again, and she strained to force her way against the current that seethed between the two islands in front of her. Billows of snow were falling, hissing like embers as they met the waves. Luce began to sing, trying to call a countercurrent the way she'd done before. If she could just make her way between those islands she might have a better chance of finding shelter.

The song-current came at her call, but this time it wasn't strong enough. The thrust of the water was still carrying her backwards, and the towering waves lifted and dropped her again and again. Each time the blow would knock all the breath from her lungs, and her voice would die until she could manage to reach the surface and seize another quick inhalation. Luce realized she'd never seen a storm like this before. It was fierce and unyielding, intolerant of any effort she could make to fight it.

An ice floe pitched at her so suddenly that she had no time to duck out of its path. With a sudden instinctive lunge Luce threw herself on top of the white coarse surface instead, almost skidding straight off its far side before she managed to get a grip on the jagged edges. The floe was longer than her body and roughly triangular, tapering to an end narrow enough that she could wrap her arms partway around it. She gasped in relief. Wildly as the floe bucked, harsh and dizzying as it was to ride it like a raft, it was still wonderful to stop struggling with the water. She let her tail go limp, let her fins flop over the brink. Shooting stars of pain coursed through her muscles, and she felt herself shuddering from sheer exhaustion.

So many waves were crashing over her that there was no chance her tail would dry out, at least. She pressed her cheek against the ice and accepted that the storm was stronger than she was. It was senseless to pretend she could fight it, and she closed her eyes and surrendered.

Luce clung hard to her ice floe as it lurched on wildly through frothing darkness that could be either night or day. She had no idea where she was going.

* * *

Again and again Luce drifted into a murky half-sleep, only to catch herself with a jolt as she began to slip from the ice floe that carried her. Sliding into these black, mountain-steep waves would probably kill her. She was so exhausted that she didn't think she'd be able to keep swimming long before her strength gave out and she sank weakly to impossible depths. Sometimes at the top of a tall surge she'd take advantage of the height by quickly scanning the horizon, but she couldn't see land any-where. Nothing but the rollicking waves, the flying gouts of foam and maddened snow.

She fell into a kind of trance, letting her mind lunge and spin with her body. Sometimes she saw white bursts of light on the inside of her closed lids; at other moments she thought she heard Nausicaa's voice. Her arms were racked with cramps and seemed paralyzed in their endless grip on the ice. Luce couldn't understand how she still had the strength to hold on, hour after hour. At one point her hands seemed to melt into an icy liquid and she almost let them give way, almost yielded to a fall with no end.

What matters is that you made the choice to save me as you did, Nausicaa whispered in Luce's ear. Her voice was so vivid and warm that Luce couldn't tell if it was dream or reality, but it broke through her trance and brought her back to awareness of her loosening hands. She tightened her grip on the floe again until its ragged edges scraped the soft skin of her inner arms.

It also mattered if she made the choice to save *herself*, Luce thought. And she was sure that Nausicaa would agree with her.

At some point the water turned strangely warm. At some point the floe stopped its feverish lunging and only pranced gently, knocking against a rocky pinnacle that stuck straight up out of the water. The wind still shrieked, but it seemed to pass by above without striking her anymore. More important, the waves barely sloshed across her tail. Luce looked up in a daze and realized that she'd arrived at a small conical island with a few dense patches of steeply leaning spruce and an uneven coast. Everything was padded in thick snow. The island didn't seem to be part of the Aleutian chain. There was nothing in sight but water, and far in the distance a dark blue line that could be either land or a ribbon of settling storm clouds.

Luce tumbled off the floe into shallow water. She'd barely

managed to drag herself to a spot where she could rest her head on the shore before she was seized by sleep.

* * *

There was a dull rattling noise. Luce shook herself, annoyed at the sound's intrusion on her sleep. She wanted to dream on, unmoving, for a hundred years. Her cheek squeezed harder against the pebble shore as if that could make the sound go away. That seemed to help, and Luce drifted again, dimly aware that there was something strange about the air here, the wind. The warmth of the water soothed her, and there was a vague whispering licking in and out of the breeze. There were sounds that were almost words, but she couldn't make out what they were trying to tell her. She slept on, dreaming that she was pressing her ear against the page of a whispering book, unable to understand the story.

The crunching noise came back, and this time her irritation was sharper. "Cut it out," Luce murmured. It was a regular, repeating sound of small pebbles grinding together. Then her eyes flashed wide open, taking in the feeble daylight, and she froze. That was the sound of human footsteps, and they weren't so far away. As lightly and silently as she could Luce slid back under the water, her heart throbbing frantically. There was no way to tell if she'd been seen. She skimmed behind the rocky pinnacle she'd knocked against the day before and then let her head glide upward very slowly until her eyes hovered just above the glinting skin of the water. She kept her movements as light and soft as drifting seaweed so that she wouldn't attract attention and peered around the edge of the rock.

A hunched human figure stood on the beach some thirty feet away from her. Clumps of brownish hair hid his face, and his tall frame was so heavily swaddled in crudely stitched-together seal skins that he barely looked human at all. His feet were wrapped in strips of fur bound together with grayish strands that Luce realized were probably dried intestines. He walked with a slow, shambling gait, his matted beard swaying. If he'd noticed Luce he gave no sign of it. Instead he just shuffled tiredly to the water's edge and stood there, staring down with sullen concentration.

The murmuring in the wind seemed to gather itself just a bit tighter, knot into sounds that were somehow closer to becoming actual words, though Luce still couldn't make them out. An electrical prickling brushed through her skin. Whatever it was she was hearing, she was sure she wasn't imagining it. The tone became a little softer, more like a whirl of blurred human voices; it sounded like a troop of invisible dancers who kept whispering insistently as they spun. Luce thought there was something disturbingly familiar about those voices. Hearing them felt like trying to recapture a lost memory. The memory kept purring and buzzing and hinting at itself but always stayed just out of reach . . .

She could hear the voices gusting in from all over the island, but they didn't pay any attention to her. Instead they seemed to concentrate around the ragged man, hissing and cooing to him. His face remained stock-still and expressionless even as the water in front of him began to eddy. The waves bubbled and coiled, and Luce could make out the flash of bright scales just below the surface. The whispering grew louder, bubbled like the water, then abruptly expired in a shrill hiss that sounded somehow like a command. There was a flash of leaping silver and translucent fins, and Luce couldn't stifle a gasp. A large pink-silver fish crashed down hard just inches from the man's feet. It beat its iridescent tail against the beach, its body arching and falling. The man bent and seized the fish with one hand then casually swung its head against the rocks, knocking it unconscious.

"Okay, already," the ragged man said loudly, staring into the whispering air just ahead of him. "At least let me have some peace while I eat, all right?"

Luce's tail gave an uncontrollable flip, sending up a shower of bright water, and a small sharp cry burst from her throat. The man didn't seem to notice. He was already straggling away from her, up the hill and into the woods, small dislodged rocks skittering down the slope behind him. Luce watched helplessly as he left. There was obviously some unknown magic at work here, but beyond that she didn't know what to think. After a while she saw a thin coil of smoke rising from the far side of the island and knew that the man was cooking his fish over an open flame.

There was something in the tone of those whispering voices that suggested faded memories, sleepless nights, and things lost forever. But the voices also suggested something more specific to Luce—or *someone*. The voices had seemed to be nudging at her, trying to recall someone to her. She just couldn't quite tell who it was.

But the man's voice had also seemed astonishingly similar to another voice Luce had once loved. And in his case she had no trouble recognizing whose it was.

He'd sounded exactly like her father.

19

Voices Remembered

Luce spent the next several days circling the island, getting her bearings and searching for the man she'd seen. Her memory of hearing her father's voice mingled with the muttering voices of the island, blurring and shifting until she wasn't sure what to think. Maybe the voices had unsettled her mind, colored her thoughts, tricked her. Probably that hadn't really been her father's voice at all, and the castaway living here was a stranger. After all, it seemed crazy to hope that her father could have made it to this obscure island after the *High and Mighty* went down. And even if he had, what were the odds that she'd have somehow washed up in the exact same spot? But if there was any chance, however slight, that Andrew Korchak was miraculously still alive and that she'd found him again—Luce could hardly let herself think about it—she'd do whatever it took to bring him safely home.

Sometimes she'd catch sight of the man in the distance, his shapeless figure perched on an outcropping of rock or pacing along a beach. But by the time she'd raced to the spot he was always gone, always climbing inland where she couldn't follow, and she'd go back to exploring. It was something to do, something to keep herself from thinking too much and sliding into alternating bouts of frantic hope and sluggish moodiness.

The island wasn't all that big, really, and the temperature of the water surrounding it varied from patches of uncomfortable, upwelling heat to areas that were almost as cold as it had been in her home territory. It was warm enough, though, that the shores were free of clinging ice. Ice floes drifted past, but there was none of the rubbery nilas that had formed in her old cave. It took Luce a day to realize that there must be underwater volcanic vents and that the steam she saw rising between rocks high on the island probably came from some kind of hot spring. The tiny waterfall she found in a bend of the coast was much warmer than the surrounding air and gave off an unpleasant mineral stench she couldn't identify.

The jagged coast bent into deep rocky inlets sheltered from crashing waves, then opened onto stretches of pebble beach. Shellfish massed along the shore, growing in heaps near the warm zones. Even if Luce spent the whole winter here there would definitely be plenty to eat. When she dove down to inspect the crevices where the hot water gushed, she found spiky, pink-legged, lobsterlike creatures; anemones with crimson extrusions like pulsing mouths; and ruffled, gelatinous animals in shades of mauve and saffron. She'd never seen anything like them before. She found strands of kelp and began wearing its leaves as a bikini top in case the man saw her again. There were no caves she could find, but other than that the island was an excellent place for her to wait out the winter.

Her only concern was the possibility that the man might come across her while she was asleep; even the island's most secret crevices wouldn't be completely inaccessible to a human. It seemed clear that the man was alone in this place, or as alone as he could be when every passing breeze carried swirls of formless chattering. But Luce had to admit to herself that he might be insane, even dangerous. And if he was some kind of sorcerer—which seemed fairly likely after the bizarre episode with the fish—she couldn't be certain that her own powers would be a match for his.

It would be better if he didn't realize she was here. Not until she could be completely sure.

* * *

The horizon was always lost behind choking clouds and webs of mist. But Luce was almost certain she'd seen a remote stripe of land when she'd first arrived, though she couldn't guess if it had been Russia or Alaska. Luce didn't like to admit she was frightened, but the idea of trying to return home in the spring seemed a little daunting. She lay sprawled in the hazy blue daylight, scanning the far horizon and hoping to catch sight of that distant land again. She was back on the same beach where she'd collapsed on her arrival, eating seaweed and daydreaming about Dorian. Assuming today was a weekday he was probably sitting in a classroom right now, drawing in the margins of his notebook as he half listened to the teacher. He would be thinking of her, sketching pictures of her face . . .

Something snapped in the woods at her back, and Luce spun around. The fur-clad man was standing twenty feet away under a shabby, half-dead birch tree. He was looking straight at her, though his face stayed strangely blank. The breeze was alive with whisperings, warm suggestions of excitement, and again Luce had the sinking, hungry sense that she knew more than one of those voices from *somewhere*.

Luce stared at the man. His face was mostly concealed by dangling clumps of hair and by his matted beard, but she could see his eyes. Wry and smart, the color of cinnamon. Luce tried to call out to him, but her throat felt like one big knot and no sound came.

He wasn't even looking at her anymore. His gaze drifted somewhere over her head, and his mouth tightened with annoyance.

"Oh, that's not right," Andrew Korchak complained vaguely to the air. "That's just going too far!"

The floating voices seemed agitated. They sounded as if they were engaged in a passionate conversation, whispering urgent confidences into one another's invisible, shapeless ears. And Luce was more certain than ever that the voices were gathered around her father, circling him like a swarm of bees. And though she couldn't have explained why, she also had the distinct impression that the voices were suddenly *aware* of her, and that they hadn't been before. Cold ran through her body like a sickness and she struggled to regain control of herself. She had to say *something*.

"Dad?" Luce finally managed, but the word cracked in her throat. Her father stayed where he was, dully striped by the shadow of the birch tree. He didn't so much as glance at her.

"I told you," he snapped at the air, waving one calloused hand in disgust. "That'll be *enough*."

He spun on his heel—the movement was much more energetic than the weary shambling Luce had noticed before—and stalked back up the hill.

Luce gazed after him, torn by shock and grief and, as a few wisps of muttering air grazed against her face, by an icy panic that squeezed up inside her and crawled like fingers over her heart. Garbled whispers began to leak into her ears and dance under her skull. She could feel a kind of frothing breath glide across her tongue and explore her throat. Luce gasped, horrified at the awareness that there was no way she could fight this shapeless invasion of her body. For the first time Luce began to sense a few distinct phrases in the muttering flow that echoed through her head. *"Battery's going,"* Luce thought she heard, and *"getting too small for her."* Then, *"If I didn't love you so damned much . . ."* Somehow it was worse to know what they were saying, and a long, unwilled shriek unraveled through the air.

Only in the abrupt silence that followed did Luce understand that she was the one who'd screamed. There was a kind of lull as the strands of wind gradually vacated her head. She could feel them go, hissing out of her nostrils and cascading over her lower lip. Tears flooded her cheeks. Her heart was beating so fast that it felt like one sustained, rolling roar in her chest. More than anything she wanted to dive, to slash away from this haunted, hideous place and never return. But as long as her father was trapped here that was the one thing she couldn't even consider doing . . .

The muttering winds backed off a little, and Luce could

hear them hissing again as if they were debating something. And Luce's terror began to yield to rage. Whatever these airy presences were they had control of her father, and they'd torn his mind apart until it seemed that he couldn't even recognize his own *daughter* anymore. She could hear a cluster of voices just above the steeply sloping beach and feel a subtle flickering motion in the air as they approached her again. Luce sat up straight, low waves curling around her waist, and faced in the voices' direction. It was hard to glare at them when they were invisible, but she did her best. They stopped in front of her, moaning and sighing, and Luce got the distinct impression that they were making an unaccustomed effort.

"*Child of Proteus,*" one crackled, old-sounding voice breathed distinctly, and a fingertip of oily wind stroked along Luce's closed lips. "*We have no need of you.*"

A sensation like freezing gusts of static swept through Luce's skin, and at the same time outrage flared inside her. What did she care what these uncanny voices needed?

"*We have the man. We have the memory. We have the man,*" the voice pursued. Its speech was halting and ragged, as if forming these words was an act of strenuous labor. "*He has lost much. We do not need you here.*" Now the voice sounded very determined; its tone was that of someone entirely convinced that everything was settled and that no further argument was possible. Luce considered the best way to respond, but she could already hear the airy babble sailing away from her. The ash-colored grass at the top of the beach churned in one abrupt swirl as it passed. The voices were almost at the edge of the forest. They were heading the same way her father had gone.

"Wait," Luce called after them. Her voice still sounded strange, broken and peculiarly empty. "What *are* you?"

There was no response. The empty gray sky rolled over the island's snowy peak, and the sickly trees groaned and fidgeted in the wind. They bent as if they were trying to scratch themselves and couldn't quite reach the spot that itched so terribly. Everything was gray and ash and dull, sad green apart from a few blots of golden lichen growing on the boulders. Still, Luce realized, the day was a little brighter than it had been recently, and it seemed to be lasting longer as well. The night's door was starting to swing slowly open again.

A miserable thought occurred to Luce: she'd blamed Catarina for murdering her father. Even worse, Miriam had committed suicide in the belief that the mermaids were responsible for making Luce an orphan. And now Luce knew that wasn't true at all.

Her father was still alive, and dark, delicate, vulnerable Miriam—Miriam who'd cared for Luce and tried to be friends with her—had died for nothing.

* * *

Each day the sun flung itself a bit higher above the horizon. Each day the patch of brightness where the sun burned behind endless clouds hovered for a little longer before dusky blue swallowed the sea again. Luce circled the island restlessly, always looking for her father. But it was soon clear that he was looking out for her as well. Whenever Luce glimpsed him on a distant beach he'd be scanning the waves, and the instant he caught sight of her he'd hunch his shoulders angrily and stomp off into the woods. It was impossible for Luce to guess how much he understood about the girl in the water, but two things were obvious: he was determined to avoid her, and he'd figured out that she couldn't follow him inland. Luce got the impression that he came to the beach now only to get fish and then left as quickly as he could.

Even the voices didn't pay any more attention to her, though she sometimes heard them jostling and sighing in the trees or tumbling like a cluster of argumentative molecules along the beaches. Usually the noise of their chattering meant that her father was somewhere nearby, and Luce would dart along searching for him. If she saw his bundled shape through the snow-laced trees she'd call out to him. Each time he'd act as if he hadn't heard her, and each time her hope would crack again. It wasn't that her heart broke, exactly; Luce clung stubbornly to the idea that eventually she'd get her father back to the mainland, even if she had no idea how she'd manage it. But every time he ignored her call it was as if a fresh hairline fracture ran through her, a fine trace of pain, until her chest seemed to be webbed through and through by thin, cutting wires. And these moments of grief were all that relieved the tedium of her days.

Luce spent her time daydreaming, mulling over memories of her childhood with her father, of more recent times with Dorian and Nausicaa, Dana and Catarina. She couldn't even soothe her frustration by singing. There was no way she could be sure her father wouldn't hear her, and he was already a broken man, spirit-needled, ridden by the gasp and twitter of bodiless voices. Even a healthy human could easily go completely insane at the onslaught of mermaid song. Dorian could withstand it as long as

Luce was careful, but he was exceptional. Luce couldn't bear to think of what her song might do to her father in his damaged condition.

The days slowly brightened, and the approach of spring struck Luce as inexplicably threatening. But the waves were still dotted by pack ice, though not nearly as much of it as there had been back in her home territory, and the wind was still bitterly cold. Storms rolled through now and then, though in the comfort of the island's sheltering coves Luce didn't mind them at all. Spring might be coming but it was still far away, and Luce told herself that she'd definitely rescue her father in time to keep her promise to Dorian and be home as soon as the ice broke up. It might be late January now, or maybe it was already February. She had at least another month.

And if she had to be a little late, well, Dorian would wait for her. Wouldn't he?

* * *

One day Luce woke to a dab of sunlight playing on her face and looked up to see a rip in the clouds and behind it a patch of sweet, pale, porcelain blue, utterly different from the murky dusk blue she'd lived in for months now. She stretched luxuriantly for a minute. For all her dread of the coming spring, that bolt of sunlight and clear sky sent exhilaration coursing through her body. She thought of swimming far out—far enough that there was no chance her father would hear her—and letting her pent-up song shimmer up to meet the pale sun. She was in her favorite little cove, its small beach tucked between two tongues of rock. Luce rolled onto her stomach and looked at the wet stones gleaming in the unexpected sunlight. The golden shine was interrupted by the shadows of a few birch trees high above her and by another lumpier shadow that Luce couldn't identify. Possibly it was the shade thrown by a small boulder with a few ferns swaying on its crest, though now that she thought of it, she didn't remember any boulders up there.

The shadow-shape tipped like something shifting its weight. Luce realized that what she'd taken for the shadow of ferns was cast instead by wind-stirred hair. And with the shadow's movement came a sudden burst of breezy muttering.

Luce froze and forced herself not to look up right away. If she stared straight at him she was sure he'd bolt again. Instead she pushed herself up on her elbows and gazed into the clouds, slowly tilting her head until she could just see him out of the corner of her eye. He was crouching up on the rocky shelf to her left, no more than fifteen feet away, shapeless in his mass of furs. And he was watching her. Maybe, Luce realized with a rush of anxiety and longing, he'd been watching her for hours as she slept. Above her the whirlwind of voices gabbled and spun. Then another, stronger voice interrupted them.

"You know," Andrew Korchak snapped irritably, "my Lucette wasn't actually that pretty. Beautiful girl, okay, but not like *that*. And I don't know where you got the idea she had a tail!"

So he *did* recognize her, at least in some confused way. He just didn't believe that what he was seeing was really his daughter. Very gradually and gently Luce turned her head a little farther. Her stomach clenched so tight it felt like wadded foil, nauseous and aching. Anything she said might send him running again, but at the same time she couldn't let the opportunity to finally speak with him slip away from her. "If you'll talk to me," Luce said softly, "I'll tell you about the tail. I'll tell you everything that's happened to me, and then we can try to figure out how to get you out of here." And at last she turned far enough to meet his eyes.

She knew he must have heard her—he just wasn't that far away—but from the blank look on his face it seemed as if she hadn't spoken or as if her words were meaningless. His eyes slipped around, always focusing just over the top of her head or just to the side of her face. He looked tired and much older than Luce remembered. Gray knots mixed with his matted brown curls, but his warm cinnamon eyes were still the same. Clouds gusted across the sun so that his face flared with golden light and then dimmed again, and for a minute he hunched there unspeaking.

"I've been waiting for you to knock it off," he said at last. "Bad enough you take Luce's voice and torture me with it all the time. I know how completely I let her down without that! But now using her face, too . . ." He shook his head. "It's too mean. It's just too damned cruel. I'm about ready to starve myself to death so I don't have to *see* this anymore!"

Luce's eyes burned with tears. "You *never* let me down! I won't let you say that you did." It was horrible to realize that her presence on the island was tormenting him this way. "Dad, I know you don't believe it, and it *is* hard to believe that I found you like this, but it's really, *really* me! I'm your daughter, Luce. Lucette Gray Korchak. My mother was Alyssa Gray, and you loved her so much, and she died when I was just four, and we were both there with her when it happened . . ."

Did he hear her this time? Something sparked deep in the vacancy of his eyes.

And, Luce realized, he wasn't the only one that heard her. The cloud of voices was spinning faster, fizzling with agitation. Luce suddenly remembered the sound of wasps drunk on the fermented apples in autumn at a campground where they'd stayed. The windy gibbering got louder as if it wanted to drown her out, and then to her horror Luce suddenly recognized one of the voices in that tangled muttering. It was her own voice, but higher, fresher and more childish than it was now: the voice she'd had as a much younger girl. Luce listened, mesmerized and sickened, trying to catch what her voice was saying, what evil things it might be murmuring into his ears—

Andrew Korchak pitched a rock. It just missed Luce's shoulder and splashed down in the water behind her, jarring her from the dark dreaminess that had flooded her mind. "I'm warning you!" her father snapped in exasperation. "Now, I know you need to keep me alive. How long would you have to wait to get yourself a new sucker way out here? So don't *push* me!"

He started to stand up. Luce gaped up in desperation. Would he ever let her talk to him again? She cast around wildly for something she could say, anything that might convince him . . . "I'll prove it to you! I'll tell you something only the two of us could know about, something we both remember . . ."

That seemed to surprise him, and he stared straight at her for the first time. A look of furious incredulity burned in his eyes. "Now that's a joke," her father snarled at last. "Like there's *anything* I remember that you don't know about, when you've been feeding off my brains for the last two years!"

Luce stared back and saw that tears were streaming into his snarled beard. He stood up, breathing hard, and scowled around at the empty sea. He looked dazed, and Luce saw him teetering as he walked off into the woods, knocking into the snow-laden trees so that clumps of white dropped to the earth behind him.

Then Luce was left alone with the invisible voices. They hummed toward her in a rattling cloud, throwing up flecks of snow and dead grass. Voices tore at the air like a hawk ripping into a still-struggling rabbit, then poured down over the shelf of rock to jostle around Luce's head and scream straight into her mind.

They were enraged.

20

Something Real

"It's exactly like you thought!" The young agent with the shaved head had practically thrown himself across Ben Ellison's desk, and he was twitching with excitement. "We followed up on that geoelectric survey you ordered. Searched all the caves that showed up on the scan. The divers found two caves with under-water entrances and all kinds of stuff in them, like they'd been inhabited—the bigger one you can only get to through a tunnel that opens up seven fathoms under the waterline at *low* tide! No way it was people who dragged all that junk in there! We're still working on an inventory. But one thing's for sure: these tails like to *party*. Empty liquor bottles all over the place."

Ben Ellison nodded wearily. Ever since the Secretary of Defense had decided to join forces with the FBI and throw as many resources as he could into tracking down the mermaids,

Ellison had been working until well past midnight every night and then getting up again by five. The clock in the corner of his computer's screen showed that it was already after one in the morning. He was so tired that he couldn't even remember this young man's name, and he didn't particularly want to. It was all he could do to tolerate the hordes of incompetents who'd been assigned to work under him recently; keeping track of who they all were seemed like an unnecessary bother. He didn't plan to stay in Anchorage any longer than he had to, anyway. "And the other cave?"

"A lot smaller. A lot less stuff. But what's so incredible about that one—you're not going to believe this—I brought the items they found to show you, because it's too nuts unless you see it for yourself . . ."

Ellison was mildly annoyed by the suggestion that there was anything he couldn't believe, and he glared impatiently as the pale young man hoisted a black leather duffle onto the desk and unzipped it, pulling out a small portfolio. At first Ellison winced at just how predictable the contents were. In fact, the portfolio held exactly what he'd been bitterly sure the search would turn up, sooner or later: Dorian's drawings, creased and rumpled but utterly unmistakable, all showing the same dark-haired mermaid whose portrait Ellison kept neatly folded in an inside pocket.

Ellison looked up. "You say these weren't in the main cave?"

"Nope. In a way smaller one, almost forty miles down the coast. But Agent Ellison, the drawings weren't all that was in it . . ." The young man was unfolding something bulky with his pale, nervous hands, and there was a glow of obvious triumph on his face and a smirk twisting his chapped lips. "Look!" It was an olive wool parka, salt-stained and mildewed, with a bright orange lining. At first Ellison didn't see what was remarkable about it until the pale hands waved it directly in his face and he saw the heavy black letters traveling down one sleeve.

"Dorian," Ellison sighed. There was no way he could protect the boy now.

"Dorian! You see . . . Doesn't that prove . . . It's like Smitt kept saying: Dorian Hurst has been in collusion with them . . . maybe plotting . . ."

"It shows he's under their influence at least." Ellison kept his voice measured. He wanted to defend Dorian, but he couldn't afford to sound like he cared too much. "Not surprising, considering what we know about the power they have. Those are Dorian's drawings as well."

"They . . . his drawings?"

"Yes. I found similar ones in his room. I noted that in my report at the time." Ellison was disturbed to realize that his tone was audibly defensive. He had to be more careful, keep tighter control of himself if he didn't want people to start suspecting him of sympathizing with their quarry. "Was that all you found? In the smaller cave?"

"There's something else. I . . . Maybe you can make sense of this, because I sure can't . . ." A stack of books was hauled from the duffle bag. From the white numbered tags on their spines it was immediately obvious that they were library books.

Puzzled as he was, Ellison couldn't help smiling. "I imagine those are overdue?"

The young agent didn't seem to think that was funny. "They're way overdue, yeah. And get this . . ." The young agent assumed an air of great significance. "They're all checked out in Dorian Hurst's name!"

Ellison felt a rush of exhaustion so intense that it threatened to sweep him into unconsciousness, and he leaned his head on his hand and gazed through half-closed lids at his keyboard and the scattered papers crowding his desk. He strained to understand the implications of everything he was learning, but his thoughts bent with dreamlike illogic. Maybe the separate caves meant that Dorian's girlfriend lived apart from the other mermaids, or maybe she just kept a secret stash. Maybe the books had been brought to the cave by seals.

"Agent Ellison?"

He shook himself. "Yes?"

"There is . . . I mean . . . You'd agree that there's absolutely no possibility that one of these tails knows how to *read*, right?" The young agent almost tittered the last words, but there was a look of anxious uncertainty in his eyes.

Ellison flinched with annoyance. The young man's shrill tone grated on him, and he found the words distasteful as well. He wasn't surprised that Secretary Moreland had taken to calling the mermaids "tails." Moreland was a crude man, and it was the kind of ugly, demeaning language that Ellison expected from him. But there was no reason everyone else should copy him.

Instead of answering, he reached to pull a thick, glossy book off the stack in front of him. *The Complete Novels of Jane Austen*. It struck him as an incongruous choice for a fifteen-year-old boy. The pages were warped, and the cover's image of a carriage passing among lush trees was dotted with mold. Ellison turned the volume in his hands, wondering what it meant. Something was sticking out between the pages, and he opened the book to see what it was. A leathery brown strip of dried seaweed fell onto his desk.

A bookmark, Ellison realized.

Had Dorian been teaching her how to read? Had he also taught her English? When Ellison had watched Dorian and the mermaid together he'd been a good distance away, wearing excellent noise-canceling headphones in case she started singing, but there were moments when her lips were certainly moving; it might have been some kind of English lesson. If she'd mastered human language already, well, she was an astoundingly quick learner. But Ellison preferred this idea to any of the unthinkable alternatives. Still, it was hard to see how a mermaid could enjoy Jane Austen or even have the foggiest idea of what her stories were talking about. A mermaid would have no way to comprehend descriptions of horses or houses, dresses or dining tables . . .

The young agent stared slack-jawed at the dried seaweed, then turned to Ellison. "That isn't . . ." he began, and then gulped pitifully.

"I wouldn't make too many assumptions about what the possibilities are here," Ellison told him as coolly as he could. "At this point we all need to keep our minds open and simply consider the evidence." He felt a little sick, though. His *daughter* liked Jane Austen. Once again he thought what a terrible shame it was that Dorian hadn't followed through on Ellison's request for an introduction to this mermaid. Ellison couldn't imagine anything more fascinating than actually talking to her and hearing what she might say for herself or about her life in the sea. Her reasons for killing . . .

Blearily Ellison glanced at the other books and then began to laugh. *Our Endangered Seas, Moby-Dick* . . .

"We don't need to consider possibilities that are crazy!" the young agent shrieked. "Some freak of a tail was *not* reading Jane Austen!"

Once he got some sleep, Ellison thought, he'd see about having this idiot reassigned to some much less important investigation. But he'd have to remember who the hell he was first. And, he recalled with an effort, there was something else he needed to know. Something urgent. He rubbed his hand across his face and then remembered.

"These caves were both iced over?" Ellison asked.

It took the young agent a moment to catch up with the change of subject, but then he nodded his stubbly head. "Foot-thick ice in both of them, yeah. The teams had to use drills to open up a way through to the shore. Rotten conditions everyone's been working in."

"And of course . . ." Ellison pursued. "Of course I would have been informed immediately if there was any indication that the inhabitants were still using these caves or that they'd been in them recently? Any sign that . . ." He couldn't think clearly enough to finish the sentence.

"Oh—the caves were abandoned weeks ago!" The shaved head nodded emphatically. "*That's* obvious."

"Why obvious?"

"Well—the ice, the garbage. Mold on everything . . ."

"So you're also making the assumption that mermaids are good housekeepers, then? They don't read Jane Austen, and they certainly can't stand a mess?" Ellison asked sarcastically, but he didn't actually care about the answer, and he barely listened to the sputtering reply.

If the mermaids were gone, even temporarily, then he didn't need to keep worrying that Dorian would be murdered. At least not for now. In the morning he'd give orders to have both caves continually monitored in case the mermaids returned.

The stubble-headed young man was still talking as Ellison got up, not pretending to pay attention anymore, and dropped to lie flat on his back on the worn beige carpet. He didn't even know if the gray haze that clouded his mind was sleep.

* * *

Steve and Ryan had been bickering over their new lyrics for so long that Dorian got bored and slumped down in an armchair in the corner, his sketchbook propped on his knees. Drawing Luce felt like falling into a familiar dream: a long, wave-rocked story that always seemed to pick up where it had left off but never actually got any further along, much less reached a conclusion. There was the same dark, spiky hair taking shape now on the page; the same long, smoky eyes; the mouth he'd kissed until the icy air numbed the rest of his face and all he'd felt was her. He hadn't understood how awful it was going to be: waking up every day and performing all the normal, repetitive tasks without any way to know whether or not she was still alive. Drawing her was the closest he could come to touching her. He could call to her face where it lived like a secret deep inside him and watch it emerge onto the page, a ghost formed from paper and black ink.

At first, drawing Luce had made missing her just a little

easier, eased the hollowness in his chest. Recently, though, his drawing had started to make him feel even worse, but he still couldn't stop. Now he drew the sinuous curve of her tail in one smooth stroke of black, then added the fins sweeping up behind her head. In the past whenever he'd reached into the water to stroke Luce's fins they'd curled in a shocked, sensitive way around his fingers. He remembered those fins now, pale green and translucent and sleek with silvery lights . . .

"Working on your comic book again?" Dorian hadn't noticed Zoe coming over to him. One fuzzy black sleeve of her oversized sweater brushed against his neck as she perched on the armrest and leaned in. She pulled her legs up against her chest, rubber heels digging into the upholstery, and wobbled precariously. Apart from the sweater she was wearing tight black jeans and combat boots carefully splattered with hot pink paint that matched her shoulder-length hair, at least when the dye job was fresh. Right now her hair had two inches of brown roots and streaks where the pink had faded into a peculiar peachy blond. As usual she was leaning too close to him, until she seemed to be on the verge of tumbling into his lap.

"Oh—yeah," Dorian muttered absently. Practice drawings for a graphic novel he was starting. That was what he'd told everyone. He'd also told them that his family had died in a plane crash. He wished everyone would stop asking him questions so that he could be relieved of the constant need to lie. It got tiring.

"It's not something you'd expect a guy to draw all the time. Mermaid after mermaid after mermaid. Where are all the *guns,* man? No one's going to read your story without more guns."

Zoe's voice was mocking as she bent messily out over the page, her sweater brushing across Dorian's nose as she leaned down to take a closer look. He smelled lavender soap and musty wool. "Actually it's always the same mermaid, huh? Is that like your main character? Of the whole story?"

"She's going to be. I'm still mostly doing character sketches." Dorian tried to shift away a little.

"Do you ever draw real stuff? From life?" Zoe lost her balance on the armrest and caught herself by throwing one leg across Dorian's lap so that her boot slammed into the seat cushion next to his hip, then smiled at him crookedly as she pulled the leg back much more slowly than she needed to. She was sixteen, with a snub nose and soft cheeks. Her greenish hazel eyes were round and thickly lashed, gazing into his face as if they were trying to discover something there. Dorian noticed that Steve was scowling at them from the far side of the room.

Dorian tried to act oblivious. "I mean I have. I took this community college class in Chicago where they brought in models sometimes. But I don't usually."

"Because I could pose for you. Right? Wouldn't it be more of a challenge to draw something real?" Now there was a distinct edge of contempt in Zoe's voice, and she flicked her hand toward the page on Dorian's lap. "Instead of just getting all obsessed with some *fantasy*?"

21

Forgetting

The voices roiled over Luce's head in a storm of outraged hissing. Tongues of air darted down to prod at her, squeal inside her
ears, claw her lips. Luce curled on her side with her head on the
shore, her lips pinched tight and her hands pressed over her
ears, but even so threads of wind wormed their way between
her fingers and up her nostrils until shrieking flowers seemed to
blossom in the core of her brain. The voices were too angry to
form words. They only yowled, the din they made gradually
amplifying as it beat back and forth inside her skull. Her head
ached with horrible seething pressure, and rip tides of shrill
snarling whipped the inside of her skull. Frantically Luce
thrashed her way under the water, trying to shake the voices
out of her head, but it was no use. "Stop it!" Luce yelled at
them. "Get out of me!"

To Luce's surprise the voices calmed down a little, as if they were considering this. She lay squeezed against the pebbled seabed. A spindly gray crab stalked just in front of her eyes while above her the water rippled like a low ceiling of molten glass. Luce watched the surface boil as one voice oozed back out of her ear, followed by another, then another. The tearing pressure in her head began to ease a little, and Luce broke the surface again. She was determined to hold back the screams that seemed to snake inside her throat until she couldn't be sure if they belonged to her or to the voices. She could feel whispering presences clinging around the edges of her face, nosing at her with hostile curiosity, but at least most of them were out of her head. There were just a few buzzing, muttering stragglers still wandering through her brain.

"*Child of Proteus,*" the same weary voice she'd heard before groaned. It seemed to be flicking around the rim of her left ear. "*We do not want you here! You hurt the memories. You hurt the man.*" The tone became snappish, impatient, as if the voice felt terribly put out at having to explain something so obvious. "*Leave us.*"

"What *are* you?" Luce demanded. She strained for self-control, fought a mass of tangled impulses to shout and weep and beg for mercy all at once. "I'm not leaving, so just tell me what you are!"

"*Leave!*" the voice retorted fretfully. "*Leave! With you here the man forgets sometimes to remember. With you here he thinks of the world he sees before him, of whether your face will appear in the water! We have the memories,*" it added, and this time it sounded almost plaintive.

Around Luce the other voices babbled in agreement. She couldn't make out words, but she could feel a chorus of eager emotions, all nagging and wheedling with the urge to drive her away. Luce began to feel a little less frightened. There was something pitiful about the voices, sick and uncanny as they were.

"I've got as much right to be here as you do," Luce snapped, then tried to think up some reason they would have to accept. There was one thing they definitely seemed to know about her. "Proteus gave his children the oceans. I have the right to stay wherever I want as long as I don't leave the water!" Luce didn't actually know if this was true or not, but the voices reacted instantly. She could hear them bubbling over with consternation, squeaking and hissing to one another like a litter of blind puppies that someone was poking with a stick. "You don't want to make Proteus angry," Luce added, then stopped abruptly, afraid she'd gone too far.

The voices had retreated a few feet up the beach, and suddenly Luce caught the thread of a different voice: not at all the gruff, crumbling voice that had spoken to her earlier, but a woman's, relaxed and sweet and confident. Luce knew from the first instant that she'd heard it many times before, long ago but also perhaps more recently. "If we get a little girl," the voice said clearly, "what would you think about calling her Lucette? Carly told me it means 'little light' and that's just what she's going to be for us. Our own little light in a world that . . . isn't necessarily the brightest place."

Luce felt a painful stillness seize hold of her heart, and all her efforts at self-control gave way as hot tears welled in her eyes. She understood at once what she was hearing. It was her mother. Actually, she realized, it was her father's *memory* of her mother talking to him before Luce was even born. This was what her father meant when he'd said that the voices had been "feeding on his brains," what the voices themselves meant when they told her that they had his memories . . . Luce went stone still, yearning only to hear more, to forget the world around her completely. *"Oh, now, that's real pretty,"* her father's voice answered out of the invisible swarm. *"I'm not as crazy about Lucy, though. Had a probation officer called Lucy once, and she was a serious nutjob. So if we're gonna call the little one something for short . . ."*

"Luce," Alyssa Gray said, and Luce jumped with the longing to answer her. In the next instant, though, she realized that her mother wouldn't hear her no matter how she called. The voice she'd heard was trapped in the past, but now the past was all Luce wanted. She waited in frozen silence for the conversation to continue, but it seemed to be breaking up, sinking back into senseless mutterings, scattered half-words. The whirl of voices was sliding closer to her again, but this time Luce was eager to let it come. Her lost mother was in there somewhere, the mother she barely remembered, sweet but also unexpectedly cynical. Even if Alyssa was no more than a memory, an empty wraith, Luce might finally get to know her in the only way she still could.

It wasn't Alyssa's voice that emerged from the swarm. *"Child of Proteus,"* the old, laborious voice hissed. *"Leave."* Now its tone was high-pitched and questioning and maybe, Luce thought, just a little scared. It was begging her to go.

Luce wanted to scream from sheer disappointment. She wanted to yell, *Bring my mother back!* But there was some subtle impulse that restrained her, some insight that she couldn't quite put words to. She knew only that asking the voices to repeat the past for her was the wrong thing to do. No matter how much she wanted to hear Alyssa again, it would be a terrible mistake.

It took a powerful effort of will for Luce to ignore her longing and concentrate on the present. If she was going to win her father back from the voices she had to understand them much better than she did now.

"Tell me what you *are*," Luce insisted. "I want to know."

The old voice moaned, and a dried leaf lying on the beach not far away abruptly crumpled as if crushed in an invisible fist. The other voices clacked with agitation, and bits of dead grass ripped with peculiarly sharp movements up and down the beach. The voices obviously thought she was being unreasonable, but apparently they couldn't actually *force* her to go.

"*We are your lost hopes,*" the voice explained at last. It sounded as if each word was something painfully carved from old bones. Luce suddenly understood how hard it was for the voices to do anything except repeat the past. Creating new sentences seemed to be a form of torture for them. "*We are the ring rolled away down the drain, the words you should have said, and should have said, but that you left instead under the water . . .*"

The voice gave out, its final words trailing away in exhaustion. Luce was momentarily distracted by the mention of the ring. Someone had told her a story like that once. It had been an old wedding ring that rolled away, the only memento of someone's grandmother . . . Alyssa's grandmother. Her father had dropped the ring as he and Alyssa were on their way to get married in Vegas, and Alyssa probably could have lunged and caught the ring in time if only she hadn't been holding their new baby in her arms . . .

"*Leave now?*" the voice breathed hopefully.

Once again Luce had to fight her way back to the present. What the voice had told her wasn't enough, and she couldn't afford to stop asking questions. "Why do you want the man?" Luce demanded. "Can he leave?"

That upset the voices again. They rushed at Luce, gabbling and tugging at her, but for some reason they seemed wary of actually forcing their way inside her head again. Instead they only lashed her cheeks with fronds of breath, squeaked and gibbered to her. "*And how 'bout for a boy?*" Luce suddenly heard her father's voice asking, but it was immediately swallowed by the chaos of random whisperings.

A few seconds of choked, scrambled syllables followed, then Luce's heart stopped as she heard her mother speak again. "*Oh, we'll definitely call him Peter,*" Alyssa announced, deadpan, and there was a shocked pause before her father cracked up laughing. "*You think anybody but me knows what a sharp edge you've got behind that sweet face, babe? You know Peter's nowhere close to being over you . . .*" The laughter spun around Luce's head, ruffling her hair, before it fell apart into a series of disconnected bleating sounds. Again longing stabbed through Luce; she was consumed by desire to know exactly how her mother had replied. Her words would be playful but also acerbic. And smart, and quick, and full of life . . .

"*The man,*" the crackling voice said then paused. It sounded wounded, as if Luce had deliberately said the cruelest thing possible. "*He has lost much.*" The words were becoming slurred.

Luce realized that the voice wouldn't be able to sustain the discussion much longer. It was sapped by the effort of forming new words, new thoughts. *"We have no need of you,"* it added, but now its words were so drafty and misshapen that Luce could barely make them out. The snarl of speaking winds around her head was dissolving, leaking away up the beach.

Then she was left alone again in her narrow cove, stone walls rising on both sides of her, green waves cresting in at the opening. Clouds were pouring across the sky, blotting out the fresh golden sunlight she'd seen earlier that day, and the now-voiceless wind blew a few spatters of cold rain into her face.

Rain, Luce realized after a second. Not snow.

Spring might be coming faster than she'd thought. And she wasn't any closer to rescuing her father from this nightmare of an island, this place where all his sweetest and most heartbreaking memories were constantly dragged from his mind and then flung back at him. Where he had to lose everything—his wife and his daughter and his hopes—over and over again . . .

There was something important in what the gruff spirit-voice had told her, Luce realized. It hadn't told her much, but somewhere in its jumbled words there was a hint, an unwitting clue to how she could finally get through to her father. If she could only put her finger on exactly what that hint had been, she'd know how to convince Andrew Korchak that she was real. The real, actual Luce and not just some haunting memory.

The daylight lasted for a long time.

* * *

In the days that followed things reverted to the way they'd been before, but with one important difference: Andrew Korchak still avoided his daughter, but now Luce did her best to keep out of his way, too. She hadn't forgotten his threat to starve himself to death, and she didn't want to do anything that might upset him before she figured out a plan. She slept in the most inaccessible crooks of the island and spent more of her time underwater.

A raft, Luce realized. They'd need a raft. The water would be much too cold for a human, especially once they were away from the volcanic vents that warmed certain areas around the island. A raft would help keep her father from getting hypothermia as long as he wasn't swamped in a storm. Even with a solidly built raft their escape would be extremely risky. Luce wasn't sure if she could swim all the way back to land, even by herself, without sinking from sheer exhaustion. Towing her father would just make it that much harder.

Still Luce began to collect likely-looking driftwood, especially planks, and heap them behind a rock on the beach where she'd first arrived. She was careful to do this work only at night. She didn't want him to see her. As the sun arched higher in the sky each day, as the air warmed and the sustained dusk began to yield to occasional clear skies, Luce slowly managed to accumulate a fair amount of useful-looking wood, planks and strong straight logs. Some of the planks even had rusty nails sticking out of them, and Luce tugged the nails free and then carefully straightened them by banging with a rock. The mists were receding, and Luce stared into the distance in all directions, looking for that narrow ribbon of what she'd hoped was land. It seemed to have melted with the clouds.

Getting materials for the raft together helped to take her mind off her bigger problems. She still wasn't sure how to persuade her father that she was the real Luce. And she couldn't help noticing that there were fewer ice floes in the water now. Maybe back in her home territory the first cracks were appearing in the ice along the shore. Maybe Dorian was starting to walk down to their beach every evening and look for her . . .

It hurt her to think of how worried he would be, how long the days of waiting might become. But she just couldn't help it.

* * *

Luce was sleeping in her little cove when the dream came to her.

Even as she slept she was faintly conscious of the rocking water, the stones beneath her head, and at the same time she was walking with her father through a ramshackle amusement park. The sky was dark and only a handful of colored lights still blinked randomly in odd locations. One of her father's hands held hers and in the other he clutched a long strip of paper tickets, but no matter how far they walked they couldn't find a single ride that was running. Everything was out of order, even disassembled into ungainly heaps of rusty metal parts, and Luce began to get the impression that everyone else had gone home long ago.

"Forget," a barker called out to them. Luce looked over at her: a slim woman in a red and silver striped vest with her scarlet cap pulled down to hide her face. Long, dark hair trailed out at the sides. Her voice was peculiar, crumbling and wheezy like snarled winds. "Forget, forget. Forget right here!"

The barker was standing next to a contraption that Luce couldn't identify, something tall and skinny and skeletal. But as they drew closer Luce clearly saw the word "Forget" winking in pink neon at its base.

"You want to play, don't you, Luce?" her father asked. He sounded inexplicably sarcastic, even bitter. "We've still got all these tickets. Might as well use them up. Every last one of 'em. God knows there won't be any more soon enough."

Luce glanced at him shyly. She didn't know why he was in such a foul mood, and she was afraid he'd get mad at her if she lost the game. And she would surely lose, one way or another. But it would be even worse if she refused to try. "Okay."

Her father tore off one ticket for the barker, and a huge glittery mallet slipped into Luce's hand. It was too heavy for her, and she staggered as she approached the machine. It had a tall column of light bulbs like grayish vertebrae and a big red button at the bottom, just above the blinking FORGET. Luce looked around for her father, but he wasn't there anymore. Only the barker still stood behind her, and she was much taller than she'd been before and oddly spiny-looking.

"Forget right here!" the barker breathed mournfully. She didn't sound encouraging. "Forget *me*. At least forget me enough, just enough . . . my Lucette, my little light . . ."

I don't want to forget you, though! Luce thought, but she couldn't say it. Instead she swung the mallet. It thudded down awkwardly, just grazing the side of the red button. Only two of the light bulbs flashed a feeble yellow before going out again. Again she glanced around. Now in place of the barker there was a fizzling, hissing, dead tree. The strip of tickets dangled from its naked branches, high up, and Luce could hear the moaning of seals.

"Do you think I can try again?" Luce asked nervously.

The tree didn't answer, but the pink paper tickets gusted back and forth. Luce decided to take that as a yes, and she brought the mallet up. It almost flew out of her hands as if some unexpected force was aggressively tugging it skyward, and Luce jerked back. She was determined to keep her grip on the mallet, determined to bring it smashing down . . .

"Forget," the lights winked. "Forget." There was a clang as the mallet hurled down onto the button, and a chain of golden lights shot up. Just for an instant Luce saw two more words illuminated in the darkness far above her.

TO REMEMBER! the machine flashed out at her in scarlet letters. The letters glowed and vanished so quickly that they were hardly more than a momentary burn on Luce's retinas, but she was sure she'd seen them. The park around her went black, engulfed by a swirl of midnight water, and Luce began to run frantically away. Cold water gripped her legs. She had to find her father before he drowned . . .

Luce woke panting. The sky was soft with amber dawn, and a pod of seals was playing in the waves just beyond her cove. She could see their sleek, brown bodies dipping and the curious gleam of black glass eyes watching her. One of them swam closer and snuffled gently at her tail.

"With you here," the old, broken voice had told her, "the man forgets sometimes to remember."

She finally knew what she had to do.

22

Being Human

Ryan's parents were away. It was a perfect opportunity to practice as much as they wanted with no one complaining, so Dorian
was annoyed to see that Steve and Ryan seemed more interested
in bullshitting, then eating everything in sight, then playing
video games. The band was always going to suck at this rate, and
Dorian finally stalked into the kitchen and leaned irritably on the
counter, staring out the window at the lashing rain. He couldn't
even return home until Steve decided he was ready to drive
back. He couldn't sit on the beach getting soaked, jumping at
every flicker of light on the water, constantly imagining that
each shifting reflection was a long silvery green tail or a pale
reaching hand just about to break through. The shore was almost
completely free of clinging ice now, and still Luce didn't come.
Maybe she was dead or maybe she just didn't care anymore . . .

"Heya." It was Zoe, of course. She'd come up behind him and rested a hand on his shoulder. "Dorian? Are you okay?"

Dorian felt like snapping at her and almost instantly realized that he wanted to lash out because he was mad at Luce. It wasn't Zoe's fault that his crazy mermaid girlfriend had either abandoned him or else gone and gotten herself killed. Dorian glanced over his shoulder. Zoe's sleeve had slipped back, and just for an instant Dorian could see her bare arm for the first time, blotched here and there with little round white scars. They might have been left by the tip of a burning cigarette.

Maybe she was one of those girls who maimed themselves to prove how punk they were? Zoe caught his look and jerked her hand away, and the huge fuzzy sweater flopped back into place. She was staring down now, but the tension on her face seemed like a warning not to say anything. After a moment's hesitation Dorian decided to ignore the warning. Zoe was so close that her body grazed against his as he turned to face her. She wouldn't look at him, but she didn't step back either.

"Did you do that to yourself?" Dorian asked. "Your arm?"

"Did *you* like to throw yourself down the stairs as a kid?" Zoe's voice was hostile, and she was glaring off to the side. But she was standing even closer now, tipped so that her cheek was less than an inch from Dorian's shoulder. Dorian thought of putting his arms around her—just as a friend, of course—but then he stayed where he was.

"I wasn't trying to be a jerk, Zoe . . ." He'd said the wrong thing, Dorian realized. And the fact that it *was* wrong carried implications he was barely willing to think about.

"Well, if you didn't have some serious *brain* damage, you

wouldn't ask me that!" Zoe sounded furious, but even so she suddenly pressed in and hugged him, nestling her face against his chest. Her body felt almost feverish compared to Luce's sleek chill. "If you're going to keep asking me stupid questions, we should really go somewhere else. I don't want Steve and Ryan to hear this . . ."

Dorian considered this. His brain was humming with disbelief at how horrible life could be, with vague boiling anger at whoever had hurt her and at the relentless emptiness of the world where he somehow kept on living. But for all Zoe's aggressive tone, he thought, she obviously wanted to talk in privacy. "Okay."

She caught his hand and towed him toward the little back foyer then up the stairs. It was a small house with a bedroom at each end of a narrow hallway: the one Ryan shared with his little brother to the right, their parents' room on the left. Zoe headed left and Dorian followed, feeling a little awkward now. She shut the door behind them and Dorian stared around the wood-paneled room. It was crowded with oversized furniture and knickknacks. He stood to one side as Zoe unlaced her paint-spattered boots, tossing them across the floor, and then scooted to the center of the big double bed. After a moment he sat down, trying to strike the right balance: far enough back that she wouldn't think he was hitting on her, close enough that it wouldn't seem cold. The bedspread under them was avocado green with sprouting tufts of yarn. Zoe was looking down, her freshly pink-dyed hair dragging in front of her eyes. She was twisting the tufts a little nervously. "So. What other fucked-up things do you want to ask me?"

There *was* one huge question pressing up in Dorian, but he didn't know how to ask it without sounding insane. If Zoe hadn't burned herself, if it had been someone else, then why was she still sitting there with human legs folded under her? Why hadn't she let go of her human life and flowed away into the sea with the other broken girls, with Luce and Dana and Nausicaa? Zoe watched him for a minute.

"I bet you want to ask who did it? My stepdad. He's gone now, thank *Gawd*, but my mom keeps taking him back. They've split up like a million times already." Her tone was sassy and hard, but Dorian could hear the slight wavering hidden inside it. She was back to tugging at the bedspread, staring down at it as if nothing could be more fascinating.

"At least he's not around to fuck you up now." Dorian wanted her to look at him again, but he didn't want to admit it. Now that he was paying closer attention to her, maybe there *was* something in Zoe's face, a kind of wounded defensiveness, that reminded him of the mermaids' faces. "But that isn't what I was wondering, actually." How could he say this? The urge to know pulsed in him, painfully strong. She must have felt something, some hint of the transformation, but for some reason she hadn't given in to it. Why?

"Yeah? What is it, then? You want to know if I *liked* it? You think I'm one of those masochists who gets *off* on that stuff?"

She was being deliberately bitchy. Trying to provoke him. Dorian's shoulders heaved a little as if Zoe's words were something gummy and awful sticking to his body. "Zoe, cut it *out*." It was odd to hear how weary his voice sounded.

"What?" In spite of the pissy tone she was looking at him

again, and there was a sharp flash of frightened expectation in her eyes. He couldn't help thinking that she was hoping he would say something important and afraid at the same time to let herself really hope for anything. For half a minute they just stared at each other.

"When your stepdad *did* that . . ." Dorian tried, then paused. "This might sound crazy." Zoe's eyes were rounder than ever, waiting. He tried to remember exactly how Luce had described it. "When he hurt you, like when it was the absolute worst, did you ever feel . . . like this cold feeling? Almost like your body was turning into water and you could just flow away? Get out and forget everything?"

Zoe was quiet for several seconds, but the hard front she kept up was completely gone. She looked as soft as dough, hungry and wondering. Dorian half imagined that he could see a cloud of dark sparkling hinting at itself in the air around her head. "How can you *know* about that?" she asked at last. Quietly, almost ashamed-sounding. Her eyes flicked over his body, obviously wondering if he was also hiding scars. "Was it . . . Like, were you . . ."

"Not *that* way." Dorian shook his head. "I'll tell you some shit sometime, but I never . . . I just *heard* about how it feels." He hesitated. "From my girlfriend."

Zoe hardened again, but the toughness had something pitiful in it. "Steve *said* you pretend you still have some girlfriend back in Chicago. You thought that was such a great idea, right, telling him so he'd tell me?" Her head was tipped back now, her gaze narrowed. "I know it's bullshit, okay?"

"It's not—"

"It's just some Mr. Sensitive crap so you don't have to hurt my feelings. It hurts a lot worse to be lied to, though." She glowered at him. "Just *say* you don't want me."

Dorian felt angrier at this than he could quite explain to himself. "Then how do I know about the whole turning-into-water thing? You've never told anyone about that, have you? And I'm telling you exactly how it felt for you. You didn't give in to it. But I know what would have happened if you had . . ."

Zoe lowered her face; Dorian thought that she was trying to hide her fascination. "Oh, yeah?" The bratty tone was back. "Because whatever it was also happened to your *girlfriend*?"

"Yes." Dorian still felt angry, volatile. If Luce couldn't be bothered to keep her promises, then why shouldn't he say whatever he felt like? Still, there was the question of how ridiculous it would sound.

"Awesome. What would have happened? This way the next time that bastard shoves a cigarette into my arm I'll know what my *choices* are." She sounded like she was joking, but her eyes contradicted the blithe tone; they were worried, eager, and guarded, as if she was afraid that Dorian actually knew the answer.

He looked up sharply. Her *choices*. He hadn't thought about that, but that was obviously the most important issue. Just because Zoe had stayed human so far didn't mean she would next time!

Zoe tried harder to cover her emotion. "Spill already! I'm waiting. You get so cold inside you feel like you're melting. Then what?"

Dorian kept his face hard so there was no way she could think he was kidding. "You change. If you go with the feeling, then you change. And you can't take it back, either."

"You change?" Zoe didn't exactly sound as if this came as a surprise to her; more as if it confirmed something she'd sensed all along.

"Into something else." Now Dorian was afraid she might decide he was lying, playing games with her when she was already so hurt. The idea stopped him for a moment.

"Okay." She actually smiled now, though there was something grim about it. "Like what?"

"You can't tell anyone, Zoe."

"Like *what?*"

Dorian gazed at her for a second. Maybe he'd sound like an asshole, but she needed to know the truth. It was horrible, he thought, that the girls who made that choice didn't know what they were getting into. Proteus tricked all of them, made them think that they were going to be safe and free when really they were trapped into becoming murderers; even worse, they were trapped that way forever, cold and lost and lonely. But maybe, just maybe, he could protect Zoe from that. If her stepfather came back . . . "A mermaid. The girls where that happens to them. They become mermaids. And . . . they kill a lot of people, Zoe."

What did it matter if it sounded ridiculous? Dorian thought angrily. It was true. He was telling Zoe the truth, and there was one thing certain: nobody else would. At least she'd know what she was facing.

"Mermaids. Like your girlfriend? That's what she is?" Zoe

was obviously trying to make fun of him, but she couldn't quite manage it. Dorian stared flatly into her awkward smirk. She was struggling not to accept the truth, he thought, but she couldn't keep herself from partly believing him. "She's the one you're always drawing?"

"Yeah."

"What's her name?"

Dorian hesitated. But it was a harmless enough question, really. "Luce."

"Is that short for Hallucination?" Zoe asked, deadpan. Then her lips curled into a sly smile.

Dorian couldn't help it: he cracked up laughing and soon Zoe was laughing, too. They were both leaning forward, their laughter wild with a strange kind of shared relief, tears brightening Zoe's round hazel eyes. Dorian felt like he was being a little disloyal to Luce, laughing at a joke about her. But it *was* funny—funny, he thought, in the way of things that are just a bit too true. Luce herself was real, of course, but her life in the sea sometimes seemed to Dorian like some kind of acted-out fantasy, with its queens and battles and shipwrecks. Not a hallucination exactly, but a willful waking dream that never ended. As if Luce was avoiding something.

"Actually," Dorian said when he could finally talk again, "it's short for Lucette. I don't know what her last name was, though . . ."

Something about that brought Zoe up short. She stopped giggling abruptly and wiped her eyes with her sleeve, staring at him. "Lucette? That's a pretty unusual name."

"It is unusual, yeah. But it's totally beautiful."

Zoe's eyes sparked with annoyance for a moment, then turned cautious and darkly curious. "I've only ever heard that name one time before, actually." She was examining Dorian's face, checking for his reaction. "Have you heard about that girl Lucette Korchak? From Pittley?"

Dorian wondered if she was trying to change the subject. Why would he want to hear gossip about some other girl with the same name? "Um, no. What about her?"

"Lucette Korchak? She committed suicide like a year ago. Early April. She threw herself off a cliff by the sea." Zoe was staring at him, and Dorian could feel something in his face starting to unfold, to blossom with realization. "Or some people up there think her uncle murdered her. He's this total drunk-ass creep, and there were rumors like maybe he was beating on her or something. They found her clothes scattered at the top of the cliff, but . . . they never found the body . . ."

Dorian reeled back against the bed's footboard. "Last April?" A whole year ago, now, even a little more. It *had* to be her. And he'd been living in Chicago with Emily and his parents then, not imagining anything crazier in his future than becoming a big-deal comic book artist. *Definitely* not suspecting how soon his little sister would die . . .

Zoe watched the emotions tearing through his face. "You *really* hadn't heard of her, had you? You're totally surprised."

"So?"

"So you weren't just using her name, to make me think . . . And that means, maybe . . ." Zoe seemed almost frantic now.

"Where did *you* hear about this?"

"My friend Bethany's mom is seeing this math teacher from

Pittley. Mr. Carroll. And I was over for dinner at Bethany's house, and Mr. Carroll started tripping out about that Lucette girl and how *guilty* he felt, like he knew she was having a shitty time and there were these sick rumors and he should have done more to help her. Me and Bethany kept getting more and more weirded out. But maybe—"

"Lucette Korchak didn't die!" Dorian shook his head. It was too bad they couldn't tell this Mr. Carroll the truth, though maybe the truth was still terrible enough that it wouldn't make him feel any better. Luce had lived, but she had also killed, and she was still lost in a cold sea. "Her uncle didn't murder her, but the part about him beating her is true. And then he tried to rape her . . ." Zoe flinched, hard.

"*She* told you this?" Zoe's voice buckled.

"Yeah. She told me the whole thing. How she changed . . ."

Zoe's expression had altered completely since the start of the conversation. It was wounded and open, shining with a kind of surrender. Dorian knew that she believed him completely. "God. Dorian . . . Where is she now? Luce?"

"I don't know." Saying it made Dorian feel a little sick. How long could he go on insisting that Luce was still his girlfriend? She'd proved before that she would take insane risks and that she didn't care enough about being with him to keep herself safe.

"You mean . . . How can you not *know*?"

"She had to leave. Because of the ice. And I've been waiting every night, but she hasn't come back yet . . ." Dorian grimaced as he said it.

Something in Zoe's face shifted again. "The ice has been mostly gone for like two weeks already."

"I *know* that," Dorian snapped. "I've been sitting on the beach freezing for hours every night, okay? It's not like I haven't had time to notice."

"If she really loved you, maybe she wouldn't leave you waiting around like that." Zoe stared at him uncertainly, and Dorian could almost feel the words hovering on her lips. He was sure she would leave them unsaid, swallow them down in embarrassment. She exhaled hard, then risked it: "*I* wouldn't."

Dorian looked away, flushing. But he still wanted to know. "Zoe . . ."

Suddenly she looked angry. "Whatever. You don't have the balls to say it!"

"No, I mean, what I want to know . . . You felt the change starting, right?" Dorian asked gently. The heat inside him was soft and hopeful. Maybe it was really too late for Luce, maybe she would never leave the sea, maybe she was even dead. But it wasn't too late for everyone.

"I felt it." Zoe looked down, hard and morose. "Just like melting into really cold water, like you said. Right on my bedroom floor." She looked up, her face agonized, but somehow there were still flickers of humor in her eyes. Dorian couldn't help admiring the strength of that. "I wouldn't have believed anything as retarded as this mermaid bullshit, okay? But I did feel like . . . I mean, I basically knew I could change. Into *something*."

"But you didn't."

Her pink hair trailed, and Dorian felt an impulse to stroke it back from her face.

"No. I didn't. I don't know how it worked. But I pulled back. Like, there was this moment where it was up to me . . ." Zoe's voice faltered.

"Why? That's what I need to know, Zoe." He was some-how closer to her now, and she was sitting with her legs folded under her, halfway kneeling. "Why didn't you do it?"

"Well, because . . . That's a tough question." She tried to smile at him. "Like, if being human is a problem for me . . . it's still a problem I have to deal with. You know what I mean?"

Dorian stared. "Totally."

"And so, like, my mom sucks, and my stepdad's an evil bas-tard, and there's all this crap . . . But I want to do a better job than they have?"

"A better job of being human?" Dorian asked. They were both grinning, but the room in front of him was warped by his tears.

"Yeah."

Dorian sat quiet for a minute, thinking about what Zoe had said. He loved Luce, and he knew she was incredibly coura-geous: brave enough to confront a whole tribe of enemies out for her blood, brave enough to race out through orca-infested wa-ters to save Nausicaa. But in a way her exploits seemed like the adventures of a child's fantasy life, dreamy, removed from the problems of the real world. She'd run away, where Zoe had stayed . . .

Zoe, he thought, was even braver than Luce. Zoe was the one taking the chances that *really* counted. And she would face growing up, awful as that could be.

She slid closer to him, grinning widely. "Hey, Dorian?"

"Yeah?"

"Well, aren't there . . ." Her soft, funny, completely un-magical face was only inches from his now. "Aren't there some really heavy drawbacks? To having a mermaid girlfriend? Don't you get frustrated?"

Dorian looked into Zoe's hazel eyes; he liked her, a lot, but still she was being unkind by asking that. And answering her out loud would be a huge betrayal of Luce. He couldn't do it. "Zoe . . ."

She was already straddling him, pressing him back onto the bed. Her hands were on his face, pulling up his shirt, warm and sweet and earthy, and her breath curled on his ear. "Maybe you should try a real girl."

23

Breaking Voices

The water purled around her, glittering with sunlight, as Luce lay in wait on the pebbles of the seafloor. She was a few feet away from the beach where her father sometimes came for fish, concealed by a patch of loose seaweed and by the brilliant glinting of the sun. It was her third day spent lurking under the surface waiting for him to appear. It was hard not to feel a bit depressed, to keep circling back to the same anxious thoughts. The plan she'd made might not work at all. The hours went by, the sun dashed blades of brilliant green light through the water, and Luce slipped up for air as rarely and stealthily as possible. And still he didn't come. She hadn't heard so much as a trace of muttering winds for days. What was he *doing*? Had he given up on this beach entirely? She knew she had to stay still, but it took constant concentration to keep her tail from lashing with impatience.

Then through the soft distortion of the water, Luce heard it. A girl's voice, high and tender: "*. . . none of Peter's business!*" the voice sighed. "*Mom loved you!*"

Luce remembered that conversation exactly. The voice was hers, but hers from more than two years before. Even as Luce's heart started thudding she still shook her head in disbelief that she had ever sounded so innocent, so cared-for. She couldn't repress a spasm of envy and resentment directed at that younger girl, the one who'd felt so secure in her humanity, who'd been loved and safe . . .

She fought to clear her head, to keep herself from being sucked into a whirl of painful memories. The only thing that mattered was the present: the moment directly before her, *now*, and everything that might still be saved in this moment if only she could make herself be quick and wise enough. If the voices were on the beach, then her father probably wasn't far behind. Luce tensed, ready to spring.

Footsteps. The slow crunch of pebbles, dragging and lifeless. He was there, walking closer, and the windy gibbering grew louder and more eager. It was awful to hear how vital and happy the voices sounded in contrast to her father's weary, defeated shambling. Closer, still closer. Through the veil of the water Luce could just see two dark blots at the sea's edge: his feet swaddled in dirty fur. Luce was almost choking, suddenly terrified to move. If she failed now her father might truly kill himself.

Luce gathered her determination and shot up out of the waves. But she was careful not to look at Andrew Korchak at all, keeping her eyes fixed instead on the murmuring disturbance all around him. "I need to talk to you!" Luce announced loudly, aggressively. "Now!"

Luce knew that her younger self had never once spoken to anyone that way. She had always been shy and gentle. That was the point.

She had to be as different as possible from her father's memories of her.

He stumbled back from the water's edge in shock, but to Luce's infinite relief he didn't take off running inland. Instead he sat down hard twenty feet from the water, his mouth open and his eyes bright with pain. But he was still there. Still watching, and still *listening* . . .

"You voices, whatever you call yourselves, lost *hopes*," Luce snapped. "Get over here! You heard me."

Up on the beach her father began to moan a long, low note, holding his head. The voices babbled, gusting back and forth in astonished outrage.

"You want me to leave, right?" Luce demanded. "Then you need to start doing what I tell you, or I'll stay here on your island and mess up your memories forever. I'll hurt the memories in every way I can! Answer me!"

It was hard for her to be so abrasive, so rude. But wasn't there a hint of something different, something just a bit more awake, in her father's expression? The voices gabbled in agitation and then seemed to arrive at some agreement. Luce braced herself as they came at her: a tangle of boiling winds carrying spinning fragments of grass and torn wildflowers.

"*Child of Proteus*," the wheezing old voice gasped out, grating and vicious.

Luce cut it off.

"I am NOT the child of Proteus!" She shouted the words, and suddenly her rage wasn't an act anymore. "Don't you ever dare to call me that again!"

The voices wheezed and hissed, debris flung higher and higher in their whispering torrent. Luce knew they were astonished, beside themselves with confusion. This was her chance!

She pressed on. "You want to know whose *child* I am? I'm the daughter of Alyssa Gray and Andrew Korchak. Alyssa Gray is dead. She's nothing but memories now, and there is *nothing* I can do about that! She's gone forever." Luce knew what she had to say next, but she could barely make herself do it. It seemed so cruel, especially with her father right there listening. "I'm going to *forget* her."

Luce's hands were shaking now. Her father suddenly looked straight at her, his eyes wide with hurt. She waited with desperate hope for him to argue with her—to yell, "*Lucette! Don't say that!*" Luce could practically see the words taking shape in his eyes, but they didn't come to his lips. Not yet.

The voices came closer, an angry chaos of winds. They lashed out at her with airy tentacles, then just as suddenly pulled back. Luce's hair jerked in their grip and fell again. "*Child of . . .*" the angry old voice gasped.

Then it paused uncertainly, and Luce attacked.

"I'm also the child of Andrew Korchak. The *man* you've been keeping here. I thought he was lost forever, but he's not. He's still *alive*, and he can still have a future. He can forget Alyssa, too—forget her enough, anyway, and fall in love with someone else. And maybe he should forget *me*, and have a new child . . ." Luce gagged on the words even as she said them, and the tangled voices screamed in her ears. They were going insane; at any moment, Luce thought, they would start invading her head again. Their shrieking pierced her thoughts, and she raised her voice to make sure her father would hear her above their wailing. "But I am NOT letting you keep him!"

Then all Luce could hear was the howl of enraged voices. They pounded into her head, opened like gashes in her brain. A cloud of sand and shredded grass rose in her eyes, blocking her father from view. She kept on yelling into the storm, though she could hardly make out her own voice. "I'm Luce! I'm Lucette Korchak! You think you can keep me as a memory, but I'm here NOW, and I'm going to *make* you know who I am!" The pain rose in her head, and with the pain came a violent urge to flee, to dash away from the suffering she felt, make it *stop*. How much longer could she endure it?

Luce thought of her dream, and her mother's dreamed voice sighed in her mind. *Forget me just enough . . .* It eased the pain a little, and Luce gathered her strength again, pulled in a long breath full of grit and twisting wind. She had to do this for Alyssa. Even as she insisted on forgetting her mother she had to honor her memory in the one way she still could, by saving the man her mother had loved so completely . . .

"FORGET ME!" Luce screamed. The scream ripped up through her chest like a whirling knife, cutting through the clamor of the voices around her. Slashing them apart . . . Luce's mind seemed to burst into streamers of pain. Something like a wall hit her forehead, hard, and her hands flailed out against a cold rocking mass of stones. The whole world pitched below her, beating to a revolting rhythm, trembling like the skin of a drum. Luce's stomach turned, and acid rose in her mouth and overflowed. She coughed and gagged and felt tears drenching her face as if something had ruptured inside her.

But, she realized, the world was finally getting quieter. Either that or she was going deaf.

"*We know you . . .*" the old voice said wonderingly. "*We know you!*"

"Of course you know me," Luce rasped back. "You've been living off memories of me for two years." She squirmed down the unsteady beach, dragging herself away from the puddled vomit on the stones. The beach seemed to lunge at her face again, and she clung to it in an effort to stop it from slamming around.

"*We know you, and you are not the memory . . .*" Even as the voice spoke it was changing. It sounded warmer, more alive: it was almost her father's voice now. But it was also fading. Winds no longer seethed around her. "*Lucette?*"

Sunlight flashed on the wet rocks inches from her eyes. Luce saw a few dots of blurry red and realized that she was bleeding.

"Lucette?"

This new voice was *human*. Soft and confused. Luce was too sick to raise her head, but she could make out two fur-wrapped feet stopping just in front of her. Hands reached down and touched her shoulders, and she smelled the animal stink of seal skins. "Lucette!" The tone was getting panicky now. "It *can't* be you . . ."

Luce knew she had to look up at him. She *had* to answer,

even if the world seemed to stagger between glaring sun and devouring shadows, even if nothing would stay still.

She couldn't do it.

* * *

Luce woke to an icy, burning pain. A shivering fire sparked in all her scales, and she lashed her tail, sick with dread as she felt cold air licking her from all directions, as she writhed and strained to touch water again. The water wasn't there, but as her eyes opened she could see its gleam, the rippling of sunset colors. Something was holding her up, keeping her from reaching it. Something warm and strong and determined, and she was already screaming . . .

"Lucette. Lucette, it's okay." Her father was staring at her, stunned and sad. "It's *okay*. I . . . oh, God. I promise . . ."

He didn't know better, Luce suddenly realized. He'd taken her out of the water, and he was carrying her up the beach in his arms. But her voice was out of her control, caught in the scream, even as wind drank the last drops from her scales. She was fighting, twisting, endless convulsions gripping her tail . . .

"Put me back!" Who had said that? Luce was sure she didn't have the strength to say anything. "Please, *please* put me back . . ."

"In the water?" her father asked, surprised. There were a few more seconds of bewildering fire, then Luce felt the splash, the burning quenched by the liquid bliss of the sea. She was sobbing, and her tail swayed through the salty waves in pure relief. She rolled across the seafloor, gasping, trying to regain control of herself. From the corner of her eyes she saw him standing barefoot in the water, his shoulders hunched in sudden helpless uncertainty. "Are you . . . Lucette, if that's really . . . Are you okay?"

Luce ducked under for a moment, calming herself in the cool, fluctuating waves. When she came up she felt a bit more in command of herself. "I'm okay now." She looked up into his doubtful cinnamon eyes, his mouth pinched with worry. "I should have warned you." But she *couldn't* have warned him, not as long as he was refusing to listen to her. "I can't leave the water anymore."

He sat down at the water's edge, his legs crossed, and gazed at her with a look she couldn't decipher. Whatever it was she saw on his face, it definitely wasn't the love she longed for. She swam over and sat near him, carefully holding his gaze, and the longer they looked at each other the worse her disappointment became. He wasn't avoiding her now, but he didn't seem all that happy to see her either.

The air around them was very quiet. Luce could hear the far-off trill of a bird, but there was nothing else. No haunted mutterings moved through the wind, and Luce suddenly wondered if her father felt lonely now that the enchantment was broken.

"I guess you aren't what I thought you were," her father said after a minute. "But I know you can't really be her. Not *really*, even if I want you to be. Don't know what that *does* make you, though . . ."

Luce's pain began to shift into anger. He'd seemed to understand, but now he was shutting out the truth all over again, and after everything she'd gone through . . . She glared at him. "I'm Lucette Korchak. I'm your daughter!"

Her father shook his head and covered his eyes with his

hands. Was he trying to shut out her face, too? "Lucette is living with my brother, Peter. Back in Pittley. And I hope to God he can find the strength in his heart to treat her decently!"

His voice broke, and Luce almost reached out to hold him, then stopped. He might recoil from her touch, and she wasn't sure if she could stand that. And at the same time she was amazed by the implications of what her father had just said: the idea that her uncle Peter had hurt her out of *weakness* . . .

Maybe that was right, though. Maybe the problem with Peter was that he was simply sick and feeble, with no strength in his heart.

As tired as she was, as sick as she still felt, Luce realized her struggle wasn't over yet. She'd brought her father part of the way toward accepting the situation, but there was still further to go. And, Luce realized grimly, she was going to have to hurt him more to persuade him.

"Peter didn't find that much strength," Luce announced. Her voice came out harsh, bitter. "Not even close. Like a month after you vanished he started hitting me whenever he got drunk, and it just kept getting worse."

Her father took his hands away from his eyes, and Luce saw that he was crying. But she couldn't stop now. It was simply too incredible: that this was his own girl, his Luce, but somehow transfigured into a mermaid. He'd only accept it once he really understood what had happened to her.

"And after a year," Luce went on, forcing the words out, "he tried to rape me."

Her father let out a sharp cry, but he didn't say anything at first. His eyes were grief-stricken, wide and wavering. She could see his expression jarring between disbelief and fury. "He what?" His voice was a croak.

"He tried . . . to rape me. Peter did. On the cliffs, on that path that you take as a shortcut back from town? He shoved me down, and he started going under my clothes. That's why . . . I know you don't understand it, Dad, okay? But that's why I changed. Into what I am now." But as Luce said it she realized that wasn't the only reason she'd changed.

It had also been because she was so sure her father was dead. If she had had any hope at all that he might still come back someday, she would have clung to her humanity no matter what it cost her.

It had all been a *mistake*, and maybe she could never take it back.

Realizing that did make her feel like she wasn't necessarily responsible for fighting on behalf of the mermaids after all. At least maybe it wasn't her *biggest* responsibility.

"I'll . . ." Something dark was coming into her father's eyes. It was like watching the shape of something huge and dangerous rising to the surface of deep water. "I'll kill him. My little girl . . . when she didn't have anyone else . . ."

"You're talking about me like I'm not here," Luce pointed out. "It's not your fault that Peter . . . I missed you so *much*, but I always knew it wasn't your fault. You didn't want to leave me." Suddenly Luce understood how much emotion she'd been keeping crushed down, buried inside her chest. It had been the only way she could keep going, doing what she had to do. But now . . . Tears had started to curve around her cheeks, and he reached toward her and slowly brushed one away. It only made

Luce cry harder, but she still tried to smile. "I *like* being a mermaid. Really. You don't have to worry."

"A mermaid." His tone was disbelieving again. "You can see why . . . I might have some trouble buying that this is really happening, yeah? Can't hardly trust my own mind anymore. But even if I'm dreaming this, my God, you're a vision." He suddenly laughed, with the same warm softness Luce remembered. She was trembling as she leaned in and rested her head on his knee, ignoring the stink of his ragged furs. He gazed down, lightly running one hand over her hair. "Luce," he said after a while.

Luce fought down a sob of relief. "Yes."

He seemed confused again. "Luce. For real? My . . . How the hell did you get here, though?"

"In a storm. I was trying to go south, but the storm got too intense, so I grabbed on to an ice floe . . ." She told him the story quietly. But the miracle, Luce thought, was that he was listening, thinking about what she was saying to him. Not about the past at all. "How did *you* wind up here? Oh, I was so *sure* you were dead."

"Oh, that. Storm, too. Eight days alone in a lifeboat after the *High and Mighty* cracked up. If it hadn't rained so much, thirst would have done me in for certain. But then the lifeboat smashed to bits on the rocks right here, and they . . . those voice things were ready to pounce. Like, maybe they'd pulled me here somehow. Oh, baby doll." His old pet name for her. Luce could hardly believe it, and she squeezed his hand.

"We need to get you out of here, Dad, okay? We can build a raft." She needed to be honest with him, Luce thought. "It's going to be dangerous. Trying to tow you back to shore. If there's a storm or something I could keep you from drowning, at least for as long as I could swim myself. But you'd get hypothermia . . ."

He didn't seem interested in this part, though. Luce looked up at him and saw that he was still thinking about something else. "You say you can't leave the water? Luce . . ."

Luce had been so preoccupied with simply getting him to recognize her that she hadn't thought about how awful the truth might be for him. She kept her voice as gentle as possible. "I can't ever leave the water again." What if she could, though? But that was probably too much to hope for, and he had to know. "Dad, I'm not *human* anymore. I can't have the kind of life . . . a human girl would."

"But then . . . if you're living in the ocean . . ." He laughed, in a bleak, shocked way. "How am I supposed to bring you up?"

"You can't." Luce saw the grief rising in his face, but she plunged ahead anyway. "You need to think about . . . doing what *you* want to do. You can't bring me up. I can't live with you." *Unless* . . . But no, almost certainly no. It would be much too cruel to give him false hopes now. She considered for a moment. "I can't even *grow* up."

"What's *that* supposed to mean?" There was a hint of growling in his voice now.

"I changed on my fourteenth birthday. We—mermaids don't get any older, ever. I'm going to be fourteen forever, and I can't grow up at all."

"But"—he stared at her again. "Lucette? You're not *dead*, are you?"

Was he asking if she was something like a vampire? A ghost

with a body? "I'm not dead. I have a heartbeat. It's maybe slower than a human's, but it's there. And I still have to breathe, only not as much. And eat."

"I do those things." He smiled wryly. "Don't stop me from feeling pretty dead."

Luce glared at him. "You're not!"

"Might as well be, Lucette. If I couldn't even protect you from—" She opened her mouth to argue with him, but he held up a hand to stop her. "Listen, though. This business of you can't grow up . . . That doesn't make any sense."

He was still in denial, then. How much longer would she have to keep hurting him? "It's just how it *is* for us."

He shook his head. "No. I mean, can you still learn new things? Change your mind about stuff?" He hesitated for a second. "Love new people?"

That stopped Luce in her tracks. She'd learned more in her year of being a mermaid than she ever had as a human being. And as for loving . . . "I can still learn and everything. Definitely."

"So how can you say you're not growing up, then?" Andrew Korchak asked.

Luce was amazed by the question. Maybe he had a point. She stared silently for several moments while he watched her. Then he grinned, brash and sparkling.

"Even if you're not growing physically. I won't be getting no taller now either, but God knows I've still got some growing up to do!"

Luce laughed and threw her arms around him. It finally felt like he was really back with her. Really alive.

It was already dark by the time her father climbed inland to bring back a stick off the fire the spirits had kept lit for him. Without their help, he told Luce, he never would have survived for so long; if they were really gone he'd have to be a lot more careful. He built a new fire on the beach so he could stay near her and roasted the mussels Luce collected for him.

Luce even tried one. It was the first time she'd attempted to eat cooked food since her change, and it felt all wrong in her mouth, too hot and too gummy. Luce spat it out, and soon fell into a hazy sleep. Firelight shone red and soft even through her eyelids, and after a while she heard him stretching out to sleep on the stones not far from her. Utterly exhausted as she was, worry kept jarring through Luce's mind, keeping her awake. The journey back to land would be hard. All she wanted was to save her father, but there was a distinct risk that she could kill him in the attempt. She wasn't even sure which direction they should choose, or where to find the nearest land. With the voices watching over him, he'd at least been *safe*. It was hours before she finally slipped deeper, tumbling through levels of velvety darkness.

Very soon now she would be with Dorian again.

* * *

Luce woke to the thump of wood being dragged along the beach and looked up to see her father grinning at her. His look was playful, impish, and delighted, and Luce saw that he'd already lugged out of their hiding place a lot of the boards she'd gathered and also heaped up some other materials that had probably come from his own stash up on the hill. Luce couldn't stay worried, not seeing that look on his face.

"I'd kind of been wondering what that wood was doing there." He beamed at her. "But it was you, wasn't it, doll? Always thinking ahead."

"It was me," Luce confirmed. She couldn't remember the last time she'd felt so peaceful, so overjoyed purely by the sight of the brilliant sky.

She wasn't going to talk to anyone from the FBI, of course. But maybe she could try changing on her own sometime, only without telling either her father or Dorian her plans. If things went wrong it would be better if they never knew what had happened to her. Two out of three hundred weren't good odds, of course, but it wasn't *impossible* that she would survive. Surviving wouldn't be any more incredible than Dorian forgiving her for her part in killing his family; it wouldn't be any more incredible than finding her father alive. Maybe *incredible* was just the way life went . . . Luce wasn't about to mention the idea to her father, though. It wouldn't be fair to say anything that might make him think they could really be a family again. Not unless she was actually standing up on human legs, alive and strong and staring back at the waves she'd left behind.

"Nice work on these nails, baby doll." He was grinning uncontrollably as he gazed down at a handful of the nails she'd straightened. "One thing I did right was I taught you how to be resourceful. Make the best of things." His confidence was coming back, Luce realized, and her tail flipped from pure exuberance. He was going to be *fine*. Maybe she could even introduce him to Dorian.

"You did *everything* right, Dad." *Except for trusting Peter,* Luce thought, but she didn't say that part out loud. Then she couldn't suppress the urge to brag a little. She wanted him to be proud of her. "Some of the other mermaids even think I should be queen."

He laughed. "I don't doubt it, baby doll. They couldn't hope for a better one than you." He was looking at the pile of wood, and Luce suddenly realized that he was consumed by hope, almost delirious with excitement. After two years marooned to be this close to freedom . . . "Now, about that raft. I'll build a frame, and maybe while I'm working on that you can oil up these seal skins . . ."

24

Strange Queens

They couldn't have picked a better day for setting out. The sea was smooth and luminous, the air warm. Birds were flocking north again as Luce slipped into the harness she'd braided from long strips of hide. It had been her father's idea to pad the insides of the straps with fur so that they wouldn't chafe her shoulders. Luce checked the raft for the tenth time that day, tugging and banging on it. It seemed sturdy enough, with low boxlike sides to keep the waves from slopping in too much. Her father grinned to himself as he lowered in a heavy skin bag of fresh water along with some dried fish in a crude net of twisted grass cord.

It had taken them several days to get everything ready, but Luce was still nervous. It was a lovely day, and the waves were as low and easy as she had ever seen them, but if the weather changed for the worse she might not be able to save him. And there was no way to guess how far they had to go.

He saw the look on her face and ruffled her hair. "Lucette, doll, if something goes wrong . . ." She tried to keep her dismay from showing. "Don't ever think it was your fault, all right? I'm the one who should've studied harder in raft-building class back in high school." He grinned, but for the first time since they'd begun planning his escape Luce could hear anxiety in his voice.

It was a feeble enough joke, but Luce smiled at him. "I won't let anything happen to you." Suddenly she was positive that she'd get him to land, no matter what it took.

"Staying here isn't no kind of real life anyway," he added, but his eyes had something wistful in them as they traveled back over the island. All at once Luce understood why he looked so sad. The muttering spirits that lived in this place might have tormented him, but they had also brought his dead wife closer to him than she'd been in many years. They'd crooned to him in Alyssa's voice, day after day.

No matter how badly he wanted to escape from this place, it also must cut his heart to go. It had to feel almost like he was abandoning the woman he'd loved, or at least the last vital traces of her, the final scraps and fragments of her spirit. It didn't matter if he knew that wasn't really the case and that what he'd heard wasn't Alyssa at all. The feeling of it would still tear at him.

Luce waited quietly while he stared back toward the woods. His head was cocked, and she knew he was listening as hard as he could. Just in case Alyssa's voice spoke to him, just one last time.

The breeze stayed silent.

"I'd say south," her father said after a while. "Don't know why, but I feel like that's our best bet." He was looking away from her, trying to hide the pain on his face as he shoved the raft out and clambered aboard.

Luce was surprised. "Not east? We'll hit the coast of Alaska eventually."

"I've got this feeling the islands are gonna be closer. Don't want to wear you out, dragging this damn raft." He was trying to smile, but Luce could see how hard it was for him, and just for an instant she wondered if she had even done the right thing.

"I'm going to be under water a lot," Luce warned him. Suddenly she felt so awkward that the prospect of whipping along below the surface came as a relief. "You won't see me a lot of the time, but I won't drown." He only looked at her quizzically, his cinnamon eyes wry and sweet and sad. Luce slid deeper, and the ropes binding her to the raft went taut. Blue emptiness opened in front of her, distant milky clouds. She glanced back over her shoulder and found him staring at the island again. "Yell if you see any orcas coming."

He spun to look at her sharply; orcas obviously weren't something he'd thought about. Luce didn't want to discuss the possibility that she might be ripped apart in front of him and she dove, staying just below the surface.

Fast. It had been so long since she'd swum this fast, since curtains of glimmering bubbles had parted around her face. So long since she'd felt so free, even with the harness pulling back on her shoulders and slowing her down. The raft wasn't nearly as streamlined as Dorian's rowboat, and towing it was much harder work. Luce whipped through the glowing green waves, thinking of Dorian. In just a few days she'd feel his hands on her face again, breathe his scent, brush her lips lightly over his before she kissed him . . .

She couldn't wait to tell him everything that had happened.

Maybe it was crazy to imagine that she might be able to go back to the human life that was destroyed after her father vanished, but she couldn't entirely keep the fantasy of it out of her mind. Then she'd live with her father until she grew up, and she and Dorian would stay with each other always, but she wouldn't abandon the mermaids either.

The daydream was a little vague on the details. But possibly she could find some way to bring the humans and mermaids together before it was too late. Maybe there would never be a war at all. The fact that she and Dorian loved each other must prove that anything could happen. If the broken world was ever going to mend, if humans and mermaids were ever going to reconcile, it made sense that it would somehow start with the two of them: with the boy who was almost a land merman and the mermaid who was—Luce allowed herself to think it—almost a sea human.

* * *

After an hour or two Luce saw something blue in the far distance as she came up to breathe. She looked back at her father. "That's land all right, doll," he called, grinning at her. Luce thought she saw some other emotion hiding behind his smile, though, maybe worry or grief. What was wrong?

"We'll be there before night," Luce told him, trying to sound cheerful. "Going south was a great idea." She kept looking around the horizon apprehensively, dreading a darkening in the sky that might mean a coming storm, but there was nothing except clear blue broken by beating wings, clouds like a trail of pale dots, a few whale spouts. It was all going better than Luce had dared to hope, and she pushed on, trying to ignore her growing tiredness. Swimming was a struggle with the raft's weight tugging on her, and they still had so far to go. She twisted, trying to loosen the cramps building in her shoulders.

Again the dive, again the streaking water, the rippling light, now and then a distorted silver wall that turned into a huge school of fish as she drew nearer. The sun arched up the sky, and Luce swam through gold-green beams, watching the ribbons of shadow that seemed to pour endlessly from her outstretched hands.

On and on, concentrating on the light-streaked space ahead of her. She'd almost succeeded, Luce told herself. She'd saved her father from his living death on that island, and soon he'd understand how much he still had to hope for.

Her daydreams still needled at her, prickling her with impossible hopes. It occurred to her, though, that even if her ideas weren't crazy she still wouldn't be able to tell her father to look for her near Dorian's village. She'd never thought to ask the name.

* * *

The sun wasn't far above the horizon, and the air was tinted golden orange as they closed on the Aleutian chain. Luce could even make out a few pale, boxy shapes perched on the slope of a conical island ahead of her: almost certainly a small settlement. Her father would find other humans soon. They'd help him. When she stopped to grin back at her father now his excitement seemed genuine, without any of the hidden darkness Luce had noticed before. "My God, Luce! We've made it!"

Luce's shoulders were killing her, her tail stiff and heavy with exhaustion. She paused and looked back at him, then swam to the raft.

They were close to safety, but that also meant they were close to saying goodbye. She could see in her father's face that he might be thinking the same thing as he reached down and stroked her wet hair. "You did it, baby doll," he whispered to her. "I thought I'd die in that place, but you saved me. I am so damned proud of you."

Luce pressed her cheek against his hand. "You're happy?"

"I'm real happy." But again something grim showed on his face. "Just need to figure out what we can do about you now."

Luce flinched. "You can't worry about me . . ."

He needed to recover his hope, his sanity. Trying to raise a mermaid daughter couldn't possibly help with that, Luce thought. Much as she hated the idea, it would be better for him to forget about her completely, at least unless the day came when she could *walk* up to him and . . . The look on his face was tense, distant.

"There's something coming!" he hissed abruptly. "Luce, under the water!"

Luce's reflexes took over and she dove in a spasm of fear. Dimly she heard her father's cry and the thud as he threw himself belly-down on the tilting raft. A surge of terror sped her heart, spasmed through her tail, but she could feel the raft's drag slowing her unbearably. Land was so *close* now. The island's dark peak loomed in her eyes, and she fought to reach it. Under normal conditions she could easily outswim an orca, but Luce realized with horror that the extra weight would hold her back too much. She strained to drive herself harder, but she seemed to be swimming through something thick and inhibiting, gray honey taking the place of cool water. Her tail was so cramped and tired that it twitched awkwardly as she tried to accelerate. And in the corners of her eyes she could see shadow-shapes closing in . . .

They came from the sides, not from below as she'd feared. And even in her panic Luce realized the shapes were too small to be orcas. Dolphins, then? For a fraction of a second she was ready to scream from sheer relief.

Her relief died as other dark shapes darted below her and she saw that she was surrounded. They weren't just too small to be orcas: they were also too quick, too graceful and sinuous, and a faint glow slicked their skin. Anais would love nothing more than to murder Luce's father in front of her . . . Luce wove from side to side, looking for a way through the closing ring of mermaids. There was a flash and a blur, and a pair of dark Inuit eyes stared straight into hers. Who *was* that? Hands seized Luce's shoulders from the sides, and the dark-eyed mermaid jerked her head, signaling them upward. Luce thrashed as they tugged her to the surface. The gold of sunset flecked the sea in all directions, and there was that beckoning island. It was so close now that Luce could make out a ramshackle old dock.

Luce stared around in the golden light, catching one quick glimpse of her father's appalled face. Half a dozen mermaids pressed around her, their hands tight on her arms to keep her from escaping, and Luce realized that she didn't recognize any of them.

"Okay," the Inuit mermaid snapped. Her round cheeks glowed tan, and her almond eyes flashed. She was the only one not gripping Luce: their queen, obviously. "I've got some questions for you."

Luce glanced back at her father again, trying to warn him with her eyes to keep silent. He looked too stunned to say anything; at least Luce *hoped* he was.

"Are you new at this or something?" the dark mermaid snarled, drawing Luce's attention back to her. "Metaskaza?"

Luce stared at her and then looked around at her followers. All their faces were hard, unyielding, gorgeous in the evening light. "Let us go."

Two of the mermaid guards jerked her in response, about as roughly as they could without it counting as a violation of the timahk. "You didn't answer my question," the Inuit queen observed.

Luce glared back at her. "I'm not metaskaza."

"And you haven't been living on your own since you changed? This isn't, like, the first time you've met other mermaids?"

"No." Luce tried to think fast. She could call a wave to throw these mermaids out of her path. That kind of singing wasn't meant to harm humans, and it was just possible that her father would be able to withstand it, but the risk was terrible.

And even then this strange tribe would be sure to chase after her, and she definitely wouldn't be able to outrace them. Not encumbered as she was by the raft.

"Cool." The queen considered this. "Looks like you're running out of excuses, doesn't it?" Luce braced herself, ready to spring, as the queen cocked her head at the raft. "Last question, then. What's with the *human?*"

Luce exhaled, trying to calm the impulse to fight. Furious as she felt at being thwarted with land so close, violence wouldn't help her father. Maybe these mermaids wouldn't care what Luce had to say, but she needed to try. "He's my dad."

Murmurs of surprise came from the other mermaids. Luce watched them look around at one another, and a few swiveled their heads to see the events that had made Luce change. "It wasn't *him*, anyway," one of them whispered. "But still . . ."

"You know that doesn't matter!" someone yelped behind Luce. Luce turned to look at her, a girl with masses of wavy, honey-colored hair and a face that would have been sweet if it weren't so bleak and miserable. "No fraternizing with humans. It doesn't matter who they are!"

Luce glowered at her. "It matters to *me*. I'm taking him back to shore, and I'm not letting *anyone* stop me."

The queen touched her arm sympathetically. "I'm really sorry. Look, I understand it's your dad; you still love him. But we can't let you do that. There's no way." Luce turned on her with such a dark blaze in her eyes that the queen recoiled a little. This was it, then. Luce had never dreamed she might kill one of her fellow mermaids, but if that was what it took . . . "I'm really sorry about this," the queen said again. "Everyone hold her. Get her tail. Jessie?" She cocked her head at the honey-haired girl. "Want to do the honors?"

Jessie shot Luce a look; Luce couldn't tell if it was meant to be defiant or apologetic. Then Jessie gazed down sadly at the water's surface. Anyone would have thought that she was thinking of something completely different, but Luce could feel the crushing expectation of the mermaids around her. Nails dug into Luce's arm, and girls pulled in shivering breaths. Jessie's soft pink lips opened, and the air began to melt like butter. It dripped with sounds too beautiful for any human mind to bear, and Luce glanced back to see her father staggering to his feet. His gaze was veiled, milky, already drowning in impossible dreams. She had only moments.

No choice, Luce thought vaguely. *No other way*. Her own emotions were rising in Jessie's voice, higher and fiercer by the moment, and even before Luce had quite realized what she was doing those feelings had transformed themselves into a song of stabbing brilliance, so sharp and piercing that the sun's glare seemed to dull by comparison. The sea swelled in Luce's cry. Everything around Luce slowed into a kind of drowning light, but the light was made of pure music, and that music was an unceasing, magnificent scream. The strange mermaids had half a second to gape at her with a mixture of terror and admiration. Then waves like giant hands caught them by their wrists, their tails, wrenching them away from her; fins tumbled, flashing sunset at every turn, and plunged from strange heights. The water seemed to obey her will even before she was consciously aware of what she wanted. Luce felt herself in the sound that cut off Jessie's singing as a tendril of water wrapped around her neck and silenced her; she felt herself, her *music*, fused into rolling waters forty feet high that threw mermaid bodies apart.

There was another shriek as the Inuit queen crashed down just in front of Luce. Luce allowed herself one quick glance backwards to make sure her father was still on the raft; his limp body lay face-down on the planks. Then she was hurling toward the island again, fading music curling in her chest and tears she couldn't control dissolving in the rushing sea. There was no way to guess what that assaulting music had done to her father's mind and no time to stop and check on him. But she was in so much pain. Her movements were sloppy and unhinged, and already that strange tribe was after her again.

"Wait!" Luce heard someone shouting behind her. The cry shivered and refracted through the water, pounding at her head from all sides, and Luce drove herself on. "Wait up! Queen Luce! We didn't know it was you!"

Luce's tail convulsed painfully. She couldn't help slowing for a moment, and her whole body wobbled with the green waves around her. Hands were closing on her again, but much more gently this time. She broke the surface with a gasp. "I *won't* let you hurt him! Not after . . . I mean, he was lost for so long; it's so incredible that I found him again . . ."

"We won't," the dark queen promised softly. Her arm was already halfway around Luce's shoulders, and Luce couldn't decide whether to be angry or to give in to the comfort of that touch. "It's all okay. I'm Queen Sedna. Look, Luce, we've *heard* about you . . ." Sedna faltered, and Luce saw the other mermaids gaping at her as if they could hardly believe it. Sedna gazed back at them with a sudden flash of authority. "She can do what she wants."

"We're talking about some human," Jessie objected. She was still rubbing her throat, but she didn't seem to be really hurt. "Sedna, you know it's not *right*—"

"She's a friend of Nausicaa's!" Queen Sedna snapped back. "And think about it, Jessie: she's also an enemy of that rotten *sika bitch* . . . Have you thought at all about how happy that *sika* will be if we do anything to upset Luce? You want to do Anais some huge favor? After she killed your *sister*?"

Luce was still gasping, overwhelmed by storming emotions, breathless with weariness. But her mind was clearing enough for her to understand two things: a lot had happened while she'd been stalled at her father's island, and if her father was safe it was thanks, in some unimaginable way, to Nausicaa. "What . . . are you talking about?" Luce managed.

Sedna smiled at her. "Wow. It's a long story."

All the stories are long, Luce thought. She suddenly missed Nausicaa so much that something seemed to crumple deep in her chest.

"But *still* . . ." Jessie kept trying to argue. "It's not like the timahk makes exceptions for anyone, Sedna."

"Oh, for Crissake." Sedna rolled her eyes. "What*ever*. We can do this." *Do what?* Luce thought. She tensed again, but Sedna was still grinning. "Luce, okay, so has your dad there ever heard you sing?"

Luce started. Of course he must have heard both Jessie and Luce singing just a few minutes before, but it seemed like Sedna had decided to ignore that. It could only be deliberate, and Luce started grinning back into the queen's sparkling eyes. "Absolutely not."

Sedna raised her eyebrows at Jessie. "See? So where's the problem?"

"Well—*her.*" Jessie gazed around at the tribe for support then pivoted her eyes slowly to fix on Luce. "*She's* the problem. Queen *Luce.* Okay, Sedna, even if . . . Singing or not, she's still been fraternizing with humans. You know what the timahk says! We can't just let her get *away* with that. Not even . . . You know how much I want to get back at Anais, but—"

"There's the timahk, all right," Sedna pronounced definitely. "But there's also common sense! God, Jessie, we're talking about the girl's dad here." Luce found herself liking Sedna more by the second. She looked anxiously back at her father, but he was sprawled unconscious with his head crooked awkwardly sideways, the edge of a board digging into his cheek.

"Queen Sedna? Thank you so much . . . for understanding. I need to go make sure he's okay." Sedna and Jessie were busy glaring at each other, tails flicking, and Luce skimmed away from them. In a moment her hands were in her father's hair, gripping his arms, and she was shaking him. At least he was breathing, even if he wheezed like some kind of broken toy. "Please. Dad, please. Don't you dare . . ." *lose your mind,* Luce thought, but she was too afraid to say it. "You need to live! You need to be okay, and happy, and . . ." *grow up for me. Since I can't.*

A sliver of cinnamon eyes gleamed at her. "Lucette. What kind of world *is* this?"

Luce beamed in relief. "The same kind it was ten minutes ago. You just fainted." *If only that's all it is,* Luce thought.

"It's *not* the same! It's new, always new. Every second. Like waking up on some kind of hard diamond planet."

He was delirious, Luce decided. She stroked his matted hair and murmured to him, even as she wondered at what he had said. Always new?

Nausicaa certainly didn't think so. But even Nausicaa wasn't right *all* the time.

"Let's get you to shore," Luce whispered. "We're almost there. You'll be safe . . ." She forced herself to start swimming. Her tail was a snarl of pain, and her shoulders screamed as the ropes snapped taut again, but they would reach land in only a few minutes.

"Come back and talk to us when you're done with that, okay?" Sedna called after her.

Luce looked around and smiled, and the glow on Sedna's face told Luce that Sedna understood how utterly grateful she was. From the limp way Jessie held herself Luce thought she was starting to back down. Sedna would handle the situation fine, Luce felt sure. She was a real queen.

The raft finally ran aground a bit too close to the village for Luce's comfort, but she was too tired to care. She flung her upper body onto the beach as her father scrambled ashore, staring all around him as if he really were seeing glinting diamond facets in all the trees. Smoke blue dusk blurred the waving grass. "Oh, Luce! It's hard to trust it, but it's all so beautiful!" He pulled himself upright and staggered a few dizzy steps, and Luce slipped the harness off her shoulders. Blood raced back into her arms like a hundred spinning razors, and she stretched and closed her eyes for a moment to fight the pain.

How could she possibly say goodbye now? But there was Dorian, and she'd already made him wait for so long. It was cruel. He must be so worried about her, maybe even afraid that she was dead.

Her father twirled messily, still clearly half-maddened by his brush with enchantment. *"It's so beautiful!* I'll never ask where I am again. Luce, baby doll, wherever it is, you brought me to it!" He was shouting, and Luce glanced nervously toward the shining windows of that tiny village: tiny enough that any disturbance would attract attention instantly. *Humans* would come. Already Luce caught sight of yellow light abruptly slicing from an opening door. Someone was calling and a dog barked.

"Dad? I'm going to . . . I have to go. In just a minute." Another door opened as if it were answering the first. They'd definitely heard him, then. "I—we have to say goodbye. It might be a long time—"

"No!" He staggered into the water, and Luce gaped in alarm. "No, doll, I'm going to do right by you this time. I swear it. Now that I've found you again, I'm going to change everything."

She could already hear faint footsteps, and the barking was getting louder. A blot of yellow from a swinging flashlight crisscrossed a path; it wasn't all that far away. "You *can't.* You've—done everything you can for me, and I love you so much, but I have to go." Luce heard the childish appeal rising in her voice. As if she was begging him to forgive her.

"How am I even going to reach you? Lucette, you can't just—"

"I have to." She considered the problem, but there was no

time to come up with a good solution. "Make sure Peter always knows where you are. That way, if I ever . . . I'll have a way to find you."

Her father snorted. "Don't think Peter will want to do me a lot of favors. Not when I get done with him."

She didn't actually want him to hurt Peter, but this hardly seemed like the moment to start an argument. "I'll find you somehow." She sounded like Nausicaa, Luce thought. "Don't wait for me, don't worry, just do whatever you can to be happy . . ." She could hear men chattering, their rapid steps, the skittering sound of the dog breaking into a run. The flashlight's beam suddenly swept across her eyes as the men turned onto the beach. She didn't think they'd seen her, but they would very soon.

"Hey." The man was heavyset and lumbering against the twilit sky. "Thought we heard something. Who's there?"

She couldn't hug her father properly while he was standing. She settled for squeezing his knees. Everything she'd promised him might be a lie. Luce had to choke down a wild cry of grief as she realized that she might never see him again.

The water closed around her, but she couldn't bring herself to speed away. Instead she hovered under the surface just offshore. "LUCE!"

"Hey there." Dimly Luce could hear the strange man's whistle of surprise and she knew he'd spotted the crude raft. "You *okay*, man? Looks like you've been through a rough patch . . ."

"LUCE!" her father screamed. His steps splashed in the water, but Luce was sure the strangers were restraining him. "LUCE! Oh, come back!"

"Luce isn't here, old guy," the man's voice soothed. "Just you."

* * *

Queen Sedna and the others caught up with Luce twenty minutes later. She was swimming lethargically under the water, her whole body trembling from a mixture of fatigue and heartbreak. She barely registered the presence of the other mermaids as they flocked around her, guiding her to a safe cove on the next island over. Luce drowsed on the beach as the other mermaids ate dinner, their chattering voices mingling with the wash of thickening darkness.

"Don't you think she needs some food, too?"

"I don't know, I think we should let her sleep . . ."

"You think Nausicaa is right about her? Like, of course what she did was incredible, but . . ."

"I trust Nausicaa more than anyone I've ever known." Luce thought the voice was Sedna's, but maybe she was already dreaming. "If she calls somebody 'the future of the mermaids,' I don't know, I kind of tend to believe that she knows what she's talking about."

"Anyone Anais hates *that* much has to be special at least."

"I think they've lost us. We're not going to catch them now."

"*She'll* know. She can show us where they live."

Luce watched curved shapes like glowing seals in a midnight tide. Her father stepped out of the sea, his hair clean and his beard shaved, and threw back water like a shining cloak. He was safe now, and Luce slept.

* * *

Luce woke to another clear morning. She still felt hopelessly weak and drained, but her tail flipped at the thought of getting back to Dorian. Something thwacked on a rock near her head, and Luce opened her eyes to see Sedna offering her a mussel. Luce noticed that three fingers were partly missing on the hand reaching toward her; they looked hacked-off, the stumps oddly angled, though they had clearly healed long ago. Luce and Sedna were alone together, and Luce wondered hazily where the other girls had gone.

"Hey, Luce. How are you feeling?"

"Awful." Luce smiled at her and sat up, taking the food. She was so hungry that it felt like a kind of illness. "Thank you, Sedna." They watched each other for a minute: a little warily, but Luce knew they were already friends. "You said you know Nausicaa?" Sudden hope rose in Luce. "How about Violet and Dana?"

"Violet and Dana? I don't think I've heard of them, no." Luce stifled her disappointment as Sedna went on talking. What had happened to the two fleeing mermaids? "But I've known Nausicaa for a *long* time. Like maybe every ten or twenty years she comes through my territory, and she usually stays awhile . . ."

Luce had assumed that Sedna was a fairly new mermaid, but clearly that wasn't true. "You've been in the water that long?" Luce was still a little wobbly. It took an effort to stay focused.

"Well, not like *Nausicaa* long." Sedna smiled. "But born-

1852 long? Kidnapped-by-sadistic-fur-trappers long? Yeah. And I've been queen south of here for at least sixty years."

It was funny, then, that Sedna's way of talking was so modern. Probably it was something she did on purpose; maybe she thought it was important to stay up to date. Sedna watched her, black eyes deep and alert, black hair glossy in the fresh sunlight. Her skin was a lush, glowing gold, almost the color of a dawn sky.

"I said, 'south of here.' On the far side of the Aleutians, like pretty near Canada even. Most of the tribe is still there now."

Luce was confused. "Okay."

"Don't you want to know why we're so far out of our territory?"

Luce ran a hand over her face. "I already know. You're chasing Anais. Maybe the rest of my old tribe, too . . ." It was coming back to her. "They must have run into you after they migrated down the coast? You said Anais murdered Jessie's sister."

"That doesn't surprise you? Fiona was just a larva, but she and Jessie changed together, and we'd kept Fiona safe for years. You can believe a mermaid—even a *sika*—would do something so outrageous? It's the kind of thing you'd expect from humans, and not even all of *them* . . ."

"It doesn't surprise me at all," Luce said wearily. It was depressing to be reminded of Anais. "She's killed larvae before. She probably didn't care whose sister it was."

"Oh, she *cared!*" Sedna's fury was building. "She cared! She did it to get back at us, and she went out of her way to hurt us as much as she could. When we catch her I'm going to expel her myself, and I'm going to make sure there are orcas all around first. Even if I have to personally draw the orcas there with bait, I'll make sure of it!" Sedna's tone was grim, and Luce knew this wasn't an idle threat. "We knew the bitch was *sika*, but we just felt so *sorry* for the mermaids with her. They seemed so scared and miserable, like they were all about to crack up completely, and we made the mistake of taking them in. Those girls are really crazy, though."

Luce's head reeled a little. She wanted to think about Dorian and her father, not about whatever awful things Anais had done. But still . . . "What happened?"

"Well, we're a strict tribe. We don't take down more than four or five ships a year, max, and I have a rule about only doing it when there's a big enough storm that it won't look suspicious."

Luce was impressed. Keeping the mermaids' longing to kill under such tight discipline couldn't be easy, she knew, even if she wished that they wouldn't sink ships at all. She looked at Sedna with sudden respect, but Sedna was too furious to meet her eyes.

"So I explained all that to them when they showed up, right? And for a while they were mostly okay. But then they started just ignoring me! Like they weren't in my territory at all!" Sedna was indignant at the memory. "They were attacking ships in this insane, random way, so I told them to get the hell out. And they did, but before they left—"

"They threw Fiona on shore," Luce finished. She felt nauseous. It was such a hideous, vicious thing to do, even for Anais. "But why do you think they ran back this way? Wouldn't it be more likely for them to keep traveling south?"

Sedna shook her head. "A few of the littlest girls snuck back to us. Begged us to let them join our tribe. And they said Anais didn't want to risk meeting any more tribes that already had queens of their own, so she was just dragging them all back to their old territory. Anais kept talking about all the stuff they'd left in their cave, anyway . . . Luce? What's wrong?"

Luce clung to the shore, greenish lights flashing in her eyes as the blood drained from her head. All her joyful fantasies of peace with the humans suddenly weighed on her in a new way, steely and threatening. "They *can't* go back!"

"Who else is going to put up with them?" Sedna asked flippantly.

"No—Sedna—no, this is *horrible*. I know Anais deserves it, but the rest of them . . . Rachel, Kayley . . ."

Sedna stared at her, utterly bewildered. "Um, Luce? Want to make sense?"

"It's not safe for them to go back there. I think—no, I'm *sure*—the human police up there know about us—"

"The humans *what*?"

Luce gazed back at her numbly. "They know, Sedna. At least a few of them do. We're not a total secret anymore."

"You'd better take that back!" Sedna shrieked. Her tail was writhing in midair, ready to strike, and Luce jerked away from her. "You'd better— You *can't* be right!"

"I saw them plant a camera. Divers. They stuck it to a wall underwater, hidden, right next to the beach where we ate," Luce insisted. "Sedna, *don't* bring your mermaids up there!"

"Humans lose cameras all the time!"

"Sedna, please!" Luce yelled. "That camera wasn't lost. It

was planted on purpose. Do you think I'm telling you this so you won't go punish Anais? After she tried to kill me *and* my closest friends?"

"You might be," Sedna murmured, but Luce could tell she didn't believe it. Her black eyes flicked fearfully around the placid silver waves.

"Maybe I am wrong," Luce groaned. She tried to feel convinced. "Maybe I'm crazy, and everything is just the same as it's always been. But Sedna, if I'm right about this . . ."

Luce watched Sedna's face twisting and suddenly knew that, no matter how much Sedna wanted justice, she wasn't about to lead her followers into so much potential danger.

"Queen Luce?"

Luce couldn't answer at first. Instead she watched Sedna fighting to compose herself. Everything was too painful, too out of control. Even if Luce raced desperately to her old tribe and warned them again to get out, they'd be more likely to murder her than to listen to her. But even so . . . "I should hurry back there, Sedna. I should try to do *something*."

Before it's too late, Luce thought. *Before something so terrible happens that we can't ever fix it.*

Sedna exhaled, hard, and looked straight into her eyes. "Goodbye, then, Luce. I really hope we'll see you . . ." She trailed off abruptly.

But Sedna didn't need to say the last word out loud for Luce to know what it was.

Alive.

25

Till Human Voices Wake Us

The journey back took two long, tiring days. Luce's thoughts flurried on in a dreamlike whirl of images: sometimes Dorian was kissing her, sometimes Anais had a knife at her throat. She'd made up her mind that she was going to do something, anything, to get her old tribe out of danger, but she had no idea how she could actually help. Not when they were all so certain that she was their enemy. Anais would treat anything Luce said as a joke, and the rest of the tribe seemed to be utterly under Anais's control, too intimidated to even question her. Had they really stood by and let her murder Fiona? Had they *known*?

But maybe she had some time to come up with a plan. As long as the tribe didn't bring down any more ships, maybe the humans wouldn't realize mermaids were still living near there or maybe the humans wouldn't do anything to hurt them after all. Luce did her best to find the idea comforting, but when the coastline finally began to bend into familiar cliffs and zigzags she only grew more anxious. It was already late at night, much too late to look for Dorian, and the sky was moody and starless. Luce made her way to the inlet that sheltered her own small cave. She felt entirely depleted, ready to sleep for days. In just a few moments she would be resting with her head on Dorian's old jacket, and she sighed gratefully as she turned toward the cave's entrance. The entrance was usually completely submerged, but the tide tonight was exceptionally low: low enough that a sliver of jet emptiness showed above the lapping water.

Then Luce stopped short. Something froze her where she was, some thrum of agitation. It was like a silent noise she couldn't put a name to, a stiffness in the way the night held itself, an indrawn breath. Luce hovered in the water, her tail barely stirring, and listened.

All she could hear was the savage drumming of her own heart, the light repetitive slosh of waves on rocky walls. But for some reason the quiet did nothing to ease her terror.

She was being irrational, Luce told herself as she backed slowly away from the dark hollow in the rock. Silly and cowardly. She should be ashamed to let her fears control her this way.

Luce skimmed out of the inlet, still insulting herself in her thoughts, but even so she stayed under the surface as she went. She needed to leave a message for Dorian: something simple, something that would make sense only to him. She'd spell out I'M HOME in pebbles on the edge of the dock where he kept the rowboat tied. Then, Luce thought, she'd go sleep in that shallow cave where she used to take him, the one with the fallen tree spanning the water.

That would be almost like being with him again.

* * *

When Luce woke the sun glared near the center of the sky, so high that she knew it must be noon and also not so long after the spring equinox. It could even be early May. She started. She had no way to guess if this was a school day or a weekend, and Dorian might be waiting for her at the beach already. He could have been sitting there for hours, frustrated and impatient. Luce shook herself, stretching her tired muscles, and sped off without even stopping for breakfast. Worried as she still was about the tribe, she felt that the water was streaked with happiness, and each familiar boulder, each leaning spruce, was a reminder of him. She was so glad to be home.

Dorian wasn't at the beach, though two small children were playing there, watched over by their mother. Maybe he knew there'd be too many people around, and he was planning to meet her after dark?

Luce went to get something to eat and waited nervously. Maybe Dorian hadn't found her message? What if he was seriously angry with her for being so late? She knew she had to think up a plan—some way to protect her old tribe—but as the day wore on she just couldn't concentrate. She watched a pair of sea otters playing not far from her. They were beautiful animals and Luce usually adored them, but today they bothered her. They treated their joy so *casually*, as if it weren't something rare and precious, something you could lose at any moment.

For the first time it occurred to her that Dorian might have even moved away. How could he let her know?

* * *

"Hi." It was early dusk when Dorian finally walked down the beach's slope, pebbles grinding under his sneakers, his face secretive and unsmiling. Luce's happiness at seeing him turned into something clammy and unsettled, twisting in her stomach. She lay against the beach, but he didn't drop to his knees to reach for her, didn't even come close enough to let her touch him. "You broke your promise. The water's been pretty clear for a month already."

Luce moaned inside as she heard his voice, so beloved but so thick with resentment. "Dorian! I know it seems . . . But I came back as soon as I could. A lot happened." Why wouldn't he at least hold her?

"You had to do something heroic? Have some big dramatic adventure? Save someone's *life*?" His sneer made Luce cringe. "Whatever. It doesn't matter what it was. You abandoned me again—"

"I found my dad alive!" Luce blurted. Dorian's face shifted, his eyes widening and his tensed mouth dropping, and Luce went on frantically. He'd forgive her once he understood. "I'm so sorry you had to wait, but I—got blown out into nowhere in a storm, and there was this island, and my dad was living there as a castaway! He didn't die! And . . .." Luce wasn't sure how to explain. "It wasn't easy to get him out of there. Dorian, I missed you all the time, but I only managed to get him back to shore a few days ago. And then I came straight here."

Dorian's expression wavered a little. There was a hint of softening as he stared at her desperate face, and one hand drifted slightly forward as if he wanted to touch her. Luce waited for him, gazing up at his ochre eyes in the blue light, his dark blond hair tangling in the breeze. Then he stopped where he was, and Luce turned cold with dread.

"It doesn't matter," Dorian repeated. He sounded just a bit gentler now, but that didn't help at all. "It's too late, Luce."

"It *can't* be. You couldn't expect me to leave him stranded! Dorian, please . . ."

"You're not listening to me, Luce! It's too late. If you'd only come back here before, it never would have happened, but . . ."

"But what?"

Dorian stared straight at her. His hands were clenched. "I'm with someone else now."

"You . . ." A *human*, Luce thought. *Zoe*. It seemed impossible, but there was Dorian's set brutal face. "Are you in love with her?"

Dorian sighed. "Honestly? Not really. But I like her a *lot*."

Luce felt a fresh jolt of hope. She opened her mouth to say something, to ask something important, but Dorian glowered and interrupted her.

"But maybe that's what I want, Luce. I like it that I'm *not* all in love with her, and that she's *not* freakishly beautiful, and that there's nothing magic about her! Maybe I like it that, whatever I feel around her, I never have to wonder where my feelings are *coming* from . . ."

"I can't help that," Luce whispered. She heard a kind of subliminal droning, a scream-song buried in her heart. She was afraid to let her voice come out at all in case the scream took over.

"You what?"

"I . . . can't help being magic. I can't help what my face is like now, or that you think—"

"You *could* have helped it, though," Dorian snarled. "You had a choice!" He hesitated for a second but then went on, lashing her with the words. "So did Zoe. She could have changed, too, but instead she decided to stay human and deal with all the *real* problems! Instead of just being some kid forever, and playing at all this heroic crap . . ."

Luce was too stunned to even be angry. The scream seethed inside her, and she gaped at Dorian in bitter astonishment. Her problems weren't *real*? Rescuing her father wasn't real, the risk of war with the humans wasn't real, Anais committing murder wasn't—

"That's an *insane* thing to say." Luce's voice was still very quiet. "I was saving my *father*."

Dorian gazed at her thoughtfully, and for a few seconds he didn't say anything. He opened his mouth and paused, as if the words he was thinking were too cruel to be voiced. Then he halfway smiled.

"I'll never get to save *my* father."

The scream fought harder now, trying to get out. Luce couldn't say anything, and she felt too broken to move.

"Luce, listen . . ."

She gaped at him, her face crumpling from the struggle not to scream or cry.

"I won't sing back," Dorian announced.

Luce clutched the shore. She didn't understand at first.

Dorian watched her, then spoke again. "If you want to kill me for this, you can. I won't sing back." He actually grinned: the impish, defiant grin Luce had loved so much. "Now's your big chance! It's a one-time offer, though, so you better—"

His grin fell away. He shouldn't *say* that to her, Luce thought, not when her voice was already so close to overpowering her, when she could hardly keep it restrained . . .

The note rose up, velvety and piercing at the same time, and hovered for a moment like a living star. The beginning of the death song, of Luce's song of enchantment, so fiercely beautiful that the air itself seemed to crystallize into pure longing.

Luce watched Dorian bite his lip, hard, and close his eyes. Preparing himself. As her song tumbled down the scale she could feel his mind falling with it, letting go of everything, giving in to that feeling of absolute forgiveness . . . But nobody was actually forgiven now, were they? He took his first steps into the sea, and even as she sang Luce was weeping uncontrollably. But he *should* die for what he'd done to her, and even if he shouldn't, the song was too powerful for her to call it back. The boundaries of her own mind seemed to disintegrate in that torrent of violent music.

Waves parted around Dorian's chest, slapped at his shoulders. His back was turned to Luce now, but she could hear his labored breathing. Even without trying to defend himself he still had much more resistance than a normal human would. But arrogant as he was, he didn't have *enough*.

He took another step forward. Two. Luce could feel his thoughts as she sang: his mother was there smiling at him with such tenderness; the air ran with streaming colors, and his mind winged outward to feel the whole world beckoning him home . . . Maybe, Luce tried to tell herself, maybe it was better this way. Maybe this was the *only* way things between them could have ended all along. Dorian staggered as the first wave crashed across the top of his head.

I hope you will be the one . . . a voice suddenly murmured in Luce's mind. Even in the trance of her singing Luce wanted to reach for that voice, to pull it closer. The death song swirled through her, trying to drive the voice back, but all at once she thought that maybe, just maybe drowning Dorian *wasn't* the only possibility left for her. Dimly Luce felt herself make some terrible effort. Her body rocked, lunged . . .

. . . who discovers the strength . . .

Was she still singing? Luce couldn't tell anymore. All she could recognize now was that voice, Nausicaa's voice, and with it a burning, unbearable pain. Heat licked at her scales, and the sting pierced deep. Like knives of pure sun slashing into her.

. . . to make a different choice . . .

Luce wasn't singing anymore. Instead she was screaming from horrifying pain, her body racked by icy fire. She was still lying at the edge of the beach, but she'd swung around far enough to throw her tail out of the water. Convulsions beat through her, her tail slapping so hard that rocks flew in all directions. Dorian was running toward her through the drag of the water, not enchanted at all anymore, his hands pressed tight over his ears. Luce felt him seize her spasming tail in both arms and then stagger sideways, pulling her with him.

Pulling her back into the sea.

Luce gasped and choked, tears streaming over her face, and Dorian stood drenched and trembling in the water nearby. He was gazing at her as she flailed, as that awful burning cooled. Luce wouldn't look at him.

"Why did you *stop?*" Dorian whispered. Plaintively, childishly. Luce found his babyish tone utterly sickening. She was dishonored, humiliated, shattered. She'd let Nausicaa leave without her, she'd betrayed Dana and abandoned her father. For *this?*

Luce hated him then. Her pride flared, dark and scathing. Dorian wasn't even worth killing. And as for everything she'd hoped might still be possible . . .

She'd imagined perfect, shared *forgiveness,* Luce thought with disgust. She'd wanted *reconciliation,* of all things, with *humans.* Now it seemed like the sickest joke she'd ever heard. And she'd even thought of risking death to turn *into* one of these creatures, who betrayed so readily, who never seemed to have more than half a heart . . .

Her body was already rippling without her having to consciously control it.

She was gone.

* * *

Dorian stumbled back a short distance and sat down. The waves leaped in front of him, foam streaking their always-descending curls. Was she really gone? Forever?

Running footsteps sounded in the distance, coming closer. Dorian didn't move. Whatever it was, it wasn't his problem. All this human stuff just wasn't his problem. The footsteps thudded onto the beach with a loud clatter of dislodged stones.

"Dorian! Oh, thank God. But you're soaking wet!"

Slowly Dorian turned his head. Ben Ellison ran toward

him, eyes urgent, and reeled to a stop as he registered Dorian's miserable face. Ellison stared around the beach, obviously puzzled. "Dorian, I was looking for you, and then I heard—I thought—wasn't someone screaming?"

"Oh." Dorian turned back to gaze at the waves again. "That wasn't me. It was Luce." He nodded toward the breakers. Ellison followed the gesture and teetered slightly as he grasped what it meant. "If you're worrying about her, she's probably fine."

"*Luce.* That's her name? That's why I was looking for you." Ellison stood unsteadily, considering, and then sat down close to Dorian. "There's something I wanted you to tell her if she came back, your girlfriend."

"She's not my girlfriend anymore. I'm not going to be telling her anything." Dorian felt shocked by the words even as he spoke them. Could they really be true? "I just broke up with her."

Ellison looked flabbergasted. "You just *what?*" He paused, his face working strangely. "And you're still here? I would have sworn that *breaking up* with a mermaid was a guaranteed way to get yourself killed."

Dorian exhaled. There was no reason now not to say whatever he felt like. Ellison knew; the whole FBI probably knew. "I *offered.* I told her to go ahead and drown me if she felt like it." Dorian glowered at the midnight blue waves and pitched a rock. "She wouldn't *do* it."

"You offered yourself up for murder?" Again that odd chewing motion passed through Ellison's worn face. "Why would you do such a thing?"

Dorian didn't answer. The wind on his sopping clothes chilled him, but he didn't want to move. An idea came to Ellison; his voice grew more animated. "Was it that you used to be so deeply in love with her that it seemed like the only way you could honor that lost connection? A grand gesture . . ."

Dorian rubbed his face against his knees and groaned. He'd thought Ellison was smarter than this, and he looked up bleakly into the older man's face. "No. I offered because I'm *still* in love with her." Dorian wanted to let go. He wanted to sway in that blue darkness, melt into song. "I more than offered, actually. I tried to *make* her do it, and she still wouldn't!"

Dorian knew it was true when he heard himself say it. He'd hurt Luce that way to control her, drive her to murder. And she'd *wanted* to; she'd started . . . But somehow she'd held back.

"But then if you still love her . . ."

"It was never going to work!" Dorian exploded. "You don't understand. She'll just run off and abandon me whenever she thinks there's something more important. And she doesn't even *want* to grow up, and she doesn't care what that's going to do to me. I talked to her and talked to her about it, but she won't even *try* to turn human again!"

Dorian caught himself and buried his face in his arms. He was determined not to burst out crying, determined to get a grip on himself, but he could feel his control slipping. He couldn't afford to meet Ellison's eyes, and for several moments they were both silent. Then Dorian felt a hand touch his shoulder, and he flinched in annoyance. He was in no mood to accept anyone's sympathy, Ben Ellison's least of all.

The hand was shaking. Dorian turned his head, but at first he couldn't identify the look on Ellison's face. Could that be horror?

"Again?" Ellison asked.

His cell phone started ringing.

* * *

Nausicaa had been right all along. Luce had been an idiot not to listen to her. But even if Nausicaa was gone now, it wasn't too late for Luce to do what her friend had wanted. She'd hurry back to her old tribe's cave and formally challenge Anais in front of everyone. If they attacked her, fine, she would fight. If they didn't she'd shame Anais by proving once and for all who the true queen was, and then she'd lead anyone who would come with her south and away from here. They'd leave for good, start over somewhere new, and maybe Luce would even find Nausicaa.

It was better to think about her plan than about how degraded she was. She'd been foolish enough to put her trust in a human, and he had utterly failed her. He couldn't even wait one *month* past the melting of the ice before he'd thrown himself at someone else. He was shallow, faithless, empty . . . just like all of them were.

Luce sped up the coast, blind to the streaking night blue bubbles, blind to the refracting starlight.

Anais had no idea what she was up against.

* * *

As Luce drew near the cave that had once been her home the water changed. It felt subtly unclean, sticky, and it licked her with a faint, sweet, metallic stench. It was disgusting. Had Anais dragged back so much garbage that it had actually begun fouling the sea? The water looked murkier, too, with a brownish tint, and it only seemed to get worse as Luce slipped into the deep underwater tunnel that led to the cave. Now the water didn't just stink. It *tasted* vile, too, with a slick tang, a raw-meat flavor as if a seal had just been torn apart. It was so revolting that Luce could hardly make herself keep going. How could the other mermaids stand it?

Hadn't she once tasted something like this before? Luce fought down the hideous memory, water stained and sticky as orcas leaped, as a tiny hand floated by . . .

Maybe the tribe had deserted this cave, though. It was oddly silent as Luce reached the spot where the rocky walls widened. The pollution was getting thicker, too: the water was actually *red*.

Luce gasped with the first shock of understanding, then gagged as the blood-drenched water flooded her mouth. She broke the surface sputtering, spitting, trying to get that taste *out* . . .

It *couldn't* be real. It couldn't.

A milky leg floated right in front of her, toes wrinkled and grayish pink. It was bobbing by itself in the filthy water, and Luce saw the ragged flesh where it had separated from its body, pale bone protruding like a snapped-off branch. Luce spun, trying somehow not to see—

That open neck, blood still burbling slowly up through dark tubes. A pink, gleaming bubble swelled at the top of one tube, filled by the air still rising from a dead girl's lungs. Luce twisted again.

Rivulets of crimson dripped down the rocks. A chest wound gaped wide between flat, childish breasts; Luce thought she saw the heart . . . There, a pile of intestines hung from a pale brown stomach . . . Inches away two blue eyes stared into nothingness, but the face below them was missing . . .

There were no tails anywhere, though. For half an instant Luce persuaded herself that no mermaids had died, that Anais had ripped apart a group of humans. Luce was still telling herself that when she turned and jumped wildly back as she saw Rachel's weak, babyish face. It was split open down the middle, fragments of her skull sticking to her cheeks, and her blond hair was clotted with blood. That elegant brown foot belonged to *Jenna*; those pale curls led to Samantha's severed head . . .

No, Luce thought. It couldn't be true. The mermaids could defend themselves. If anyone attacked them they would sing. Their enemies would all drown . . .

Get out of here, Luce told herself. *Get out get out get out.* She couldn't move, couldn't scream.

They'll come back! Lucette, go!

The red water turned and whipped past her, the fouled tunnel streaked, then opened. Gray shapes approached: sharks, drawn by the stench. Luce lashed her tail, racing, the sour-sweet taste of blood still glutting her mouth. She gulped in mouthful after mouthful of salt water and spat it out again, trying to cleanse herself. It didn't help, though; nothing helped, nothing could *ever* help. She was in the wild open sea near the cliffs, but the sea was corrupted, slimy with death. She ruptured up through the waves and inhaled, staring frantically around at the endless night . . .

It's starting, Luce thought, but she barely understood the words. *It's starting, it's starting* . . .

Something black and fast. On the water's surface, not below it. Luce didn't even hear it coming until it was almost on top of her, until the helmeted men on board were shouting, hefting huge black guns—until a pointed silver blade whizzed past, nicking her shoulder. A line of blood appeared. More filth for the water.

Without thinking about what she was doing, Luce screamed to the sea. It answered her, rising into what might have almost seemed to be a natural rogue wave sixty feet tall if it didn't leap straight for the black boat. It came at the men, furious and purposeful, and Luce could hear their small tinny screams drowned out by her own enormous voice, shriek and song at once. The boat was thrown high above her so fast that she could barely follow it, rolling upside down as it slammed into the cliffs. Its hull crunched like a mussel shell, and kicking men dropped into the suddenly outracing swirl. There were rocks in the water; they might survive . . .

Why should she care? All of them were murderers. The mermaids lay slaughtered, and these men were responsible.

No. *She* was. The guilt was hers. She had known in her heart that this moment was coming. If she'd only listened to Dana, to Nausicaa, only led the tribe away in time, instead of letting herself be fooled by some human's thoughtless words . . .

It's starting, Luce told herself again. She was swimming underwater so quickly that all she could feel was speed. This time she understood what that meant. *The war. It's starting. We'll have to fight* . . .

How could they fight, though, when the humans had found a way to block the power of their songs? *Those helmets* . . .

Everything was broken; everything was destroyed. But she couldn't collapse, couldn't allow herself to give in and die. *South. Go south; warn Sedna. Warn everyone* . . .

She had to find Nausicaa.

ACKNOWLEDGMENTS

I am indebted to the following authors, whose wonderful books taught me a great deal and also informed *Waking Storms* at many points: Sylvia A. Earle's *The World Is Blue* provided me with an invaluable overview of ecological problems affecting the oceans. *The Climate Crisis* by David Archer and Stefan Rahmstorf was also helpful in this regard. Because I've never seen pack ice or nilas myself, my descriptions were largely based on what I learned from Barry H. Lopez's magnificent *Arctic Dreams*. Nausicaa's references to whaling, especially to hunting blue whales with exploding harpoons, were drawn from Philip Hoare's *The Whale*. Alaska Geographic's book *The Bering Sea* offered background information on declining seal populations in the region and the consequent behavior of orcas deprived of their usual prey. An excerpt from Dick Russell's *The Eye of the Whale*, published in the *New York Times*, inspired the description of the gray whales' migration. Any factual errors or whimsical deviations from accepted reality are entirely my responsibility, not theirs.

Gratitude is also due to everyone at Houghton Mifflin Harcourt, especially to the Best Editor Ever, Julie Tibbott; to the Best Agent Ever, Kent D. Wolf; and as always to the Awesomest Husband of All Time, Todd Polenberg.

SARAH PORTER is the author of *Lost Voices, Waking Storms,* and *The Twice Lost*. She is also an artist and a freelance public school teacher. Sarah and her husband live in Brooklyn, New York. Visit Sarah's Watery Den online at **www.sarahporterbooks.com.**

A war between humans and mermaids is raging in the exhilarating conclusion to the Lost Voices trilogy.

Mermaids have been sinking ships and drowning humans for centuries, and now the government is determined to put an end to the mermaid problem—by slaughtering all of them. Luce, one mermaid with exceptionally threatening abilities, becomes their number-one target, hunted as she flees down the coast toward San Francisco.

There she finds hundreds of mermaids living in exile under the docks of the bay. These are the Twice Lost: once-human girls lost the first time when a trauma turned them into mermaids, and lost the second time when they broke mermaid law and were rejected by their tribes. Luce is stunned when they elect her as their leader. But she won't be their queen. She'll be their general. And they will become the Twice Lost Army—because this is war.

Turn the page for a sneak peek at *The Twice Lost*.

1

The Tank

"Hello," the young man in the lab coat purred into a round speaker, his hands fidgeting. Ripples of azure light reflected on his cheeks. "Are you awake?" There was no response. He stood with a few other stiff-backed men, among them the nation's secretary of defense, in a room divided in half by a wall of thick—and perfectly soundproof—glass. Behind the glass was something that resembled the kind of fake habitat found in a zoo, like an enclosure for keeping penguins or seals. Bubbling salt water filled most of the tank to a depth of about five feet, but on the right there was an artificial shore of baby blue cement sloping down into the water. That was where the resemblance to a zoo display ended, though. A giant flat-screen television blazed high on the wall above the tank's deep end, playing what appeared to be a reality show about rich teenagers. Flouncy pink satin cushions were heaped along the shore just above the waterline, and a large white dresser decorated with golden scrolls perched on a ledge at the back. Various electronic gadgets were scattered on the cement, but beyond the clutter the tank gave no sign of being inhabited. "You have a very important visitor today, so . . . your full cooperation . . ."

The crowd behind him shifted impatiently, and the young

man flinched as if he could feel their disapproval pricking his skin. "Getting on with it! I'm going to be turning on your microphone so you can talk to these men. But I have to warn you . . ." Far back in the tank something sky blue and pearlescent flicked up for a moment from behind a pile of cushions. For a second the young man's voice grated to a halt, and he stared urgently before he mastered himself enough to keep going. "We've programmed the computer to recognize any hint of singing. If you try anything, it will send out an electric shock automatically. A pretty severe one. All right? I'd like you to be on . . ." There was that blue flash again, and a trace of rippling gold. "On . . . your best behavior, please." He turned to look at the secretary of defense and offered a tight, ingratiating smile. Then he flicked a switch in a small control panel set into the glass beside the speaker. "Please meet the United States secretary of defense. Secretary Moreland?"

Moreland leaned toward the glass, an odd expression rippling over his heavy reddish face with its sagging jowls. His white hair shone like meringue above his gleaming pate. "Anais," he snapped, then waited, scowling, for a reply. It didn't come. "I'd suggest you get your damned tail over here. You're our little mermaid now."

The sky blue tail rose above the water again, twitching irritably. Pinkish iridescence shone on its scales, and the cushions stirred as a golden head shifted up into view. Dreamy azure eyes turned to gaze through the glass. Several of the men stepped forward as if involuntarily, and others visibly braced themselves. She shook herself, and her inhuman beauty came at them like a living wave. Moreland's smirk tightened, and his upper lip jerked sharply higher to expose his perfect teeth. "Hello, there."

"Hi." She examined Moreland's crisp, expensive suit with a trace of approval. "Are you really important?"

It was hard to tell if Moreland was leering or snarling in response. "Oh, I'd say so."

"Then I only want to talk to *you*." She scanned the other men disdainfully. "Having all these people staring at me makes me feel so shy!"

She didn't look shy, but Moreland nodded almost indulgently. He made a quick motion to the young man in the lab coat, who hurried to tap at the control panel, cutting off Anais's sound. "Do you mind, gentlemen?" Moreland asked.

"We can observe through the monitors in the next room?" the lab-coated man asked anxiously. "She is—I mean—I am her primary handler, and I should know—"

"Oh, I don't think so." Moreland's lip hiked up again. "I don't think you should observe. I'd like to allow *her*"—he cocked his head toward the tank, where Anais, piqued at not being able to hear what they were saying, was now swimming toward the glass—"a chance to confide in me. Privately."

"But—of course you're aware, Mr. Secretary, that she's suffered some very serious trauma. Those mermaids she was living with, all . . ."

"A fragile flower," Moreland agreed, grinning horribly. "I'll use my most delicate touch."

The young lab-coated man didn't look particularly reassured, but he still nodded. "The blue switch controls sound going into her side. The red cuts her off over here. Given the precautions we've taken, though—"

"Thank you, Mr. . . ."

"Hackett. Charles."

"Thank you, Mr. Hackett. I'll let you know when I need your assistance."

Anais was tapping, though inaudibly, on her side of the glass. She was supporting herself in the deepest water with a slight circulating motion of her fins so that her face and shoulders floated just above the surface. Her golden hair rippled and shone around her, and she looked sulky and eager. Hackett gave her a coy little smile and a wave as he turned to leave. "Even *without* any singing," one of the men observed as they walked to the door, "she's still remarkably . . ."

"Remarkably?" one of his companions asked archly, eyebrows raised.

"Compelling, I would say."

"I'd use a different term, frankly."

Secretary Moreland didn't watch them go. Instead he was staring fixedly into Anais's blue eyes, though the look on his face didn't exactly suggest attraction. It was somewhere between caressing and murderous, and a smirk kept tweaking his lips. Once everyone was gone he reached to flip the sound back on, still keeping his gaze locked on Anais's face. "Better now, tadpole?"

Anais pouted. Her lips were slick with strawberry pink gloss. "You have a problem."

"I'd say there are some other—you really can't call them people—some other nasty animals who have much bigger problems these days. You should be very, very thankful that we're taking such good care of you. When you could be in the same mess as your little killing-machine friends . . ."

Anais shrugged impatiently, sending a quick surge through the water around her. Her hair lapped at her shoulders. She was wearing a sparkly, sky blue tank top that matched her tail almost perfectly, and diamond studs sparked in her ears. "I don't care about that! Charlie told me about that boat of yours that got trashed."

"Charlie?"

"Mr. Hackett. He said there was a big wave that came out of nowhere and, like, *totaled* the boat with your guys on it, after . . ." Anais suddenly seemed a bit uncomfortable. "After . . . I surrendered. I knew you'd want to *talk* to one of us, if we just acted nicer. And—"

"That wave didn't come out of nowhere, I think, tadpole. You shouldn't assume that Mr. Hackett's information is entirely reliable."

"That's what I'm trying to *tell* you!" Anais was getting exasperated. "I just didn't want to tell . . . Mr. Hackett because I didn't think he could really do anything. I figured it all out. You can go and kill mermaids without the *singing* stopping you now. Right? But you don't have any way to stop her from bashing your guys with those waves. You *have* to kill her. Soon! Like, right now she's the only one who knows how to do that, but she'll probably start teaching everybody else, and then you won't be able to get rid of mermaids anymore at *all* . . ."

Secretary Moreland was clearly trying to keep his expression steady, but it wasn't working. Tiny spasms of excitement bent his features and shimmered in his eyes. "So you're claiming you know the mermaid who committed the assault on the Special Ops boat?" He paused for a moment, assessing. "Several of our men were killed. This isn't something we take at all lightly. You wouldn't want to be anything less than perfectly candid on the subject."

"Of course I know her. We had to kick her out of the tribe because all she did was cause *problems*, but then she wouldn't stop hanging around . . ." Anais's tail was swishing faster now, its pink iridescence flashing candied reflections on the glass.

Moreland looked disappointed. "So she wouldn't consider you a friend? Try to find you?"

"No way! She knows I see right through her. Though she did keep trying to get me to pay *attention* to her."

Moreland nodded. The sparks in his eyes seemed agitated. "I *see*. But you'll tell me all about her, won't you? I'd suggest you start now."

Anais leaned back from the glass with a motion that suggested someone settling into an armchair, although there was nothing but water around her, and smiled slyly. Her fins lightly stroked across the tank's blue cement floor. "That depends."

"*Does* it? On what?"

"On you letting me out of here!" Anais shook her head, golden rays of hair swinging with the movement. "I mean, I know my parents must have left me a *ton* of money. And the house! And there's a pool, and I could get our servants to come back, and—"

"Tadpole, tadpole . . ." Moreland shook his head, and his smile was much softer, much more slippery, than before. "You haven't thought this through."

"I totally have! I—"

"You aren't *human*, little tail. Not remotely."

"So?"

"So the law doesn't apply to you. Not one teeny bit. And that's including due process and inheritance law. Legally you don't exist. There's no provision in the law for leaving a house to a precious little monster . . ."

This clearly hadn't occurred to Anais before. Her eyes widened in dismay and her mouth opened onto a round darkness that seemed to threaten the unleashing of terrible music. Moreland grinned stonily and raised his eyebrows at her. She paused and glanced around her tank, then shut her mouth again.

"Exactly," he hissed. Anais scowled. "But you don't like this troublemaker mermaid, do you? She absolutely deserves to die, doesn't she?"

Anais was still sulking. "Of course she deserves it!"

"So maybe helping us track her down would be worth your time anyway. I promise you we'll tear her guts right out. Maybe we'll even take our time doing it. Remember, legal protections don't apply to her either, and we're very, very annoyed with her."

Anais cocked her head, brazenly intrigued. "You *should* be. She's a bitch, and she's really nuts. And just, like, *weird*."

"Tell me her name." Moreland's voice was suddenly rough.

"Luce." Anais spat it out.

A shadow passed through his pale eyes. "Luce. I believe I've heard her mentioned before. And what about her . . . *human* name? Do you know that much?"

"Will you at least show me *pictures*? Once you kill her?"

"Oh, certainly. Probably even video. We'll watch it together. It will be my great pleasure. Virtue should always be rewarded." Aqua light from the tank gleamed on Moreland's wet teeth as he spoke.

"Lucette . . ." Anais visibly struggled to remember. "She said it . . . No, *Catarina* said it once when they were fighting. Lucette Kip . . . No. Lucette Korchak?"

"A very good beginning, Anais." Moreland smiled. "You know, at first I wasn't sure your information was reliable. But I'm beginning to think we can come to an understanding after all."

"What about Sedna? Will you at least make sure you kill her, too? And Dana, and Violet."

"Sedna was the leader of the group you identified? In southern Alaska?"

"Yeah. She—"

"Ah, but that's why I didn't think we could trust you, my dear. We couldn't find any trace of mermaids anywhere near the location you described to us. Unless you can do better, I'm afraid I won't be able to show you video of Sedna's dismemberment."

"I told you the truth." Anais's pout tightened moodily, and her head tipped sideways. "I bet Luce got there first. I bet she *warned* them."

Moreland nodded, a bit curtly. "Very possibly. I need you to understand something, Anais. It won't be easy, and it won't happen anytime soon. But if you help us enough, I might eventually see my way to . . . encouraging special consideration of your case. Maybe a judge could be persuaded that you deserve your inheritance after all, in view of your services to your country."

Anais mulled this, her blue fins rippling irritably. Then her face changed completely. All at once she beamed with gentle innocence. "Of *course* I'll help. It isn't safe for anyone to have Luce swimming around out there! She'll just kill so *many* of your men if no one stops her!"

"Quite so." Moreland's tongue slid across his bluish teeth, and his eyes widened with a fake sincerity that almost equaled Anais's, except that his smile kept twisting into a leer. Every tiny disturbance of the water sent greenish light crawling across his stiff white hair. "We're very grateful for your patriotism. Now, did . . . Lucette ever mention the name Dorian to you? Dorian Hurst?"

"Who?" Anais asked. Her confusion looked genuine enough.

Moreland was disappointed again, but Anais suddenly leaned forward in excitement. "Wait, wait, wait! A guy? You're saying that Luce was seeing a *human guy*? That is so sick!" She squealed with laughter. "And she thought she was supposed to be queen!

Oh, I can't wait to tell . . ." Anais's laughter faltered abruptly, and she looked down.

Moreland observed her for a long moment. His gray eyes were covetous, cold. "Oh, but there's no one left to tell, is there, tadpole? The abominations who would have liked to hear your gossip about Lucette and her human boyfriend are all dead." He gazed at her with something that might have almost passed for compassion. "We destroyed every last one of them in front of you. And even as we speak the teams are out there, hunting down other groups of your kind."

"I didn't *want* to be a mermaid!" Anais snarled. "I never wanted to! They're not my kind! I loved being human. Everything was so *perfect* . . ."

Moreland considered this. "You didn't want to be a mermaid. Were you somehow changed against your will?"

"Of course I was!" Anais was staring down, plainly on the verge of tears. Maybe they were even real.

The secretary of defense didn't look convinced. "Then who changed you?"

"Luce did it." It came out in a sullen whimper. "She *forced* me, but I . . ."

"That's *very* sad." Moreland stared at Anais for a few more moments. Now that she wasn't looking at him, he examined her stunning form with a mixture of hungry fascination and naked loathing. "Well, then, it's a very fortunate thing that you're living with humans again, isn't it? You can talk to us. Now, what you said before, about this Luce . . ."